Hearts and Minds

AMANDA CRAIG

Little, Brown

LITTLE, BROWN

First published in Great Britain in 2009 by Little, Brown

Copyright © Amanda Craig 2009

The moral right of the author has been asserted.

Lines from T. S. Eliot's *The Waste Land* from *Collected Poems* © the Estate of
T. S. Eliot, quoted by kind permission of the publishers, Faber and Faber Ltd.

A CIP catalogue record for this book
is available from the British Library.

Hardback ISBN: 978-0-316-72483-8
C-format ISBN: 978-1-4087-0190-4

Typeset in Goudy by M Rules
Printed and bound in Great Britain by
Clays Ltd, St Ives plc

Papers used by Little, Brown are natural, renewable and
recyclable products sourced from well-managed forests and certified in
accordance with the rules of the Forest Stewardship Council.

Mixed Sources
Product group from well-managed
forests and other controlled sources
www.fsc.org Cert no. SGS-COC-004081
© 1996 Forest Stewardship Council
FSC

Little, Brown
An imprint of
Little, Brown Book Group
100 Victoria Embankment
London EC4Y 0DY

An Hachette UK Company
www.hachette.co.uk

www.littlebrown.co.uk

Hearts and Minds

To my father

. . . among the multitudes
Of that huge city, oftentimes was seen
Affectingly set forth, more than elsewhere
Is possible, the unity of men,
One spirit over ignorance and vice
Predominant, in good and evil hearts
One sense for moral judgements, as one eye
For the sun's light . . .

William Wordsworth, *The Prelude*

It is the mind which creates the world about us, and even though
we stand side by side in the same meadow, my eyes will never see
what is beheld by yours. My heart will never stir to the emotion
with which yours is touched.

George Gissing

Unreal City,
Under the brown fog of a winter dawn,
A crowd flowed over London Bridge, so many,
I had not thought death had undone so many.
Sighs, short and infrequent, were exhaled,
And each man fixed his eyes before his feet.

T. S. Eliot, *The Waste Land*

Preface

Uneasy City

At night, even in these dead months of the year, the city is never wholly dark. Its shadows twitch with a harsh orange light that glows and fades, fades and glows, as the pulse of electric power courses through its body like dreams. The sour air, breathed in and out by eight million lungs, stained by exhaust pipes and strained through ventilators, is never clean, although, after a time, you no longer notice its bitter taste and smell. The dust of ages swirls and falls, staining walls, darkening glass, coating surfaces, clogging lungs. Bricks, leaves, paper, food, bones and skin all decay, reduced to almost invisible specks that accumulate into the eternal dust of London.

The only times the city can breathe freely is when a wind blows in from a far-off place, bringing with it gulls and the cries of the sea, or a fresh sweet air from the west. But this city is a world of its own, a country within a country. People are used to taking the old and making it new; and used, too, to taking the new and making it old. Every glass of water from its taps, it is said, has passed six times through the kidneys of another, and every scrap of its land has been trodden on, fought over, dug up and broken down for centuries. Yet fresh water wells up, too, from under roads and buildings so that the buried landscape beneath is never quite forgotten. This place could almost be countryside, for here its streams fall into ponds rather than hidden pipes or channels. It is here that the murderer has come to hide the body.

The woman is a great deal heavier than he had expected. Perhaps he has been stupid not to put the body in the boot of the car and dump it far away; only, he knows how easily the police can find out the number plates of passing vehicles in the vicinity of a murder. Sticking to well-known routes that he always takes is wiser. This side of the Heath has few CCTV cameras, and he's waited a long time in the side road for people to leave – not that many are around on a winter's night, with the wind shrilling in the bare branches like distant alarms. He's satisfied with his choice. All the same, dragging the grey mailbag out of the back seat and onto the grassy bank is almost too much for one person. He should have kept her semi-conscious, instead of strangling her when he had the opportunity. It had been so quick and easy, like killing a chicken; and of course quite silent.

He knows just where he wants to put the bag. There is an area by the Ponds, a nature reserve fenced off from people and dogs but not from the wilder inhabitants like foxes, where a body could lie and rot for years without ever being discovered. The place stinks already, being clogged with mud and mire, and nobody will notice a little extra smell. The plan had been made more or less on the spur of the moment, but it seems a good one to him, although he is still worried about whether she has tricked him. No time to check, yet . . . The man grunts and lurches, hating her even more than in life, and his hatred gives him strength so that when he gives a final heave over the railings the body flies through the air and lands with a splash.

For a moment, it seems as if it won't work. He watches anxiously, all the time alert for any other people, while the bag seems to waver as if uncertain. Then, to his relief, it sinks down, making a plopping noise that is almost comical as the air inside escapes. Something moves on the bank, and he freezes, but it's only a water bird, labouring along the edges, alarmed by the disturbance. Finally, the bag disappears from sight, leaving the water of the pond undisturbed but for the skeletal forms of bare trees and shrubs, which occasionally draw their twigs across its depths like long bony fingers, and sigh.

The woman had survived many trials long before the one that had taken her life. She had been young and strong and attractive. She had possessed a good brain, which had enabled her to learn a new language, a language that was itself a fusion of many other tongues, and which she believed would bring her, miraculously, to a better future. She had been like so many Londoners, a person who did not fit in anywhere else, and who had come to the city hoping to find a new beginning. Now, though, she is just one more discarded thing which will be counted as lost, if she is counted at all.

1

Waking

Even in sleep, Polly is conscious of guilt. Like a splinter forcing its way to the surface of her skin, it throbs just below the level of consciousness until she wakes. Drowsily, she listens to the occasional rattle of the sash window in its frame and the creak of floorboards, until the pressure in her bladder forces her up.

Walking with the cautious, shuffling tread of one who knows the floor is mined with Warhammer figurines, she gropes her way to the bathroom. The central heating is off and the blind up, showing her the upper half of a wide, tree-lined street in the dim orange street-light. Two rows of seemingly identical, flat-fronted, white-stuccoed early-Victorian houses face each other, each subtly different, like Darwin's finches on the Galapagos Islands. Polly, with her potted olive tree, Farrow & Ball paintwork and Smeg fridge, is a relatively recent arrival, for half the street is gentrified and half still owned by the council. She feels at ease here, on the scruffy edge of Islington and Camden Town: something she had never felt during her marriage in Fulham. She chose it because it is close to where she grew up, and also to where she now works as a solicitor in a firm specialising in human-rights cases. Although the house (bought following her divorce) is comfortable and pretty, and her children go to private schools, she earns a modest salary, having taken almost a decade out of full-time employment when her children were young.

Theo, her ex-husband, is a very different kind of lawyer. He works in the City, and hates London.

'This town has had it good for a decade, but now the party's over,' he likes to say. 'Its infrastructure, transport system, education, policing and security all suck. I'm telling you, Polly, people are talking seriously about relocating to Geneva.'

By 'people', Theo always means those like himself, who earn a minimum of a million pounds a year; the rest do not exist. Polly, though, is obdurate. Vague presentiments of danger have been a part of every Londoner's life for the past five years, but Theo's alarmism is ludicrous. He sees threats everywhere, and couldn't understand why nobody else had even bothered to buy duct tape after 9/11.

'Dad's weird about people, isn't he?' Robbie had remarked after a weekend away with his father. 'He thinks people wear towels on their heads to blow up planes.'

'The thing about Daddy's country is, they didn't live through two world wars and the IRA bombs,' Polly told him. 'They're paranoid about the rest of the world.'

Theo had been amazed to discover just how deeply Americans were now hated by the British. He returns this hatred with interest. He wants to take Tania and Robbie back to the States, to whisk them into the kind of sprawling suburban New England home which his colleagues live in, complete with Mexican maids and a swimming pool.

'Theo, that simply isn't the way British people live,' Polly had said.

She has window locks and a London bar on her doors, but refuses to have a burglar alarm, though Theo has insisted she have a panic button installed.

'You're a woman living with my children, and I have the right to insist that they have some protection,' he'd said.

'Burglars can't break in,' Polly had told him. 'We're very safe here, the windows are all toughened glass, and besides, this is a friendly house – can't you feel?'

Theo had looked at her as if she was an idiot, and perhaps it is silly of her to believe this, but Polly doesn't care. She's free, and this house belongs to her.

There is a distant *whoosh* from the timed boiler, and the underfloor pipes begin to creak and tap, as if the house is stretching its body. Polly returns to bed, luxuriating in her solitude. Christmas in California without the children had been amazing; the house in Pacific Palisades, with its swimming pool and landscaped gardens, had given her a glimpse of a different world. Her lover, Bill Shade, is a scriptwriter in Hollywood, and wants her to move in with him, but Polly is resistant. She has just got her career back; she can read detective novels until late at night instead of having someone moaning about the light; she can spend the weekend without a scrap of make-up on her face; she can spread out to enjoy the cool expanses of her mattress.

Polly thinks gratefully of Iryna overhead. Bill has teased her about the way her life is dependent on cheap foreign labour, and she is conscious of the irony that, while her professional life often consists of helping refugees and illegal immigrants, her ability to do so depends upon exploiting them.

'Is it for this that Shakespeare penned his immortal plays, Smith developed his economic theories and Berners-Lee invented the internet: so that your strawberries can be picked by Eastern Europeans, your streets swept by Serbs, your laundry ironed by Pakistanis, and your garden manicured by an Italian?' Bill says. Yes: but by far the most important is Iryna, who works twenty-five hours per week for seventy pounds, not counting babysitting or the school holidays. Iryna does the housework, collects Robbie from school, cooks the children their tea, makes sure they do their homework and, in short, performs all the boring chores of being a housewife and mother that Polly has dropped because of her job. She loves her children, and yet she can't deny that when she goes back to work on a

Monday morning she is always relieved to leave them behind until eight p.m.

'This is my rock, Iryna,' is how Polly introduces her; or else, 'This is Iryna, my right hand.'

It isn't as if Polly hasn't done this work herself. She knows how to vacuum, iron shirts and wash dishes; will still sew on name-tapes, cook children's teas, and trudge around museums; she has felt her well-trained legal brain click gears like a rusty bicycle while singing 'Here We Go Looby-Loo' for the thousandth time. Being able to battle with the Home Office is like child's play compared with real child's play, but without Iryna she simply couldn't manage. With Iryna, life is good. Polly had taken her without a reference, in response to an ad, and she feels a warm glow to think of how nicely she has accommodated her. The British are not good at welcoming foreigners into their homes, but Iryna not only has a large, light room with a TV, fridge and microwave, she has her own bathroom – whereas Polly shares hers with the children.

Placid, pleasant and pretty, Iryna reminds Polly of a Russian doll. Polly sometimes wonders whether she has ever had a boyfriend, because she never brings anyone home. She certainly has an active social life, going out in the morning and evening, but it never inter-feres with her work. Polly is relieved to see her looking well and rested again following a two-week break of house-sitting while they were all away on holiday, because just before Christmas she had been pale and listless, and Polly worried that she was homesick. Now, however, she is back to normal, and no cobweb or dust-ball is safe from the probing nozzle of the vacuum cleaner. The washing machine whirls with its almost silent, high-pitched giggle, tossing its contents one way then the other, the children's supper sizzles golden-brown under the grill, and Polly herself eats their leftovers for her own supper. Iryna is like Adam Smith's invisible hand: she does it all, then disappears.

It is only a minor worry that, being Russian, she happens to be illegal.

Polly falls back into a sleep so profound that it is like falling into black water. Down, down, and then the radio alarm hooks her back up, panicked. The *Today* programme splutters on about the Iraq War and the failings of the Prime Minister, while Polly stomps up the stairs, trying not to remember that dazzling May morning over a decade ago when Labour had won and the country seemed so full of passionate hope.

'Wake up!' she calls, going into each child's room and switching on their lights.

Now the hour-long struggle begins. Tania slumbers on in the languor of adolescence, her skin covered with a pearly sheen of sweat as Polly kisses her, but Robbie stirs and burrows deeper into his duvet. Polly notices with annoyance that Iryna has not put out his school clothes for him.

'Time to get up, my angel.'

'I hate school,' says Robbie, lashing out as his mother pulls the duvet off him.

'I hate Mondays,' says Tania, in turn. 'And I hate you.'

'Tough,' says Polly. 'Get dressed, or you'll be going to school in pyjamas.'

Each weekday morning, she has to make sure the children are dressed, fed, clean, have done their homework and get to school on time before going to her office. It does not sound like much, but there are days when she feels like she can't stand another minute of it.

'Robbie, you *still* haven't got your shoes on! Put them on, or you're going to school in your socks.'

'Why do I have to go to school? Why can't I stay with you?'

Polly sighs. She is trying to cram a full working day into eight hours, and she keeps her watch five minutes fast in order to get to any appointment, tricking herself into tiny panic attacks that are like the miniature muffled explosions in a combustion engine.

'Outside this country, and also in it, are millions and millions of people who would kill to have what you do here,' she says. 'They are

9

clever, fantastically hard-working and they are all learning English. When you grow up, you're going to be competing with them for places at university, and for jobs.'

'Yeah, yeah,' says Tania, rudely.

'You *have* to do this stuff,' said Polly, slapping Weetabix on the table. 'If you don't get good marks, you'll never go to university, and if you don't go to university you'll end up flipping burgers and—'

'You mean if I don't read, I could have all the burgers I could eat, every day?'

'Then you'd get fat, Robbie,' says Tania, with horror.

'Who gives? But why must I learn *French*? Or *any* language when everyone in the world wants to learn English?' says Robbie, who won't even drink orange juice if it has bits.

'Because otherwise you won't know what they're saying about you in secret,' says Tania.

Polly smiles, for this is a far better answer than she could have given. Then her heart jumps with the clock, for they have just forty-eight seconds left to get out of the door. Where are their coats?

'How should I know?' Robbie answers, calmly.

'You *must* have them! It's freezing, it's January, you can't go out today without a coat. Look, I'm wearing my heaviest one again.'

'I don't see why you make such a fuss,' Robbie complains. 'It's not *that* cold outside.'

'I am a Jewish mother,' says Polly. 'My dying words will be, "Put a jumper on."'

'Mum, all mothers are Jewish mothers, only they don't make such a fuss as you,' says Tania.

'I can't find my school tie,' Polly's son complains. 'Iryna's hidden it.'

'Iryna!' Polly calls up the stairs. The girl is supposed to be down by now. No answer, and Robbie will be punished if he turns up without a school tie. She races upstairs to fish one out of the laundry basket, already nauseous with stress.

'I hate you!' Tania screams. 'I'm going to miss the school bus, and it's *all your fault!*'

Outside, Polly takes off like a rocket. They have only three minutes as a margin of error, never enough.

'Oh, damn and blast!' she says, trying to text Iryna at a traffic light. 'I wonder where she is?'

The car surges forward. It is only a momentary release of frustration because a second later her undercarriage hits a speed cushion with a bang. Polly dreams long tedious dreams in which she does the school run, endlessly grinding up Highgate Hill to the bus stop for Tania's school. But now, at last, she is passing Highgate Cemetery and Karl Marx's tomb, racing past the ornate iron gates of Waterlow Park, out of Pond Square and then, just in time, she stops in front of the school bus.

'Love you,' Polly says, drawing up.

'Huh!' says Tania, slipping off to join the gaggle of other girls in uniform. Every day, when she goes back into the heart of London, Polly thinks how glad she is that her children will be out in the suburbs, where it is leafy and safe.

Onwards for her second chore. The tree-lined street in West Hampstead where Robbie's prep school is situated heaves and throbs with huge cars disgorging tiny uniformed children bowed antlike beneath the weight of their rucksacks, sports kits and musical instruments. Polly sits behind the wheel, squashed between giant gleaming chrome fenders and exhaust pipes pumping out a continual shimmer of pollutants, while Robbie chants out French verbs with the hopelessness of a novice monk. There! With a spurt of adrenalin, she darts her little car forward, lights flashing, and reverses.

'Out! I have to get to work.'

'Wait, Mummy, wait!' Robbie cries. 'I haven't got my shoe on properly.'

'I can't wait, darling. I have a court case.'

'Why do you care about bloody foreigners more than about your own children?' he says.

'They aren't bloody foreigners. They are people like us, who are just less lucky,' Polly says. He doesn't understand: how can he? Like all these sweet innocents, he will only ever visit the Third World as a tourist. But Polly had taken in compassion and fear with her mother's milk. She has nightmares about running away from torture and death with her children, just like some of her clients. In this dream she is always running to escape the Nazis, while the children drag on her arms like twin stones.

Back along Hampstead Lane, and already the ringtone of her mobile is drilling through her skull. It must be Iryna. One-handed, Polly fishes for her phone, but finds its screen blank. For a moment, she wonders if the jarring, persistent wail building up and up and up is the noise of her own stress, made audible.

It is only as it becomes louder, and the cars ahead of her pull over like the waters of the Red Sea dividing, that she realises it is a police car, lurching past in the opposite direction, blue lights flashing, and vanishing towards Hampstead Heath.

2

Freewheeling Is What Life Is About

Just before dawn Ian has got up, groaning to himself, in order to cycle through the grey streets and get to work. Behind him, buried in a white goose-feather duvet and embroidered pillowcases, lies Candice.

He hadn't meant to spend the night with her in West Hampstead, but somehow the drink after her return from South Africa had turned into a reunion. Pump, pump, pump go his legs, pushing the bicycle uphill, and pump goes his heart, pulsing hot blood through his body. He is twenty-eight years old; he has had sex three times in the past twelve hours, and an Innocent smoothie for breakfast; life should be good. The brief exhilaration of solitude, and speed, blow away his sleepiness. Christmas decorations are still up in Hampstead Village, strung overhead in sagging lines of lit bulbs. They always look so attractive at first, he thinks, and so banal after the event.

This patch of London, which he now knows well, is perhaps a twentieth of its total size, and all hill. Ian has hardly ventured into the centre, and has never crossed the Thames. His horizons are bounded by what he sees: Hampstead, Highgate, Camden, Islington, Hackney and Finsbury Park, places that were once villages, vanished fields and rivers now lost under brick and tarmac. To the south, City office blocks are illuminated in delicate rectangles and spires of light against the dim sky. To the east lies Hampstead Heath, in shadow. Ian presses uphill, past red-brick mansions and white Victorian villas, past the eccentricity of Jack Straw's Castle, then along Spaniard's Road in a streak of triumph for one mile of beautifully easy road. Already he is encountering the cars of early commuters, swishing into the city from the suburbs.

It takes him a little longer to go to work by this route, but it is pleasanter and safer than cutting down through Camden Town to the East End. Leafless trees arch over him, shadow against shadow; he surprises foxes, rabbits and many birds. This is his second British winter, the one that's supposed to break his will to stay. Ian could have chosen to go back to South Africa for Christmas, and seen his mother and stepfather, but freewheeling is what life is about. The wind whips in his face and hair. To be cutting through the cold air like a blade, to be in motion, gives him a rare sense of self-definition.

Ian is not sure what he wants out of being in Britain, but some of it is to do with meeting his father, and some with professional quali- fication. He's not entirely purposeless, which helps. He has seen other Antipodeans and South Africans arriving, full of optimism, and watched them falter before the cold, the wet, the grey, the indif- ference. Having lived under burning blue skies every day of his life, he understands that it changes something inside you when you are cut off from the air and light. How can people live like this? Ian's housemates keep asking. There are many answers. Money is one of them. Whatever their backgrounds, they do the crap jobs, like nurs- ing and teaching, bar-keeping and nannying, that British people don't want to do themselves.

'You should look around,' Candice had urged him last night. 'You can do better.'

'Oh, I will,' Ian had said. 'Eventually.'

'Admit it, you're terminally lazy. You always wait for people to come to you, sweetie.'

Laziness, or apathy, is his besetting sin, he knows. He hasn't even got his act together about travelling to the Continent yet; maybe not having to queue for a Schengen visa (the one thing his British father had bestowed upon him) is part of it. To his housemates, London is just a means to an end, a jumping-off point and a playground. To Candice it's home. Ian hasn't decided yet which it is for him.

He can feel the greyness gnawing him like a dog at a bone, stripping the easy, laid-back self-assurance. November and December were bad enough, but there are at least two more months to endure before any hope of spring. Right now, everything seems frozen. He has not made contact with his father; the excuse being that he is still finding his feet. He has his own life, though before he left his mother made him enter her ex-husband's number in his mobile.

'Put it down, darling, just in case. You have to have an ICE number, In Case of Emergency, now that you can be blown up by terrorists at any moment,' she said.

'I'm an adult, Mom, in case you hadn't noticed.'

'I had, but I won't have a moment's peace unless you do.'

Ian begins the smooth glide that dips down and around Kenwood House. Its creamy neoclassical façade overlooking an artificial lake looks like something from a tourist brochure or a fairy tale. Away above Highgate the long rolls of grey cloud that have lain like dust under a bed are flushing crimson and orange, acid yellow and green. Brighter and brighter they become, until within seconds the whole of the eastern sky has become a dazzle of gold and pink.

Before him, the city centre lies cupped between two hills, like a bowl of jewels. There is the twisting glass digit of the Gherkin, and the fragile diamond bracelet of the London Eye; there the miniature crown of St Paul's, the ruby on top of Canary Wharf, all growing slowly larger as he speeds towards them. Over to the east, where Ian works, lies the City within the city, a place where so many millions and billions are traded daily that it has the income of another country, all thanks to an accident of history that means that international business is largely conducted in English.

15

It's a view he's particularly interested in right now, because he has been writing a play over the holidays for his class to perform. It's a romp about Dick Whittington and his Cat – not a pantomime, but an adventure with lots of parts for the whole of Year Eight which he has dashed off over Christmas. He's always loved the story, not just about the cat which unexpectedly makes poor Dick's fortune but because of the moment when Dick, utterly disheartened, is climbing up Highgate Hill and hears the bells of London: *Turn again, Dick Whittington, thrice Mayor of London*.

Something about that bit always makes him feel strange. It's a fairy tale, of course, but how often do people get the chance to make a single, life-changing decision? Ian's choice to leave South Africa has turned into a policy of drift. Instead of boldly marching off like Dick Whittington, he had simply flown over, on the modern equivalent to the Grand Tour of Europe. Instead of cultural pursuits, however, what he did at first was get drunk and have as much sex as possible while living in conditions of total squalor. Everyone behaved like this, when Travelling. It was different for those who settled here – they became the most upright of citizens, or maybe they just got middle-aged. But for most of Ian's contemporaries, London is a playground consisting of other South Africans and Antipodeans, in which encounters with actual British people are a purely economic necessity.

Up above the Heath an aeroplane glints, bright white in the sun that has not yet touched the land. A robin perches on a twig, and whistles piercingly as he passes. He had been amazed the first time he had seen one, a tiny brown bird with its bright flush of red feathers on the breast; it was familiar from cards, and as fantastical to him as a zebra or a giraffe would be to an Englishman. His pupils are always asking him about the African jungle, where they imagine he has grown up with lions (and tigers). He's tried to explain that the only times he has seen such beasts have been in safari parks, and that he's from a city; but they prefer to think that he spent his time swinging through trees, like Tarzan.

'You even look a bit like him, sir,' said the cheekiest boy. 'You know, in the cartoon.'

He had told Candice this. She laughed and agreed.

'Get a haircut,' she said.

'Oh? What are teachers supposed to look like?'

'They wear suits.'

'A suit would kill me,' Ian said, seriously.

Candice is thirty-two, an age difference which doesn't matter except that she has had a string of failed romances, all of which seem to have ended badly. Ian is a little worried that she's going to count him as one. He's tried to make it clear that, as his best friend Mick says, he's 'only passing through', but Candice seems to think otherwise. She's circling him, just like that aeroplane, looking for a landing slot; but Ian won't respond. He hates rules, and being here is his chance to break free.

Cycling, for instance, is illegal on the Heath, and once or twice along this path he has been stopped by the police, and cautioned. Ian hates this, though they are never as intimidating as the police back home; he can't believe that they still don't carry guns, just truncheons. So much about British life is comical, really.

Gravity takes control of his bike, gliding over puddles blind with ice. They splinter with a satisfying crunch under his wheels. Squirrels, questing for acorns, freeze like question marks. Imported from Canada over a hundred years ago, they are everywhere, riffling through the sheaves of dry fallen leaves so that whole glades flicker with the furtive motion of gamblers shuffling cards. Londoners hate them; they pose a threat to the indigenous reds which now survive only in remote, protected areas of Britain.

Ian is warm now, his tendons stretching and easing. At this hour there are only joggers, and a few dedicated dog-walkers. The leafless oaks and beeches overhead are centuries old; frosted grass slopes its moth-eaten velvet up to Parliament Hill. Magpies call, a metallic, rattling sound like a clockwork toy being wound up, as they hunt the exotic bright green parakeets that survive, somehow, in this climate.

London is said to keep a couple of degrees warmer than the rest of the country, and perhaps that's what makes the difference. Their high-pitched shrieks have a monotonous, irritating sound that sets his teeth on edge, but they are beautiful to see when in flight, teasing the heavy, predatory crows in much the same way that the Bangladeshi boys at his school do the Afro-Caribbeans. Thinking of his working week, he sighs. Two more terms to go until he qualifies, and then he can work anywhere in the world.

The ponds he is passing smell rank, draining off the muddy hillside into a series of pale oblongs fringed by stinking reeds, decomposing leaves and black iron railings. It is a sinister spot, and his least favourite part of the ride. Further along, there are natural pools formed by the rising springs of the River Fleet, some of which are used by swimmers. The idea of swimming in freezing, filthy water teeming with rats is another English eccentricity. Some are apparently so devoted to their hobby that they will swim even in the depths of winter, when ice has formed on the surface.

A flock of crows rise, cawing harshly, from the woods. As Ian approaches the end of the tunnel of trees, he sees that the dark waters ahead ripple with ribbons of white and blue. Sirens are approaching in a wince of light. A police car is bumping down the long hill behind him, its wail redoubled by echoes. He slows, and gets off his bike, sighing.

The police are not interested in him, however. Two more police cars pass, and an ambulance. Ian, puzzled, frowns. Some accident ahead; perhaps another cyclist knocked down by a car. A plump middle-aged woman and her son, wearing the uniform of a private school, call their small dog to heel, and watch.

'What's wrong?'

'I don't know,' she says.

'There's something in the pond, Mum.'

The boy, excited, cranes forward. The pond, which lies between the Ladies' Pond and the Men's, is frequented only by birds. The sun is still not up above the trees, and the valley is in shadow. There is a huddle of figures in fluorescent jackets gathered round something which is being lifted out of a rowing boat. What is it? A bag of rubbish? A dead dog?

The woman behind Ian draws in a breath and says sharply, 'Come away now, we haven't got all day.'

Ian can hear the boy's shrill voice, protesting. He feels rooted to the spot, aware that he is about to see something horrible, but unable to comprehend what this might be. The blue lights whirl, silently. Then, at last, the rising sun touches the pool, turning its waters a deep viscous red, as if it were warm blood: but the body being lifted onto a stretcher is white – as white as marble, and as cold.

3

Invisible Men

There is nothing for it, Job has to run the engine. He can't stand the cold any longer. Huddled inside his jacket, he sips the polystyrene cup of milkless tea that is his breakfast, and broods on his many misfortunes. At the control centre he can at least boil a kettle – as long as he and the other drivers bring their own tea bags and sugar – but he can't hang around. The tiny, steamy waiting room is full of drivers, all chatting to each other in their own language, and he knows he isn't wanted. They get the first jobs, the ones Mo, the controller, assures customers 'will be there in five minutes, hundred per cent'. Job comes last. He hardly ever gets the lucrative trips to Stansted or Gatwick airports, the regular business that keeps the other men and their families afloat.

All the same, he's lucky to get this work. When he'd walked in, Mo had been short of drivers because it was Ramadan. Job had presented his Zimbabwean driver's licence, hopelessly, and Mo had only asked, 'Are you a Muslim?'

'No,' Job said, though he had felt tempted to answer yes.

'Are you a believer?'

'Yes, sir,' Job had said. At that, Mo had given him a job. He is an immensely fat man, and Pakistani like all the other men at Ace Minicabs, but not averse to having someone who wouldn't complain. Besides, Job has no dependants in this country. He can do the kind of driving jobs that family men, and decent Muslims, don't want.

Job's colleagues marry young, and take their duties seriously, working long hours. They never drink, are polite and honest, and one or two turn to Mecca and pray at noon in the tiny waiting room. But they are not friendly, and he has no friends there. Job tries not to mind, for he had not particularly expected even companionship. Only Job is lonelier still, because he has been abandoned by God and is outside His grace. So, instead, he listens to the BBC World Service News. It is almost as authoritative, and full of pain and reproach.

Waiting for a fare is agonising. He looks along the dull street, then into the mirror keeping a wary eye out for traffic wardens, who will ticket him if they can, and flexes his icy feet. Mid-morning, with an hour to go before he switches jobs, he thinks. Job has driven a silent, scowling man into the City at six a.m., and a frantic woman whose car broke down during the school run, but now he is back at the office off York Way, praying for his luck to change. If he doesn't make at least ten fares a day he can't cover the rental for the car, let alone rent for his tiny room, and food. His other job is the one that he uses to send money back to his wife, Munisha.

He has a photograph of her wearing one of her pretty sprigged dresses in his wallet, and another of them both on their wedding day in his room, and they are like maps of a country which he has forgotten. In the beginning, they talked on their mobile phones every week, but now she has left Harare, and he has not heard from her since two months before Christmas. Job heaves a gusty sigh, which turns to trickling moisture as soon as it hits the windscreen. When he refused to buy a Zanu-PF card, years ago, he had had no idea that it would lead to this cold country, to the crackle of static in his ears and the buzz-saw rasp of anxiety in his head. Every night he has nightmares, not just about prison but about being forced to walk through passport control, out of Britain, and be ejected back into hell.

21

'Two-three, two-three, where are you, two-three, over?'

'Outside the office, sir, over,' Job says to Mo's voice.

'Just checking, two-three, over.'

The other men all have names, but Job is referred to as 'two-three'. Some, like Job, also do second jobs – in their cases, working in Indian restaurants nearby – but they have each other as well. Job never fails to smile at them all, and two of them do grudgingly include him in the conversations, partly, he suspects, to practise their English. Kamal, Shamsur, Azam, Humayun, Ahmed, Tariq and Iqbal are all from the same area of Pakistan, and some, like Tariq, have sons who are following them into the same work. Their English is generally poor – so much so that they can only work as minicab drivers thanks to SatNav, which means they can find the most obscure street in the city provided they have the full postcode. Job, who speaks perfect English, can't afford anything fancier than an A–Z, though in truth he has learnt so many roads and routes by now that he usually doesn't need to look in it.

The A–Z is one of those examples of order and helpfulness that underpin British life. Job likes looking at it, just as a work of art. He loves the roads warning you to SLOW, the pedestrian crossings, the traffic lights, and even the speed cameras. Everyone else hates them, because they have not, as Job has, lived and driven in a place without law.

Job sighs, and flexes his legs as the warm air starts pumping out of the engine. It is a strange way to make a living, but it is cash in hand and that is what he needs most. He has to keep the car immaculate and make sure he looks clean and neat, even though he has nothing to wash in but an old cracked basin. He is saving in order to buy himself a false EU passport, and for three hundred pounds he has now obtained a fake British driving licence, which is essential. Everything costs so much, but the money he sends back to Zimbabwe every month, which would not even pay a week's rent or food here, is all that is keeping his wife and sister's family alive.

'There is food in the markets, but none we can buy without dol-lars,' Munisha told him. 'Every day, inflation makes what we earn less and less. My salary will not even buy us a head of corn.'

Come to me, come to me here, he begged, but there is no money. She is stuck, unless like thousands of others she makes the dangerous crossing to South Africa.

'If things get no better, that is what we shall try to do,' she said, the last time they were able to speak. He has tried calling her mobile number, but it doesn't even ring. Perhaps there is no electricity to recharge it, or perhaps she is out of range. He has to believe this, rather than the alternatives. All the same, when he watches the news about his country on TV, he is always looking for her. She and his sister had given him every dollar they had to get him out of the country, like the birds that King Lear described – the pelicans, giving blood from their own breasts in order to feed their children. Job has found an illustrated book about birds in one of the second-hand bookshops that he haunts in his spare time, and looked pelicans up. He had been disappointed to find them not just hideously ugly, with huge bag-like beaks, but white.

When Job arrived at Heathrow airport, he fully intended to claim asylum. He had the scars from his beatings still fresh on his back and legs, all the documentation he could gather together as proof – which was not much. How can you prove you were attacked for not voting a particular way? He was not even a member of a trade union – which had of course been banned too – only a young student, who had been arrested and imprisoned for wanting democracy. Then, ahead of him in the queue, he had heard someone else from Zimbabwe claim asylum at the passport control. The officer hissed, 'You people aren't wanted here, don't you understand?'

The expression on her square pink face had taken him right back to his beatings. He entered on a student visa, enrolled in a college which never taught a single student. Every African Job knows has entered on a student visa. There are African tourists, of course. He has seen them, stepping out of limousines and gliding along Bond

Street: the wives of dictators and kings whose money is sent out of Africa. But Job lives in a very different kind of city.

In Harare, too, there were rich areas where the lawns were immaculate and nobody went hungry, and poor areas where now people drank water from open sewers. Here, people are more mixed up although the place where Job lives is all poor people because it is an estate. Although Job only has a tiny room, he likes the grass all around it, with some trees and flower beds, and even a small play area – all luxuries where he comes from.

'You know the only rule you need to know to get on in this country?' one of his employers told him. 'Never complain, never explain. Keep your mouth shut, mind your own business, and nobody will even know you're here.'

Nobody else will do what Job and his kind do, and doing it makes them invisible men as it is. Rubbish must be collected and roads swept, crops picked and chickens plucked, cars washed and offices cleaned, elderly nursed and children watched. If you are willing to accept two pounds fifty an hour instead of the minimum wage, if you are polite, punctual, professional and above all humble, then people will give you work. It's called the black market, though at least half those who work in it are white.

Job needs the toilet. He knows the others don't like him using it, but where else is he to go? The tiny lobby has three battered chairs to sit on, and here, lingering, he sees Tariq, a middle-aged driver with bad teeth, looking depressed.

'A bad morning, two-three.'

'You took your sons in again?'

Tariq nods. 'There are too many drug-dealers at the gates.'

'You are right to do this,' Job says. 'You cannot risk your family.'

'They are bad, these Somalis.'

He glares at Job, broodingly, and Job wonders whether Tariq thinks that he too is Somali; it seems to him that few people make the distinction between one African country and another. Job's skin is lighter, in fact, than that of many of the other drivers.

Nevertheless, they look down on him, and he will never share so much as a cup of tea with them.

Back in his car, he tries to concentrate on the newspaper that he picked up outside the Zimbabwean Embassy. Underneath a photograph of a child with a belly full of air, the headline says:

STAND UP AND BE COUNTED!
Day by day, inch by inch, yard by yard, it's hard. Enough is
enough! Sokwanele! Zvakwana!
You, who with pride, resilience, courage and patriotism have so far
carried the national independence torch and aspiration – STAND
UP AND BE COUNTED.
You, who are the power, you, who are the life and the nation's
backbone – ARISE TO THE CALL.
Shed the fear, wipe the tear, brave the storm and lift your
expectations higher. Cry, our beloved country, cry!
Demonstrate your rights which are enshrined in the universal law
of human rights and liberties, and endorsed in the spirit of
brotherhood and the Holy Scriptures. It is not only your right to be
free, but also the will of the Almighty.

It is all so noble, so fearless, and it will do absolutely nothing. Job has been reading calls like it ever since he left his country. But when you are young, he thinks, you have no idea what the old and cruel can do to you.

'Two-three, two-three, do you copy?'

'Yes, sir. I'm right here.'

'I have a fare to pick up from Barnsbury, travelling to the centre. A Mrs Noble, pick up from number twenty-seven.'

He listens to the directions, and takes off. The traffic is heaving with impatience and anger all around King's Cross, and in the middle of it all there is the usual scramble to make way for an ambulance screaming past, followed by a police car. Buses, lorries, taxis, motorbikes, cycles and private cars are all welded into a single stream of metal and flesh oozing towards the centre. Every day it's the same. The buses steam with the sheer numbers of people trying to get to work.

How is it possible to be so crowded, and yet so lonely? Job sometimes feels that, without the touch of another human being, he will wither and shrivel. He lives in a society entirely composed of men. White people, and especially women, treat him as an extension of his car, which he can understand because to get into a vehicle with a strange man is not something any woman would necessarily feel comfortable about.

The address that Mo has given him is close to where he lives. He can see mothers walking their children to school, the women in long, dun-coloured robes and headscarves, or completely covered in black veils. Their children run ahead, warmly dressed in pink fluffy anoraks or blue coats, looking happy and well fed. They will be from other, war-torn places, or perhaps descended from refugees yet further back in time.

Somehow they have got the indefinite right to remain, Job thinks enviously. They will grow up as Britons, whereas people like himself whose history has been intimately intertwined with this country are denied it. They will have free health care, schooling, housing; they will be rocked in the cradle of the state while he falls endlessly through the air, with nobody to catch him.

4

She Hopes She Doesn't Look Too Young

Anna slumps on the seat, feeling the metallic vibrations of the ferry through her bones like a presentiment of disaster. The January crossing has been terrible, with the floor seeming to tilt in every direction, so terrible that for much of it she thought death would be a relief. She has never before been conscious of her body as something separate from herself, capable of revolt and a profound, animal misery. The bottle of water given to her had come up as bile, and the sour taste in her mouth hurts her teeth, but worst of all is the nausea, poisoning her stomach and head. Her trainers are soaked in vomit.

The other girls are trying to sleep on the hard moulded seats, while older travellers get drunk on duty-free alcohol and take photographs of each other in bedraggled red hats decorated with tinsel. For hours, they have endured the stuffy, squeaking bus that thundered across Europe, stopping and starting when the driver wanted to relieve himself in a lay-by but rarely pausing to let them do the same. Now they are all on the ferry, the plumbing is better and they can move around more, but the feelings are worse. Knowing that she is cut off from the rest of Europe by this interminable expanse of angry grey water is making her family feel far more remote than she had

27

ever thought they would. Good, she thinks. If this is what it takes to be independent, she is glad.

Natalya winks at her. This enormous boat, with its tiers of levels and smell of oil and salt, would be terrifying if she were alone, but Natalya has organised it well. All her life, Anna has been the one to organise others: her little brother Pyotr, her sisters (actually her aunt's three children), Katya, Olga and Raisa, besides looking after Granny Vera while her own mother worked herself into exhaustion in her job. She has never had a childhood, she feels, resentfully, and they never loved her.

When she announced her decision to go to London with Natalya, her mother, surprisingly, had burst into tears, saying she was too young. Anna suspects it was the thought of losing her services rather than herself that caused this.

'She's fifteen,' her grandmother said. 'By her age, I was the same. Let her go.'

Anna's grandmother has always hated Anna's mother, and Anna has picked up something of this, for her mother's opposition to her going only made her more eager.

'Why do you deny me this chance?' she asked, angry and tearful. 'Don't you trust me?'

'You are a good, kind girl, Anna, and I fear for you,' her mother said; but Natalya told her she was far too pretty to be stuck in a dump like Lutsk, and that made all the difference.

Although the long, long hours of the journey are boring, Anna is excited. At last she is out of the Ukraine! She hopes she doesn't look too young; in the ferry toilets, she reapplies her eyeliner and mascara, and wishes she could cover her skin in a thick flesh-coloured foundation and powder like the others. Her ears look childishly unadorned, and she looks with envy at the big silver hoops that another girl is wearing. If she could only have big silver hoops in her own ears, how happy she would be! The other girl must be British, and Anna studies her with interest and envy, noting how bright and skimpy her clothes are. Anna is amazed by everything: the white ship as big as the apartment block where her family lived – how did it stay afloat? Why didn't it fall over on its side, or sink with the weight of all the lorries, buses and cars in its base? It seems miraculous, but so does a Christmas tree made of artificial needles nearby, which softly changes colour from red to violet to blue to green. She thinks she'll never tire of watching it.

I had to get away, she thinks. There is nothing for her in Lutsk, no jobs, no money, no hope. It was the same for her father. It was either Britain or Poland, and in Poland the only jobs men got were to replace the workers who had come to Britain, so what was the point?

They are all around the same age, teenagers who have watched each other out of the corners of their eyes. Anna has shared her eye-liner with one girl, and lent a hair-clip to another, and in doing so they have exchanged information, shyly, over the past few days. Some are being brought over by their boyfriends, some by friends and some by agencies, but all are coming together on the bus. To get to England, to London, is the dream of all. They have tried out halting English phrases on each other.

'How many years are you?'

'I yam fifteen,' Anna says.

'What is your work?'

'I am very strong. I am hotel chambermaid. What is your name?'

'My name is Valentina.'

At school they had been taught Russian – as if anyone with any sense would want to work *there*. Russia had even stolen the earth of her country, the deep, rich black earth in which any crop would grow. If there are any jobs in Russia, they will be for Russians, she thinks; so she hardly bothered to learn it. English is the key. Natalya says so too.

'I think if you come to London, you could be a model. It happens, you know.'

Of course Anna knows. All Ukrainian girls know about Olga Kurylenko, who is in the new James Bond movie, and used to be a model.

'You must have many boyfriends,' Natalya remarks admiringly, and Anna, because she does not want to seem like a child, blushes and nods, not daring to say that she has never so much as held a boy's hand.

'Many English men are lonely. Maybe you would like to go out with one?'

'Maybe,' Anna says. Some of the girls on the bus have a hard, flirtatious look and dress less modestly than she does. Anxious not to seem provincial, she undoes a button on her blouse.

They are in England. The creaking see-saw of the ferry stops, and the call goes out for everyone to go below and get onto their vehicle. The Ukrainians pile onto their bus, and when it rolls down the ramps in the darkness Anna tries to see if it feels different. She wants there to be something distinctive about this new country, but all she can see is the light of the docks, and some warehouses which look the same the world over. Their passports are checked, and everyone holds their breath, smiling and pretending to be tourists. It must be a good time to come in, because the official is yawning and tired at the end of the night.

Now, at last, they are moving. The road is smoother, perhaps, but the dim orange lights show little. Still, orange is the colour of hope in her country. She thinks of the pictures she had seen of London in a film on TV. It is a green place where beautiful people spend their lives falling in love in flower-filled gardens. Anna has butterflies in her empty stomach, just thinking about it. Everyone is excited, and some girls even have cameras with which they take pictures to send their families. Eventually, they pass more and more buildings – small houses on their own, and huge advertisements, and then office blocks on either side, and more houses. She can't get used to how different they all are from what she is used to, and the immensity of it all, but it isn't even London.

Now, after increasingly frequent stops and starts, the bus grinds to a halt at a lay-by on the motorway. Some other cars are parked there, with their lights on and their engines running. These will be their new employers, the ones for whom having the correct paperwork will not matter, because of England's great need for hotel chambermaids, nannies and waitresses. There is a long, slow hissing sound in the silence, as the bus's pneumatic brakes relax. Then the doors are opened, and the air rushes in, damp and sweet. The girls gasp, stretch and twist, like fish in a net, under the dull red light of dawn.

Dimly, Anna understands that money is changing hands as, fuddled by sleep, the girls collect their bags and are taken off into cars. Natalya has told her that this is part of the service, that the agents pay to collect her and will take a percentage of her earnings.

'Will you be there too?' Anna asked. 'Will you be at my new job?'

'Me? Oh no!' Natalya laughed, as if the very idea was ridiculous. 'You will make your own friends. London is a very friendly city.'

'You are Anna?' says a man in Russian. She is a little surprised by this; somehow, she had expected an English person to be there.

There are two of them, as big as bears. They are called Sergei and Dmitri, and wear black leather jackets and identical gold chains round their necks. They stare at her. Anna has seen this expression before. Maybe her clothes and make-up aren't so bad, she thinks.

Sergei opens the door to a big car, black and shiny as a boot. Dmitri starts the engine at once, and Anna leans back. She has never been in a car like this before, and is delighted. She strokes the furry plush of the upholstery. How Pyotr would love this, she thinks. Maybe I can find him a toy as soft as this, a dog perhaps or a little cat . . .

'Put your seat belt on. It is illegal to travel without one.'

Sergei's voice is harsh and glottal, and she obeys with trembling fingers. The wide webbing cuts into her breasts and neck, and feels too tight, and she is afraid she might vomit again in the warm air.

The big black car with its tinted windows swishes along the motorway and enters the city. By now, the sun has risen, and Anna can see more and more wonderful things. She can't take it all in: the endless buildings, the billboards on the walls flip-flopping to form one picture after another, the shops brilliant with colour, the churches, the little parks, the faces rushing past. There is so much! Where are their old men and women? There is not one person who looks like her grandmother here, but there are people with skin as brown as wood or as black as charcoal; people with narrow eyes or broad noses or hair like wool. She is used to people who all look alike, and these are all unalike.

The car is like a moving room, with deep, soft seats. Music shouts from its speakers, and luxurious warm air plays over Anna's face. She is a little uncomfortable having the two men in the car, but she looks out of the window, at streets hung with dazzling lights and decorations. It's like looking into a book of fairy tales. She is so happy, she forgets she is tired and thirsty and that they have not even offered her something to drink.

'What does SALE mean?'

The men – so alike that she thinks they must be brothers – turn fractionally towards her.

'No talking.'

Chastened, Anna shrinks back. She mustn't offend them. Natalya has told her that, once in England, she will be a criminal because she will be working without a visa.

'This is why they must keep your passport. If you are found with your passport, you will go to prison.'

At last the car draws up outside a row of old houses on a hill. The bottom third of the houses is painted white, and the top is brick. They get out, and Sergei holds Anna's arm as they go up the steps as if he sees how sick she still feels. Dmitri gets out a key and jabs it into a big door, turning it impatiently. Inside, it is wide but dirty. I am in an *English* house, Anna thinks, and her excitement makes her forget her discomfort. At some point in the journey the sun has come out and now, for a few moments, the hall is lit up with specks of dazzling dust, all dancing and swirling in uncountable millions. A long time ago, she believed that every one of those points of glittering brightness was a minute angel, watching over her. Into this cloud of gold, Anna sees a shape descending.

It is a woman. The light has got into her pale hair and made it glow around her head. The woman is slim, wearing a long, shapeless coat like a robe, and she is smiling. Anna looks up at her, wonderingly.

'I'm Katie,' the woman says in English, and Anna smiles back. 'I live in the apartment upstairs.'

Anna is reassured, although Sergei is gripping her so hard now that she almost cries out. A melodious, questioning gabble comes out of the woman's mouth, too fast to follow. The men growl back. Anna can't understand what they say, but she recognises the tone, which is hostile.

Dmitri has unlocked a door and pushes Anna towards the flat that it opens into. When they are inside he says in Russian, 'Never draw attention to yourself again. Never smile at foreigners.'

'I'm sorry. I forgot.'

The men say nothing. There are two women on the black PVC couch in front of a TV in the front room. Anna looks at them, wondering who they are. They wear very short skirts, a lot of make-up and tight tops which cling to their bodies. One is blonde and the other dark. They ignore Anna completely, though the blonde one looks up and grins vaguely at Dmitri.

'Hey.'

'Hello, baby,' he says in English. Anna knows these words; it's what boys called out to her.

The front window has a grey net curtain in it, and on the other side are thick iron bars. Behind is a passage and another room, but there is an internal stair she can see to a floor below. It's a strange, comfortless place. The walls have pictures of half-dressed women on it that make her flush and avert her eyes at once, because they are holding their glistening, oiled breasts out like fruit, and some are bent over with their legs spread, parting their shaved crotches.

A twist of unease grows and coils in Anna's guts. They are men, and men like these kinds of pictures, she thinks; but she dislikes them.

33

She wonders why men never see that the girls' expressions are hateful.

The dark girl snickers. She has her eyes on the TV, where brightly coloured little people are running about, trying to build a machine out of scrap metal.

'Please,' says Anna, her need now becoming too urgent. 'Where is the toilet?'

'In there,' says Sergei. 'It has a shower.'

He jerks his head, and Anna picks up her bag and scurries down a short passage lit by a single naked bulb to a small room. She wedges the door shut (it has no lock, for some reason), uses the toilet, then twists the shower tap on the tile wall. A surprisingly forceful spray shoots out, and drenches her. She takes off her trainers, peels off her stinking clothes, and steps in. I am being baptised, she tells herself; I am becoming British.

It is cold, but the room fills with steam. Anna, clean and happy, begins to sing.

> *'Ti skazala shto v vivtorok*
> *Potseluyesh raziv sorok*
> *A ti meneh obmanula,*
> *Obmanula tai zabula.*
>
> *You told me that on Tuesday*
> *You would kiss me forty times,*
> *But you tricked me*
> *You tricked me and forgot me . . .'*

The door is rapped on sharply.

'Hurry up.'

She looks for a towel. There is only a worn cotton rag of a dull pink colour hanging limply from a nail. Anna does the best she can to dry herself with it. She wants to wash her trainers, but there isn't time. At least she has a change of clothes in her small rucksack. She puts these on. The smell of home, which she has never before noticed as something particular and precious, overwhelms her with nostalgia.

'It would have been better, it would have been better not to go
    walking,
It would have been better, it would have been better not to fall in
    love,
It would have been better, it would have been better not even to
    have known you . . .'

She rubs the little mirror on the wall to clear the condensation, and puts on some make-up. She doesn't look too young, does she? Perhaps everything will be fine.

Anna walks out of the toilet. The two men are standing in the doorway to the reception room.

'I can work now?' she asks, in careful English.

She hopes that it will not be for a day, so that she can rest and recover, but the men exchange a glance.

'Good,' says Sergei. 'Is better.'

There is a kind of tension between the two men. They are looking at her, and grinning.

'OK.' She draws a deep breath, and tries to look confident. She thinks how to say what she wants in English. 'I am ready.'

'Baby.'

Sergei seizes her wrists. Anna twists and struggles in his grasp, but it makes no difference. His thick hands, covered in long dark hair, are stronger than she could have imagined. He pushes and jostles her along the corridor towards the back room. There is a bed, and little else. Through the door, she glimpses the other women.

'Help, help me!' she shrieks, but Sergei looms over her, vast, solid and dark.

'It's no use pretending, *sukha*.'

'Please! You've made a mistake!'

Then he hits her, very deliberately, across the face with his hand, and she staggers back. Her head is an iron bell of pain and disbelief.

'You want this, don't you?'

'Oh, no, no, no,' Anna says, and her knees buckle as she understands.

'You owe us $5,000,' Sergei says, grinning. He pins her down with one hand, and unzips with the other. 'That's what we paid Natalya. So now you're going to pay us back, like a good girl, or your family will do it instead.'

5

Not That Kind Of Girl

Katie allows herself the luxury of a car home to Camden, because she isn't paying for it. Her life is now predicated upon thrift and self-denial, but Ivo Sponge has insisted. For such an amusing, amiable man, he can be surprisingly commanding.

'I'm in Highbury, I can drop you on the way,' he said. 'I've a mini-cab booked to collect me. Don't be ridiculous, I'm as jet-lagged as you are, and hacks should stick together.'

'I'm not a hack, I'm an editorial assistant,' Katie said.

'Whatever. Don't worry, I'm a married man and quite safe in taxis these days.'

They had sat next to each other on the flight back, and struck up a conversation because both were reading the latest issue of the *Rambler*. Grateful though she is for any excuse to avoid the subway, Katie is just a little uneasy. Ivo is the bombastic kind of journalist, and knows her boss, Quentin.

'Not the easiest of chaps to work for, I imagine,' he says, in an enquiring tone.

Katie says blandly, 'He can be quite demanding.'

'You know, what I always wonder about Quentin is how he manages all that hair,' says Ivo (whose own locks are receding somewhat). 'It must be a full-time job just keeping it under control.'

'He is very handsome, though,' says Katie.

Ivo darts her a quick, amused look. 'Aha. Do I detect an office romance?'

'Certainly not!' says Katie, indignantly. 'I'm not that kind of girl.'

'So what are you doing there?'

'It's . . . well, an experiment.'

Ivo laughs. 'Did you hear about when Trench's wife met the Prime Minister, and he asked her what she would like for Christmas?'

'No.'

'She said, "I would like a penis."'

'My goodness.' Katie can see the driver flick his gaze in her direction. He's young and has a miniature Koran dangling from his driver mirror. 'You mean – she wants a sex change?'

'No. What she meant was, she would like *happiness*. But as she's French and Roger's immoderately unfaithful, everyone thought—'

'I haven't been to a *Rambler* party yet,' Katie confesses.

'No! Everyone goes, my darling, especially now. The Prime Minister, half the Cabinet, the good and great . . . you know what they say about it?'

'What?'

'If a bomb went off there, it'd wipe out everyone who's anyone. Not that Trench is anyone.'

'I haven't met him yet.'

'He's one of those men who've risen without trace; mind you, so many press barons are like that. Max de Monde was just the same, and look what happened to him. Trench is just lucky to get someone as clever as Quentin to edit for him.'

'I wouldn't think that just owning the *Rambler* made you into a press baron,' says Katie.

'No, but it does buy you profile,' says Ivo. 'A slice of literary history, a staff composed entirely of pretty young toffs, access to the good and great – well, of course Trench would want it. It's not really a serious weekly any more, but who cares? Before, he was just another anonymous multimillionaire who'd made a packet buying up half of King's Cross before the Eurostar; now, he's someone who gets to meet Prime Ministers and tell them how to run the country.'

'Do they listen?'

'I hope not. Man's a raving nutjob . . . God, look at this cartoon! That'll have the mullahs frothing away.'

Katie looks at it, and sighs. It is one of 'Felix' Viner's, showing a man with a bomb on his head instead of a turban, saying 'Islam is a religion of peace', and it accompanies a call by the Political Editor, Mark Crawley, to close down faith schools in Britain.

'Oh dear.'

'Yes. I liked the old *Rambler*, gently purple and open to contrarian opinions across the political spectrum. But it is still read in the House. I suppose we ought to be glad some politicians *do* still read. It always punches above its weight, silly old mag.'

'My parents take it back home, you know. That's partly why I applied.'

The red-dyed road takes them round the Buckingham Palace round-about, and past St James's Park, with its exotic, brilliant pink flamingos balancing, one-legged, in the lake. It reminds Katie of a book she had loved as a child, called *Madeline in London*. Something about a little sunshine, a little rain, and everything would be all right again. She smiles, sadly. Even if she loathes Winthrop as much as she had once loved him, she doesn't think she will ever be completely all right again.

'So, you like living here?'

'Yes,' she says. 'It's different to New York, of course, but I like that.'

'Aha,' said Ivo. 'You're running away.'

'Am I so transparent?'

'Not at all. It's a common reason for American women to come to London, my wife tells me. That, or looking for Mr Darcy.'

Ivo chuckles. He's a kind man but not a good one, Katie perceives, although his flirtatiousness is rather sweet.

'I was engaged to someone. It didn't work out.'

Ivo says, with cherubic impertinence, 'So now you're thin and mad and reinventing yourself. A bold move.'

Katie shrugs. 'I got my fiancée's visa to work here for a year, and the *Rambler* job lined up, so I thought, why not?'

She keeps her tone light, but she can feel Ivo scrutinising her. She hopes, very much, that he doesn't know Winthrop's family. He's the kind of person who might.

'You think this is a safer berth?'

'England still feels . . . well, gentler and kinder.'

'Oh, but I love America,' said Ivo. 'I absolutely adore it.'

'You can't like Americans. Nobody does, these days.'

'Of course I do. I'm married to one. I'll tell you the difference between our countries: Americans think that life is serious but not hopeless; the English that life is hopeless but not serious.'

Katie suspects Ivo has trotted this joke out rather frequently. She does not say that she herself feels life to be both serious and hopeless, and that she came to Britain as an alternative to suicide.

'You take care of yourself in that snake-pit,' Ivo says.

'Is it a snake-pit?'

'My dear girl, they all are. No British institution but the media is so full of malice, envy, spite and chicanery, mixed in of course with generosity, loyalty, expertise and wit. All the most interesting people work in it, or think they do. You'll be lucky to come out alive.'

'I'm only a sort of secretary,' Katie says, truthfully.

Eventually, the minicab bumps uphill to the row of terraced houses where she lives. Agar Grove is a long, nondescript street in a kind of no-man's-land between Camden and Islington, ringed by council estates but also, like so many parts of the city, containing four or five blocks of agreeable but run-down Victorian villas. Katie's one-bedroom apartment is in one of the shabbiest of these, but the rent is only £1000 a month: more than half her salary, but worth it to live alone.

'Thank you so much,' she says, politely. 'Are you sure I can't split the bill?'

Ivo hesitates, then waves a chubby hand. 'Expenses, dear girl, expenses. I'm sure we'll meet again. Don't let Quentin bully you.'

He'll probably never remember my name, she thinks as the mini-cab pulls away. Once she had been pretty enough to be engaged to Winthrop T. Sheen III, Wall Street banker and scion of one of the richest families on the East Coast, but now she is just Katie Perry, a Cinderella in reverse who has lost her career, her fiancé and her bloom.

She opens the big, shabby black-painted door and goes into the lobby, crusted with dirty cream paint over what looks like carefully spaced blobs of dried mucus. Light falls from the opaque sash window on the half-landing, illuminating a mess. It smells of old carpet, patchouli and the sour-sweet ghosts of Chinese takeaways. This house, and a surprising number of those nearby, is owned by a property company; the comparatively low rent being compensation for the general neglect in communal areas, the ill-fitting windows and the erratic plumbing.

The floor beneath Katie's is occupied by a disc jockey, invisible and inaudible unless he plays rock music at three a.m., but the ground-floor maisonette has been empty for a while, being damp and dark and hard to let. The whole building is in a bad state. Her mail is scattered on the floor, bearing the faded ridges of at least one large shoe. A floating, disembodied sensation of exhaustion makes the long flight of stairs to the top flat seem especially vertiginous. She plods up and up, until she arrives at the featureless door which gives onto her own apartment. The frame scrapes her knuckles as she turns the keys.

It is even shabbier, dirtier and colder than she'd recollected. Books, the one thing she had shipped over in bulk, lie in haphazard piles on the floor and the sagging couch. The windows are smeared with dust on one side and dirt on the other, and the skylight in the ceiling gives onto a slab of neon grey. When she first moved in, Katie bought some red drapes from John Lewis in an attempt to brighten it up, but the drawstring tape had defeated her.

They now hang limply from hooks, like despondent bats. The view is terrific, she says silently to herself, looking out over a patchwork of wintry back gardens towards King's Cross, as far as Canary Wharf and the London Eye. It could be made more pleasant, if she had the energy to unpack. Outside the back window of her living room is a kind of shallow ledge, made by the stack of the flats below, where some previous tenant had left a couple of plastic window-boxes filled with compacted earth, and two rickety wooden chairs, perhaps to enjoy the evening sun in summer (if summer ever came to England).

Katie switches the thermostat up, and turns on Radio 3, telling herself for the hundredth time that she's lucky to have found this place. She'd been working in her new job and staying in a terrible bed-and-breakfast hotel, flat-hunting through *Loot* and gumtree.com, when she'd spotted the card advertising it for rent on the office noticeboard. As so often these days, she feels like bursting into tears, but instead takes down her jar of dried beans to soak for her evening meal. She must remember to buy orange juice and milk, because apart from a single sprouting onion her fridge is empty.

'Honey, you were just too young,' her mother had said, at Christmas. 'You have to start over. There'll be someone else.'

'I'll never find someone else. I'm hideous.'

Katie forces herself to drink herbal tea. She isn't anorexic, as her parents fear, she just can't remember what wanting anything ever again feels like. But the world won't leave her in peace. Already, her cellphone is vibrating like a trapped wasp. Several are messages for Quentin, rerouted through to her from the office because he is so frequently out, but then the familiar voice barks, 'Katie! Whilst I understand that the consumption of enormous meals is an imperative in your country, I will be producing a turkey of my own here should you fail to get on the next flight back. Beep!'

Quentin again, 'Katie! Heel! Now!'

Quentin Bredin is like all those fabled English gentlemen whom Katie had adored in novels, whose languid manner and habitual sneer conceals a host of manly virtues. So far the virtues are conspicuously absent. Famously, he rides everywhere on a Harley-Davidson motorbike, and expects her to catch his helmet as he walks in. People who don't know him believe that his views are those of an ironist, but Katie thinks they are the unvarnished truth. Quentin will sit in his boxer shorts while getting her to sew up a rip in his trousers. A born contrarian, he can not only bring himself to believe six impossible things before breakfast, but persuade a hundred thousand others to do so as well. He is vain, imperious, clever and shallow, and his charm is turned on strictly according to whim.

'I'm not coming in,' Katie reminds herself. 'I'm still on vacation.'

The next call is from Patrick, the designer. 'Katie, I know you're probably stuck somewhere over the Atlantic, but if there is any way you could hurry back ASAP it would be a good idea. Nobody has a clue about how to work Quark Express and we've just had an ad for inflatable bath cushions come in and I – coming!'

Katie sighs. Magazines, she knows from past experience, seem to act as powerful magnifying glasses on the natures of their staff, but those on the *Rambler* are outside her previous experience. As Quentin's assistant she performs a job that has no definition, but which seems to include doing everything from being the receptionist to sub-editing copy.

'Patrick,' she says to his voicemail. 'Hope you had a good vacation. My plane just landed, I'm coming in.'

Downstairs, she sees a group of people unlocking the door to the maisonette.

'Hi there! Are you the new tenants?'

They look Eastern European, she thinks. Two are men in black leather jackets, wearing gold chains round their necks, and they scowl at her, but one is a young girl with soft brown eyes and a look of puppyish anxiety. Katie smiles at her.

'I'm Katie. I live in the apartment upstairs.'

The girl smiles back, shyly.

Katie launches into her spiel. 'I've been trying to get a system

43

sorted, you know, for the mail we get? It makes sense if mine is left at the end of the shelf, there.' She puts her hand down on the hall shelf, then removes it hastily because it is thick with dust. 'Then yours could go in a pile at the other end, and the first-floor flat in the middle.'

One man is staring at her with a curious, hot, indifferent glare. It makes her feel most uncomfortable.

'Do you understand?'

'Hello, goodbye,' says the other man abruptly. He has a harsh Eastern European accent, and both men have their hair gelled up into spikes like a porcupine's quills.

'Oh, sorry,' Katie says, flustered by the feeling that she has broken yet another unspoken rule of life in London. 'Well – see you later, I guess.'

She wonders why the young girl looks confused, and why the man holding her has to grip her so tightly.

It isn't my problem, she thinks as the bus turns along her street. They are foreigners, like herself. This is why she has come to London, where nobody knows her, or cares.

6

Self-help at the Samuel Smiles

Ian often wonders whether he would not do more good for the pupils at the Samuel Smiles Secondary School if, instead of trying to teach them English, he were simply to show them how to fry an egg for breakfast. Most of them come to school with nothing more than a packet of crisps and a can of Coke in their stomachs – he cycles past the packaging in the street – and so, of course, they are unable to concentrate even at their best time of day. Ian, who has been replacing a staff teacher who had a nervous breakdown in the autumn term, is still getting to grips with who they are – a task made less easy because a number of them fail to turn up.

'This is a list of my rules,' he had told them in the first week. 'If you can find one rule that you think is stupid, and you can explain why, I'll let you off school for a day.'

He had said it firmly and pleasantly, and the bored faces had brightened a little. Needless to say, none of the boys had found a stupid rule, but that didn't stop around a third of his class playing truant. Effectively, he is here as an alternative to Borstal, not to teach. They kick off at the slightest excuse, and he is expected to bring them back into line by sheer force of personality. If he so much as taps a pupil, he risks being accused of assault. There is still time to catch most of them and get them to learn something before they became hopeless, he thinks, but he knows that the window of enlightenment is getting narrower each day. Self-help at the Samuel Smiles means keeping out of trouble, at best; at worst, it means mugging another boy for his mobile phone.

'You know, when I taught in South Africa I didn't realise that I was lucky to be able to teach.' He complains far too often, he knows.

'So why don't you leave?' Candice says. 'You could go to a private school and teach kids who really want to learn.'

'There's nothing wrong with the kids,' Ian says automatically. It's axiomatic that children are never in the wrong: teachers blame the parents, and parents the teachers. 'Besides, I have to stick it out for three terms. I need that qualification if I'm to have a career.'

Candice believes he is headed for one of the fee-paying schools around Hampstead and Highgate, where dozens of other South Africans, Australians and Kiwis seem to wind up, enjoying green fields and Olympic-sized swimming pools. Ian had gone to a school just like that in the suburbs of Jo'burg, and had done part of his teacher training at another. It is a comfortable option, and he could spend his life in it. But if he wants to travel as a teacher, or progress in the state system, then he needs to be more than an NQT or newly qualified teacher.

Ian's current school, the Samuel Smiles, is a tall, red-brick Victorian building in Hackney with high windows and vaguely Dutch gables near the roof, of the kind that is much sought after by property developers to turn into luxury flats. This run-down site should be undergoing a process of refurbishment and investment, but instead the Head is spending the money on getting security for an outbuilding that is persistently targeted by arsonists – many of them, it's said, ex-pupils. As a result, the Samuel Smiles is a wreck. Ceiling tiles fall off, fluorescent lights flicker and collapse, windows are left smashed and the ceilings of the toilets have stalactites of paper hanging from them. Ian and his colleagues teach in class-rooms which are so uncomfortable that they are probably dangerous.

'You know,' says Sally, the other supply teacher who joined around the same time as Ian, 'all that's holding this whole place up is red tape.'

'Just like Heathrow Airport,' he tells her.

'Yeah, and don't I wish I was on the flight home on days like these,' she says. Her round, bespectacled face, framed by curls of hazel hair, is despondent. She teaches maths, which most of the kids hate even more than they hate fruit, and sometimes Ian has to leave his own class to go next door and quieten down hers.

Just get them through the coursework, he tells himself. When he'd started teaching, he'd been full of ideals about wanting to inspire the new generation with a love of reading. Now they're grinding through *Of Mice and Men*, something that is on the National Curriculum and which is, like all such texts, being squeezed drier than a shrivelled raisin. They don't have to read the whole novel, short as it is; but they must answer questions on it. Ian reads it to them, hamming up each character appallingly and putting on an unconvincing American accent that makes them laugh.

'Tell me, who thinks Lennie is a smart guy?' he asks, gazing out at class after class. The sullen faces – some still eleven, some sprouting moustaches at almost thirteen – stare back. 'Amir? Omar?'

'Maybe,' says Omar, uncertainly.

'Ah, come on, he's even thicker than you are!' says Chris. With relief, the boys start shouting at each other. Everything imaginable has been done to make Ian's subject as dreary and soul-destroying as possible, so that it is less about responding to real literature and more about grammar, punctuation and comprehension.

Ian can feel that familiar mix of stress, anxiety, frustration and exhaustion rising up again, to sour the breath in his throat. 'Quiet! Quieten down, or you'll be going On Call!'

The threat is an empty one: all that will happen if he sends them

47

to see the Head is that they will wander round the corridors, either vandalising school property or beating up other pupils On Call.

'If we could only treat the little blighters like the imams do, we'd solve all our discipline problems at a stroke,' says Meager, a history teacher, in the staffroom where everyone is having a quick mug of tea during break before the bell rings.

'Do they work harder for them, then?'

Meager laughs. 'Yes, and their parents pay for them to learn! You know, this stuff about free education is where the rot set in. Literacy rates are worse than they were a hundred years ago, because you just don't value what you get for free, and you don't value what is given to you as an automatic right. I've seen this school turn from being a perfectly decent secondary modern, serving the white working class, to a dump.'

Ian dislikes Meager, who also teaches sport with him, but he has to admit that something isn't right. His classes, like almost everyone else's, are far too noisy and disruptive. Boys feeling their hormones, maybe: many of them are as tall as he is, and some of the Afro-Caribbeans are probably stronger. They slouch around in hoodies, jump over six-foot school walls and make female teachers feel threatened in the grounds.

There are tried and tested techniques. Greet them all by name as they flood in, and never let a queue build up outside his classroom door. Put the troublemakers in the front row. Remember who works well with each other, and who doesn't. Make each lesson something that can be absorbed more easily by the inattentive, their minds mostly on texting each other, gossiping or bunking off. Above all, act. Ian acts for five solid hours each day. He is tough, he can handle it; he is Slim in *Of Mice and Men*, he is Maximus in *Gladiator*, going into the arena. But actually, what helps him most is that the boys know he's big enough to give them trouble if they jostle him.

None of this is real teaching. It is simply creating the conditions in which it is possible, for five minutes, to teach. What he has to teach, far from being inspirational or useful, is the following:

Write a letter of complaint. Write a letter in response to your letter of complaint. Write a series of instructions for fire safety. Paraphrase the instructions on a leaflet.

There are general moans. Ian can feel them slipping, like a boat-load of disgruntled voyagers, off along the dark river of indifference.

'I know, they must really have taxed their brains hard to come up with such an interesting assignment. But you can still make this bit of coursework something you feel strongly about. How many of you hate where you live?'

Hands shoot up in the air. Everyone, it seems. Even Liam, one of the boys he has most trouble with, stops jigging about.

'Omar, what's wrong with yours?'

'It's shit, man. All council housing is shit.'

'OK, but you need to tell me why.'

'The lifts is broken, the lights is broken, the stairs stink of piss and there's gangs bustin' my dad's car.'

'We live next to a bunch of fucking nutters,' says Hanif. 'They play the TV so loud I can't sleep.'

'Right. So you need to write a letter to someone on the council in charge of housing – let's call him Mr—'

'Mr Dickhead!'

The class bursts out laughing.

'Mr Jones,' says Ian firmly, 'because I looked up who's in charge in this borough, that's his real name, and you can actually send him the letter. You know, if you send a letter, the council *has* to do something about it? Tell him that the lifts ARE broken, the lights ARE broken, and say you expect him to do something about it.'

'Yeah, but what's the point?' asks Amir. He is one of the brighter boys, Pakistani, with the line of a moustache coming on his upper lip. 'They won't do nothin' about it.'

'You need to know how to write a letter to get a job,' says Ian. 'You can't just send a text.'

Odion says, 'We don't get good jobs, man. That's for white people.'

'No, it's not. Anybody can get a good job in this country, as long as they work hard.'

There are mutters of disbelief and resentment. 'Look, these are your lives. Nobody can stop you realising your dreams. Nobody can make you marry against your will, put you in prison without a trial or deny you freedom of speech. Yes, Dylan?'

'Sir, that's not true is it, sir? If I call Amir a Paki bastard, I get sent to prison, but if he calls me names—'

There is a lot of shouting.

'Yes, well, if you called him that it would make you look stupid,' says Ian. 'You don't want people to think that, do you?'

Everyone assumes he must be racist the moment they hear his South African accent. One bloke he'd met in a pub, an Englishman, had blamed him personally for apartheid, and said, 'Admit it, you all beat black people with a whip every day.'

Ian had answered, 'Only every other day, not counting public holidays.'

He misses home so much that some days it's like a toothache. The older generation fled apartheid; the next one, crime; but his own are simply trying to gain employment. They pride themselves on being members of the Rainbow Generation, where colour no longer matters, but they feel trapped between two worlds. White graduates know that they can't regard Africa as a permanent home, but it's ingrained in them to feel it is. Candice is a dentist, working in a glossy practice in Hampstead; her family have been here for over a decade, and she still talks of Africa as 'home'.

What am I going to do? Ian thinks, as he strives to get them to lay out their letters correctly. One option is becoming clearer to him, if he chooses to take it.

'You know, most of my friends are married,' Candice said, before she went away.

'People here stay single until they're in their thirties,' he pointed out.

'That's why they have so many fertility problems.'

50

'You've got a way to go, I'd say.'

'You know, you could at least try living with me, instead of sticking in that dump. You can't really enjoy living with Mick the Slug and the lesbians.'

'They're my friends, Candy.'

Ian has enough on his plate at work, and he's still shaken from seeing the dead body on the Heath. It isn't the kind of thing you expect in London, he thinks. Nobody here automatically locks their car door as soon as they get in; you can walk around at night without being mugged; you don't need to live on a compound just in case you're burgled. In South Africa everyone knows someone who's been burgled and everyone knows someone who was murdered. Even now, London is a city that seems innocent and fearless.

Before he left Jo'burg, Ian taught in some of its poorest slums. It had been a charity job, but one of his most rewarding experiences. The kids knew that their only way out was through education, they wanted so much to learn. He couldn't get a job there, because of being white, but to him it is shocking to find British classrooms starved of books and overcrowded by poor children – not that, by African standards, these kids are poor.

'Why don' he knife Curley?' Omar asks, apropos the Steinbeck novel. 'He's gay, i'nt'e?'

There was a general hum of agreement. Ian says, 'He's got his fists.'

'Yeah, but a blade's better,' Omar says. They like this kind of discussion.

'Not if you're Lennie. Not if you know how to use them,' Ian says. 'That's half the problem with Lennie, isn't it? Steinbeck shows us that he doesn't know his own strength. How many of you have got into fights?'

All the boys put their hands up. They want to talk about their fights, and Ian knows he has seconds in which to switch their attention away from this and back onto *Of Mice and Men*.

'Well, remember you've got two legs for a reason. The best option in a fight is just to run away.'

The year has barely begun, and already teenagers are dying from stab wounds. Ian gets through his next two classes, then spends the break patrolling the playground. Don't fight, run away. Knives will get you killed. Maybe it will never sink in. Two kids have taken the blades out of pencil sharpeners, and think it funny to go around threatening to cut other kids. Someone else has a chain as a weapon. Just photocopying the four pages from *Of Mice and Men* that he needs to teach has taken a prodigious effort, because teachers continually squabble over who gets to use the copier first. The Samuel Smiles does not have enough class readers, which is one of its many short-term economies. Somehow, he's supposed to be able to get them through a scene of *Macbeth* next. He doesn't even want to think about that.

Sally, also on playground duty, looks pale and exhausted.

'I don't know how much longer I can stick it,' she mutters. 'This is a dreadful school, truly dreadful.'

'You want to move on?'

'They're all just as bad as each other.' She laughs, hysterically. 'Maybe I should go work as a nanny. Then I'd just have a couple of spoilt brats instead of a hundred.'

During a break, Ian stares at the TV screen in the staffroom. There, suddenly, on the news, is a picture of the Ponds at Hampstead Heath, followed by a photograph of a young woman with lank dark hair and the remote, glassy stare of the dead. It has to be the one he had seen on his way to work. He leans forward, wondering who she was. The newscaster informs them, brightly, that she was in her early twenties and probably of East European origin. Ian thinks she looks like hundreds or even thousands of others that he sees, waitressing in cafés, walking children in prams, taking tickets or serving in shops. He wonders whether anyone will even know her name.

7

A House of Cards

Once the police cars have passed, the traffic continues its slow crawl. The endless stream of smart, new, expensive cars fills Polly with appalled fascination. It's insane, she thinks; pumping out carbon monoxide just so that we can each sit in our own space, listening to our own music, thinking our own thoughts. She gives way to people she thinks need a break: other mums, other drivers of small battered cars, buses. The ones she will never let in are white vans, and those big show-off BMWs which could crush her battered Golf and not even notice it. But the car behind her is playing music so loudly that, even with the windows up and her own radio on, she can feel the vibrations through the road. Her temper rises. As she comes down Dartmouth Park Hill, a cyclist cuts across the road just in front of her bonnet.

'Idiot!' she yells out of the window.

He lifts a hand, either in abuse or apology. In Polly's childhood, people told each other off all the time but now they are petrified of the consequences if they draw any kind of attention to themselves. She watches the cyclist skim down the hill, trying to calm down by switching on Radio 4. Polly adores Radio 4. She has often thought that it's the thing that makes her proudest about being British, with its robust inquiry into all matters political, and its good-humoured but incisive expression of opinion. There is a discussion on the *Today* programme about whether anti-Semitism is rising.

'Of course it isn't, idiot,' says Polly, aloud; then wonders whether this is just her own perception. London isn't like New York – her American friends like Ellen can't understand why people here don't make any fuss about Passover and Yom Kippur – but apart from those weird Orthodox families who have to drive Volvos to accommodate their hats, Jews look and behave like everyone else. Her mother's family have been living in London since the 1930s, and are as English as her father's family.

'You can tell who the cleverest of us were because we got out early,' her maternal grandmother liked to say complacently. 'We could see what was happening, unlike some.'

It is the kind of attitude that still makes Polly furious. It's so easy, she thinks, to believe that others deserve their fate, and the fact was that if nobody bothered to help other people then the worst would always happen. Polly is still hurt by Tania's recent remark:

'Your trouble is, you think your farts smell of roses.'

It was typically obnoxious of her teenaged daughter, and most untrue. Everyone Polly works with is in the right, which is to say the Left. An unusual number of the lawyers Polly works with are the descendants of races that had suffered – but then, she reflects, what race has not? Go back in history, and who has not been trampled on, raped, exiled, enslaved? Sometimes, when she sees all her colleagues earnestly discussing some piece in the *Guardian* or the *New Statesman*, she does wonder whether their world view might not be a little too narrow.

Every morning, as she returns home to catch the bus into work, Polly sees families from the neighbouring estate walk slowly to the local primary school. As they glide along in their long dun robes, heads veiled, they smile and chat in their own tongue. Polly can't but prefer them to the white ones, who shriek, 'Don't fucking do that or I'll fucking kill you!' at every step.

Polly feels perfectly at ease about living in such a mixed area, but others who have lived in her street for much longer eye these families, and mutter about 'white flight'. One old man, a retired postman, has told her that he carries a switchblade 'just in case the bastards have a go'.

It is useless to talk to these people about why their new neighbours might want to be in Britain, or tell them that they may have even more fear of violence than white people. Their minds are made up on the matter: foreigners are here to grab benefits, jobs and free housing. In any case, they are not the ones lawyers have to persuade. Polly has a hearing at Rosebery Avenue, one of the many that will pay her about two thousand pounds for weeks of work. Most of her cases involve this, because for the past ten years the government has solved the problem of immigration by simply lifting its controls, and now they are trying to shut the door again. Nobody can decide whether, in a country whose indigenous population is ageing and falling, having uncounted thousands of young people from elsewhere is a good or bad thing. At present, the Home Office is bent on returning about two planeloads of immigrants out of Britain a week, simply to make it look as if they are still in control of the situation, while cutting Legal Aid. Mostly, the ones they pick on are women and children, who are the easiest to track down, and who are the poorest and most defenceless. These are the people Polly tries to help.

'But Mum, why don't you do the kind of law that Dad does?' Robbie once asked.

'Because somebody needs to do this kind.'

'You could make so much more money, though.'

'Yes, I know. Only money isn't everything.'

'It is a lot, though, isn't it? I mean, you could just not work and have Dad pay.'

'Oh, I could, could I?'

Yes, at one point in her marriage, she had tried that. The career break had meant she slid off the ladder she had been on; it was only because she had kept up a little pro bono work for the Medical Foundation that she had got her present job at Stern & Wiseman. If Polly helps immigrants, it is just as arguable that they help her. All the lawyers working in her field are women, and many are divorcees. They are at the bottom of the firms, on the mummy track, without hope of ever making partner. All the same, she is managing to keep it all going. There are days like today, when she has got the children off and knows she has a clear ten hours of work ahead, when she feels quite triumphant.

Polly parks the car, and goes up the front steps to collect her brief-case before catching the bus into the centre. She inserts the key into the door, but it's already unlocked. Polly frowns. Surely she dead-locked it automatically on leaving?

'Iryna?' she calls. There is no answer from indoors.

Polly looks at her watch, and hesitates. Supposing Iryna is ill? Supposing she is lying in bed, unable to reply? There is just time to dash upstairs and check. If Iryna can't collect Robbie from school, then Polly needs to find an alternative, fast. Her world, which moments ago felt so pleasantly safe, is a house of cards: take out one, and it comes tumbling down.

She runs to the top of the stairs. Iryna's door, adorned with a perky pencil self-portrait, is closed. It is one of the nicest rooms in the house, comfortably furnished as a little self-contained bedsit. Polly has seen too many other people's au pairs expected to share the family bathroom and live in a room the size of a cupboard; but she looks after her help. Iryna has a very good deal out of their arrange-ment, in addition to her seventy pounds a week. She has even got Polly's old mobile phone, because Iryna arrived with nothing but a suitcase full of terrible Russian clothes.

'Iryna?'

She taps, and the door swings open.

'Oh, no,' says Polly.

It is immediately clear what has happened. The room, normally so neat, is a mess of paper, wire coat hangers and crumpled sheets. The large battered suitcase that has lived on top of the cupboard is gone, and so are Iryna's clothes, and the little painted icon she had hung above her bed. It could not have looked worse, Polly thinks, if it had been tossed by the police. There is no farewell note, no explanation, just abandonment. She feels her legs give, and sits down on the bed, devastated.

What has she done to make Iryna run away? Stunned, Polly thinks back over recent exchanges. Had Iryna felt lonely? Homesick? Resentful? Has she offended her in some way? Paid her too little? Could her request for the children to be given some broccoli with their food, even if they won't eat it, have given offence? True, Iryna is supposed to do two hours of cleaning every day, but she isn't overworked. She, Polly, is about to be so, however.

Already, Polly can feel the burden of domesticity sagging her shoulders. A fine film of dust is gathering on surfaces, and the lump of self-pity rising in her throat is almost the size of the bulge in the laundry basket. What on earth can she tell the children? They will be so upset.

'Why have you done this to me?' she asks aloud, almost in tears. 'Why didn't you tell me something was wrong?'

Iryna had seemed perfectly self-contained and contented. Eastern European girls did not seem to mind travelling in buses across vast tracts of the Continent, they were astoundingly sanguine about living hugger-mugger with people they'd never met before, and Polly, like many women of her generation, simply cannot square the circle without them.

Increasingly uneasy, Polly goes to her dressing table and opens her box of jewellery. Theo had never given her much, but it was all special to her. Her pearl necklace is there, and the string of polished amethysts . . . but where is her diamond engagement ring? Polly tips out the contents of the box, and searches. She knows, even as she does so, what she will discover.

The diamond ring from Tiffany's rises in her mind with holographic accuracy. Fool, fool, to have left it where it was so easy to steal! Polly feels tears rise in her eyes, not at the loss of its value (which is considerable) but at the loss of all the memories it represented. She does wear it sometimes, even though it's got a bit big on her finger since her divorce, and it always makes her feel good about herself, as expensive jewellery is supposed to. Is she stupid to feel like this? It's the one object of real value she has ever been given, the one thing besides her children that is left from a wrecked marriage.

She glances down outside, and at once her fury redoubles, for she sees her car is being given a ticket by a traffic warden. Outraged, she runs out.

'Wait! Stop! Can't you see I have a resident's permit?'

The traffic warden turns a face as hard as mahogany to her and utters, 'Parking suspended for tree-pruning on this side of the street.'

Too late, Polly sees the yellow boxes that had been strapped to lamp-posts for a fortnight, each bearing a sign she had forgotten about.

'Oh, for God's sake! I'm a resident and only left it outside my house *for five minutes.*'

'I can't cancel it now it's issued.'

He slaps a sticky plastic envelope, yellow and black like a wasp's arse, on her windscreen, and moves on.

For a moment Polly wants to scream. Vile traffic Nazis! She is sure he is laughing at her distress, that he must hate her just for having a car and a nice house.

She is too angry to catch the bus, and she's going to be late for her court hearing. Miserably, she finds the number of her local minicab firm, and asks if they have a driver in her area.

'Five minutes,' says a crackling voice. 'We will promise you that, one hundred per cent.'

Again and again Polly tries to call Iryna's mobile while she waits, only to get the standard answering-service message. It's stupid to

58

keep hoping she'll return. When her car arrives, she doesn't even look at the driver, but stares out of her window at the busy street, where the British go about their daily business, taking it for granted that they will never be arrested for not voting the right way, praying the right way, dressing the right way or for belonging to a different tribe. Unlike Polly's clients, they will not be raped, or see their children hacked to pieces, or everything they possess stolen. They take freedom with their daily bread, and never think to thank those who guard their civil liberties. So why has *she* been the one kicked in the teeth?

She sighs, checking her watch.

'You in a hurry, madam?'

'I'm due in court in twenty minutes,' said Polly, curtly. She is angry with everyone, and doesn't want to have a conversation. 'Can you get me there in time?'

'I will do all I can,' the driver says, shooting smartly round King's Cross. 'May I ask, madam, are you a lawyer?'

'Yes.' She is trying, politely, to convey her stress. At least he doesn't have his radio on.

'That is a good business to be in.'

'It has its moments.' Then, feeling she has been too dismissive, 'Have you been here long?'

In the driver's mirror she sees the whites of his eyes.

'A while, yes. I would like to go back to my country, but things are too bad there.'

'Where are you from?'

'Zimbabwe.'

'I'm sorry,' says Polly.

They arrive on time, and in her relief she thrusts a ten-pound note at him.

'You have given me too much money, madam,' he says. 'The fare from your house to here is eight pounds.'

Polly, in the act of closing her purse, pauses. An honest man: how refreshing.

'Well – keep the change.'

'Thank you, madam. If you ever need a good driver, ask for number two-three.'

'I will. Good luck.'

She gets out, and runs like a hunted creature to her court hearing.

8

Job's Jobs

Job is feeling lucky again, for the woman lawyer gave him two pounds more than the fee she had agreed with Mo. On such small pieces of good fortune the graces of his life depend. He had read so much about London in the works of Charles Dickens, but this city is nothing like what he had imagined. He thought it would be like the rich districts of Harare, with long white houses and sprinklers on the lawns, but instead of spreading out horizontally the buildings here are all vertical. There is a constant pressure on space, and at times, when he lies on his bed late at night, he imagines himself being pushed up, like a ball in a jet of water.

All the time he has been here, he has sent back as much as he can to his wife and sister, queuing at the Western Union office between other Africans. Sometimes, Job has a vision of English banknotes flying in a steady stream, out of this small terrier-shaped island and over to the sad elephant's head of Africa. He can tell that many Londoners do not like this; he has even heard them complain to each other about how foreign shopkeepers 'put nothing back into the community'. Yet he has seen white British men begging in the streets, claiming to be homeless and hungry. He wonders whether they really know what these words mean.

Job has been both, but now he works a sixteen-hour day, every day. Apart from minicabbing, Job's second job is working in the AA Carwash underneath a railway bridge near King's Cross. This is where he goes in the mid-morning and mid-afternoon, when mini-cabbing slackens off.

Since Job arrived in the UK, vast areas of wasteland in North London have been lifted up, turned over, pounded down and built upon in preparation for the Eurotunnel station at St Pancras, and the new high-speed rail connection to Europe. Already, an area that was largely frequented by prostitutes and drug dealers has become less steeped in vice, though when he drives through late at night he can still see streetwalkers negotiating with men, and couples in steamed-up cars. By day, however, it is becoming ever more slick, as money works its magic. Blocks of apartments have been constructed along the canal, trees have been planted, and almost every month it seems as if something new is happening.

The AA Carwash is squeezed into an obscure corner of this unceasing ferment. It is a tenebrous, echoing space of blank blackened bricks and dripping pipes, with a semicircular drive of pocked and spotted concrete, so that cars can come in from the north and go out again to the south, into the city centre. Rainwater collects in puddles where the concrete has been patched with tarmac, and crusts of darkness scab the walls behind loops of black electric cable, left hanging for an unknown purpose. Everything at the AA Carwash is sunk in age and decrepitude, apart from its staff, who are young. The oldest person there is probably Job himself, and he is only twenty-two.

There are no mechanical brushes here, only buckets and sponges and vacuum cleaners wielded by men in overalls the colour of wet ashes. It was a mystery at first to Job why anyone should prefer human beings rather than the drama of big, whirling blue brushes that descend and ascend mechanically onto a car. Yet not only are people better cleaners, they are cheaper. They cost less than a machine, for they earn two pounds an hour, performing the same repetitive motions until they get deported, get sick or move on.

Like Job, the other washers arrived in the UK as students, and many genuinely want to study. They soon found, however, that they couldn't afford the fees, though two are supporting younger brothers through college in the hope that at least one family member may make a better life here. Job, who has no such family ties, both pities them for their responsibilities and envies their closeness to their families. He is naturally friendly, and his loneliness aches like a wound. It is two years since he has felt a woman's skin next to his, and there are times when he misses Munisha so much that it feels like a part of him has been cut off, that she is beside him like its phantom, itching and hurting. But the only woman he sees each day is the boss's straw-haired daughter Jayne, who sits watching a small TV set and painting her nails with the St George Cross when not handing out coloured tickets indicating whether drivers had paid for an Outside Only (eight pounds), an In & Out (nine pounds), a Special (twelve pounds) or an Extra-Special (twenty pounds). Jayne never speaks to the men at the AA Carwash, who are beneath her consciousness, but she smiles and flirts with drivers, especially if they arrive in an expensive car. The seven washers are used to being ignored, and she does not bother to learn their names.

They know each others' names, however, and on days when the wind is less chill and a little sun comes out, they sit during quiet times with their backs against the wall, smoking and talking softly. All are from different parts of Africa, and all have become friendly enough once it has been established that none of them is Nigerian.

'Those low, dishonest people, they are all liars and thieves,' says Michael. He is a refugee from Eritrea whose other job is delivering laundry all over North London.

'I do not like them,' says John, the Ghanaian. 'We are not Nigerians, thank God.'

'If I were Nigerian, I would feel shame,' says Sebastien, the Rwandan.

'Nigerians feel no shame, my brother, that is why they are Nigerians,' says Michael.

'And traffic wardens,' says Job, and they laugh; for traffic wardens are a common enemy, even if you will never have a car. To be a traffic warden in London is to be the lowest order of humanity, hated by all but other traffic wardens, and it is no surprise to find that, with pleasing logic, most traffic wardens are Nigerian. Only Job understands why they really hate Nigerians. They are wealthier than other Africans, because they have oil.

'If my country had oil, like Nigeria, we would not have Mugabe,' Job says; but Michael shakes his head.

'If your country had oil, then you would have American soldiers instead of African ones.'

They all speak to each other in English, for this is the common tongue. It makes us sound like children, Job thinks, even though when he found out a little more about their past lives he discovered that some are well educated. Many have been businessmen, and still hope to resume trading, though what exactly it was they had bought or sold in their home countries remains mysterious. One or two have been used to a very different kind of life but have been reduced to mere muscle thanks to war, changes in regime or a fall from favour. They do not speak of the past, though last summer when they stripped off their ash-coloured overalls to work naked from the waist up, Job had seen that at least three others bore, like himself, the marks of torture on their torsos. They have been carved like trees, and like trees they have endured.

The problem is that, even if they were legal, their English isn't good enough or, as in his case, their qualifications are not accepted. That long, pompous degree certificate from Harare University, far from making Job sound professional, makes him sound fraudulent when he applies for jobs. Besides, he doesn't have the most precious thing of all: the right to remain indefinitely. This, known as 'the million-dollar stamp', is what everyone like himself longs to get in his or her passport. Once you get that, all doors are open.

Michael, the most intelligent (he suspects) of the men he works with at the car wash, asks him, 'Tell me, professor,' (this is Job's nickname among them, because he has his degree) 'why is English so hard? Why can't it be simpler?'

'Because it comes from other languages,' Job says. 'It's a mixture of other languages, like the British themselves.'

'So the English, they were once invaded?'

'Yes, but not for many hundreds of years.'

Everyone thinks about this for a moment, unable to imagine it.

'No wars between tribes?'

'Many hundreds of years ago,' Job says, vaguely. 'When Scotland, Wales and Ireland were separate countries. But they all came together under one king.'

Job's grasp of history is derived entirely from Shakespeare and the dim memory of a children's book called *Our Island Story*. He has read more than Jayne or her brother will ever read in their life, and yet he is shut out.

When Job left Zimbabwe, he had wept. Everyone he had ever known, everyone who had known him, everything real he had ever seen, was lost, perhaps for ever. Yet besides that, a part of him had been curious, even excited, at the idea of seeing the country whose history is so deeply intertwined with his own, and whose best literature he has studied.

Job's parents had worked for a white family, the Wisdens, who had farmed near Harare for three generations. His father had driven a tractor, and his mother had been the Wisdens' maid. Job and his sister Miriam had played with Beth Wisden, in the semi-tropical garden, with its big dogs, bright flowers and bird-haunted trees. Miriam was the eldest, and Beth the youngest, but there had been no difference between them in their games; and Job, a little older than Beth, had been appointed as her companion and protector, responsible for looking out for snakes. They had taken it in turn to ride the bicycle, push the swing, dance in and out of the jewelled rain of the sprinklers. When Job's mother baked cakes, they all had an equal share.

It had been a time of milk and honey and braiis, when the scented white tobacco flowers towered over his head, and God spoke to him like a father. Job had learnt to read with faded little books full of pictures of smiling white children going about their business in the beautiful, bright, safe place that was England. When he came across his first Shakespeare play, it had seemed like a continuation of that, even though the places were called Athens or Illyria or Padua. There were the tragedies, whose language moved him with its passion, but he had no inkling that these princes and warriors would one day come to speak to him as his heart's blood, and the star to his wandering soul. Later on, he read other books, full of fog and poverty, but there were laws, and justice prevailed. He dreamt of England, even when he got to Harare; but he had never dreamt of finding himself there.

Job closes his eyes, and the rumble of a passing lorry becomes the jolt of a tropical thunderstorm. The sky, instead of being lumpen and cold, shines and quakes like copper sheet and stretches away for ever, shaking the acacia trees. He thinks of Munisha, her infinitely soft skin, and the way the dust smelt after the rains. She is laughing at him.

'There you are! I've got us some avocados.'

The fruits are enormous, smooth dark pears. She holds them up and shows him.

'Sweets to the sweet.'

Her laughter is like water in a dry land. He leans forward to embrace her, and finds himself falling, the smile still on his face.

'Hey, professor! Wake up!'

'I am awake,' says Job, back in the wasteland.

A car rolls in. Sebastien and Michael come forward, grinning, with soapy sponges in their hands. Job can see the man inside flinch as they touch his car. Almost all white people flinch, he has noticed, because to them a black person touching their car means danger. The men know this, and smile. What can they do but look friendly? A hundred others wait to fill their rotting trainers. They spray and rinse and polish, vacuum and empty and wipe.

'*Out, out damned spot*,' Job says, polishing. 'What, will this car ne'er be clean?'

The other men giggle. They don't understand what he's quoting, but they enjoy the performance.

The best bit comes at the end, when they spray the tyres with something that makes them look black and new again. Once it is finished, Damien steps forward and collects the tip. He never does any work other than to give each car a last flourish with a dry rag: but he keeps the tip. He is the boss's son, and Jayne's brother.

The money is hardly enough to keep you alive if you only do one shift, but it is here, unlike at Ace Minicabs, that Job has his friends. A little bit of Africa grows in the grime, like the thistles that have rooted themselves in the brickwork and, with a transcendent effort, put out thorny leaves in the cracks. They share roll-ups, and talk as equals.

Job bends and reaches around the interior, the industrial vacuum cleaner roaring even louder than the trains. The owner stands nearby, watching in case any of them steals so much as a two-pence piece from under the carpet. Yet the cleaners at AA Carwash are just as nervous of drivers. There is one regular in particular who comes every Monday, rock music thudding out of his speakers, who exudes violence like sweat.

The men sing along with the radio, hoping that the Lexus won't arrive, but here he is, Job thinks. The driver gets out and lounges by the wall, watching as they jump into action. Job sends his vacuum nozzle into the interior with vigour, wrinkling his nose at the reek of vomit. Sometimes the car smells of bad things; and sometimes he finds twists of foil that he is pretty sure come from drugs. The men never comment on these, even to each other. Job sometimes wonders what else the dark plush of the upholstery and carpets conceals; occasionally, the car gets an Extra-Special, which means a deep-cleaning of the interior 'guaranteed to lift every stain'.

They polish and spray and polish again, bending and twisting in their faded overalls, then stop expectantly.

'Hey, you!' says the man in a harsh, accented voice. Thickset, dough-faced, with black bristling hair and a black leather jacket, he always walks round the car as it is being waxed. Job and the other cleaners never dare look him in the eye. Job steps forward with his rag and a bottle of white spirit to polish away a fingerprint on the door. The car is as shiny as a mirror.

'No – this one!' hisses the man. There, on the bonnet, is a flaw in the surface.

'Bird droppings, sir,' says Job, apologetically.

'You think I am fucking fool?'

'No, sir, no.'

'You think I donnow you tryin' cheat me?'

'It is a bird dropping.' Job tries to think of a word the man will understand. 'Guano. Poop. Bird shit. You know?'

'So get it off.'

'It eats into the metal if you leave it more than a day. I'm sorry, sir.'

The man walks up to Job, and puts the point of a knife next to his neck. It happens so quickly that there is no time to react, but Job's heart seems to stop. He stands very still, hardly breathing. Job looks the Russian in the eye. *Wherefore do the wicked live, become old, yea, are mighty in power?* he asks God, bitterly. He has faced down men like this before. The man smiles. He slowly withdraws the knife.

'Monkey-man,' he says contemptuously, and leaves.

Job drives back to the minicab office, still trembling. A trickle of something warm goes down his neck. The knife has nicked him.

Mo eyes him from the booth. He misses nothing, squatting there all day. The drivers, all bearded, examine Job in mild surprise.

'I had a customer draw a knife on me just now,' Job explains. The skin itches and burns where he was cut, and he dabs at it with a square of toilet paper. He worries about his skin. Ever since winter came, and the raw winds, he has been afflicted with rashes.

'A fare?'

'No. At the car wash.'

The other two drivers look uneasy, and mutter to each other. They are civilised men, their indignant backs seem to say, and do not want to know about such matters.

'I am unlucky,' Job says to them.

Mo is wheedling on the phone, saying, 'I have another very good driver, madam. My cousin's son.' But the voice at the other end of the line persists, and when it rings off, Mo says, 'Two-three, I have got you a very good job.'

9

The Bars Never Move

The ceiling has a big crack in it, like a river winding across a field of dirty ice. The ice is deep but scratched here and there with little swirls and eddies. It stretches across an enormous space. There are shapes sunk in the ice, just visible, things that are locked beneath the surface: a face and two hands, pressing, pressing. Anna looks at it in vague surprise, for she almost recognises it.

Elsewhere, things are done to her body. Her mouth fills with bitter salt, her breasts are kneaded, her anus torn. If she went back into her body it would be too much to bear, and so she stays away, on the other side of the ice, where she can observe what is happening and not hear her own whimpers. The first man almost splits her in half, pushing until something pops inside her and gives way in a flood of blood. He collapses almost at the same moment, and she wonders whether he is going to die, too; but it seems that this is not to be the case.

'Little bitch, I could have sold you for one thousand pounds if I'd known,' he says.

He does it again, and then the other man does it too. It feels as if it will never end, as if it is quite impersonal – although, of course, it is all too personal as well. Anna had not known men were like this, so angry and heavy, grunting and bristly, with their piggy eyes and sour breath. She almost pities them, to be ruled by this piece of flesh, which they shake in her face as something to worship but which is just very, very ugly. Surely, men hide it away out of shame, for although she has seen her brother naked she had never seen her father. Are they all like this, or were these two deformed? It makes her think of mushrooms, foul-smelling and musty, and when each collapses in a pool of slime, they become calmer, quieter, less dangerous for a while as if she somehow takes their rage into herself.

She had not been ignorant of people like this. But Natalya had been so insistent that Anna was going to a new future that it had not even crossed Anna's mind to question why anyone would want to offer an unknown teenager a job in another country. Hadn't her mother tried to warn her? She has nobody but herself to blame.

You are a good, kind girl, Anna, and I fear for you. Well, how should she have known?

Anna couldn't remember a time when she hadn't been the one cooking and cleaning and changing nappies. She'd been the Little Mother to several children, all younger than herself, and by the time she'd turned fifteen she'd been desperate. She had finished school, and there was no hope of any further education or training; yet, even in Lutsk, she could see from the TV that there was more to life than school and drudgery. But then Natalya had found her and befriended her, telling her about the wonderful times she could have in London, and the money she could send home to her mother. Why stay behind in the Ukraine as an extra mouth to feed? Katya was twelve, and could take over.

She had never had a friend like Natalya before: someone who had travelled, who was older and more sophisticated, who told her she had a bigger future in which dreams could come true.

'I used to be like you, stuck in this dead place – and I got out. Now look at me! Look at this, and this and this! Would I have got them if I'd stayed here, on the edge of Chernobyl? Anything is better than this, Anna!'

Natalya had been older than Anna at school, and Anna had dim memories of her not being all that popular, but that was before she had left home. Now everyone envied her. She told Anna she was a talent scout for an agency, that she had been looking round for pretty young girls to be waitresses in London, where there was such a need for them that the agency had paid for her to come back to the Ukraine. She was only in the area for a week, but that had been all it had taken for Anna to be set on fire with longing at her descriptions. Natalya told her that the city was full of Ukrainians working for English pounds, having a great time. London was all that Lutsk was not, a place of unlimited wealth and opportunity with a queen who rode around in a golden carriage, and all the shops and clothes and clubs she could possibly want. Anna was enthralled. Her friend had sealed her promise with the gift of a wand of mascara that made Anna's lashes look even longer and thicker, and had helped her with everything, including her passport application and visa.

'You will go as a tourist, so you must pretend you have money,' Natalya said.

'How do I do that?'

'I will lend you the clothes, and teach you what to say.'

It had been an adventure, right up to the point of getting her visa from the British Embassy in Kyiv. Even that city had awed her, with its size and speed, and she had almost been too frightened to speak during her interview with the hushed stern officials. But by the end of the summer her visa had come through, and when Natalya returned for Christmas she was ready. Natalya had recommended the service which ran a bus for girls like Anna who were coming to Britain; although the fare cost all her granny's savings.

'You don't want to have to find your way around alone, do you?' Natalya said. 'It's OK to come with me. I will show you everything you need.'

Now Anna understands that she has been tricked. Natalya has sold her to these men, and perhaps the others on the bus and the ferry have been sold too – by their boyfriends, by their best friends, by somebody. Maybe some of them knew what they were coming to; Anna remembers the hard looks on some faces, looks that had puzzled her. Maybe they too are going through exactly the same things, in a communion of violation. The rape takes hours, or minutes. She looks at the walls, which have a brown pattern on them like spiders hanging down in rows, at the ceiling, or the pillow. Sometimes, she can't breathe. Maybe she'll faint. But she doesn't.

Eventually the men get up and leave.

There is silence in the next room, apart from the TV set which shouts on. Anna lies like a dead thing. Then she gets up, slowly and stiffly, with blood running down her bruised thighs, and limps to the toilet. She is distantly aware that her face is white in the mirror, and her eyes are staring out of twin pits of shadow. She dabs at herself with paper, and then with the rank pink hand-towel that is still hanging where she left it after her shower. She would drink bleach, if it were possible, only there isn't any.

Anna leaves the toilet. It is too cold, and she hurts too much to stay still. The other two girls are still in the front room, smoking and watching TV, though the men have gone. She doesn't want to meet their gazes, nor they hers. They have shared this shame, they can do nothing for her.

Eventually the blonde one says, 'You speak English?'

Anna nods, slowly.

'Good,' says the blonde. 'Eat. He doesn't always get us food.'

They divide a kind of round flat bread with tomato sauce from a box. Anna eats and drinks automatically. Her body is ravenous. The women light fresh cigarettes, and the blonde asks, 'Where are you from?'

Anna whispers, 'Ukraine.'

'Me, Albania. Drita. Her, Moldova. Cristina.' she says. Cristina snickers to herself, her stare back on the television. She has not said a word, and looks mad, or drunk, scratching her forearms. Anna has seen crazy people and pitied them, but now she is one of them.

She looks around surreptitiously. There is no obvious way out. Both girls wear skimpy tops and miniskirts despite the cold, and their heavy make-up conceals the fact that they are probably only a couple of years older than herself. They are shivering. The airless room is oppressive. Its windows shake and rattle each time a lorry or bus goes past, but she can see that the bars never move.

'Did you know? Before you came?'

Drita nods, and says in her deep, hoarse voice, 'I knew I would be prostitute. I was prostitute in Albania. There is no work, no money, nothing. I thought, in England it will be OK. I will have money. Maybe I meet nice mans. But nobody is telling me that it would be so many, or that Sergei, he takes all the money.'

'Do they ever let you out?'

Drita smiles sourly. 'No. They let Cristina out, though.'

'Why her, and not you?'

'Cristina, she loooves heroin.'

Cristina's head comes up at the word. Her pale, dull face breaks into a brief enchanting smile.

'You have some?'

Drita ignores her. 'Sergei, he brings. I smoke a little. Otherwise, I go crazy. But I am not an addict. So the brothers know that if they let me out, I go.'

Anna feels crazy already. This conversation in broken English, which she has to translate into her own language to understand, then translate back to speak, is hard work for her but it's also a distraction from her body's pain. She has tried to make a pad to soak up the blood, but it keeps coming in a thin, foul-smelling trickle.

She looks at the door.

'Is locked,' says Drita. 'Same as in the other place.'

'There is another place?'

Drita says, 'Kill Burn.'

The name means nothing to Anna. She is in a prison; and yet, when she remembers the angel-woman who had come down the stairs from the floor above and smiled at her, she is puzzled. Was she like Natalya? Was everyone either a whore or a pimp?

'Sergei will bring more men for you.'

Anna utters the question that is uppermost in her mind. 'How many?'

'Twenty a day. Sometimes more, at weekends, most times less.'

'They will kill me.'

Drita laughs. 'No. You will live.'

Anna can't imagine it.

'They are men,' says Drita, shrugging contemptuously. 'White, brown, black, fat, thin. Is better if you pretend you like it. They come quick, and go. Sergei is happy, you make more money. You will get regular customers.'

'It will kill me,' Anna murmurs.

'No.'

'I must get out. Please, help me.'

The blonde looks at her with fathomless despair. 'You are prostitute now, always prostitute. If you leave, they kill your family. Or your family will kill you.'

'Do they lock the door every time?'

'It would not matter if they left it open. You have no passport, no money. They will find you. Where would you go?'

Where would she go? Anna has not the faintest idea. It is the middle of winter, and the cold, though nothing like the cold of the Ukraine, is bitter. Nobody has even seen her arrive, and nobody will believe her if she tells them what has just been done to her. She has nothing and is nobody.

Outside, the cold dark skies press against the window. It is like being at the end of the world; but instead, Anna is at its heart.

10

At the Rambler

The 274 bus is nimble and quick, taking Katie down into Camden Town and along the outer rim of Regent's Park before steaming along towards Oxford Street. Even in her jet-lagged state, she recognises local London landmarks with melancholy pleasure. Here is the row of Greek restaurants opposite a plaque to Dickens; then the pretty, pastel-coloured Victorian villas round Primrose Hill, which she had first seen in the cartoon of A Hundred and One Dalmatians. Past the statue of St George, energetically spearing a dragon almost facing the burnished dome of the mosque; and the straight drive down into Baker Street, where a man in a Victorian policeman's uniform waits outside the non-existent Sherlock Holmes's non-existent flat 221B for the delectation of tourists. She can't blame them. The real London would, for her, always be overlaid by its literature, which smooths away every unpleasantness much as a layer of old varnish subdues yet enriches a painting.

The bus is crowded: students, commuters, elderly people, women with children, tourists, travellers, shoppers, all talking in a dozen different languages. Katie has her iPod in her ears and Angela Hewitt playing Bach's French Suites to block them out. As long as she has music, the bus is charming. She ponders Ivo Sponge. She has a vague feeling that she ought to know more about him, but the British media, with its feuds, alliances, personalities and obsessions, is a special study. Katie doesn't have the time or the energy. She needs to skim across life like those thin, spindly insects which skate over the meniscus of a pond, never breaking the surface tension, because if she can just get through this year and regain some self-confidence, then she may start to get better.

The *Rambler* magazine is housed in a tall terraced building in need of repair. Bought from the bankrupted estate of the disgraced media magnate Max de Monde over a decade ago, its alcoholic but aristocratic editor had survived for another five years before being fired to make way for Quentin Bredin. He is, according to gossip, the only member of staff to be paid properly, although his columns for the *Daily Chronicle* also net him a small fortune, and his distinctive appearances on TV quiz shows have made him a minor celebrity. There are even rumours that he may one day go into politics, although he is too maverick a figure to have come out in favour of any party to date. The magazine itself is, however, severely underfunded by its proprietor, Roger Trench. He keeps a luxurious flat at the top of the building for company whom his wife refuses to entertain, but the rest of the structure seems not to have changed since the 1930s. Its radiators, painted the colour of gravy, are barely functioning, its computers are riddled with viruses, its toilets clank and all its staff are in *Debrett's Peerage*.

Quentin had explained to Katie, in the days when he still spoke to her, how matters were arranged.

'The fact is, we pay a hundred pounds for an article, which means that writers only write for us at the beginning of their careers, when they're desperate, or at the end, when it no longer matters. So everyone here, from the advertising manager to the secretary, has a private income. I pick up the kind of talent that comes through knowing the right people.'

'So is it all nepotism?'

'Not entirely. The *Rambler*, you see, positions itself as the unofficial opposition to whichever government is in power. It's a British institution. People go on to great things from here.'

Katie goes up the steps to the scarred front door, which is if anything in even worse condition than that of her flat. Over it is a fanlight shaped like a collapsed umbrella, and to one side, behind an iron boot-scraper, huddle six bottles of skimmed milk, veined like marble because nobody but herself ever brings it into the office. There is also, she sees with a sinking heart, a small bearded man in glasses and a long striped scarf, hovering. Katie recognises him. It is Eric Claud, the persistent poet. He haunts a number of magazines, seemingly on a rota, and is almost certainly mad.

'Hi. More submissions?'

He thrusts a brown padded envelope into her hands.

'I'll see that the editor gets it,' she says, kindly.

Inside, the narrow hall is crowded. Every tread of the rickety uncarpeted stairs has padded envelopes, books or sheaves of paper piled on it, deposited by Books and Arts on the ground floor. With a movement of agility remarkable in one so rotund, the little man slips past her.

'KATIE!' Quentin bellows. 'Where have you been?'

He emerges from his office on the first floor, glaring down at them. Then, slowly, he raises his arm and points accusingly at the figure beside her.

'*Is that a poet?*'

Mesmerised, Katie and the little man nod. Quentin swells with awful fury.

'Out! OUT! Get out!'

'But if you would just – people say—'

Quentin seizes a stick from the umbrella stand by his door and descends, making elegant fencing motions.

'We-do-not-publish-poetry!'

The poet, with a terrified squeal, bolts.

Restored to humour, Quentin says, 'Worse than rats. If you ever let another poet in, Katie, you're fired.'

'Sorry,' Katie mutters. Already she has displeased him.

A row of faces, resembling the disembodied heads of angels, appear over the banisters of the next floor up.

'Ooh, Quentin,' says one, 'you're so gorgeous when you're angry.'

'Was it a particularly *odious* poet?' says the next.

'The one who writes about nipples and cunts?'

'I've no objection to pornography, but I will not abide bad verse,' says Quentin.

The faces dissolve into giggles. Cecilia, Cassandra, Jocasta and Araminta, the belles of the *Rambler*, keep up a perpetual flirtation with Quentin although only one, Cecilia, is actually sleeping with him as far as anyone knows. She does the *Rambler* arts blog about the launches and parties she goes to, and is related to European royalty. The week she arrived, Katie was asked to clear her desk and move to another one. Cecilia now sits in full view of Quentin across the landing.

'I'm sorry I'm late,' says Katie. 'I need another coffee and then I'll get going.'

Quentin's features settle into a kind of saurian sulk. 'I do depend on at least *one* person in the office working, you know.'

This is the strange thing about the *Rambler*, and from what Katie gathers it is by no means unexceptional in the British media. In her previous job, Ivy League graduates thought themselves lucky to get jobs as coffee-makers, and were expected to worm their way up by a mixture of blazing talent and round-the-clock dedication to fact-checking. This was how she herself had worked, with colleagues she liked and respected, and who were drawn from many different races and cultures. There, fact-checking was an honourable job; here, an airy disregard for truth makes the weekly visitation by the magazine lawyer a formality.

'Nobody but an idiot would want to draw attention to *that*!' is Quentin's cry; though, as Katie and the lawyer remind him, idiots still exist, and sue for libel.

To her, the other members of staff are not quite human, and it seems that they are odd even to their own kind. Justin, the Arts Editor, explained to her that in their families 'being born with brains is a little like having an extra toe or a cleft palate'. Perhaps it's this that makes Katie fond of them, despite their persistent coolness to her and their continual exchange of gossip about the smallest details of their friends and relations to which she can make no addition.

All the same, they seem relieved to see her.

'The cavalry arrives,' says Patrick. 'I was getting a trifle bored of telling people who phoned that you were stuck on the lavatory.'

Katie knows he's trying to embarrass or annoy her, and smiles warmly.

'How was your vacation?'

'Vile. You?'

'Same. Not,' she adds hastily, 'that I don't love my family.'

'You are so lucky to have your parents,' says Cecilia. 'My father died when I was three.'

'Jet ski,' Patrick whispers, snickering.

'Poor thing,' Katie murmurs back.

'Oh, he was just some bodyguard.'

Patrick is wearing a pair of tight pink leopard-print trousers, a leather waistcoat and pointed leather boots. Katie looks at these, and sighs.

'Only making the most of my assets,' Patrick retorts. 'You know, you should try it.'

'Actually, I'd better start earning my salary.'

'Oh, bugger that,' Patrick says. 'Nobody is doing this for the money, darling. Look at the place.'

One corner is taken up with the Great Cham's chair, in which Cecilia's miniature pug dog, Boswell, is snoring, warmed by a shaft of thin winter sun. The grimy Georgian windows are thick with dust and yellow stains, and Reynolds's celebrated portrait of Dr Johnson, peering moon-faced at a book, could be any one of the employees trying to read. The *Rambler*'s staff is vigorous in its defence of smokers' rights, and they still light up in the upstairs room of the pub down the road where the magazine has its famous weekly lunches. Katie tries not to wave her hand or cough too much.

'Meet anyone interesting?'

'I encountered someone called Ivo Sponge on the flight over. Do you know him?'

'Ivo! Good God, he's a legend.'

Justin, the Arts Editor, who has been hovering nearby, more for the tortured pleasure of being in Patrick's company than anything, looks livelier.

'Of course I know Ivo. Everyone does,' he says in his low, melancholy voice.

'Really? Is he famous?'

'Well, his expense accounts are *legendary*. Now, of course, he's editor-at-large on some rag across the Atlantic, which pays him pots of money,' Justin says. 'I tell you, if Ivo were editor, Trench wouldn't know what had hit him. He'd get rid of the Tobys for a start.'

'Shh, he might hear you.'

The temporary helpers are all called 'Tobys', because they are public schoolboys with floppy hair whose parents know Quentin, and who are trying to get a day or two of work experience before or after university. They remind Katie of Labrador puppies, and are as adorable as they are useless. The present Toby approaches them nervously.

'Er, there doesn't seem to be any copy to input.'

'That's because nobody comes in before eleven,' says Patrick, witheringly. It's true, but ten minutes later the office is crowded. Cassandra walks in bearing three bags from Bond Street, saying, 'Not another bloody invitation! Really! Who does he think he is?'

Across the landing, Quentin is bellowing, 'No, Lottie, I will *not* tolerate a parents' evening! You'll have to go by yourself.'

'So, sorry to be stupid about this, but how does the magazine actually get produced?' the Toby asks.

'Oh,' Patrick tells him airily, 'by us fairies, you know.'

'You know, it's a mystery to me, too,' Katie says. 'I have nightmares about going to news-stands and seeing *Ramblers* which are just blank pages.'

'I get over a hundred unsolicited pieces a week, so there's always something good,' says Minty cheerfully. 'Panga's sent in another rant about gypsies invading his estate.'

Justin looks around disapprovingly. 'God, this place is *filthy*! You know, I even found a used condom in the bin last week?'

'Whose, do you suppose?'

'It can't be Quentin, he's got a sofa in his office. Practically the casting couch.'

'Well, who wouldn't prefer a little hurly-burly on the chaise longue compared with the deep, deep comfort of the double bed?' says Patrick.

Katie thinks about the two years she spent living with Winthrop before finding him on the couch with her best friend a week before her wedding. She is getting better at looking down on her past, as if it were one of those computer games like The Sims that her nephews like playing: miniature mental images of herself and Winthrop in their apartment, entertaining, watching TV, working, telephoning, getting dressed, having sex but somehow never really talking. How could she possibly have thought they were going to stay together? What had she been thinking – that she would just morph into a perfect banker's wife? That's the worst thing, the total loss of judgement. She hadn't liked his friends, nor they her; she had loathed his parents and they her – nothing had been right about it except that Winthrop had been ready to get married and she was available at the right time and place. That was all it took, really. He had not wanted to be posted to London, having briefly been at a public school in England and hated it, whereas she remembered the wonderful year in her childhood when her parents had taught in London. Perhaps that is why it has always seemed like a good place to run to. Her thoughts are jerked back by Patrick's voice.

'By the way, Katie, you've got to sack the cleaner. I absolutely refuse to sit at my desk in Dolce & Gabbana when it hasn't been cleaned!'

'Has anyone phoned the agency?' Katie asks, busily tapping instructions into her keyboard.

'They won't have a clue. What is she, Polish?'

'Something,' says Katie.

'Probably gone off to work in a Pret A Manger.'

'Why?'

'Who in their right mind would want to clean offices, except wogs?' says Mark Crawley, in his bellicose way. He has returned from the House of Commons in a particularly bad mood. Katie had learnt that, where most of the young people on the staff are on the way up, to better jobs on national newspapers, the opposite is true of Crawley. He had once been married to the daughter of the *Rambler's* former proprietor, Max de Monde, but his career has been under a cloud ever since his divorce, and nobody much likes him although he is said to be clever. An arrogant, sneering, perpetually irate man, he makes no secret of his ambition to replace Quentin in the editor's seat.

'Look at it,' he says. 'It's falling apart. We should stop clinging on to the past, and move.'

'Trench can't afford it,' Jocasta says.

'If only Panga had stepped in! He's so rich he wouldn't even notice.'

'You know what Panga says about magazines: they are worse than yachts. That's why he wouldn't buy it. He may look like a playboy but he's smart as a whip.'

'God knows what we'll do if Trench pulls the plug. I mean, I *have* to have two years here on my CV before moving on,' says Minty. She's the Books Editor, and sifts from among the hundred or so hardbacks sent each week those that will be of specific interest to the *Rambler's* readership. These, Katie has discovered, are not necessarily the best of their kind, but those which are either by a member of the aristocracy, about a member of the aristocracy, or, at a pinch, defending traditional British values. Traditional British values always need defending, apparently, because they are under continual assault from the rest of the world – which, by definition, does not read the *Rambler*.

Everyone is suddenly working hard, because Quentin has struck the gong for conference. The noise reverberates through the building.

'Oh, well, good riddance,' says Crawley. 'In a couple more years, the police will be patrolling our shores with gunboats trying to keep Johnny Foreigner from flooding in, but meanwhile let's see if we can at least get one who can clean, shall we?'

'I wonder whether she's decided to stick exclusively to the shag-pad?' Jocasta muses.

'The what?'

'Oh, you know. Trench's flat, for the occasions when he's too "tired" to go home.'

'Ew, gross,' Katie says.

'Oh, come on, Katie, every rich man is like that, you know.'

Katie is silent. She does, indeed, know all too well.

11

In the War Zone

Ian is reading an English class a chapter about White Fang being beaten by his new master. Although over half the class comes from a culture which fears and hates dogs, the violence transfixes them, just as he had hoped. If he could do *this* book as a set text . . . but then it would probably be ruined too. What they like is its samizdat quality.

'How does it end, sir?' Bilal asks.

'You can read it yourself.'

They always want to jump to the end of a story that they enjoy. There is no concept of waiting for good things, or of good things being worth the wait. Perhaps he's no better: after all, he'd jumped straight back into his affair with Candice. He has to admit, the sex is great even if it feels weirdly like rock-climbing, the other thing they do together.

Next door, he can hear Sally screaming herself hoarse as she tries to teach maths. 'What – is – a – fraction?'

It's like going into battle, every lesson, and Ian's just not battle-hardened. He's always reading about the responsibility that British teachers carry, how on top of crowd control they have to teach kids basic manners that their parents somehow forgot to instil, oh, and a sense of patriotism. How is someone like him supposed to be winning over hearts and minds when half the time they don't even bother to turn up? If the media are to be believed, people think that all teachers are lazy, or incompetent. They think that it's somehow the fault of teachers that one in five adults in the country is functionally illiterate. Nobody blames the parents, which in South Africa would be the first thing.

'Why do people have children,' Candice demands on hearing some of his stories, 'if they just can't be bothered to teach them the basics before school?'

'I don't know. Maybe we just do things differently. When I speak to their parents, I often have to do so with the child as translator. So you can imagine how teaching English isn't exactly easy.'

'I thought it was just, like, reading books and writing about them,' Candice says.

'If only. My lessons have to be about performing DARTS, or Directed Activities Related to Texts, anything *but* reading,' he says. 'A book isn't a book, it's an opportunity for a DART. I'm not supposed to get them to think about *Of Mice and Men* as a great novel; it's a vehicle to investigate the American Depression. Actually, it's a vehicle for the DVD, only the player got stolen.'

Ian has set aside seven minutes of each lesson to read aloud to them a book they might enjoy. Even so, there are interruptions.

'You have a girlfriend, sir?'

He knows better than to answer, asking them to write a page describing their own favourite animal, because of Steinbeck's Lennie and his obsession with rabbits. Some begin writing immediately, a good sign. The ones in front – the troublemakers – manage to scrawl a couple of sentences. Nadif sits staring at the piece of paper before him.

'Can you write English?' Ian asks, quietly. Some of the Bangladeshi boys have particular difficulties because, he discovered to his amazement, there is no alphabet in Silheti. But Nadif is from some other country. He tries to remember which.

Nadif mutters, 'Yeah.'

'Are you having problems?'

'No.'

Ian looks at what Nadif does, ten minutes later. He has been drawing scenes of stick soldiers firing guns, and figures falling over in a hail of bullets and blood.

'Are any of these animals?' Ian asks, sternly.

The boy raises his head.

'It is my mother and brothers being killed by soldiers in my village,' he says, in a sad, precise voice. 'They were killed as animals are killed.'

'Stop that at once! Stop it!' Sally's voice shrieks through the walls.

Violence is part of these children's lives, so no wonder they are suspicious, aggressive and rude, bullying each other and their teachers. Ian knows that Sally is having a harder time of it, but he can't spare the time or energy to help her. If he leaves his class, it will erupt in turn. When the bell shrills at the end of the mid-morning, it always feels like he's only just made it. How can he help someone like Nadif? He'd asked with whom he was living, and learnt that it was with an uncle; but the uncle ran a laundry business, and the boy was not only exhausted but had burns on his hands from ironing.

'My best chance of life is to be here,' Nadif said when Ian asked if he could help. It's probably true, and yet what a life! The mixture of guilt, anger and hopelessness makes him sigh.

After lunch he goes out into the cindery yard which is the playground, football pitch and exercise area. Surrounded by a high wire fence, it is perhaps a foretaste of things to come for some. There is a pair of big Afro-Caribbean boys blocking something from sight by the bike shed. Ian strongly suspects they are extracting lunch money, and makes a point of walking over whenever he sees them bunch together. It's like watching the behaviour of gazelles in the bush, he thinks. Kids like Cameron and Delano are born predators, and Amir and his younger brother Chandra are unmistakably the prey.

'You gay, then, fat face?' he overhears, before they see him and fall silent.

'What's up?' Ian asks. He feels their hatred of him, as they avoid his gaze, shifting from foot to foot. He looks at Amir, who hangs his head.

'Jus' hangin', sir.'

Cameron and Delano, who try to block him from view, are fully grown, with the baggy trousers and idiot baseball caps too many boys in the school affect; at fourteen, both have long sideburns and moustaches. Delano rarely turns up at school, and rumour has it he is a drugs runner. The under-sixteens are valuable to dealers because if caught they get a lesser sentence; even Ian knows this. On the other hand, they could just be having a perfectly innocent conversation. The look on the younger boys' faces convinces him otherwise.

'I don't know what's going on here,' Ian says. 'But if there's any violence, or threats of violence, then I will punish those responsible.'

'You dissin' us, man?' says Delano.

'No, I'm warning you not to bother other pupils,' Ian says. Amir looks frail and miserable. He may be gay, which to these boys is a term of abuse, but it's equally likely that he is being picked on for being quiet.

'We was just havin' a chat, friendly like.'

'It didn't look friendly to me. What was it about?'

They won't say. Ian folds his arms in frustration.

'Amir, there's something I want to go through with you about your homework,' he says. It's an excuse to extract him from the group without losing face, and they know it.

'If you're having a problem with those guys, tell me,' he says quietly, when they are out of earshot.

'No problem, sir.'

'What are things like at home?'

'My family are good Muslim people, sir,' he says, in the monotonous tone of one repeating a lesson; and it probably is, thinks Ian sadly. Would it really be better to be in one of London's worst schools than a school in Pakistan? He doesn't know the answer. What he does know is that of the various ethnic groups, Pakistani, Afro-Caribbean and Bangladeshi boys are the worst-performing. All are strongly represented here, and all fail to flourish. Thirty to a class, four classes to a year, how can it possibly work? Without a Head, the school is rudderless and totally lacking in direction. As so often, with places like these, nobody wants the responsibility; the Governors simply cannot find anyone.

There are just so many of them, Ian thinks: a thousand teenage boys, all penned up in a small space, whooping and pounding along the corridors to freedom at the end of the day. The smell of curry, sweaty trainers and creosote makes it a pleasure to get out into the cold night air on his bike and pedal back to Finsbury Park. His brief-case is leaden with papers to mark and lessons to prepare, but at least he's survived another day.

Ian's home is a terraced brick house with three bedrooms, rented from a Greek guy who is doing up a series of equally unprepossessing places in the area. They have it cheap, until the developer gets round to putting in proper central heating and a new kitchen and bath-room. Ian shares with three other people, all Aussies. The two girls, Liza and Kim, keep different hours. Liza is a doctor doing locum work and Kim is a nurse. They are cheerful and friendly, but younger than himself. The other is the Slug, as Candice calls him.

As he lets himself in, Ian can hear a loud burp from the kitchen.

'Hi, Mick,' says Ian.

'G'day.'

'You've been abroad?' he asks, seeing Mick's rucksack in the corner. The house is full of friends and strangers, dropping by or crashing out, but Mick has been absent for a week.

'Nah.' Mick grins. 'There's this company, see, they give you two grand a week for sitting in a hotel room all day, watching TV, eating and playing video games.'

'What are they paying you for?' Ian asks, enviously.

'Drugs, man, only they're paying me instead of the other way around! I've done it before, no worries. Half the time you get a placebo anyway.' Mick shambles out of the kitchen, leaving a scatter of aluminium curry trays in his wake, then puts his head round the door. 'How's Candy?'

'Fine.'

'Lovely sheila. She's wasted on you.' Mick winks, and disappears.

'Remember to flush!' Ian calls, throwing the trays in the trash.

Mick is messy, lazy and careless with other people's property, but Ian would far rather live with him than with some of the people he's house-shared with before, who tended to have their own labelled shelf and insisted on having a kitty for foodstuffs like milk. He's been over for longer than Ian, and it was just pure luck that Ian had answered an ad on the gumtree website and they'd clicked. Ian likes cooking for more than one person, and so do the girls. When they get pissed off at Mick he takes them all out to the pub where he pulls beer, and then he pays for their meals. Once a month they have a party.

Ian takes the bulging black bin-liner out to the front garden, a tiny patch of ground given over to metal trash cans, taking care to replace the lid because otherwise the bags get ripped open by urban foxes. The foxes are everywhere, walking along the streets in daylight as boldly as if they were dogs, and he almost admires their insouciance. If nothing else, London has taught him how to look after himself, he thinks, because it was almost a moral duty to employ a maid in Africa. He'd earned a salary, paid his taxes, owned a small house and a car back home and all the time he'd never ironed his own shirts, sewn on a button or done the dishes.

He catches sight of himself in the darkened glass of the living-room windows. Despite the English diet of beer and takeaways he's kept himself in shape. Just as well, considering the prickling hostility he's had to face down today from Cameron and Delano.

'They're animals, just animals,' Sally had said, when he'd eventually waded in to help her.

'They do kick off more just before lunch.'

'It's all the time! They don't want to learn, most of them, and the

90

few who do get bullied. You know what they're all showing each other on their mobiles?'

'No.'

'It's this clip from a porn film, called *Teach the Teacher*, about this young woman teacher on her first day. She gets . . . well, it's not going to add to the culture of respect.'

Ian had been horrified. 'Can't you confiscate their mobiles? They're supposed not to have them on in class.'

'You think I could wrestle them to the ground, Ian? Be my guest.'

But in Finsbury Park, all is quiet – or as quiet as the city is likely to get. He has cycled home through the maze of housing, old and new, thrilled as he always is by the density and antiquity of London. Every turning seems pregnant with possibilities, with stories; he loves the tall thin Georgian buildings of Islington and the old pubs and warehouses, the small parks where people congregate to walk or play with their families, the Victorian terraces and busy late-night shops. Candice won't stay the night here, partly because it's too squalid for her and partly because she loathes the Slug ('that dretful guy' as she calls him). Ian isn't sorry about this. He has a ton of marking to get through, and wants to keep going on his play.

There is noise, and the smell of cooking from neighbouring houses: stew, curry, sauces from around the world. On one side of them is a professional musician called Viner, and right now Ian can hear a difficult passage being practised again and again and again, so that its beauty becomes a torment. Often, when cycling along at night, he catches glimpses of all the lives happening in other houses, and other streets: people cooking, walking babies up and down, watching TV, quarrelling, or just looking out as he looks in. So many lives, all going on, not quite touching, all so different yet, he thinks, linked by place and time and a surprising degree of helpfulness once they realised you were OK. He's signed for Viner's parcels, and returned footballs from the messy front garden; they all chat to neighbours when they go to Mehmet's, the tiny shop run by a Turk on the corner. He thinks of the dead body that he saw on the Heath, and wonders who misses the person it once was.

12

Such a Banal Problem

Finding a new au pair is like childbirth, Polly thinks: you forget each time how excruciating the process is until you are in the middle of it. She is stuck with no childcare, in the worst time of year. 'Nobody wants to be here in January,' says an au-pair agency; as if she doesn't know that already.

It is such a banal problem, and yet life-consuming. Men never have it, of course. She can't work full-time without cover, and without full-time work she has no income, and no future independent of motherhood. She will be back at square one, drudging as if she didn't have a law degree or anything other than a womb. She keeps her hurt and anger over Iryna's departure in a separate compartment of her mind; the children's bewilderment is more painful.

'But *why* did she leave without saying goodbye?' Robbie asks plaintively.

'I don't know, darling. Maybe she had a family problem.'

'She was worried about her sister,' Tania remarks.

'I'm sure we'll hear from her soon,' Polly says, trying to reassure them. 'After all, we still hear from your other old nannies and au pairs, don't we?'

'But I don't remember them, and I do her,' Robbie says.

'Never mind, darlings. I'll be around to help you until we find a replacement.'

'But Mum, how can you? You don't know anything about us!'

Polly had given up work for seven long years to look after her children when they were small. But children's memories are short, and their ingratitude is boundless. There is, as her generation has found to its cost, no such thing as quality time. For the past three years, Iryna has been there for them and Polly has not. She can order groceries on the internet, access emails on her BlackBerry and have a link from office to home but she still has to put in the hours at Stern & Wiseman or she will get the sack. She has clients on the verge of being deported, victims of torture, children in foster care and cases that actually earn her firm a bit of money and she also has her own family to support. She had thought she had got the fine balance between heart and mind about right, but it seems that nobody is happy with her performance.

'You know,' one woman partner says to her, smoothly, 'we all have families, but we just don't let them intrude in our lives.'

It is all very well for her, Polly thinks resentfully. *She* has hot-and-cold running Filipinas to service her three tow-haired children and her perfect house. When Polly walks through the lobby of her firm's offices, with its blond-wood floors and large photographs of important victories, she finds it hard to believe that she herself works in something little bigger than a cupboard, on behalf of the poorest and most desperate. Of course, Sam Stern takes on the big high-profile cases, defending Cabinet Ministers and football stars, the cases that bring in serious profits; he also does pro-bono work for Amnesty, defending people in far-flung parts of the Commonwealth where there are still death penalties. He is a kind man, and Polly wants so much to deserve his trust, because he gave her a second chance when no other law firm would. Going out to meet a barrister, Polly finds herself in the lift with Stern. She blushes when he smiles at her, because she has a bit of a crush on Sam, if she's honest. He's one of those solid oak-like lawyers, a man whose probity and integrity have led him to attack the government on Iraq and civil liberties, and he moves in the highest circles of the Left.

'Hello, Polly. I haven't seen you for a while. Do you know each other? Roger, this is Polly, one of my brightest solicitors; Polly, Roger Trench, proprietor of the *Rambler*.'

Polly smiles politely at a florid middle-aged man who resembles a Roman emperor in a suit. She doesn't read the *Rambler*, which she considers a frightful rag, but he must be a client.

'Always come to Sam when I need a spot of advice,' the man says. 'It's like turning left rather than right when one boards an aeroplane, you know.'

'How's work?' Stern asks her, benignly.

'Fine.' Polly, always anxious, adds, 'I've a spot of bother with an au pair who's left suddenly, but I'm keeping going.'

'Ah, yes,' Stern says vaguely. 'Well, you'll get it sorted.'

Polly does interviews over the phone in her lunch hour, and on the bus to and from work; she takes calls on her mobile while driving to collect Robbie from school and while boiling pasta for tea. Most of her applicants, or supplicants, can barely speak English; when she tests those who attempt her standard question (*What would you do if my child became unconscious?*) some become angry and confused and ring off.

'Can't you get Theo to pay for a proper housekeeper?' Bill asks, during one of their late-night conversations. 'Or just pay for one yourself?'

Polly sighs. Although Bill isn't doing as well as he hoped in Hollywood, he still has a vastly inflated idea, after ten years there, of what is actually possible for a single mother.

'Theo doesn't want me to work. He has old-fashioned ideas about how I should stay at home, and I can't afford to pay more than an au pair's salary.'

'My ex-wives always employed an army of Mexicans.'

'Yes, it's the same all over, isn't it?' Polly says. 'Strange, isn't it, the way it never affects fathers this way.'

The biggest single problem is collecting Robbie, bringing him home, and making sure that he and Tania are given their tea. Her mother lives too far away; and Theo is, predictably, 'not in a position to help out'. Her younger sister Lucy is equally unavailable. In desperation, Polly even rings a couple of neighbouring mothers whose children go to Robbie's prep school, and begs. But she is long out of the favours market, and now she has gone back to work she has crossed the divide between the working and non-working mums.

'I'm sorry, but I'm having a manicure then,' says one; and another pleads her Pilates class. Whom can she call on? At last she tries Hemani, her best and oldest friend, and now, since her marriage to Theo's middle brother Daniel, Tania and Robbie's aunt. Normally, Hemani is rushed off her feet as a doctor, but Polly remembers she has just started her maternity leave.

'Of course I can collect Robbie!' Hemani exclaims when Polly asks. 'No problem.'

'Bless you,' Polly says. Everything in her body relaxes. 'I have a court hearing today, and my au pair has walked out on me.'

Hemani sighs in sympathy. 'God, we've all been there! I'm enjoying the rest, I can tell you, Poll. The poor old Nash is doomed.'

'I thought the Health Service was getting loads more money pumped into it?'

'It's a drop in the ocean. Do you know, we have one case of tuberculosis a day at my hospital? All from the Third World. We'd eradicated it here, and now it's back because we don't even demand health checks at passport control.'

'Hemani!' exclaims Polly. 'Surely you don't really mean that?'

'The last case I had before I went on leave was this man from Nigeria who was going blind. He'd got AIDS and had been using his wife's anti-retroviral drugs, prescribed by the NHS for her. So she's dying, because she didn't get the medication, and he's disabled because the drugs weren't meant for him. And because I had to deal

95

with him I can't treat poor old pensioners with glaucoma, who've paid their taxes all their lives. It's insane.'

'Awful,' says Polly, thinking how right-wing Hemani has become. It's strange: all the white people she knows are liberal Left-wing professionals, but all the Asians like Hemani are the opposite. They argue that uncontrolled immigration is bad for Britain, and so it is: but how can you draw the line at your own feet just because you were lucky? Isn't it as horrible to die of starvation as from political persecution? Of course, she can see that there are economic migrants as well as the sort she defends – yet isn't that just what a country needs, adults with the energy to make a fresh start? If only she could find one herself, given that no girl from the EU will glance at what she has to offer. Bring me your tired, your poor, your hungry, because they're the ones who'll look after your kids for less than the minimum wage and be thankful for it, she thinks.

In between trying to prepare witness statements, and briefing a barrister on an asylum case for an Albanian scholarship student who has been detained in the third year of her studies at Imperial, Polly has rung two agencies, outlining her requirements. As usual, she is assured by bright adenoidal voices that they had 'some lovely girls' on their books, and as usual, they turn out not to be.

How difficult can it be to find another Iryna? Very, it seems. For over a fortnight, the wretched of every nation flow through Polly's door, wanting to look after her children in return for bed, board and (admittedly) a tiny weekly wage in British pounds that, translated into their own currency, seems like a decent living. Some bring bunches of flowers, as if these would persuade her, and some rant on about their Christian faith, or their existing family, and almost all of them smell horrible. I cannot let you look after my children, Polly thinks, and I can't live with you in my home. She is miserable and desperate, but not yet *that* miserable or desperate.

'You just *don't understand*!' Robbie screams when she is trying to sort out his sports kit. She hasn't read a newspaper or watched TV for weeks because of chores.

'I'm sorry, darling, I am trying but I'm just so tired.'

'You're always bloody tired,' Tania says. 'You shouldn't have had children.'

Had they talked like this to Iryna? Was that why she'd left?

'I'm not your servant,' Polly says, angrily. 'You should know how to make your own beds, and cook.'

'But why should I?' Tania says. 'I've got schoolwork, and I'm going to have a career.'

Polly sits with another client, a teenager who had been dumped at Heathrow by his father as a child, and left there. It is something a good many Africans now do, because they can at least be certain that this way their child might survive a few more years. Despite X-rays and medical examinations, nobody is quite sure how old the boy is, but once he's over seventeen he can be deported. The problem is that he has no passport, and no documentation to say where he came from. Attempts to speak to him in various African languages were met with stony silence, though he spoke a little French and from this the Home Office have deduced that he might be from Cameroon. He now speaks excellent English, passing six GCSEs with A grades; he is well liked, polite, honest, gentle and local people have got up a petition asking for him to be allowed to stay. It is, however, unlikely that he will be.

'How are you, Ben?'

'Okay.'

'You're at the Samuel Smiles, I see.'

'Yes.'

'They seem to think very highly of you.'

He smiles, shyly. 'I work, that's all.'

Polly wishes she could show him to Tania, to make her realise how lucky she is: only the two halves of her life never meet. She knows about the Samuel Smiles, if only because it's bottom of the league tables, just as her own children's schools are at the top. How this boy has managed to flourish despite the adverse conditions is something she can't begin to imagine.

Polly has marshalled all she can about conditions in Cameroon, which is now a democracy, though a very unstable one, and points out that there is no evidence that Ben even comes from there. He has not lived with his natural parents since he was six, and would be sent back to a place where he has no connections, memories or means of earning a living. The judge – a pale, refined man – listens to it all wearily, and Polly's adversary, a Home Office man with cropped hair and a stud in one ear (as if, Polly thinks, that could make him less boring!) makes his case in turn. Each side has bundles of paper to present to the judge, but despite evidence from Ben's teachers and foster parents, it seems unlikely he will stay. Polly argues for a postponement, on the grounds that it is not absolutely certain that Ben is seventeen. She gets it: a huge relief, but only a temporary one.

'We'll think what to do next,' she says. 'At least you can sit your A levels.'

'All I want is to go to college, to work hard and live a good life,' Ben says quietly, when they go down the lift together. 'I'm not asking for any handouts. This is my country. I don't have any other.'

Polly goes back to her office in a vile temper. Yesterday, she instructed a barrister to defend a Kenyan who she knows is a crook. Because he has money, and an advocate, he will be allowed to stay. There are murderers and terrorists who invoke their human rights, and who are not deported because they come from dangerous countries, while innocent, law-abiding, hard-working people who have simply had the misfortune to be born in the wrong country are like lambs to the slaughter. She has represented Ben for two years, and although she has barely covered her costs in doing so, she will go on fighting for him until there is nothing left. If she fails, he will be sent to Yarl's Wood or Harmondsworth detention centre and forcibly deported in a plane. Maybe I should offer *him* a job as my au pair, she thinks crossly.

I need to work, I *need* to work runs through her head like the rattle of the trains that go deep underground beneath her house. To lose her job would be to sacrifice all her sacrifices, would be to give in to all those people who told her when she was growing up that women's education was pointless because they stopped work when they had families. She knows she will probably never become a partner, and her children will never stop resenting her for working so much and earning so little, and yet she has to keep going.

When Iryna had walked in off the street four years ago, Polly had been in an even deeper crisis. Getting divorced, going house-hunting, finding the children's new schools and getting her own life back on track had preoccupied her more than whether or not Iryna was legal. The girl had worn a terrible grey anorak, and her face had been alarmingly pale, but she had been sane, intelligent and clean. She had no references, she said, because her previous employers were treating her badly and didn't even know she was planning to leave.

'They pay me one week's money when I have worked for one month.'

It was a familiar story. Polly always wondered how much hatred her country was storing up for treating migrant workers in this way; she had heard of women who turned off the heating when they went on holiday, leaving their au pairs to freeze, and who never fed them properly.

'I like this house,' Iryna said, in her glottal accent, looking at the kitchen. 'Is nice.'

Then she did what no other interviewee had done, and examined the pictures that Tania and Robbie had stuck to the wall. They were the usual products of wild imagination: dragons, pirate ships, volcanoes, fairies with insect wings.

'In my country, we tell stories like these,' she said. 'The bird of fire, the hut on chicken legs, Baba Yaga. Do your children know these?'

'I'm not sure,' said Polly, 'but they sound like the kind of story they enjoy.'

It was a bit like going on a blind date, Polly thought, but it worked. Iryna had vacuumed the stairs on her first day and made perfect chips for the children. Nothing seemed to upset her.

'*Chort!*' she would exclaim, and that was all. After a few months she had blossomed. Her cheeks turned pink, her hair glossy, and she sang as she dusted. Polly revelled in her new freedom. She could work late, go out to the cinema and, once she began the affair with Bill, stay with him when he was over from LA; occasionally, they even went away to his house in Tuscany for a long weekend while Iryna was paid overtime to look after the children alone. The issue of visas was never mentioned. Polly had learnt long ago that there was no word for 'privacy' in Russian, and this made her especially careful never to intrude on Iryna, or examine her room when she was out. She thought of Iryna as a part of the family – or very nearly. They had exchanged birthday and Christmas presents, had laughed over the children, had discussed art . . .

Another thought strikes Polly.

'Does Iryna have a boyfriend?'

'Of course she did. We met him,' says Tania.

'He'd come round when she did babysitting,' Robbie adds.

Polly is astonished, then furious. 'You know babysitters aren't allowed to have boyfriends round!'

'Why not?'

Polly says defensively, 'Because I don't want to have strange men in the house.'

'Well, he was a stranger at first,' Robbie points out. 'But then we got to know him, and he was perfectly nice. Gheorghe always brought us Mars Bars.'

Polly files this information away, while trying to sort out the problem of collecting Robbie. After some thought, she remembers the young Zimbabwean driver she had had on the day Iryna disappeared, and rings the company. He is on the doorstep within ten minutes, smiling.

'Come in – I want you to meet my son, so that you can both recognise each other tomorrow,' says Polly. 'But I don't know your name.'

'My name is Job, madam,' he says. His deep, gentle voice makes her think of honey.

'Please, do come in.' He steps just into the hall, respectfully. 'Say hello, Robbie.'

Shyly, Robbie obeys her.

'You will take care, won't you?' she said anxiously. 'He's only ten.'

Job seems sensible and reliable, though Polly worries that he won't make Robbie fasten his seat belt.

She goes upstairs, carrying a big basket of clean clothes, and then starts to do more cleaning of the spare room. Iryna has left a lot of rubbish behind. A photograph of her is wedged in the side of a drawer. It must have been taken before she came to England, Polly thinks, for in the picture Iryna is still greyish, hugging a much younger, prettier girl frozen in a flash of teeth and startled eyes, a sister perhaps. Polly takes the photograph, and puts it in her purse. What had Iryna got up to all those hours when she was not at home? The abandoned room gives no clues among the elastic bands, cotton buds, and candles. In a jam jar holding old pens and pencils there are a couple of matchbooks with the words *The Giant Bread & Cheese* printed on them. Polly recognises it as a gastropub, not far from her office. Could Iryna have had a job there? Could it be one of her haunts?

Maybe, she thinks, I'll pay it a visit.

13

Broken English

How is it possible that there are so many men who want this? Anna wonders, spitting and rinsing into the small white china basin of her cubicle once again. She is getting better at it, thinking of them as goats to be milked, quickly and efficiently. Another and another and another: each so different, yet each so drearily the same. Thick or thin, long or short, turkey necks and turkey wattles: how ugly men are, and how in thrall to their vile bodies. She has no illusions that their lust has anything to do with *her*: she is a means to an end, that is all. They never look her in the face, even when slobbering at it. They would be just as well served by a plastic doll (and she knows, now, that such dolls exist, life-sized, with round cartoon mouths and startled eyes), only they want the touch of young flesh.

Anna's bewilderment and fear has long since changed into contempt. How stupid men are, she thinks; stupid and weak to be the prisoners of this part of the body, with its blind eye always searching so greedily for what was inside her. Some are absorbed in their own pleasure, and those are the easiest because they demand little, their eyes averted. The worst are the ones who take longer, hissing and growling long strings of words she doesn't understand, though she recognises the voice of hatred. Bitch, cock, cunt, fuck, arse, yes, suck hard, yes, they say in thick monotonous whispers, muttering the same things over and over in a frenzy until they are seized by the spasm that renders them limp and small again. Anna's limited English has expanded to accommodate these new words, once she understands that they will make them hurry up. They like to pretend that it is she who is making them do this, rather than they who force it on her; that she deliberately tempts them to the acts that cause her pain and humiliation; that she asks for it all.

Very quickly, Anna herself has come to believe this, too. After all, she wasn't a fool; she knew that girls could be trafficked and sold into prostitution. Even in Lutsk, she should have known that Natalya with her smart new clothes and her story about the good jobs to be had in London was just a scout to find other young girls; Drita, who had been caught the same way, told her that Natalya probably had a child who was kept hostage. 'Unless,' she added, 'she is doing it for the money. Everything here is about money.'

Anna has been raped by up to thirty men a day, every day, and she never gets any of the money that they pay to do this though the men are charged fifty a time. The only difference is that after the first few days she is moved from the flat to a brothel on a busy high street where more men will visit. The journey takes place in the same black car that had fetched her from the bus, and now her feelings on looking out of the window are so different it is as if she were another person. She knows that she passes through a place called Camden Lock because there is a bridge with the words painted on it, and it terrifies her. The shops have strange things poking out from their fronts – a giant boot, a rocking chair, a Chinese dragon – and the dummies with their black-painted eyes and jagged black clothes are scarcely less frightening than the people walking around with studs of metal in their faces. Who *are* these people? The only Briton she ever saw on TV was its Queen, who was always waving, brightly dressed and covered in jewels. That was all the TV in other countries ever showed about Britain, apparently.

The new brothel, Poshlust, advertises itself in pink neon writing as a massage parlour and sauna, and sits on top of a fish-and-chip shop in a place the girls say is Kill Burn. When Anna translates these two words she becomes even more frightened, because none of them have any doubts that the two men are capable of the first, and their favourite game when bored is putting their cigarettes out on the girls. To add to their misery, the smells of frying fish-oil waft upwards, tormenting their empty stomachs, and sometimes schoolboys dare each other to bounce on the mat at the foot of the stairs and make the bell jangle.

'Sons of whores,' says Lena. 'But one day they will be clients.'

Lena is the woman who sits on the front desk. She is some kind of partner in the business, according to Drita; she takes the money, keeps the accounts and hands out pills.

Routine will numb even the most loathsome life. The men Anna dreads most are Sergei and Dmitri. She has healed in some places, but it hurts to go to the toilet, and no matter how she lies she feels permanently bruised. A whore's most precious possession, she has learnt, is a tube of KY jelly. Lena told her that, in a good mood. The brothel issues its clients with condoms, but there are those who will always pay her to do without; if she agrees, she risks getting HIV. Anna has been told about the danger of disease, but this is the only money of her own that she can earn, and what is her life worth anyway in this place? In any case, not all of them even ask, or pay. The moment the cubicle door is closed, they think she's like a piece of meat.

Often, in her home, Anna had wondered about what it would be like to do it with a man. She had giggled and whispered stories about boys, as all girls do, and at night when alone had discovered certain drowsy, pleasurable sensations that her body could give her. She had wondered whether everyone made this discovery, which was never talked about as far as she knew, but in London it seems to be the principal industry. Everything she sees in the brothel – the TV stations, the magazines, the posters – is about masturbation, though they pretend it's about sex.

One or two girls are allowed to work in hotels, and they are envied; a girl called Galina is a particular favourite of a rich man. All the others hate Galina, because she gets to go with only one man, and is even allowed to keep some money. He is a regular customer of Poshlust, and has some business arrangement with it, Lena hints; he's crazy about Galina, to the management's relief. There is a lot of competition in prostitution.

'Too many Brazilians,' Lena says, disgusted. The Brazilians are cutting into their profits, and they have the reputation of being sexier. All the girls at the brothel are from Eastern Europe: Albania, Romania, Lithuania, Moldova, Croatia, Russia and the Ukraine. Though they speak Russian to varying degrees, among themselves they speak broken English. Anna is the youngest, for now.

'Maybe you will be lucky, get oligarch,' Lena tells her. 'Maybe you get rich man, too.'

Some of the older girls were prostitutes before they came to Britain, and aspire to be lapdancers; they speak of the profits to be made at 'gentlemen's clubs' in the city centre, where businessmen stuff fifty-pound notes between your breasts. But, they tell Anna, you have to look like a model to get work there, and the competition is too fierce, with students and real dancers vying to fill any vacancies. All the brothel girls have is their youth, and health, and their desperation to avoid being beaten or sent back home. There is no other future for them now, for they can never go back.

'If I go back, my family they kill me,' says Marija, the Croatian.

Lena is a great reader of magazines, the sort that show happy Hollywood film stars with perfect white teeth celebrating their romantic choices beneath rocking palm trees on semi-tropical beaches. She urges Anna to be cheerful.

'You may be prostitute now, but one day, maybe celebrity come knocking on your door. I see many, many girls from my country like this. Anything can happen.'

'It already has,' says Anna.

'What did you think you would be in England?'

'A cook,' Anna mutters.

Lena gives them all pills to take, every morning. 'Here, take these. You don't want to make a baby, do you?'

Anna takes hers, and swallows obediently. The ice around her thickens. Nothing matters; but the next day, Drita stops her.

'You want to be like the rest?' Drita asks her quietly.

'I don't know.'

'If you take the pills, they make you stupid. Pretend to swallow.'

'Why are you telling me this?'

'You are not an addict. That's how they keep me, like dog on a chain.' Drita laughs, bitterly. She is full of a savage, cynical sense of humour. Anna likes her, until she finds her small cache of money has gone. The next time she sees Drita, stoned, she knows who took it.

'You took my money.'

Drita shrugs. 'So? I had it done to me. In a few weeks, you will do the same.'

Anna bites her lip in order not to cry. The cruelty of the men is something she expects, but the cruelty of other girls is worse. 'I would sooner die.'

Drita looks at her sceptically. If Anna were determined, she could smash through the window and fall fifty feet onto the railway track at the back. But she isn't, and won't. 'Nobody stays here long. In one year, they sell you on to another place. When you are twenty, you look like old woman.'

Five years, Anna thinks. It is impossible to think of surviving this even five more days, but somehow she has to. She has to learn how to squeeze her insides so that it's over quicker, to simulate all the joy that is her despair. She has to learn how to cope with the rotten breath, the filthy hands, the rank bodies. The dirt offends her almost to the point of madness. Her own family had shared a bathroom in their block of flats with five other families, but everyone had washed, even in the winter. Here, no one is clean; Lena, at least, provides them with a basin on the wall as part of the service, but few use it even after. They are like pigs in mud.

'I used to be a cleaner,' Lena tells Anna. 'I was cleaning Arsenal stadium until three in the morning. I earn one hundred pounds a week, I am so tired I could fall down by the end, and a Russian in my house, she said, try this and you earn three hundred pounds a day. So I become prostitute.'

Lena grins her broad, gappy grin. She had been successful enough to have a flat, which she had shared with another Russian, until her cocaine addiction got her kicked out. Now she is in business with the brothers, but mostly with Sergei, who provides her drugs. Her attitude to the girls is both maternal and brutal. She is the one who brings them food, pills and medicine, and she is the one who sizes them up and gives them new clothes. The drugs, of course, they have to earn.

In a part of herself, Anna is still the girl who loves clothes and make-up. It's the strangest thing: alone, the girls in the brothel will brush each other's hair and paint each other's nails as if they are at school. They are young, and vanity dies hard.

'Is better if you relax,' Lena tells Anna. 'The men like you more if you look happy.'

Through the thin partition walls, Anna can hear some of the other girls make noises – Uh-uh-uh – or say, in a mechanical way, 'Yes – yes – yes, baby!'

What idiot could believe these are sounds of ecstasy?

Sergei beats them all if he thinks they are wasting time, taking care never to mark their faces but to hit their breasts or thighs with a length of electric flex. He is more and more foul-tempered. The cold weather and post-Christmas slump mean less business, and less cocaine.

'You want to know why girls are better than drugs?' he says. 'Drugs can only be sold once.'

He and Dmitri drink instead – not vodka, like the men back home, but whisky. Even the smell of it makes Anna gag, but they love it.

'Visky!' they say, and knock back shots of it in glass tumblers.

Drinking, though, puts them in a worse temper.

'Why you look sad, bitch?' Sergei shouts at Anna. 'You like your new country? New country, where you owe me money!'

Anna suddenly blurts, 'I have earned much more than five thousand pounds by now! Let me go.'

She has worked it out. Sergei looms over her. He has been waiting for an excuse to explode. 'So, little Ukrainian *suka* can count?'

He begins to land blow after blow on her shoulders and legs, and she curls up, terrified. 'How many is that, bitch? Five? Ten? Twelve?'

Anna sobs, a ball of bone and pain. Sergei wrenches one of her arms up. He is so strong that there is no resisting it.

The other girls watch, dumbly, as with an audible snap he breaks one of her fingers. The pain is like lightning. Anna opens her mouth, and howls like a dog. Sergei raises his fist for a blow whose imminence she can only sense because her eyes are streaking tears, but just as he is about to hit her again the doorbell rings. They look up at the video-entryphone screen. A man has stepped on the mat and is coming up the stairs. They fall silent, Anna cradling her hand and trying to muffle her sobs.

'Another one. Those black motherfuckers can't get enough white meat.'

Sergei presses the buzzer, and Anna, trembling, stands up.

14

Katie at the Wigmore

Katie's sources of spiritual refreshment in London are not as many or varied as they once were, but they include something new. Her office is within walking distance of the Wigmore Hall, and on Fridays, when the magazine is out, she feels entitled to take a longer lunch break to go to recitals there. This is also the day when the more favoured of Quentin's staff get invited, along with various members of the good and great, to partake of lunch in the private dining room of the Giant Bread & Cheese, a pub just along the road from the office. Katie has yet to be invited. She knows the reason for this: she is not glamorous enough. Had she married Winthrop and become the multimillionaire daughter-in-law of a Senator it would have been a different matter, but in herself she just doesn't register.

'You see, Trench expects a certain return for his investment,' Justin has explained. 'He likes rubbing shoulders with the movers and shakers, and you—'

'It's OK, I'm good with that,' she had said hastily. 'Really.'

Given her feeling of being too hideous and too dull for anyone to want to talk to, lunch is an ordeal that Katie is especially happy to pass on. The only thing in her life which she can control is eating, and as her ribs rise out of her flesh, her sensation of detachment has made hopelessness bearable. Katie's desk is the only one in the *Rambler* office to be meticulously neat and clear of extraneous paper; even Quentin admits his correspondence has never been dealt with so efficiently.

The doorbell rings. Another delivery, she thinks, impatient to be off. Just opening the padded envelopes with their unsolicited pieces and unreadable books is almost a full-time job, and as she goes downstairs she sees the dark face of a delivery boy outside.

'Do you want me to sign for it?'

'I was told to deliver it to the editor's office.'

'He's not in. You can leave it on his desk, if you want.'

The boy tramps up the stairs behind her as she returns to her own desk. As soon as he leaves, she sets off, barely pausing to buy a smoothie and an apple for lunch.

What Katie hungers for is music. This has taken her by surprise; for although she learnt to play the piano moderately well a long time ago and always liked listening to concerts and the opera, she was never crazy for it. But shortly after arriving in London, Katie had discovered Radio 3, and one thing had led to another so that now she is usually the youngest person in a room full of grey and white heads. What do *they* get out of it? Is it a purely intellectual pleasure, or is it the memory of the strength and pain of passionate feeling? Her parents, whose long and contented marriage had not prepared her for disappointment, loved the high, lonesome sounds of bluegrass music which suggested that they, too, had known times of trouble. Or perhaps – and this alarms her most – you go on feeling just as anguished, just as confused at seventy as you do at twenty-seven. For this is what she hears when she listens to Bach, Schubert, Mozart, Debussy, Chopin and Beethoven. To her, music is all about containing love, and pain, and loss.

The Wigmore is too small for big orchestral pieces. Its recitals are all of sonatas, preludes, études; the intimate, internal music that addresses her directly. Now that she has been flayed, she feels it as never before. There is also the charm of place, for its glories belong to another age. She imagines meeting the Schlegel sisters in *Howards End*, or a minor character from Anthony Powell. Everything about it, from its rich acoustics to the glowing gold mosaic of its Art Nouveau Apollo surrounded by angels, enchants her with a confident, opulent reverence for high art that had presumably existed in New York, but which she had never taken advantage of. The plush seats, the air of hushed anticipation, the soft multilingual murmur of other music lovers – some of whom, she surmises, must have come to London specially to hear this or that performer – all speak of a mode of existence that transcends ordinary life.

Today there is Couperin and Chopin, to be broadcast on Radio 3 as a lunchtime concert. The performer, Viner, is someone she hasn't heard of but who is supposed to be a rising star as a soloist. He comes onto the stage wearing a sharp black suit and a Byronic scowl beneath wild, dark curls, but his looks seem somehow to fade the moment he begins playing, as if all the beauty of his face drains into his hands.

Those hands! Katie can see them reflected in the lid of the Steinway, even longer and thinner than her own. She always forgets about how live music is at least in part a visual experience, and that the drama of seeing a performer play amplifies what is heard. His expressions change constantly; sometimes he seems to be in the middle of an intense conversation with the composer, and sometimes he seems as remote as a priest praying to his god. Yet it is Viner's hands that fascinate her most. Their motion, darting and flickering up and down the keyboard like two white fish in a river of darkness, hypnotises her, even as the music unfolds its story.

She is not familiar with Couperin. At first the pieces sound playful, almost like half-remembered nursery songs, and she feels self-conscious and on edge, thinking: he's all peacock brilliance, without feeling. But time after time, the melody turns on a hair, jumps a key or an octave, and amazes her. One piece especially almost stops her heart, and it's clear that not only does the pianist love it but everyone in the concert hall does too, for that special quality of listening which is particular to the Wigmore blossoms like a great flower. Nobody coughs, or rustles, or shifts by so much as an inch, but they seem to hold their breath as the ravishing sounds transfix them. What *are* the Mysterious Barricades? Are they real or imaginary, between people or between the world and the spirit? The broken chords and weak beats are perplexing, like someone approaching a being they desire yet fear, but underneath there is the same strength as in Bach. The sky darkens overhead, and the glow of the burnished figures above intensifies. It is worth being alive.

The first half ends, and at once there is a rumble of coughs, rising in every throat as the audience stirs. An elderly, balding man with a magnificent nose who is sitting just in front of her opens his eyes; beside him, a woman with severely cropped grey hair and a pair of silver coffee-bean earrings begins chatting animatedly to an actor Katie recognises from a TV series – one of those slick thrillers that are watched by the entire nation on Monday nights. Benedick something, she thinks. Beside him, she recognises a journalist called Georgina Hunter who sometimes came to lunch at the magazine. She would never have guessed the elegant, frivolous Georgina to be musical, but then music yokes together the most unlikely people. Winthrop, of course, had never liked any kind but rock.

Suddenly, Katie feels a wince of fright. Of course, she has only met him once, but she is almost sure that, next to Georgina, she recognises the profile of Daniel Noble, Winthrop's half-brother. It is a few years since she's seen him, but unlike herself he has scarcely changed. The realisation that she is going to have to talk to them crashes around inside her hollowed-out stomach, even as the pianist embarks on the famous first chord of Chopin's *Barcarolle*.

Katie clenches her fists, her mood shattered. What is Daniel doing here? Is he spying on her? She knows from one or two mutual friends that her ex still asks about her, presumably out of malign curiosity rather than guilt. On the other hand, one of the few things she knows about Daniel is that he is very musical. Wretchedly, she wonders whether the pianist too feels the panic and distress that she is experiencing, or whether it is just technique, a matter of nerve and touch and speed. The audience are listening with that extra level of pleasure and alertness, but perhaps the pianist can remain as indifferent as a god while producing these rippling modulations, the long nightingale-like trills of the *rubato*. The pattern shifts from anguish to ecstasy, like someone knowing they are going to die and transcending mortality. Serene, exultant, it falls away into a silence that seems to reverberate with new strength.

I *won't* run away from Daniel, she decides. The music has shown me that. After the applause, prolonged and enthusiastic, she finds herself shuffling out along the aisle. Her gaze, inevitably, meets Georgina Hunter's.

'Hello!' Georgina exclaims pleasantly. 'Wasn't that wonderful?'

'Yes,' says Katie, adding: 'Just what I needed before heading back to the office.'

'You work at the *Spectator*, don't you?'

'No, the *Rambler*,' says Katie.

Now Daniel, who also seems to be in the party, is looking at her in a mildly puzzled way.

'Don't I – oh, hi, hi Katie! How are you doing?' says Daniel.

'You know each other?' Georgina asks, surprised.

'We're kind of related,' says Daniel, adding in a lower voice, 'I heard you and Win split up. I'm sorry.'

The others move on towards the hall.

'Thank you,' says Katie, stiffly. 'I heard you'd gotten married.'

'My wife's expecting our first child,' he says, with such touching pride that she knows at once that her fears are groundless. 'She's on maternity leave right now. Hemani!'

A woman turns, and waits for them in the lobby. She is hugely pregnant and exquisite, Katie thinks, like an Indian goddess.

'Hi.'

'I am so very pleased to meet you.'

Katie is struck by the warmth of their greeting. It is so utterly

113

different from anything she expected, or indeed has encountered during her time in England.

'I'm sorry we never met before,' she says, impulsively.

Daniel asks, 'Katie, are you living in London?'

'Well, I am, in fact,' says Katie. 'I live in Camden Town.'

'That's not far from us! You must come to supper before the baby arrives.'

'Oh. Thanks, I'd like that.'

To her surprise, she finds it is true. Winthrop had always sneered at his middle brother as 'the useless nerd-brain'; but she's pleased and flattered by the invitation, not least because, in the entire time she has lived in this city, nobody has ever before asked her into their home.

'Seriously. Give me your number. This is ours.'

She switches on her cellphone again, which means Quentin's incessant, querulous demands will shortly begin to arrive. Sure enough, it begins buzzing with texts and voicemail messages.

'Problems?'

'Oh, just work. You know. Daniel, it's great to see you and I'd love to catch up, but I must run.'

She rushes off, hypnotised by her cellphone screen.

'Turnbull & Asser suit?'

'My latte was insufficiently macchiato.'

'NEVER put Dominic Piston through to me.'

'Katie, buy wedding anniversary present Selfridges.'

On and on and on it goes. Whatever she does for him is never right. Patiently and politely she will find the suit, the coffee, the excuse, the present, on top of her official duties, and he never thinks of thanking her. Getting reimbursed is another nightmare.

'You know, Quentin's last assistant spent every lunch break in tears,' Patrick had told her in his mocking lilt. 'People are taking bets on how long it will take you to crack.'

'He is pretty cranky at times.'

'You should stand up to him more, instead of being a shrinking violet.'

'I figure that would only make him more persnickety.'

In truth, Quentin's spite does not trouble her as much as his hali-tosis. The rest of the staff, by common agreement, never pick up his telephone. It is ringing when Katie returns to the office, and she just looks at it.

'If it's his landline it can't be too important,' she says aloud.

'How do you suppose his mistresses stand it?' Patrick wonders. 'I mean, I know he's quite fit for an old man but you'd think the smell would make them pass out.'

'Perhaps that's his secret. He just breathes on them,' says Minty.

'The new cleaner never cleans the phones,' Jocasta complains. 'She's the most frightful slut, and I'm not sure she didn't pinch my Chanel sunglasses.'

'What happened to what's-her-face?'

'The Russian?'

Katie shrugs. She is preoccupied with fact-checking, her default job. 'The agency said they'd find us a permanent replacement, but it's January.'

'Too true. God, if I were them I'd spend all of this month and the next somewhere warm and sunny,' sighs Patrick.

Justin clears his throat.

'I have a friend with a riad in Marrakesh, if you're interested.'

'No, thanks.'

Katie sees the older man flinch. Justin can work out at the gym every day; he knows everything there is to be known about Wagner, Damien Hirst and Henry Green, but he is still a bald man in his forties whom the others find comical. Only Mark Crawley, the Political Editor, is more pompous.

'God, wouldn't you rather be anywhere but here?' exclaims Cecilia, yawning and looking out of the window. 'At least I'm off to Paris for the weekend.'

'Somewhere nice?'

'Of course.'

She would always be going to nice places, and Katie knows that

115

the person Cecilia is probably going with is Quentin, because she herself contacted the Press Office at a luxury Parisian hotel in order to obtain a free suite for her boss there, while his wife and family go to their farm in the West Country. Everyone at the *Rambler* seems to have a second home as well as a flat or house in either Notting Hill or Chelsea. (Justin, who has a flat in the Albany, is the exception.) When Minty had heard that Katie was living in North London, she exclaimed with a shudder, 'Isn't that full of intellectuals?'

Katie likes books and music and museums, but when she discovered she was pretty she had resented that part of herself, and seen Winthrop's easy charm and extravagance as an escape from it. She had coloured at her colleagues' surprise at her address; and it's true that, when she had come over as a fiancée to find an apartment or a house to rent while Winthrop was posted to London, she looked in very different places: a mews cottage in Belgravia had been her choice for them. But perhaps that too would have been frowned upon. Katie thinks again of the music she had heard at lunchtime, the *Mysterious Barricades*. They are just like what she too encounters as she negotiates this strange culture, at once so familiar and so foreign.

15

A *Polite English Fiction*

Job knows he is doing a foolish thing, coming to this place, but he can't go on any more. The years without his wife have made him desperate. The touch of a woman's hand, the softness of her flesh, the chink of light between her thighs is what he daydreams of continually. He has tried to be a good and faithful husband, but he can feel that he will die if he continues like this. Munisha will understand, if I ever see her again, he thinks; and besides, she will never know. I will be careful, I will not catch a disease, I will just pay some woman some money and then I will be better. For years, his warm and active imagination has enabled him to remain faithful; like Nicholas Nickleby's, it can thrive on very slight and sparing food. But now even that is exhausted.

Job has a little more money these days, thanks to the regular work of picking Robbie up from school. He likes the boy, with his unmistakable look of a child who is loved, and he likes Polly, who always looks so anxious. She is one of those Englishwomen who is like a small bird, all softness and busyness. Job is sorry for her because she has no husband to help her.

'I just wish I could find this girl,' she says, from the back seat. 'It's maddening.'

'May I ask, madam, why you are seeking her?'

'She used to work for me, and she's disappeared.'

'I too have lost someone,' Job says, nodding. 'My wife.'

'Have you told the police?'

'No,' he says, sighing. 'She has disappeared in Harare.'

'Mine was my au pair,' says Polly.

'I do not know this word.'

'She is someone who lives in your home and looks after it and your children for a few hours every day in return.'

'Ah. Like a maid?'

'Yes, I suppose so.'

Job thinks of how, little by little, his mother had become bitter because they did not even have running water in their hut, like the Wisdens in their big house. It was different for Job, in the beginning, because he and his sister had been allowed to play with Beth. *Such dear little piccaninnies*, the white people had called them, and although he remembered the phrase he had been too innocent to register the insult, though his mother had. She was old enough to remember the wars, and the way white people had tried to prevent Independence, while all Job and Miriam cared about was having fun. But then, when he was twelve, it had all changed. He had grown up, and become the size he is now, and the Wisdens didn't want him to play with Beth any more.

Polly is saying, 'Au pairs come from abroad, and aren't trained, so they – well, they cost a lot less, but they learn English and live in your house as part of the family. I thought I had a really good one, only she's disappeared.'

'I am missing my wife,' says Job. 'I do not know if she is dead or alive. We have a very bad president in my country.'

'I know.'

'That, there, is where I live now.'

Polly looks out at the tall, shabby grey concrete building he points to. 'Oh, I know this place!' she exclaims.

118

'You have been there?'

'Er – no, not exactly. I can see it from my house, that's all.'

'One day, perhaps, you might like to visit me,' Job says.

'One day, perhaps,' she replies.

He knows that she never will, though they pretend to each other, in the way of the British, that they are equals. It's one of those polite English fictions of equality that are like grease on a wheel shaft. She talks to him in a friendly, interested way; she's surprised to find that he reads Dickens and Shakespeare. Perhaps the kind of Africans she defends are not like him, though he tells her that people in his country learn English now in order to read these authors.

Poor people do live differently in Britain. They have so many things that it seems to drive out thought. Job would never have dreamt he could one day drive a car like the one he leases from Mo, for instance. Nor would he have believed that he might have a TV set, thrown out because it was an old, bulky design instead of the flat-screen ones everyone expects. Also, there is so much culture available for free. Job has walked, amazed, round every museum he can find on Sundays, where people from all over the globe wander in to enjoy the most beautiful paintings, inventions, buildings. He can't join a public library, but the cheapness of second-hand paperbacks on stalls and in charity shops almost makes him weak. There is an abundance of everything – food dropped half-eaten on the pavement that goes to feed birds or rats – and yet a consciousness of nothing. He thinks of the city conjured for him by Dickens; that foggy, dark place riddled with crime and yet suffused with kindness and courage. He had been a little disappointed when he arrived to find the soot had been scoured away during the last century, and no horse-drawn carriages. Yet there were still men like Bill Sikes, with their dogs and violence. He sees them right outside his home.

Home for Job is now a tiny room with only a sink to drink from and wash in, and the noise of police sirens and traffic wailing and sighing in a continuous susurration below. Damp blooms on the walls, outlining new continents – as if those who live here, in the

119

perpetual stench of urine, beer, sour milk and cinders, need any more reminders of what they have lost. Job's own room is sub-let from another foreigner, in a kind of food chain of privation and opportunism. There is a whole family next to Job, sleeping on a floor that is all a heaving, twanging mattress. He doesn't even know where they are from because they speak no English, but he suspects it is the Gambia. On his other side are two sisters from Turkey, and then a young couple from somewhere in the Indian subcontinent. Intimately acquainted with each other's bowel movements and cooking smells, his fellow tenants mind their own business, and when they pass each other silently on the stairs or in the corridor they keep their heads down. They bang on his door when he shouts out from his nightmares and he bangs on theirs if they quarrel or fail to quieten a baby, but otherwise they pretend not to exist, which is another polite English fiction.

But the worst of all are the other sounds – the sounds couples make together, when alone in the dark. Job can't stand listening to them, and being reminded of his wife. His stomach is full, but his heart is empty.

The pink neon sign flashes POSHLUST and advertises sunbeds and massage. Job looks up doubtfully, but other men have told him, with smiles, that this is the place to go. It is not at all like the way it had been in Zimbabwe, where women sat outside their huts all along the road, calling softly and enticingly at passing men on their way to work, then lay down with them on a single bed. They were not bad women, and they did it to feed their families. Many men used them in a willing exchange, whose only real risk was that they might catch the sickness. But they did not cost too much. These ones, the men at the carwash told him, are expensive because they are young, and white.

'But they are good, my brother,' Michael says, with a reminiscent smile. 'You know?'

Job steps on the doormat, and a bell jangles. Nothing happens for a moment, and Job wonders whether he's come to the right place. When a police car rocks past, siren shrieking, he shrinks back into his jacket like a snail into its shell. He becomes aware that he's being looked at through a video entryphone and he grins, hopefully. With a vicious buzz, the door clicks open. Inside, a flight of stairs leads up to the first floor. He goes up, wondering how many other men have done this before him. On each tread, the brown carpet is worn down to its backing.

Job pushes the door at the top of the stairs, and another bell clatters. Inside, there is a desk, and a round-faced blonde woman, heavily made-up, painting her nails. She looks at him, unsmiling. He can hear the thump of pop music coming through the white wall behind her.

'Fifty for full body massage, thirty for a rub,' says the blonde. She looks as bored as Jayne at the AA Carwash.

Job has it. He takes out his wallet and counts out five ten-pound notes.

'I would like the full.'

'The girls are waiting for you,' the woman says. She hands him a small packet, with a silhouette of a naked couple kissing.

'You will need to wear this.'

Job takes the packet of condoms, and at that moment he forgets everything. Blood surges through his body, harder and hotter and stronger than before. He is like a dog following its nose, blindly, panting with eagerness.

The blonde jerks her head, indicating the door behind her.

'Enjoy.'

It is like going into a shop, but a shop selling girls. There is very little furniture, just a black PVC sofa, and a muted flat-screen TV set playing a pornographic film overhead. The temperature is warm, so much so that Job begins to sweat, and the rich grassy smell of his own body excites him still more. He relaxes. He has paid his money. He will have a good time.

'I am looking for a woman.'

121

There are four girls, and one man, whom Job barely looks at. Would it be that one? She looks tall and strong. Or maybe the plumper one, with the breasts and hips.

'Anna, you take him,' says the man.

A girl stands up. She is very young and pretty, dressed in a thin, short white nylon dress, like a nurse's. It has a long zip down the front, low enough for him to see the faint swell of her breasts. Job has a vague impression of her face, because his body is clamouring to thrust into hers; but then she sniffs. It is a very small sniff, almost inaudible beneath the noise of the TV set, but Job hears it, and sees the stain of tears on her cheeks.

Uncertain, he glances from her to the man, who has looked away. Job recognises him at once. It is the driver who held a knife to his throat at the car wash, the driver who called him 'monkey-man'. Appalled, he turns himself. What will he do if he recognises me? Job wonders. Will he cut me again?

'Come, please,' says the girl, abruptly. Her voice is hoarse, and he can tell that she is foreign. It had not occurred to him that, of course, he would not get an English girl. He wants nothing more than to get out of the room, and follows her.

Job walks upstairs on trembling legs, confused and alarmed. So this is what the man in the black Lexus does for a living! It doesn't surprise him at all. What is of more importance is that at any moment the Russian will cut him like a pig if he remembers Job's face. He is one of those white men who hate black people, maybe, or who hates everyone. The memory of the big knife that appeared in the man's hand is vivid. Job looks around for a way out, but there is none, just a corridor with a row of doors. When Anna opens one, he slips inside with a sense of finding temporary safety.

He sees a cubicle containing a bed with a fitted sheet and a sink. There is a view out the back window of some railway tracks at the bottom of a deep gully of brick.

The girl sits on the bed and takes off her dress. She wears a black lace bra and panties that are more like pieces of string than cloth. Her flesh is startlingly white. Job, embarrassed, looks out of the window, at the railway tracks where pale, tattered rags of plastic flutter in the chill air like small ghosts. The tracks make a pattern of intersecting triangles, and he thinks of all the lives that come together, briefly, in this place, before dividing again on parallel but separate journeys. Even as Job feels the strangeness of this, there is a tinkling sound, as if something fragile is being slowly shattered. The sound, rhythmic and insistent, rises in volume until, in a clatter of cogs and a rumble of wheels, a train passes by, long and dun, pouring itself out of the city in a great curve of motion.

Anna yanks down the blind. Job sighs.

'I give you massage now,' she says, tonelessly.

Job stares at her. Two thoughts collide in his head. One is that the last time he had seen a white girl with so few clothes on, it had been Beth Wisden. His best friend and playfellow had had just the same withdrawn, hopeless expression on her face as this girl Anna has now. The other is quite simply that he wants what he has paid for. His body is throbbing with a confluence of confusion, anger, curiosity, guilt, lust and sorrow.

He says, 'Have you hurt your hand?'

She looks at him, and then at her hand, puzzled. 'Is nothing.'

But he had seen the little finger hanging loose. 'No, it is broken,' he says. 'I know.'

'How do you know?'

Job takes off his shirt, turns his back, and shows her his naked torso, the scars like small dark stars on it, from the cigarette burns. 'This is how I know.'

Anna sits down on the bed. The atmosphere between them has changed. 'Please, I must do this work.'

Her head averted, she reaches out with her good hand, and slips it inside his trousers. Job's penis stiffens, but he says, quietly, 'No. You cannot do this, my sister.'

'I *have* to.'

123

'Why?'

'Sergei—'

She does not know how to say it, so he asks, 'You are a prisoner?'

Anna nods.

'Leave him.'

'I have no papers,' she whispers.

'But you can buy papers. You must make a lot of money from – from this?'

She almost laughs. 'He takes it all. Sergei, Dmitri and Lena, they take all the money.'

Job sits down on the bed beside her, shaken. Nothing is as he believed. He is, after all, one of the lucky ones. He can choose to walk out of here, he who had once been in prison; he can walk out of his jobs and find other ones; and he gives only the strength of his body, not its sweetness.

'I will not hurt you, I promise. Let me see your hand.'

Very slowly, she holds it out to him. The last of his lust vanishes.

'You need to see a doctor.'

'No.'

'A hospital does not ask questions.'

'You don't understand. He will not . . . I cannot leave this place.'

She is so young, Job thinks, and the thought of what he nearly did to her makes him sick. He thinks of Beth Wisden. She could even be the same age, this Anna.

'I can bandage it. If you allow me.'

There are no bandages, and nothing to make a splint. Job tears his T-shirt, which is thin but clean, into strips.

'Hurry, hurry,' Anna says.

Her ears, sharper than his, have caught the sound of footsteps.

'Ah,' she calls in a high-pitched voice, 'ah!'

'Yeah!' says Job, understanding. 'Oh, baby!'

He winds the strips of cloth tightly around her hand, binding two fingers together. The footsteps recede, just as the splint is done.

'My hand does not hurt. So much,' says Anna. She looks at Job doubtfully, and he can see layer upon layer of distrust sliding back over her features, hardening them.

'Anna, does anybody know you are here? Do you have family?'

Her face closes at once. 'You must go now.'

'I want to help you.'

'Tell Sergei you like me. That is the only way you can help.'

Job rises, then turns. 'Little sister, I will find a way to get you out. I will come back,' he says.

16

Ian Has An Accident

Clogged with about twenty pairs of shoes, two backpacks and a black bag of rubbish that hasn't been properly tied, the narrow hall of the house in Finsbury Park is an assault course. Ian is going to Candice's parents' for a brunch party, and is late. He really doesn't want this, but he's fed up with being dull at the weekends as well as during the week. The Verhovens are, besides, seriously wealthy people, and Candice has told him to pack his swimming trunks. He hasn't, but he needs to buy a present for his hostess. Even if it will no doubt be inadequate, and cost him more than he feels comfortable about spending, he can't arrive empty-handed. It's probably the thing that annoys him most about the Aussies who doss with them, that they take and never give back.

This is one way of finding out who I really am, he thinks: by making sure of what I'm not. It feels like progress, of sorts.

'Hello, Ian.'

Mehmet, the nice, round-faced owner of the corner shop, has crammed more food into his tiny store than Ian would have considered possible. He works seven days a week, from seven a.m. until midnight, and as well as stocking wonderful Turkish food he has what the Travellers consider to be the best line in organic stuff. Ian buys a box of Green & Black's chocolates, hoping these are posh enough for his hostess. He returns to shave and make himself look respectable. They won't like his having long hair, but tough.

From inside the living room comes the sound of snores; some friends of Mick's are dossing on the thin, foam-filled sofa bed. Ian, who has already found all the breakfast cereal gone and no milk in the fridge, heaves a sigh. Next door, the incessant piano practice has begun again; even Bach can irritate, Ian thinks. At least the young men who live on the other side of his house are very quiet. Ian looked into their front window once at dusk and saw all four of them prostrate on their knees; he wondered whether they were holding some form of exercise class before realising that they were Muslims, praying. Kim and Liza dislike them because, they say, the men 'radiate hostility', but then both are always alert for signs of antipathy towards them as a gay couple. The Slug is far more sympathetic to them than Ian expected, but for his own reasons.

'They're just a couple of sheilas who are into each other. If I were them, I would be too,' he said, with a dreamy look in his eye. 'Maybe I'm just a lezzie in the wrong body.'

Ian laughed. 'I don't think that's really your problem, Mick.'

The subject of his thoughts appears from the living room.

'Off again?' the Slug asks. He is wearing a necklace of beads, an old vest and a jockstrap. It's hard to believe he can pull anyone in this, but he is (as even Candice admits) seriously fit.

'I'm seeing Candy's parents for lunch.'

The Slug whistles.

'You lucky bastard.'

'It's just brunch, Mick.'

'Yeah, sure.'

'How many in there?' Ian asks, jerking his head at the living room.

'Only two. Gorgeous, and guess what? They're—'

'Just ask them not to use my razor, please? I'm covered in cuts because someone used it to shave their legs.'

127

'I think I must have been given a new kind of Viagra, my last drug test,' the Slug says, ignoring this. 'I keep wanting to shag—'

'Yes, well,' says Ian, hurriedly. 'Some other time.'

'I'm telling you, any time you want to earn two grand in a hurry, mate, you try this drugs gig. All you do is sit around in luxury for a couple of days watching movies.'

'Thanks. Maybe when supply teaching palls, I'll give it a whirl.'

Candice's parents live outside Highgate Village, in a modern, gated estate: squat, detached brick houses, surrounded by clots of clipped shrubs. Ian can see Porsches, BMWs, a silver Mercedes and Candice's customised Mini, parked on the gravelled drive. Annoyed, he chains his bicycle to one of the concrete neo-classical pillars of the porch, then yanks the bell-pull beside the door. It is answered by the Verhovens' maid.

'Hello.'

'Hello, sir.'

It's like being transported back home. The maid lets him into the wide, white marble-tiled hall. A vast vase of orange and violet flowers like cockatoos' heads towers above the tray of champagne on an antique sideboard. Ian can feel his palms sweating as he holds his box of chocolates in their paper bag. Beyond, the drawing room is a flotilla of white sofas. Almost everything in the Verhovens' house is white. Only their staff are black.

'Darling, you're late,' says Candice, kissing him. She wears a tiny dress which shows off her tan, and her thick blonde hair has been ironed as straight as a doll's. 'Mummy, come and say hello to my boyfriend.'

'Ian, my dear.'

Mrs Verhoven is an older and more manicured version of her own daughter, with beautiful legs. The house, the garden, the food reflect her domestic expertise. Ian has never seen her without heavy gold chains round her neck and wrists; Candice says jokingly that each time her father buys one for his mistress, her mother gets a piece of jewellery too. Ian gives her his box of chocolates, and although she thanks him smilingly he knows at once he's made a mistake. A woman like this probably never touches chocolate; she'd give it to the maid.

'What a handsome couple you make.'

'Leave him, Mummy, he's mine,' says Candice archly. She tucks her hand into his; it is small and soft and manicured, with a large pink diamond on one finger.

'I remember your mother at university.'

'You were contemporaries?'

Mrs Verhoven looks horrified.

'Do I look that old? She was a lecturer on one of my courses.'

Ian's mother and stepfather would have laughed at this kind of party, he knows. They had been anti-apartheid campaigners, and although apartheid had ended when Ian was ten he had never felt comfortable with the kind of people the Verhovens were. Of course, Candice pointed out that as a businessman her father did more good for the Rainbow Nation than any political protesters. Beside her, he is introduced to a sprinkling of politicians in the room, a couple of minor celebrities with South African connections he recognises from TV, and other members of her family. Everyone apart from Candice and himself is middle-aged, and glossy with prosperity. Perhaps this is the point of inviting me, Ian thinks. Perhaps she thinks I'll be impressed by it, or perhaps she herself wants something more.

'It must be hard for you,' he says softly to her as they help themselves to the buffet lunch, a lavish selection of roast meats and salads. The food is the best he's eaten for weeks, and the wine is a KWV vintage. It is really good, and for several minutes he loses himself in the simple animal pleasure of freshness and ripeness. Luxury is something that he misses: like Candice's flat, the house is so clean, well ordered and bright that he doesn't feel as if he's in England. Winter sun slices through the wide windows, glazing the food to the shiny luminescence of a Dutch still life and picking out the painstaking brushwork

129

of an enormous and violently pink hibiscus flower hung behind the table.

'What's hard?'

'Being with me. You should be off with a hedge fund manager, not a teacher,' says Ian, trying not to look at the painting. It looks more and more like a diagram of female genitalia.

'Oh, I went out with one, and he was always asleep by nine p.m.,' she says. 'No fun.'

'Mick sends his regards.'

Candice giggles. 'The Slug . . . hey, he's not my type. Look, there's Daddy coming over with Roger Trench. He's the most boring man in the world, and a complete sex maniac.'

Ian tactfully covers her retreat by walking towards his host. Both Verhoven and Trench have the look of men who prefer to spend their lives in suits, because even their casual clothes have a militaristic cut. Candice's father is holding forth in his clipped Afrikaans accent.

'What I despise is the attitude, the world is a lovely place and so is everyone in it. The British government is just unbelievably stupid, and the *Rambler* can't attack them often enough in my view. What do you say, young man? Candy's boyfriend is a teacher in some state school, he knows what I'm talking about.'

There are polite murmurs of horror.

'How brave of you,' says another woman. She looks as appalled as if she's just heard that Ian worked as a handler of dangerous animals. 'One hears such dretful things about British teenagers.'

'It isn't so bad,' says Ian. 'They're just kids, you know.'

'But the behaviour, the illiteracy, the violence!'

'Oh, sure,' says Ian. He's drunk too much, he realises. 'They aren't all like that, though. There are some really nice kids, too. They're no different from adults, really.'

'I can't stand all this political correctness,' says Verhoven. 'Not being able to call a blackboard a blackboard.'

'Actually, they're all whiteboards now,' says Ian.

There is a ripple of amusement, as though he's made a joke.

'Why can't you get a job in a private school instead?' asks Trench, as if there must be something wrong with Ian.

'Yes, I could. But there are just as many problem kids there, you know.'

Verhoven's blunt face looks sceptical. 'The problem as I see it is that too many people in this country want something for nothing.'

There is a general murmur of agreement. What is the collective noun for white South Africans, Ian thinks: a complaint? Even here, it seems, they aren't happy.

'London is really going downhill, I'm afraid,' says Trench. 'You know they've stopped over thirty terrorist attacks since 7/7? Sooner or later someone will get through and then, my friends, it'll be Armageddon.'

'Oh, but it isn't just the centre that's dangerous. We had a murder only a couple of weeks ago,' says Mrs Verhoven. 'Some poor woman was fished out of one of the Ponds on the Heath.'

'I know, I went right past when they were taking her body out,' says Ian.

'Did you? You never told me!' says Candice. 'Now, isn't that typical of a man!'

'I suppose I didn't want to freak you out.'

The women shiver, and Trench and Verhoven look irritated. The latter says heavily, 'Thank goodness we can keep away from that kind of trouble. I don't even like you living away from home, Candy.'

'Daddy, it's only West Hampstead, not Brixton, you know.'

Ian stays for two hours, increasingly uncomfortable. He really doesn't like this kind of party. The people bore him with their received opinions, recycled from the columns of right-wing newspapers. There are no books, not unless you count blocky thrillers of the kind probably picked up in airport lounges as an alternative to magazines; he feels the absence of culture, or of kindness, as if it were a kind of airlessness. In one room he enters there is a TV as big as a cinema screen, where a handful of bored blond children are watching *Big Brother*.

'Wouldn't you rather play outside?' he asks.

'We don't play,' says a girl.

'Aren't there any good DVDs?'

'Everything sucks,' says a boy.

Ian retires. They aren't his problem, he thinks, though they will be somebody else's. Of course, as soon as he's got his training certificate he won't have to worry about the kids he teaches, either. He'll be free as air; he can teach in Australia or New Zealand, or the Far East; it's his ticket out of bondage just so long as he can stick the Samuel Smiles for another two terms.

'I'm sorry,' Candice says. 'I've been neglecting you to talk to Daddy's friends.'

'I must go, I'm afraid,' he says.

'Oh, but you haven't swum in the pool yet,' exclaims Candice, with a pout.

Several of the Verhovens' guests have brought swimming costumes, the better to enjoy the heated turquoise pool steaming slightly in the conservatory. He sees Trench belly-dive and splash a couple of wincing teenaged girls.

'I don't want to.'

'We could always sneak upstairs to my bedroom,' Candice whispers.

'No, I must go, really,' says Ian, though his body responds with moronic enthusiasm. She coaxes him upstairs.

'You are so naughty,' he whispers.

'Not naughty enough,' she whispers back.

There is something kinky about doing it in her bedroom. It's still made up like a little girl's room, with a pink doll's-house and pink sprigged curtains, and a dressing table with a flounce. Ian looks at these as Candice straddles him, and wonders if she has really chosen to keep it like this. It's so weird if she has. Ian himself is a confused mess of impulses and personalities, so he can scarcely condemn her, but afterwards he feels ashamed. Perhaps this is what he likes about teaching teenagers: they make him sure he is an adult.

'You know . . .' Candice says pensively. 'It's my birthday next week.'

'It is?'

'Yes. I'm going to be thirty-three.'

He can't think why she's telling him this. 'You don't look it.'

'No, I hope not.' She smiles at him, her pearly-white dentist's teeth gleaming. 'But it does make me realise, well . . .'

'Well, what?'

'Don't you think about what it'd be like to start a family? I mean, by my age my mother had had three kids. You'd be a great dad, I think.'

'I don't know about that.' Ian doesn't want to remind her that he's only twenty-eight, and just passing through. 'I've never even met my real father, you know. He walked out on us when I was a baby. That's one of the reasons why I came to London.'

'Really?'

'Yes, he lives here. I'm supposed to get in touch, but I haven't got around to it.'

'OK.' Candice looks thoughtful. 'Maybe you should, you know—'

At that moment one of the blond boys he'd seen downstairs bursts into the bedroom, closely followed by the angry maid.

'I'm telling you, Mister Charles, you are not to do this—!'

The boy looks at them in disgust, sticks his tongue out at Candice clutching the duvet and leaves just before the pillow she throws hits him.

'Maybe not,' Ian says, laughing at her fury.

Ian pedals back through the Heath. Away from Candy's family, he feels bad about disliking them, about his disrespectful thoughts. She's not stupid, and she's right, he ought to contact his father instead of wimping out.

Ian pushes forward against a slight incline as the road rises. The sense of resistance is satisfying, because if he can't propel his students forward he can at least propel himself. Harder, harder. He treads down on the pedals, as if grinding his heels into the difficulties he faces, forcing his body to work harder.

Suddenly, sickeningly, there is a sense of something giving way. The sky turns upside down, he's flying with the iron taste of blood in his mouth, and then the world, like his wheels, is spinning and the road leaps up to smash his face.

17

A Bottomless Pit of Fear

Polly sits in bed, reading her emails. The spam keeps coming relent-lessly. A hundred people a day try to sell her Viagra, or gain access to her bank account. There are tales from orphaned sons and widowed wives, promising millions of dollars in return for her partnerships or assistance; there are tales of assassination, murder, injustice and coer-cion that almost make her admire the ingenuity of the writers. Do they really believe she is so stupid as to trust total strangers? Perhaps that is all Britain ever seems to them, a bottomless pit of fear, greed and stupidity. Each year, no matter how many firewalls she installs, the spam keeps coming from all over the world, bent on stealing her identity or her money. If they can't enter Britain in person, they'll do it through cyberspace, she thinks.

Meanwhile, the case of her Ugandan asylum seeker is reaching a climax. Dembe had fled to Britain in 2002, when government agents working for President Museveni broke into her family's home and beat up her father, a supporter of the Forum for Democratic Change. Dembe had never seen her parents or her three brothers again, and she herself had been taken away and repeatedly raped by soldiers. Kept under guard as a soldier's 'wife' for a year, she had been freed by friends of her father's, who had raised the three thousand dollars to smuggle her out of Uganda to Britain. She is HIV positive as a result of being raped, and only drugs have kept her from developing AIDS. Within six months of arriving in the UK, she had given birth; the child, too, is infected, and yet he is the only thing Polly's client has left to love. Despite all her suffering, Dembe has become the subject of a deportation order; last week, it was the agents of the British Secretary of State who broke down her door and took Dembe to Yarl's Wood. Dembe fought them so ferociously that she broke a policeman's nose, and received a black eye herself.

'I'll kill myself and my son before we go back,' she told Polly, when she finally got through to her. 'I will never go on that plane. They will torture my child in front of me, and we will both die.'

Polly has applied for a Judicial Review of the case, but fears it might not be lodged in time. She likes Dembe, whom she has met several times at the Hackney Women's Refuge, but even if she did not she would still do her best to save her and her son. It is the kind of case that makes her proud to be a lawyer, even if it's also what keeps her poor.

'I don't understand,' Dembe, distraught and incredulous, says. 'I thought that this country stood for justice, and that as a democracy it would understand my people's fight for freedom. I thought you were better than us, but you help these bad men.'

Polly can't utter what she knows is true. No matter how quickly they learn English, or how hard they work, people like Dembe are not wanted, because they are black. Their children are less likely to integrate and do well than, say, Poles, according to common perception; so most of Polly's clients are from Africa. The women she tries to help get no council housing or income support – though they are widely attacked for having both – and have fewer resources than men. Dembe is such a quiet, gentle woman; thoughtful, courageous and honest. She has supported herself as a seamstress, she goes to church, her son was born in Britain and is now in primary school. There is no question about whether or not her story is true, but she has been picked as a sacrifice to the tabloids. It's essential for the government to be seen to be doing something about immigrants.

Polly has been using all the networks she can think of to beg supporters to fax British Airways not to fly Dembe and her son out of the country. Sometimes all the protest and publicity achieve nothing, and it comes down to the individual consciences of the airline staff, who can be moved to refuse take-off. Does it always come down to that, the conscience of the individual? People have stopped believing this; it seems so old-fashioned, like those ludicrous, ponderous Victorian paintings about morality.

It's after midnight, and Polly's head is ringing with exhaustion. What she'd like is to read a couple of pages of her detective story, and comfort herself with a fairy tale in which criminals are actually brought to justice. There had been a time, perhaps seven years ago, when people like her had been ashamed of reading such tales, and the preferred form had been novels in which nothing much happened. But then it had become hideously clear that they were living a very different kind of story, in which far too much happened and nobody knew what to think about it. Everything is a mess, Polly thinks. She spends her lunch-hours talking on the phone to young women with minimal English, and her working life trying to organise her home. In desperation, she has even hired a cleaner from an agency to start tomorrow, at twice the price for half the hours. She has no choice if she wants to keep her job.

'We all know you have personal problems, but you should have had them sorted by now,' says the same senior partner who had told her off before.

Polly remembers the anorexic Romanian, the Croatian with a tight T-shirt emblazoned with UP FOR IT across her chest, the one with dirty nails and platform shoes, the Turkish girl in a head-scarf, the one with a tongue stud, the dwarf, the one with the moustache, the very fat one who just sat and smiled. It had been inconceivable that she would allow any of them to look after her children.

137

'Well, maybe,' she says. 'But seeing that my last au pair turned out to be a thief I'd rather find someone honest.'

Her anger towards Iryna for dumping her in this situation has grown. She keeps feeling that there is something she's forgotten, but she's too exhausted and cross to think what.

Ping! goes her email softly. Another au pair, she thinks, but it's Bill Shade. At least he can't see her in her glasses and flannelette night-gown; the webcam is switched off.

'*I miss you,*' writes Bill. '*How are you, Pollyanna?*'

'*I miss you too. Still no au pair. When are you going to come over?*'

'*When I finish the new script. Can't you take a break?*'

That's their eternal problem. Bill wants Polly to move to Los Angeles, she wants him to return to London, only he has a show about detectives working undercover that is being piloted. I could give up again, and have another baby, she thinks. She adores Bill, but she just can't allow herself to make the same mistake that she did in her marriage and become a surrendered wife.

There is a faint noise. It sounds like something falling on the floor. Probably Tania, tossing restlessly in bed, she thinks. As a teenager, her daughter finds it hard to go to sleep and harder to wake up. Polly pauses in her answer, and some animal instinct makes her keep totally still, listening.

'*Hello??*'

Polly is about to reply when another sound makes her sit bolt upright. The creak comes from the stair to the half-basement, the one that makes a noise when someone treads on it. She freezes. As the only adult in the house, she is conscious of being a degree more vulnerable than before, and sometimes this does play on her nerves.

'*Bill, I—*'

Her fingers continue their soft rattle on the keyboard. Surely she must have imagined it?

Her ears feel as if they're stretching out on elastic cords, while at the same time she tries to reassure herself that her old house is just creaking as the radiators cool. That faint, indefinable sound comes to her again, however: a discordant note among the soft, familiar plaints of her home.

She is being burgled.

Polly shoots out of bed.

'Get out! Get out!' she shrieks. 'You bastard, I can hear you, get out!'

A wave of fury carries her running down the stairs to the hall. The door leading into the basement is open, and she can feel the weight of the intruder on the squeaky step on the other side of the partition. Her sprint must have caught him by surprise, for she slams the door shut, and bolts it. On the other side of the wooden panel, the stair creaks more loudly.

'I've called the police,' she lies, panting. There is no answer. Her heart slows. Maybe I've just imagined it, she thinks. Then, for the first time in her life, Polly understands what it means when people say they feel their spine crawling with fear. All the tiny hairs on her back are standing erect, because on the other side of the door she can hear someone breathing.

'Go *away*,' she says. 'Just leave.'

Her legs feel weak and trembling, and she wonders whether she is going to faint. But then the knob begins to rattle, and the sound galvanises her into action again. Idiot! She can't get to a telephone, but she has something else six feet away, by the front door.

Running back along the hall on feet slippery with fright, Polly punches the panic button, thanking Theo in a moment of purest gratitude for insisting that she have this installed. His American paranoia about crime, far from being risible, was entirely reasonable given that she is a single mother with two children, living alone. Oh, God, if anything happens to Tania or Robbie – she can't bear it. What a fool she has been, not to have a proper burglar alarm! A bright red light on the panic button begins to flash, but there is no noise. She watches it, and it seems as if her heart is going on and off in time with its pulse. How long before the police get here? Three minutes? Five? Twenty? Without warning, the door to the basement

139

is rattled on its hinges, and there is a low grunting. It sounds like a monster from a dream.

Polly is astonished to notice that what she feels most is not fear, but anger. Her indignation that someone should dare to do this, to violate the sanctum of her nice North London house in this rude way is burning as brightly as a magnesium flare. She'll *kill* this man if she can. She looks round for a weapon.

There is a thud. One of the thin panels begins to splinter. Polly shrieks, as a man's black-gloved fist punches through the opening. It protrudes through the hole for a moment, then begins groping for the bolt. More splintering, and now an arm is through, an arm in a black leather sleeve.

Upstairs, the voice of her son wails, 'Mummy? Mummy, where are you?'

'Stay in your room!' she shouts.

But, of course, Robbie doesn't. He is a child of his time, disobedient and wilful, and he comes running down the stairs, twining his soft, slim child's arms around her nightdress like strangling ivy, staring at the black arm.

'Is it a bad man, Mummy?'

He has reverted to the nightmares he used to have. Polly pushes him away so violently that he reels into the kitchen next door. She seizes a heavy enamelled frying pan from the kitchen stove.

'Go *away*!'

Robbie looks at her, stunned at the rejection, and his mouth opens to howl. She thinks of Dembe, fighting four policemen. They are both small women, but if Dembe can break a policeman's nose then so can she.

'Hide in the kitchen, Robbie, and shut up. Understand?'

Polly grips the pan. Clever Polly and the Stupid Wolf, she thinks. This man is the Stupid Wolf, he's barged into her house just like one and now all those summers of developing a good backhand at tennis may have a practical use, although this enamelled frying pan (Le Creuset, a wedding present) is heavier than a racquet and he is coming now and there is no time to think so she raises the pan and slices it down just as the door crashes open.

Clang! Polly staggers a little from the force of her own blow. It connects with a jarring thud that feels like an electric shock up her arm. She drops the frying pan on the floor without meaning to, whimpering with pain. The intruder, his head partly protected by a balaclava, seems barely to notice, but she can see his face. She hopes he's going to fall down, but instead he says, 'Give it to me!'

He has a thick, accented voice. She can see his eyes glaring at her. He's white, and thick-set, unshaven.

'I'm not giving you anything, you fucking bastard.'

He hesitates, and she glares at him. She's almost laughing, the adrenalin is so strong, though it does cross her mind that she might be about to die. Then, before she can understand what has happened, he's gone, withdrawing into the shadows of the basement just before there's a screech of brakes and a flashing of blue lights.

'Police – open up!'

'Mummy, Mummy,' Robbie squeaks. 'Are you bleeding, Mummy?'

'Police! Mrs Noble, are you inside? Can you answer?'

There is a huge shadow on the other side of the half-glazed front door. Polly walks towards it, stiffly. Her right arm and shoulder are hurting like blazes.

'We're OK, hang on, I'm unlocking the door.'

How wonderful it is to have two enormous men in flak jackets to protect you, Polly thinks, comforting and sane and on her side, tracking the intruder down the street with an Alsatian dog! She has always seen the police as the enemy, but right now she could kiss them. Robbie, quite recovered, is chattering away, his imagination embroidering the events so that they tackled the man together with their light sabres. They are calm and professional.

'Did he hurt you, madam? Do you need an ambulance?'

No, she explains; it was she who had hurt him. It is his blood staining her Farrow & Ball paintwork, and her frying pan, which they ask her to 'give to the SOCOs as evidence'. (Scene of Crime

Officers, they explain, when she looks bewildered.) The officer in charge takes notes.

'You were brave to tackle him. We'd never advise it for the public, of course.'

'If his DNA is on record, we'll get him,' says the SOCO, bagging up her frying pan. They take her through her story again; it already seems remote and dreamlike. Something is puzzling them.

'We've been all round the house to check where he might have got in, Mrs Noble, and he seems to have gained entry without damaging any doors or windows,' says a policeman. There are two of them, one filling in forms, the other talking on the radio to the dog handler.

'I don't see how,' says Polly. 'I lock the front door and the basement automatically, after I come home from work, and nobody else – oh!'

A horrible thought strikes her.

'You've remembered something?'

'My au pair – Iryna,' says Polly, with reluctance. 'She left us recently, and never gave back the keys. I should have got the locks changed, but . . . I've been so busy . . .'

'I see.' The two policemen exchange glances. They ask her Iryna's surname, which Polly remembers, and her date of birth, which she doesn't.

'She's Russian,' she adds guiltily.

'We're not Immigration, Mrs Noble. We're only interested in a possible criminal offence. Does she have a boyfriend?'

'Yes, although I never met him.'

'Any idea what his name was?'

Robbie pipes, 'He's called Gheorghe.'

'And you haven't seen him hanging around?'

'No, though I've been a bit worried,' Polly says. 'She just disappeared, about three weeks ago.'

'Any quarrels? Any problems between you?'

'No.'

142

She's still reluctant to tell them about the lost engagement ring. It could all be a misunderstanding, and a coincidence. She can feel Robbie listening.

When Polly finally gets rid of everyone, she is too exhausted to sleep. Her laptop is still on, its screen-saver showing a peaceful picture of rolling green hills beneath a blue sky. She must send Bill an email, but right now she is more worried by other things. She can get her locks changed, and a burglar alarm installed, but there is a growing certainty in her mind that Iryna hasn't just left. Something is wrong, really wrong. The only thing is, she doesn't know what.

18

The Business of Surviving

Like a pantomime horse, the *Rambler* is divided into a front half (devoted to politics) and a back half (devoted to the arts). These maintain a sense of mutual loathing, yoked together by mutual dependency, so that the readers' letters page is, in every sense, a kind of hinge on which each past issue hangs. This is Katie's main source of entertainment during the weekly conference, where she is a barely noticed presence. The editor of the front half is Mark Crawley. Ambition pours off him; if handicapped by arrogance and malice, he is also admired as a columnist on a national newspaper. Believing that devoting any space to the arts is a waste of time, he vents his frustration on the Arts Editor, Justin Vest, who gets more mulish by the month. Crawley is insistent that the way to build circulation is to publish on-line, free.

'If it's free, none of our readers will read it.'

'They will if we have less airy-fairy tossers and more meat,' says Crawley.

'One is not limited to apes dragging their knuckles along the ground, if that's what you mean,' Vest drawls.

'My dear chap, our readership doesn't give a toss about another fringe-theatre company performing Cocteau on stilts.'

'Quentin, I fail to see why I should endure these *ad hominem* attacks, but you know as well as I do that what holds circulation back are those unutterably boring parliamentary sketches that poor Mark insists on. We need jokes, not lectures.'

'Some people don't *need* jokes, they *are* them.'

'You're both essential,' says Quentin smoothly. He looks at them both over his half-moon glasses, and gives his famously charming, almost shy smile. Katie thinks how handsome he would be, were it not for the petulance of his mouth. Cecilia is gazing at Quentin round-eyed. Poor girl! The whole office knows about their 'secret' affair, and sniggers over it in private, not least because Quentin will never leave his wife, Lottie, who is independently wealthy and the sister of some sort of lord.

They are all seated in a semicircle round the editor's desk, impatient to get conference over with. It is Friday, and the weekly lunch at the Giant Bread & Cheese next door beckons, with a handful of special guests and amusing contributors.

Quentin adds, 'The *Rambler* may be perceived as a political weekly, but its history is one of the most distinguished in literature. Remember who our founder was.'

Here, the assembled editors, nearly all of whom are men, raise their eyes piously to the portrait of Dr Johnson, solid and bewigged, over the mantelpiece.

'Doesn't look a happy bunny, does he?' Cecilia murmurs.

Katie stifles a smile. The fusty warren of offices, with their faded Turkey carpets, their portraits of Bagehot, Queen Victoria and Dr Johnson and the elephant's-foot umbrella stand; the perennial squabbles over space and politics; the eccentric opinions and shambolic operations – they all still charm her as an essence of Englishness. Lying on the sofa at her parents' house in Connecticut after her breakdown, the magazine had seemed as comforting as the voice of Mary Poppins, and as brisk.

She is not, however, part of the team. Though she can chat to Patrick (in a good mood) and Cecilia (in a bad one) it is dawning on her that she has now spent nine months in a foreign city without making a single friend. Her loneliness is undermined by the active social life enjoyed by the inhabitants of the ground-floor flat, who have a constant stream of visitors in the evening and weekends.

Vest insists, 'The magazine is not, and never has been, for any distinct political agenda.'

'If you're talking about Panga—'

Everyone groans. Panga is the *Rambler*'s longest-serving columnist, and nothing unites the disparate halves of the magazine so much as the mention of his name. A louche, boisterous Malaysian playboy whose time at a variety of top British public schools and striking good looks ensure him an entry to high-octane circles, he is detested by the more liberal readership for his views on women, homosexuals, global warming and the Iraq War. The rest adore him.

'I can't discuss Panga,' says Quentin, warily. 'Let me remind you that when this magazine was facing financial ruin following Max de Monde's untimely decease he was the one who found us our present proprietor.'

'I suppose it's marginally better than being owned by Panga himself—' says Justin.

'I did ask,' says Quentin. 'He told me that owning the *Rambler* would be even more expensive than keeping a string of polo ponies, and he preferred the latter as more obedient.'

Everyone looks glum.

'I've got a month of full-page ads booked,' says Simon, the Advertising Manager.

'From whom?'

'Stannah Stairlifts.'

There is a general groan.

'Why not De Beers, at least?' says Justin. There is no answer to this, for they all know that, like the rest of the print media, they are part of a dying culture.

'If we did podcasts—' says Crawley, resuming his attack.

'What have you got for your lead next week, Justin?' Quentin asks, tactfully.

'Mary Quinn on the decline of biography,' says Justin.

'Excellent. The decline of anything is always good,' says Quentin.

'Er, why's that?' the Toby ventures, pushing back the floppy blond hair that all British public schoolboys seem to have.

Justin says, as if to an idiot, 'It makes everyone else *feel better*.'

'Oh, right. Right. Yes, of course,' says the Toby, blushing scarlet.

With that, everyone but Katie and Cecilia troop off to the pub.

Cecilia makes a habit of sobbing with willowy abandon in the ladies' loo, with the hand dryer on to muffle the sound even though nobody is left in the office.

'I'd even marry Ivo *Sponge*,' Cecilia says.

'Isn't he married already?' Katie asks.

'Yes, to Ellen Von Berg, the cow, though she does lovely shoes. All I want,' says Cecilia, dolefully, 'is to find a nice man and have babies. Why is it so 'ard?'

'You might not find that marriage is all it's made out to be,' says Katie.

Cecilia gives a very Gallic shrug, as if to say, What would Katie know?

Katie thinks about this, tramping round Hampstead Heath at the weekend. She has come out the other side of what Cecilia wants, in a way. Her sense of herself as an independent, autonomous being is still fragile, but she is on the verge of finding something good about it. Her poverty means that she spends much of her Sundays in public places, to save on heating, but she also likes being free to do the kind of cultural activities that Winthrop never tolerated. He would go to such things only to see and be seen, and although she had told herself that she was enlightening him, the truth was that he had been darkening her own mind.

To be solitary is not the same as to be lonely, she thinks, wandering round Kenwood House. She loves one particular painting, a Vermeer of a young woman in a yellow fur-trimmed dress playing the guitar. There are other treasures there, but she keeps returning to the figure of the young woman who is smiling, whether at an onlooker or because she is simply content to be alone Katie can never decide. If you were to meet her in real life, she would probably be quite plain, but here she is beautiful, because she is happy.

Will I ever be happy again? Katie wonders. She feels that she was once made to be so, but may have lost her capacity for it. At times like these she is able to probe her feelings, as gently as if they lay beneath a painful scab that might become reinfected. She can't bear to remember the intimacies she once shared, the things she said to Winthrop and he to her. Winthrop is still present by his absence, so that even when most preoccupied Katie is conscious of him, and of her exact geographical position relative to New York. She needs her busy, silly new job and her solitary existence. She values the peace of her shabby little flat – though this is, of late, frequently broken by men buzzing on her intercom to speak to one of the new tenants on the ground floor. Lucky I'm out so much, she thinks. Even so, it's starting to get quite annoying.

The great old trees, livid with brilliant moss in the low sunlight, tick past. Katie doesn't remember what it looked like in summer, because she'd arrived in such a haze of misery, but the Heath is exquisite at any season. Families walk and talk in groups; couples pass, keeping pace together; dogs bound up to sniff and lick each other, and every now and again the sky is rent by the slash and screech of parakeets, exotic and graceful against the pearlescent wintry sky.

I never saw a wild thing feel sorry for itself, she thinks, remembering the poem. Well, birds just didn't have enough of a brain to feel self-conscious, she could hear her father, a high-school biology teacher, point out patiently. Maybe they just got on with the business of surviving. Everything about living was about surviving; even the *Rambler* was, in its genteel, ridiculous way, fighting for its life. If only its circulation would pick up! No wonder everyone was so grumpy and poorly paid.

Katie comes out onto Hampstead Lane, a wide road edged with large villas and many plane trees. The constant flicker of passing people and cars is stimulating yet exhausting. She needs to eat more, but how can you want food if you have no hope of anything good happening to you? It's like make-up and pretty clothes and all the other paraphernalia of femininity. What is the point? Being briefly pretty is what got her into all this trouble. Today she has eaten a bowl of bran flakes and skim milk, which should be OK. The exercise had warmed her, but she does feel tired. I should catch the bus back, she thinks.

Her cellphone rings. It's a number she doesn't recognise, perhaps re-routed from the office. Who on earth could want to speak to her on a Sunday?

'Hello?' says a clipped British voice. 'I am trying to get in touch with Quentin Bredin.'

'I'm his assistant.'

'This is the police. We've just dialled this as an emergency number on the mobile of a young man who has had an accident.'

'Oh my God. Who? Where?'

The police give her the address, and a brief description.

'I've no idea who he is, but I'll try to get hold of Quentin,' says Katie.

The address is just on the other side of the Heath, and she hails a passing taxi, at once excited and nervous. Quentin doesn't pick up his home line. Katie wonders whether the man is a relation, and is relieved that she has enough cash on her to pay for a cab.

The accident is already causing the traffic to slow down when she gets there. Katie jumps out of her cab and looks at the sprawl of limbs, horrified. A policewoman is kneeling beside the victim, her radio crackling. Katie introduces herself.

'Do you recognise this person?'

It's hard to tell. She can tell the man is young, but that's all. His face is dark with blood and grit.

'Can you give us his name?'

Katie shakes her head. The sight of blood, still spreading rapidly on the tarmac, makes her nauseous.

'I've left a message on my boss's landline, but he hasn't rung back.'

The tarmac is icy. Katie can see that the man can't be moved, but she wonders why nobody has thought to give him any covering. The policewoman is talking to the ambulance, and her colleague is directing the Sunday crawl of traffic. Impatiently, Katie takes off her own coat and puts it over him. The cold is painful, but she is overcome with a passionate wish to help. He's a big, strong man, but she pities him so much that she feels tears prick her eyes. It's never meant to be like this, she thinks. Why don't accidents ever happen to bad people? Why is it the good ones who get cancer, or their heads smashed in? It's such hard work being good, you'd think there would be some reward for it, only there doesn't seem to be. But in the face of pain, it doesn't matter, they just need help, she thinks. Maybe Winthrop had been in a bad place of his own, and hadn't meant to hurt her so much. Maybe she was truly just collateral damage.

The police are still trying to find out more.

'What's your name?' the policewoman asks, but the man is slipping in and out of consciousness. Katie takes his hand in her own thin one. It is large, and well shaped, but too cold.

'Stay awake,' she says. 'You need to stay awake.'

Why was that, though? Was it that, once entered, the pull of unconsciousness was so seductive that you wouldn't choose to return? She can well believe it.

The man murmurs, 'Ian.'

The policewoman asks, briskly, 'How old are you, Ian?'

He says, with an effort, 'Twenty-eight.'

'What do you do?'

'I'm – a teacher.'

He has an accent that isn't English, Katie notices. She isn't good at accents, but she does hear a lilt – maybe Scottish or Irish, it's quite soft. She can see the tiny dark hair follicles in his cheeks.

'The ambulance is coming,' says the policewoman. 'Ian, how old are you?'

'Twenty-eight.'

Her colleague has been inspecting the bicycle, and the pavement. There, in the middle of it, is a perfectly round hole.

'Bloody drain cover's been nicked. These people, they're stealing scrap metal everywhere – copper telephone wires, lead off church roofs, drain covers, you name it. China and India, they can't get enough legally so they pay people who nick ours in order to make us cheap fridges. Still –' straightening up '– he shouldn't have been riding on the pavements. Teach him a lesson, poor sod.'

Katie crouches down, irritated. 'Where are you from, Ian?' she asks.

'South Africa. Jo'burg.'

'Do you have any family here?'

He mutters something.

'Quentin? Quentin *Bredin*? Is that why his number was on your cellphone?'

'He's my father,' Ian says, and faints.

19

There Is Nothing Else For You Here

Job's visit has begun to change something in Anna. The river of ice that has kept her frozen is melting, releasing a dark cloud of filth just as it does in the rivers at home when the winter begins to end. Her thoughts are full of grief and blame and remorse, so that when Sergei burns her with his cigarettes she almost (but not quite) welcomes the pain as her punishment. Yet even in this darkness she remembers Job's quiet, gentle voice calling her his sister.

Anna had not loved her own sisters. In fact, she had resented them more and more as she grew up, especially as they were really her cousins. Katya, Olga and Raisa. They were all round her like a ball and chain, constantly underfoot, demanding and boring, and her resentment at not being allowed any freedom had made her feel she was going to burst. But now she remembers other things about them: how they had made her strong, because they in their weakness looked up to her. They loved me and I never knew it, she thinks, because I didn't know that I loved them. She had thought that she hated her mother; now she sees that she had never known her, that her mother had had no choice but to work as she did. But it is

152

Granny Vera, her wrinkled old face, framed by a headscarf, who is the one she remembers most clearly.

Vera had encouraged her to leave home.

'What is there for you here if you stay?' she had said. 'Nothing. You will find some clod of a boy and waste your life having his babies, and that will be your life just as it was mine and your mother's. There is nothing else for you here; the earth is poisoned, the road leads only to despair. You are a hard worker and a good cook, Anna; get out while you're young and strong.'

Get out, get out, Anna . . . When Anna wakes from troubled dreams, late in the morning, she can hear her granny's creaking voice in the brakes of cars passing down the high street below. Vera had survived the bitter winter of Stalin's death camps, the Ukrainian Holocaust that had murdered at least ten million people, three million of them children. She told Anna how, in a place where hunger was so terrible that people resorted to cannibalism, she had realised that the only important thing was the will to live.

The bad thing about Job's visit is that hope is painful, more painful than the broken finger which remains splinted to its partner, throbbing and aching at the slightest movement. Every time she sees her hand, bound in a splint, she thinks of him. His skin had been so smooth, apart from where it was scarred, as if it had no hairs on it. She would not have thought less of him if he had taken her, for it was what she expected all men to do. Maybe she would have liked it, just because he was kind. Not all the women pimped by Sergei are repulsed by sex. Lena, for instance, says she enjoys it – perhaps it is not so bad with only a few clients, or even just with Sergei. Those like Anna, who are often in such pain that they can hardly move, are in hell.

She could throw herself out of the window, or smash a light bulb and slash her wrists, and end it. Only she can't, because she remembers Vera.

'The Jews make such a fuss about their Holocaust that nobody remembers ours, but it was much bigger,' Vera would say between puffs of acrid tobacco smoke. '*Never* forget, Anna! I survived the camps, and I survived the winters, when my village was buried so deep in snow that all you could see was the gold cross on the top of the church. We had four months a year living underneath the snow, and when we came out we were so thin and hungry that we ate grass.'

Anna was frightened of her granny, but admired her deeply. Vera had seen babies tossed into trains by starving parents desperate for them to survive; people eating dogs, cats, birds and leaves off the trees while the grain they had grown was surrounded by barbed wire and exported to Russia. The breadbasket of Europe had been turned into a gigantic concentration camp, but Vera had lived. She would never say how. She was withered and terrible, with a beard and three teeth like Baba Yaga in the fairy tales, full of hatred for everything but the patch of land out of which she coaxed food, and her own descendants. Yet she had loved Anna, and Anna loved her.

'You are a clever girl, Anna. I can see that you've inherited some brains from me, and there's a spirit in there which isn't meant to stay idle. Go, and when you come back you will have made something for me to see.'

Anna knows that if she shows any sign of intelligence here, both the men and the girls will turn on her. As the youngest of the whores, she receives a sort of weary kindness from the older ones, especially Drita, who talks to her sometimes in her hoarse, coarse voice. Drita and Cristina are still working at the Camden place, but they come round every day to the other brothel to score drugs – Sergei and Dmitri have obviously decided that it's now safe to let Drita out too. She's clearly as addicted as Cristina is to heroin. When they come to the massage parlour, yawning and scratching themselves, desperate for the next fix, they are irritable and best avoided, but soon after it even Cristina smiles. The pimps have them streetwalking on slow nights, because of the drugs. So it goes round and round, Anna thinks: the girls addicted to drugs, the men addicted to sex.

'Do you ever think that, one day, this may be over?' she asks Drita in a low voice. 'That you could find a boyfriend who would know nothing about this?'

Drita gives a harsh laugh. 'Men are such fools, they believe anything. But how to forget myself — that's something other.'

Drita is pregnant – she has done what they all do for extra money, only more often, and now her belly is swelling into a hard round lump.

'She'll have to get rid of it,' says Lena. 'There's no point keeping her, not unless we sell the baby. Maybe we do that.'

Drita, to Anna's surprise, weeps when told this.

Lena says to Drita, angrily, 'You think you are the first to have this problem? Fine, keep it, go on the streets. You think you can stay alive on your own, with no Lena?'

'*Otebis, koshka*,' Drita says, with hatred.

Lena answers, in her glutinous English, 'Sure, I am piece of shit but so are you. You think you can be prostitute alone? You go back to Albania, or you see doctor.'

'OK,' Drita says. 'I see doctor.'

'Will you really do it?' Anna asks, in a whisper. The girls are sitting on the black PVC couch in the room behind the lobby. Overhead, the TV is switched on to the news. Business is non-existent in the morning, and the girls want to learn better English. Two middle-aged men announce the latest casualties in Iraq, the latest economic forecast, the latest consequence of global warming. It is always bad, the news. Anna looks to see whether there is anything about the Ukraine; even a glimpse of Russia makes her tearful. But there is nothing.

Drita says, 'I lie to her. I will leave, and go on the streets.'

Anna looks outside the window, at the iron train tracks, and shivers uncontrollably. How did she ever imagine she would find any other job but this in a city where she barely speaks the language? Maybe this life is the only one she can have; maybe it's the only one she deserves.

'Can you go back?'

'To Albania? No. There is nothing. Why else come here?'

Anna had once seen what happened in the chicken run when her grandmother drew a white line in the ground. Although there was no food, the chickens all ran to the line and began pecking at it, unable to stop. We are like those chickens, Anna thinks. We can't lift our heads from the line that men draw, even if it starves us. The line is their fear of Sergei and Dmitri, of being beaten up so badly that they'll be smashed for ever, or even killed. The excruciating pain of her finger's being snapped is enough to keep her with her head down.

There is, though, another reason, which is Lena's pills. They must take them if they don't want to get pregnant like Drita, and also to suppress their periods, she reminds them. 'Is bad for business,' Lena says, in a bright, cheerful voice, as if she were their teacher giving them a treat. She likes dressing in pink, and her dyed blonde hair is scraped back off her broad Slavic face with pink elastic and pompoms, which make her look grotesque. Drita had palmed hers from the first, which is why she is in the state she is now.

How can I get out before I become like them? Anna also palms the pills, hoarding them in a twist of paper. Somehow, they may be useful. She thinks about escaping, while the clients pant and groan and swear above her, grinding to a climax which she urges on with a tired show of enthusiasm. They have the same look in their eyes that she has seen in mating dogs, a glazed, absent gaze, turned inward. If I told them I'm fifteen, if I asked whether they had a daughter or a sister my age, would they stop, she wonders. No, they would not. Only Job has seen her as a person. Perhaps he was just covering up for impotence; or perhaps she dreamt him. She almost began to believe this, but for the scrap of bandage round her finger.

Drita winces.

'Does your baby hurt you?' Anna asks.

'Sometimes.'

'What does it feel like?'

'Like I am the sea.'

Drita strokes her belly, and Anna sees how the flesh ripples and rolls from underneath, like something rising out of water. Amazed, Anna thinks, There is a real person in there.

Drita smiles, grimly.

'Already, he kicks me. But he is mine. I will not kill him, or give him to them. You know what they do to babies, people like Sergei, when they sell them?'

'No. I no want to know. So you leave?'

'I try.'

The idea of escape is increasingly at the back of Anna's mind but, short of becoming an addict herself, she can't see how it is possible. To get out onto the street she would have to get past Lena, Sergei or Dmitri, for one of them is always on guard, and all are bigger and stronger than she is.

'Who was here before me?' she asks Drita. It has occurred to her that, with five cubicles in this brothel, and only four other girls, plus two in the Agar Grove flat, she must have come to replace someone. What happened to her?'

'Galina. She lives with an important client.'

'Sergei?'

'No!' Drita laughs scornfully. 'Sergei and Dmitri, they are his dogs. Sometimes he has parties in his big house. Maybe you go there. Maybe you will be lucky too.'

Anna aches to be free, to use her body rather than be used. Outside, tangled trees growing on the sides of the railway embankment to the back of the brothel glint with brown buds; birds sing more loudly; a faint scum of green grows among the rubbish. Even if it never snows, and the skies are unendingly grey, spring is approaching months earlier than it does in the Ukraine. At home, there will still be ice and snow . . . How she yearns for it!

Pigeons tumble through the air, struggling on the whistling winds, whipped by swirls and lashes of rain. It seems impossible that anything so frail can keep going against all that force and fury, and yet they do. Like all prisoners, she envies birds. Oh, she thinks, if I could throw myself out and fly away! But even if I did escape, where would I go? I have no passport, no papers, and hardly any money. I would have nowhere to go.

In her rough way, Lena takes care of them. She makes sure, for instance, that clients buy condoms although these are not always used; there are small washbasins in each cubicle so that clients and girls can wash, and a couple of showers. Perhaps it had once been a legitimate massage parlour, because there is even a sunbed, which the Russians like to use. Lena loves the artificial rays; her chunky orange body, naked apart from a black G-string and an eye-mask, lying under the intense blue light, is a familiar sight to them all. She lies there during the hour that Drita scrounges what little she can in preparation for going on the streets. Drita is already shaking from her desperation for heroin. She looks ill, her skin drawn tight over her thin face.

'I wish I had some to give you,' Anna says softly.

Drita wipes her face with her hands, her make-up smeared.

'I'll be OK. I feel bad, but I can do this.'

'At least you can get out,' Anna says softly. 'I miss my family so much . . .'

'If you give me money, I will post a letter to them.'

'What will I say? That I have become a whore?'

'Don't be stupid,' says Drita, with a flash of spirit.

Anna doesn't believe Drita will spend the money on anything other than her next fix, but into her mind comes the memory of her mother's anxious face, and Vera's. She has to hope that Drita will at least buy one small stamp.

'Wait.'

She finds a piece of paper and an old envelope, then writes her mother's address on it.

'You promise me, on your baby, you will send my letter?'

'I promise,' Drita says, taking the ten-pound note that Anna hands her and putting it in her bra.

Carefully, quickly, Anna begins to compose the lies.

Dear Mother,

    I am well, and I have a job. England is a wonderful country . . .

20

Who Would Leave Himself Defenceless?

Jean-Paul has been deported to Cameroon. At the AA Carwash, the mood is a mixture of fearfulness and relief: if somebody else has been caught, maybe it won't be their own turn just yet. It reminds them, however, just how frail their position is. The AA Carwash has created jobs out of nothing, just as the degraded landscape all around them somehow manages to breed wild flowers, Job thinks.

'We should get sick,' says Michael, during the morning shift. 'They let you stay if you are HIV positive.'

'I have heard of people who inject themselves with blood, to catch the disease,' says Simon.

'But that will kill you,' says Job.

The wire fence around the car wash vibrates gently, in tune with the road, in tune with the trains arriving from Europe on the brick railway arches overhead.

'My brother, I am a dead man if I am made to go back, so what is the difference?' says Simon. 'We are all dead men. We cannot help our families, the people we love, we are nameless and powerless.'

He had come over on the 'scenic route', as it is called, smuggled in through the Canary Islands after crossing the deserts of Senegal and the sea between North Africa and the tiny pinpricks still owned by Spain that are the destination of thousands of Africans trying to enter Europe.

'There were so many people, all in a boat,' he told Job. 'For a day and two nights we went on like this. No food, no toilet, no water. People became so desperate they drank from the sea, even though it made them crazy. We were almost dead when we arrived. It took me another year to get to England and claim asylum. I cannot live in Senegal, but they think I have made this journey just so I can live on thirty-five pounds' worth of Asda vouchers a week.'

Job is still grateful to this country, and grateful, too, that he understands more of its ways than the others, but he agrees that its treatment of people like himself and Simon is not what he had expected. He had saved his own life, at immense cost and sacrifice to his family and possibly to himself, and he can't do anything here but lie and cheat and survive by pretending not to exist. (When Job, scouring second-hand bookshops, came across a novel called *Invisible Man* by a black American he looked at it with fascination until he realised that what Americans called invisible and what Africans did were two different things entirely.) Every night, after he has knelt to pray for Munisha and Miriam, he asks God to continue to keep him hidden.

There is his fake driver's licence, which does not (yet) require a photograph or fingerprints, and this is why he can be a driver. If only I could earn enough money to pay for a false passport, he thinks. It always came down to money. Money is freedom, money is independence, money is health, and none of them will ever have enough of it. He is not a beggar, he reminds himself. He has a room, with water clean enough to drink, and he has food. He has his health and strength and life, which the Zanu-PF had done its best to rob him of.

'To kill yourself is a sin,' says Michael. 'God has made us to live in this world.'

'If God made Africa,' says Job, 'He has left it, just as we have.'

The other men suck their teeth at this, and shake their heads. Job

160

had always imagined God looking rather like Mr Wisden – big white men with beards, who spoke fluent Shona as well as English, who were stern but just. But neither God nor Mr Wisden had been able to stop Mrs Wisden being stripped naked and made to sing Zanu-PF songs after a machete had been held to her throat. Nor had God stopped other things, which Job can only blame himself for. He shoves the nozzle of his vacuum cleaner viciously under the front seats. Sometimes he is overwhelmed by the pointlessness of what he does, sucking up dust from one place to move it to another. It will always come back, this London dust, and it coats everything no matter how hard you try. The constant destruction and erection of buildings, the exhaust from vehicles, the millions of people shedding skin, the food wrappers and the food, will always end up as grime. Even so, there is the miracle of British rain. The landscape is drained of colour, the buildings and slopes of raw earth flattened and devoid of perspectives, yet the constant drizzle of moisture will make this barren place fertile, with thick pale grass again soon.

The famine now gripping Job's country makes him despair. Even its wild animals are being exterminated. What has happened to his sister, and to Munisha? Has any of his money got through to them? Are they, like so many others, trying to escape to South Africa? That most perilous journey, which thousands attempt every day, crossing rivers infested with crocodiles, preyed on by bandits, is what he has to hope for. Job himself had a most luxurious escape by comparison with what his family face: slow starvation at home, or else the desperation of camps along the border, with the life of a slave if they get through. How can he possibly rescue them, thousands of miles away? He wrings the cloth out into his bucket as if it were Mugabe's neck.

There is a frantic tap on the window, and he starts. The driver, a middle-aged man in a suit, is pointing to a smudge of lather on the windscreen, his face clenched like a fist.

'Yes, boss!' says Job. 'Sorry, boss. This is the car of my dreams, sir.'

Job waits for the discomfort to become too much. Michael, Simon and John all polish and wipe with particular vigour.

161

The driver clears his throat. 'I had a cleaner for twenty years. She earned herself enough here to buy herself a house back in Portugal.'

'We, however, cannot go home,' Job points out.

Just as he had hoped, the man hands over a tip, a whole two-pound coin. The four men who had worked on the car exchange glances. Damien is off work today, so he can't pocket it. Jayne is squawking into her mobile, berating either the hospital or the police.

'What has happened to the boss?' Michael asks.

'He was attacked.'

Michael shakes his head. 'They ask for knives to be given up, but who will do that? Who would leave himself defenceless?'

Job wonders this when he arrives at the minicab office that afternoon. Tariq says his children carry knives, though it's hard to believe that the two boys who are sitting in the tiny waiting room, shivering miserably in their grey school anoraks, have any weapon. They look like a pair of half-frozen birds, their hair clotted in greasy feathers, their slim hands like claws.

'What's the matter?'

The younger one says miserably, 'We had to call Daddy again to pick us up from school.'

'May Allah smite them,' mutters the elder boy.

'Or Selim,' says the younger one. He looks about nine, though it's hard to tell. Job thinks of Robbie, of whom he has become fond, and his confident air that always makes him seem bigger than he is. These boys look the opposite. The muted sounds of Bangla pop come through the speakers.

'Has anyone told your father?' Job asks.

'Dad's mad wiv us – he lost a fare fetchin' us,' says the elder. 'Now he's gone, and we ain't had our tea.'

'Selim should be here. Our bruvver. But he ain't.'

Their lips are a blue-grey colour, and their eyes are shadowed.

'Wait a moment,' says Job.

He goes out into the street, and buys some milk and a packet of

162

chocolate digestives (one of the best English treats) from the Lebanese newsagent.

'Here, would you like these?' he says, breaking open the packet, and offering them. 'I'm having one myself.'

He puts the kettle on, and makes tea for them all.

'What about me?' croaks Mo's voice from the radio booth. He sits there like a bullfrog, and it's easy to forget he is there as something other than a voice on the radio until he speaks.

'Sure, boss,' says Job, though in his heart he is annoyed. The biscuits have cost him ninety-nine pence, and Mo, being perpetually greedy, helps himself to three. 'I'm sure your father or your brother will be here soon,' Job says to the boys.

They both nod, then quietly take off their rucksacks to do their homework. He reads their names on their exercise books – Amir and Chandra. What good boys, he thinks. Maybe if I had had a son, he would be like this.

'Where are you at school?'

'Samuel Smiles,' says Chandra; adding, after a pause, 'It's a shit-heap.'

Job is called out for a fare, but it is only to the centre of town and back. He drives quickly, using back routes that he knows are better than those plotted by the SatNav systems that the other drivers have. Many of them speak such poor English that they get passengers to punch in the address, and are lost without the postcode. Yet they survive, thanks to the custom of helping each other. African families help each other, too, he thinks; the same ties of kinship helped me buy the ticket out of Harare, but when we get here it all goes. We do not help each other, as Muslims do. That is the difference. He has not been back to help Anna. Guilt about this nags him.

What can he do? He can't just go and demand that the man, Sergei, should set her free. Job remembers the knife, the terrifying ferocity of Sergei's anger. He's met enough psychos and thugs in his time to recognise the kind. If he gets into any kind of trouble, he'll be found out and deported. Maybe I can just telephone the police from a phone box, he thinks. Leave an anonymous complaint. Maybe that will be enough. He delivers his passengers – a woman and two children – to Paddington Station, where the black cabs try to cut him up, as usual. Then he returns to the minicab office.

The boys are still there. The younger one is looking at a comic, but Amir is looking miserable.

'You have a problem?'

'I suck at English.'

Job looks down. 'Underline each NOUN, VERB and ADJEC-TIVE in a different colour,' says the sheet. *The black cat sat on the red mat.* He can't think of a more boring task. Job sees Amir stare at the words and bite his lip.

'Did your teacher explain what they mean?' he asks.

'Yes, but I have forgotten,' says Amir.

'Can I be of assistance?'

'I dunnow,' Amir says, mistrustfully.

Chandra says, 'My brother does not like reading and writing, only numbers.'

Amir kicks him.

'Some people are like that. Good at numbers, not so good at words. I have the opposite problem. I could not do the sums you have just done.'

Amir smiles, a sudden, dazzling flash of white which transforms his sullen face. 'One day, I hope to be an accountant.'

'That is a good job,' says Job, approvingly. 'But even if you are very good with numbers, you will still need this kind of knowledge. Maybe if you look at something more interesting it will become clear.'

Tariq enters the tiny, cramped waiting room to find Job reading them a story from *The Camden New Journal*, which is far better than any of their textbooks. The boys are fascinated by the stories, and Amir says that he didn't realise he lived in such an interesting place.

'All human life is here. One day, when you are older, you might like to try reading the works of Mr Charles Dickens,' Job says.

'What did he write?'

'Have you heard of *Oliver Twist*?'

They shake their heads.

'He's an orphan who gets adopted by a gang of criminals, and taught how to be a thief by another boy called the Artful Dodger,' Job says. 'Only he gets kidnapped, and—'

'Yeah, we know that one,' the boys say. 'Oliver's this kitten, and they're all dogs.'

'I liked it, even though dogs are *haram*.'

'I think the film may be different,' Job says tactfully. 'In the book, they are all people.'

'Books aren't as interesting as films, though,' Amir says.

'They're different. But when you get to be good at reading, you will find you can see it in your head just as if it were a film,' Job tells them. He reads stories aloud, stops whenever he gets to a word they can read, and makes them sound out the letters. Once he explains the difference between a noun, a verb and an adjective, they grasp it easily. 'You see, you can do it.'

'Wicked!' says Amir, as his father comes in. 'And that's an adjective, right?'

Job looks at Tariq, and Tariq looks back. They exchange shy, hesitant smiles.

'I'm sorry I was late,' Tariq says. 'There are police cars and ambulances all along Royal College Street.'

'Yeah,' says Mo's voice. 'I picked it up on the radio. A body in the canal.'

'We live in dangerous times.'

'Yeah,' says Mo. 'But good for business. People feel safe in mini-cabs.'

'He helped us with English,' Chandra says.

Tariq walks over to where Amir is hesitating over his homework, face screwed up in agony.

165

'They know how to do this!' Tariq is affronted. 'They are clever boys.'

Job shakes his head. 'Believe me, it is no fault of theirs,' he says. 'Your eldest son has been taught to recognise words, not sounds. It is not a good system. He would learn quickly if he were taught another way. But also, he needs to learn that reading is for pleasure.'

'What right do you have to say this, when you are not even British?' says Iqbal. He is the least friendly of all the drivers.

Job says mildly, 'In my home country, I was a teacher of English.'

'So why don't you teach here?'

Tariq turns on Iqbal, and says something sharp to him.

'He gave us chocolate biscuits, Daddy,' Chandra says.

'I hope I have not presumed too much,' says Job anxiously. He knows that there is so much that is forbidden to these men. 'They were cold and hungry—'

'Go and sit in the car,' says Tariq to his children, giving them the key. Obediently, they go out, casting apprehensive glances back at him.

Job waits. It's hard to know what Tariq thinks. He can feel the man studying him, and endures it patiently. Tariq has always been friendlier than the rest, more communicative and less mistrustful. Job never feels so alien as he does in this place, and yet the men are friendly to each other. Some are even related: they come from the same part of Pakistan, he gathers. All are second-generation, born to parents who fled not only poverty but some other kind of trouble.

'They are having problems at school,' Tariq says. 'There is a gang . . .'

'Can their teachers not help?'

Tariq laughs, shortly. 'They change all the time. Every term, new teacher. They get sick, or frightened. It is not a good school, but what can we do? Many children from many countries, and they bring the problems of those countries here. Some of the older boys are very bad, they take money from the young ones, or the quiet ones who wish to learn like my sons. So I try to take them and collect them in my car. If these other boys see there is a father, they will leave them alone. Or so I hope.'

'That is what a good father does.'

Job thinks of his own father, long dead. There had never been a time when he and his sister Miriam had been taken to school.

Tariq says abruptly, 'Do you have children?'

Job shakes his head. 'No. We were not blessed.'

'You are married?'

'My wife is still in my country, where there is great suffering. She stayed so I might leave.'

'May Allah protect her,' says Tariq.

Job nods, his eyes suddenly full of tears at the unexpected sympathy.

'Two-three, where are you, two-three?' says Mo's voice.

'I'm right here, boss.'

'Fare for you, two-three,' says Mo. 'Pick-up on Richmond Avenue for Victoria Station.'

'Mo,' says Tariq suddenly, his beard bristling, 'his name is Job.'

21

Accident and Emergency

The Accident and Emergency Room of the Royal Free Hospital, Hampstead is not at all the way it's supposed to be, Katie thinks. Though some are clasping their injuries – heads, arms, eyes – while others, like Ian, lie on trolleys, in curtained booths, nobody complains. After the drama of their arrival by ambulance, the melancholy inertia, dingy surroundings and smell of boiled cabbage amaze her equally. Nobody seems to be *doing* anything, even the nurses. Where are the doctors? Why isn't somebody looking after the patients? Why isn't it more like *ER*? Like all her countrymen, she thinks that having free, universal health care is extraordinary, an act of magnanimity almost beyond comprehension; the fact that everyone could be treated here without health insurance must surely be a relic of – what? Britain's innate moral superiority, perhaps. If so, Britain's innate bureaucratic sloth isn't doing much to help it.

Ian's lips are puffed up and split like a burst sausage, and he has either a broken nose or a black eye. Katie is really anxious for him. The bleeding is wadded by surgical cotton, and has been mostly caused by Ian's having bitten the inside of his cheek as he landed, but he needs an X-ray for his arm, and a CAT scan. He could be haemorrhaging right this minute! The reality of being responsible for a total stranger isn't one she seeks, and yet it's come to her. She wonders whether she might be sued for something she's forgotten about before she recalls that this country isn't quite as litigious as her own – yet.

His cuts have been painted with yellow iodine, which add to his hideous appearance. Curiously, she scrutinises him for familiar features and finds none. She knows her boss's face all too well, having studied it in apprehension many times, but this broken, shambolic cyclist looks nothing like the debonair editor of the *Rambler*. How could he be Quentin's son? She knows Quentin has two younger children, but they are both daughters. He has been married before, though. That must be it.

Minutes go by. Katie is starting to feel restive at having her Sunday hijacked, yet she can't walk out and leave him. She is also, admittedly, intensely curious to know more. There is still no response from Quentin; she has kept her cellphone on despite strict signs all around asking people to switch theirs off, and it has not buzzed in her pocket once.

Ian lies on the trolley, eyes closed, in a hospital gown. Katie, embarrassed to be plunged into an enforced acquaintance, find this a relief. A nurse has taken down again such details as Katie is able to give; she can only watch and wait, hardly even daring to get herself a beaker of water from the cooler. Soon, though, she becomes worried that nobody seems to be paying them any attention. She buys a Sunday newspaper, but it fails to distract her.

'This is unbelievable,' she mutters after an hour, when no doctor has come near them. 'There must be better hospitals than this in Africa.'

'Who are you?'

His eyes are brown, flecked with green, and now she can see a faint resemblance to Quentin after all.

'I'm Katie. I work for your father.'

'What happened? I've got a hell of a headache.'

'You came off your bike. The police found Quentin's number on your mobile, and his voicemail sent it through to me.'

Ian licks his dry, puffy lips. 'Could you get me something to drink?'

'Here.'

Emboldened by anxiety, Katie goes out and starts to nag at the nurses. She has a terrier-like persistence. On and on she goes, very sweetly, until she gets a nurse to come and put a drip in Ian's hand.

He mumbles, 'My arm hurts.'

'They need to X-ray it,' the nurse says cheerfully. 'Radiology is chock-a-block, I'm afraid. But you're logged into the system now – it won't take much longer.'

'You could have been killed,' says Katie. 'The police said the wheel sheared right off.'

He gives a grimace. 'Guess I won't be going into work tomorrow, then. Hell! It was a new bike.'

'I can ring your work, if you tell me the number.'

There is a pause as he tries to think of it. 'It's on my mobile. Is it here?'

'I don't know – the police have it, I guess. What's left of your clothes is in that bag.'

'I was wondering why I was wearing a nightgown.'

Ian tries to smile, and Katie looks at him warily. She hopes he isn't going to try to charm her, like his father.

'Tell me where you work.'

'I'm a teacher at the Samuel Smiles Secondary School.'

Katie raises her eyebrows. Not quite what she expected in a son of Quentin's.

'I'll leave a message for them.'

There is a pause. He says, 'So, you work with my father?'

'Yes.'

'Do you like that?'

'I guess so.'

'My mother—'

170

'Oh, should I call her?'

'No. She'll only worry and want to come over on the next plane.'

'Is she South African too?'

'Yes. She lives in Cape Town. Where are you from?'

'New York. But before that, the Midwest. My parents are teachers too.' Katie doesn't know why she added this, as it's not exactly information that would interest or impress any son of Quentin's.

An exhausted young doctor comes in with a nurse. 'I'm so, so sorry, we've been rushed off our feet—' he says apologetically.

'I was about to make a complaint,' says Katie.

'It is still under four hours, you know – we are within national guidelines for A&E. We'll soon have you sorted, um, Ian.'

He goes through Ian's symptoms again, and they push Ian's trolley to the X-ray room. The trolley squeals along the chipped linoleum. Katie is appalled at the run-down look of it all. Do they not even have hospital porters? It seems not.

A man she has only just met is revealed on a succession of photographic plates. Skull, ribcage, arms are pinned up on a light screen, one after another. Katie can see ghostly shapes, the bleached density of bone, the death's-head helmet of the skull. His heart, a glow of white, shines mistily behind winglike ribs.

The radiologist says, 'Nothing worse than a broken radius, though I'm ordering a CAT scan too. No cycling for a while, I'm afraid. You should stay overnight, in case there's concussion.'

Ian looks at Katie, questioningly. 'I'll need some things.'

'Sure,' says Katie, pushing up her glasses. 'Where do you live?'

'Finsbury Park. It's really good of you to do this for me.' He gives her the address. 'Oh, and something to read.'

'What?'

'You choose. I trust you. I teach English, if that helps.'

Katie, pleased, says, 'I'll try your father's number again.'

She goes outside.

'Yes?' says Quentin's voice impatiently.

'Quentin, it's Katie Parry from the office—'

In the background she can hear children's voices, and the clink and hum of late Sunday lunch, punctuated by laughter.

'What?'

'Your son – Ian – he's been in an accident,' she says. 'He's going to be OK, but—'

'My what? WHAT?'

'It's just a broken arm they think, but he's—'

'Who?' says Quentin.

'Ian,' says Katie patiently. 'He's South African. You do have a son, right?'

There is silence at the other end. Then Quentin says, 'You'd better come to my house.'

Ian is drifting off to sleep in the trolley, having had his arm set. Katie writes her name and mobile number on his cast and walks back along the dismal beige corridors.

She has to admit that she is curious about the way Quentin lives; how anybody conducts their lives here is still mysterious to her. Nobody has asked her to their home, perhaps because everyone seems to hate Americans. They might watch American movies, wear American clothes, even read American books but Bush and the Iraq War have made actual American people social lepers; she only has to open her mouth in some places to feel a wave of loathing directed at her. Katie is weary of pointing out that at least half her countrymen detest their President even more than Europe does, but it's no good. Those charming children's books which had lured her to this country are full of locked doors and barriers, and it does not escape her that such doors often demand that you change in some way in order to gain entry.

Quentin's home is in a street of other big houses, all built from primrose-coloured brick and white-painted stucco, with columns and porticos over the front door, and set back from the road as if wincing away in affront from the general public. Maida Vale is immaculate, but somehow dead; she can hear the susurration of a motorway flyover nearby. There are black and white chequered tiles on the path, and steps up to the wide front door, and in the early twilight she can see that the walls of the double drawing room not yet shielded by heavy drapes are painted a deep, bold crimson. She presses the round brass button of the bell, and waits. A dark-haired woman, slim as a dagger in a short skirt and a cashmere sweater, opens the door. This must be Lottie Evenlode, who (according to those who know her in the office) is far too good for her husband.

'Hi, I'm Katie – Quentin asked for me,' she says.

'Come in.'

Katie is led into a hall. There is a large antique portrait of a woman in a chartreuse ball gown above the stairs, and a scatter of children's shoes. The halogen spotlights bear no resemblance to the gas lamps of her imagination. Secretly disappointed, she concedes that Quentin must, after all, live in the twenty-first century.

'We haven't met before, have we?' Lottie says, in a glacial manner.

'No,' says Katie.

Quentin's wife scrutinises her, with veiled insolence. I didn't think you could be one of Q's mistresses,' she says, her mouth twisting. 'I always put them next to each other at dinners. They have so much in common, you see.'

Katie blushes. 'I'm not his type,' she says.

'Really? Q will make love to anything, you know,' says Lottie, and stalks out.

Katie feels sorry for her, but also intolerably weary. She wanders into the kitchen and warms her chilled hands on the radiator, then picks up a banana from a large fruit bowl, and eats it in a burst of defiance. It is sweet, and surprisingly good. When Quentin sweeps downstairs, Katie says, 'I hope you can reimburse me for the taxi because I have no money left.'

Quentin closes the door. 'Katie, I must ask for your discretion on this matter,' he says. 'The last time I saw Ian he was a baby.'

'But he *is* your son?'

Quentin paces up and down, haggard with self-pity. 'God, what a bore. I suppose I ought to visit. No, that's something I can delegate.'

'Um,' Katie says. 'It was *your number* the police called, Quentin.'

'No son of mine would prefer a visit from a middle-aged man if he could have a pretty young woman instead.'

'I'm not,' says Katie, at once.

'Not what?'

'Pretty.'

Quentin shrugs, indifferently. 'Whatever. Tell him we'll meet as soon as I can find the time.'

Which will be never, Katie thinks. How could he be so heartless? She has spent four hours with the poor man; if nothing else she will buy him a new toothbrush and clothes – it's the least she can do. She catches sight of herself in the hall mirror, and unconsciously touches her face, which is tinged with faint colour. Ian is just some guy, and nothing to do with her. But as she returns to the hospital, she feels a strange sensation, half-burning, half-thrilling; almost as if a powerful muscle that she has let atrophy is being forced to work again, long after it had been forgotten.

22

Everybody is Trying to Get This

'You won't mention the burglary, will you?' asks Polly's daughter, over breakfast. 'You know how, like, nervous her parents are about sleep-overs.'

'Darling, I'm sure they trust us by now.'

'It isn't about us. They're stressing over Rosie coming into the centre of London.'

Tania's friend Rosie is staying for a sleepover in the evening. Recently, Polly has found her home colonised in this way, so that every so often at weekends her daughter's room is transformed into a dormitory. Rosie is a lovely girl and, like almost all Tania's friends, Chinese. Every year there are more – children who are tidy and charming, and who carry off the annual school prizes with relentless success.

'I wish you two would behave more like them,' she says.

'Tania's friends are just like the aliens in *Galaxy Quest*,' remarks Robbie. 'You know – too polite to be human. Really they're squids.'

Polly laughs, guiltily. Half of her is delighted that these virtuous girls are friends with her daughter, because there is no doubt in her mind that they have encouraged her to work harder. The other half of her is in a ferment of anxiety. Rosie's family are like Jews: they believe in hard work, respect, self-reliance, tradition and the family, only much, much more so. At fourteen, Rosie and the other Chinese girls already have GCSEs in Mandarin and, according to Rosie, find European languages easy because they are all so similar. They invariably enter the school with Grade 8 on two musical instruments. Rosie's parents had escaped China, survived pirates and internment camps and set up a tiny takeaway. Twenty years later, they have made a fortune in the restaurant trade and live in a modern detached house, somewhere near Brent Cross. Tania has told her that they can't understand why Polly lives in an inner-city slum.

'That's it, Polly, all done and dusted,' says her handyman when she returns from the school run. 'I've changed your locks and here are the new keys.'

'Thanks, Terry,' Polly answers. She is still fearful, even with new keys and a burglar alarm, but tries not to dwell on it. 'It's all been such a shock. My au pair must have given her keys to the thief. I'd never have thought she'd be dishonest.'

'That's the trouble with these foreigners,' says Terry. He heaps sugar into his mug of tea, and drinks. 'I'm not being funny, but you don't know where they're coming from, do you?'

Polly fetches her purse, meekly. Everyone pays Terry cash. He can't compete with the Poles otherwise, as he likes to point out.

'I'm just glad I had the sense to buy my flat from the council when I did, so as I can leave,' he says, putting on his spectacles and licking his fingers to count the bills. 'I'm selling up. Soon as I've got the money I'm moving to Spain.'

There is no point suggesting to him that this might not be a good idea: after all, lawyers are not yet being undercut by migrant labour. Polly loads the washing machine, the price of which was no higher than the one she had bought when she was first married. It looks just the same, and bears a European trade mark, but it has been assembled on the other side of the world, just like the clothes that she is piling

176

into its drum. It can't go on, she thinks. Sooner or later, it's all going to collapse, the frenzied getting and spending. Oxford Street and the centre of town heaves with people shopping, like a bag about to split. Although there are rumours about collapsing credit, and a run on one bank, nobody takes it seriously.

'England's had it,' says Terry. 'Let the bloody foreigners take over – this isn't the place to live any more.'

'But I love England,' says Polly. 'It's all very well saying you want sun, but after a couple of weeks I find I long for rain and clouds.'

'The thing is, Polly, it's different for you,' says Terry. 'To live here, you've either got to be rich, or you've got to be on benefits.'

That evening Polly locks up carefully, yawning as she gets ready for bed. The slightest noise at night wakes her to a red haze of thundering blood and adrenalin, even with her spanking new burglar alarm system connected to the police station. Her initial triumph and excitement at having actually fought her burglar has worn off. She feels as vulnerable as if she had lost a layer of skin, and is more anxious than ever about her children's safety, though of course she has assured Rosie's parents that their daughter will be fine. Her burglar didn't seem normal, especially not as he appeared to have taken nothing from the basement. What had he meant, asking her to 'give it to me'? Had he meant money, or something else? She wonders whether Iryna had been involved with something bad – theft, perhaps, as she'd stolen her ring. Polly's faith in her own judgement about people has been rocked, and her home seems, literally, alarmed. Whenever she unlocks the door now, she is greeted by the high-pitched wail of her security system. If nothing else, she's been robbed of her peace.

'I really, really wish you were here,' she says to Bill later.

'I know. I wish could be.'

The distance that separates London from Los Angeles has never seemed greater. Polly longs for the deep, animal comfort of a protective male. Bill is short, balding, bearded, funny, the least obvious person who would turn into Action Man and yet he is *her* man, and even if he specialises in writing witty screenplays about neurotic, unsuccessful men who can't commit, she knows he'd protect her in a crisis. The real problem is that neither of them has made it, professionally. Bill has only had one hit – the series that got him out of the BBC and into Hollywood a decade ago. Although he's got work, a reputation and more money than he'd ever have earned in England, he feels a failure.

'This isn't getting any easier, is it?' she says to his image on the webcam. 'This living together apart business.'

'You won't come to me, Polly, and I can't come to you. In another time, we'd never even have met; or else you'd give up your career. That's just how it is.'

He's quoting, ironically, from the tagline of his TV show, *That's Just How It Is*, but she feels a lurch of dread.

'I can't,' she says. 'You know I can't. The children are in schools . . .'

'There are great private schools in America, actually.'

'Yes, my ex-husband always told me that too,' Polly retorts. 'They're settled in this system – I can't just uproot them after all they've been through with the divorce.'

'I want to work more in England, but this is where the work is,' says Bill.

'I know,' says Polly. 'Are you sure you really want this to continue?'

She makes herself say this, every so often, dreading rejection. How had her parents managed it? Sometimes, when she walks on Hampstead Heath with the children and sees swans flying, side by side above the dark waters of the ponds, she wonders whether she and Bill will ever achieve such communion, such purity. Their relationship has been going on now for five years, and she hasn't slept with anyone else (not that, in her late thirties, she has many offers) but he is in a business notorious for its fickleness and failed relationships.

'I hate Hollywood breasts,' he says. 'It's like lying on top of twin rocks. Besides, I'm only a scriptwriter, not a director.'

'You mean, I'm the best you can get?'

'I miss you, is what I mean,' Bill says. 'Nobody in America has skin like yours.'

Polly sees him on her webcam, smiling a little jerkily. 'That's all the sodding rain, you know.'

'Think about trying it,' he says. 'The kids are still young enough to switch.'

'Nothing is more conservative than a child,' Polly answers.

Meanwhile, she has to get on with life. The police come round to take a formal statement.

'You realise that, if we apprehend this gentleman, he may press charges against you for assault?'

'Yes. It's idiotic, isn't it?'

The detective rubs his eyes, tiredly. 'So you have no idea who he might be?'

'No.' Polly hesitates. 'My impression is that he was Eastern European.'

'And nothing was stolen?'

'Not that I can make out. Of course, there's very little of value in the basement.'

'Do you think you could make a visual identification?'

'I think so,' she says. 'I only saw him for a moment, though.'

'Right. If we can trace his DNA, or your nanny's, we'll call you up.'

'You sound as if you really want to catch him.'

The detective grins. 'Oh, we do. We hate thieves. If it were up to me I'd do what the Romans did and put people like your burglar in the Coliseum with a couple of hungry lions.'

'Just as well he'd have a lawyer like me, then,' Polly retorts. 'In case you got it wrong.'

At least Polly is able to work longer hours again. Recently, she has hired a cleaner, and this is going rather well because it turns out that Teresa can also cook the children's supper and do babysitting. Once again, Polly can put in the eleven-hour day that office life demands, even if it now costs her almost half her net income so that she can afford to work. Of course, Teresa is Brazilian, and so not legal either, though one day she might be. Eager to practise her English, her cleaner explained to Polly that she is trying to claim an ancestral passport, given that her grandparents were Portuguese and Italian.

'Everybody in Brazil is trying to get this,' she says. 'We try to find documents, but so many were destroyed in the war, is ver' difficul'.'

Polly thinks about this as the bus she's on lumbers up Camden Road. It's a long bus, of the 'bendy' design that not only frequently kills cyclists when turning, but has multiple points of entry and exit. Consequently, almost nobody bothers to pay. Polly has an uncomfortable vision of what the city might be like if all those who emigrated in the past hundred years to far-flung European colonies choose to return.

'If you stop the benefits, we all go back,' Teresa said. 'You think we don' know that if we have baby, we get a home and money?'

'But it's difficult to get, and the housing is very poor quality, you know.'

'If you have nothing, anything is better. Where I come from, people try, try again. They get sent home, they come back. In my country my mother and I, we work all day making clothes and we don' have enough to live.'

Such conversations make Polly feel depressed and guilty. Is she just a stooge? Are all her efforts pointless? Today she is going to the Medical Association in Highbury, to hear the statement of a Turkish woman who is claiming political asylum. It's unclear whether or not she's been raped back home, but even if she has been it won't help her. Polly closes her eyes, and thinks of the standard letter sent out in such cases:

You claim that you were ill-treated during detention, tortured and raped. The Secretary of State does not condone any violations of human rights which may have been committed by members of the

security forces . . . but to bring yourself within the scope of the UN
Convention, you would have to show that these incidents were not
simply the random acts of individuals, but were a sustained pattern
or campaign of persecution directed at you by the authorities.

Rape is the invisible crime committed against women, often in cultures where admitting to sex outside marriage brings the death sentence; Polly wonders how anyone can prove they were raped as a deliberate act of political persecution. Many of her clients don't even have identity papers or passports because, in the countries from which they fled, such documents are unobtainable. They know nothing about UK asylum laws; they simply want to live in a democracy, in peace . . . and yet Teresa's cynicism haunts her. If you have nothing, anything is better, even the conditions at Yarl's Wood and Harmondsworth . . . But it isn't Polly's job to make judgements, only to argue for clients.

'She's going to be late – there are problems with the trains,' says Julia, embracing Polly in the lobby of the Medical Foundation.

'If the trains were run by Poles, they would always be on time,' jokes Polly.

'There are problems with this one,' says Julia. 'There are no scars that the doctor can say are definitely the result of sustained beating. She won't talk about rape; she's Kurdish.' Julia has no children. She pours her passion into the damaged people who come to her, scavenging old clothes for them, making sure they eat properly, coaxing them to learn English and finally to talk. A psychiatrist, she once showed Polly a row of round puckered white discs on her arms, where cigarettes had been put out on her flesh in Chile.

'Well, the Turks are hoping to get into the EU, aren't they?' says Polly. 'They know they have to be more careful.'

She scrutinises her new client gravely when she arrives, breathless and apologetic. To look at, Nesrin is like a thousand other twenty-year-olds, fashionably dressed with a pretty scarf.

'I not speak good English,' Nesrin says apologetically. 'You have translator?'

181

There is a translator, a middle-aged bearded man whom Polly had noticed in the lobby, reading a novel by Orhan Pamuk. She likes coming here because it has that kind of person working for it, and is besides a building whose design induces a feeling of calm, backing onto a courtyard garden, adorned with soft grasses and sporting an ornamental pool. There are paintings – probably art therapy – by past and current clients on the walls, and heavy modern oak doors.

They sit down in Julia's small office, and Polly listens to Nesrin's statement.

Nesrin is, or was, a law student. Often, the people Polly defends are from the most privileged classes, because lawyers – like politicians, publishers and writers – are the ones who have the money and connections to get them out of their countries and into Britain. The middle class helping the middle class, she thinks; well, isn't that always the way it goes?

Polly suspects that Nesrin was involved in the PPK, the Kurdish resistance, but Nesrin denies it, as she does membership of the Communist Party – which, from the point of view of her application, is unfortunate. By her account, all she had done was take part in peaceful demonstrations in the capital. Her large eyes, rimmed with kohl, burn and brim.

'The police found me after I'd been on a demonstration for women's rights,' the translator says, in a swift monotonous voice. 'I was told to keep my head down in the van. They grabbed my hair, and pushed me down so my head hit the floor, and I knew we weren't going to court. I started screaming, kicking and hitting, and so did my boyfriend. I saw them hit him on the head with a gun, and then they must have hit me because I came around in a cell, very late at night.'

'Describe the conditions of your imprisonment.'

'There was no light in the cell, and no window, and only a bucket with water in it. This was when I knew things were going to get bad. Nothing prepares you for the terror. There was just a door with a grille, facing into a corridor, and no air apart from that. It was smaller than this room, and very hot. I am still afraid of being in a small space.'

Julia gets up, and quietly opens the door. She believes Nesrin's story, but Polly has to be more sceptical. Initially, she has to take them on trust. She thinks of Job. He, too, had been imprisoned for his politics, though he doesn't talk about it. Polly told him about the burglary, and had been touched by his indignation.

'I hope you weren't injured, madam,' he said, anxiously.

'No, I wasn't.'

'Was he foreign?'

'I don't know. It doesn't matter whether he was or wasn't.'

'Foreigners are always blamed. It's always easiest to say that evil comes from outside us,' Job said. 'But evil comes from within. I know this.'

Polly turns her thoughts back to Nesrin. The interpreter's voice is droning.

'I was dragged out by my arms, and taken to another cell, lined with white tiles, and there I was stripped naked and hosed with a high-pressure water jet. It hurt, it was like knives. I slipped and fell down, I couldn't see or hardly breathe and—'

Nesrin stops, and says something rapidly to the interpreter, who has been relaying her words in a monotone at odds with her impassioned speech. He says, 'She wishes to apologise for what she is about to say.'

'That's OK,' says Polly, wondering what this will be.

'I had my period. So there was blood all over the tiles, white and red everywhere. I had no spare underwear, and no sanitary protection. I felt as if I were no longer human.'

This is the detail that makes Polly believe her. Nesrin wouldn't invent such humiliation.

'Every day they would bring the hose, and then I would be taken out of the cell blindfolded and brought somewhere else for questioning. I was not allowed to sleep. I wanted to sleep so badly. I didn't know whether they would let me go, or kill me.'

The girl's story goes on. There are the same sordid, cruel things people always seemed to do: the dirty water, the bucket for a latrine, the beatings, the hunger strike. She had been released, but her boyfriend had spent many more weeks in prison, suspended by his arms and half-blinded. He had not been able to get out of the country, whereas Nesrin had been able to enter Britain on a student visa. Just like Iryna, Polly thinks.

'I know that there isn't a place here for everyone,' Nesrin says. 'I know you will check what I say, and perhaps disbelieve it.'

'I don't disbelieve you,' says Polly, gently. 'The trouble is, it may not be enough.'

23

Public and Private

High up on the seventh floor of the hospital, Ian is shocked at how painful and humiliating it is to be ill. He has a catheter in his penis, and a drip in his hand; his head aches and his lip has stitches in it. His face is so bruised and swollen that when he eventually hobbles to the toilet and looks in the mirror he doesn't recognise himself. It'll pass, of course; he's had a broken leg before, playing rugby, and now he has a broken arm. Still, as he lies in bed looking at the curtains that surround his bed, he feels depressed. Like every other curtain in the ward, they are covered in pastel drawings of well-known tourist landmarks from around the world: Big Ben, the Sydney Opera House, Sacré Coeur. It reminds Ian of all he has yet to see, but renders every capital equally bland and clichéd.

Being in a public ward is worse than he expected. He has heard stories from Kim and Liza, about how bad the NHS is compared to Australia, but he never imagined it would particularly affect him. There is no peace, and no privacy, and as he listens to conversations all around him he gathers that the speakers' ailments range from senile dementia to criminal assault. An old woman is left soiled in her stinking, soaking bedding, her buzzer removed because she kept using it to ask for help. A young white man is being prepped for emergency surgery after being slashed in the neck, and is giving his statement to two policemen.

'He just came at me,' he says. 'I never did nothing.'

'Our Damien would never hurt a fly,' says his sister to the constables.

'Have you ever seen your assailant before?' the police ask.

'It was just some drunk in the pub,' Damien says. 'Bloody glassed me.'

In the next cubicle, an Afro-Caribbean woman with kidney problems keeps saying the same sentence again and again. 'I've paid for this all my life,' she says loudly, in a heavy Jamaican accent. 'I've paid for this all my life.'

Opposite Ian an Asian family have gathered to feed a sick relation, as patiently as birds feed their young. As he grows hungrier, he realises why. It takes twelve hours for the system to register that you are there, and when food does arrive it is almost worse than no food at all. He looks at the children playing around their father's bed, the two girls in *salwar kameez*, telling the patient in a murmur of English and (he guesses) Gujurati what they are doing in school. The young son of the family, who looks about twelve, sits quietly reading *Animal Farm*.

Why can't I have pupils like that? Ian thinks. He knows the answer: because the kids at the Samuel Smiles don't have parents like these. They aren't bad kids, for the most part, but knowledge, literacy, enthusiasm, intellectual curiosity are lacking in their parents, and nothing about the society in which he now teaches encourages pupils to break free of their backgrounds. They grow up in bookless households. (Ian knows this because one of the first questions he'd asked them was how many books they had in the house, and the answer in every case was 'less than five'.) Everything is pitted against pupils at schools like his, including the way they are supposed to be taught, and yet they must learn or they will never be fully integrated into Britain. Ironically, the ones trying hardest are the children of asylum seekers – who are so routinely despised by other pupils that the term has become one of abuse – but who, through the concentration of desperation, tend to be the only ones who get five GCSEs or more. Is it because their parents, in the countries from which they came, tended to be professional people, or is it just that they are driven by a sense of urgency?

'If we could have a school entirely made up of refugees, we'd have the best results in the borough,' Sally the Kiwi maths teacher had remarked, and sometimes Ian had to agree. Without the Chinese, the Ethiopians, the Iranians and Poles scattered through the school, they'd be on Special Measures. He thinks of a boy he'd met briefly, one of the few to be taking A levels, who is about to be deported to a country he can't even remember or be certain he comes from. Madness! That boy, if allowed to remain, would go to university and make something of his life; he would in turn improve the lot of others simply by existing and succeeding. If only they could keep boys like that, and eject those like Cameron and Delano, they would have a chance. Only they can't, because that would be 'social exclusion'.

Ian wants to teach, he really does, but he isn't supposed to hand out anything but praise, so how are kids to learn what's right or wrong? Some boroughs even hand out treats to the especially badly behaved, claiming that those who have never been praised need it most. He's all for respecting other cultures, but he thinks there has to be more give and less take, especially in matters of religion. When he read a piece of prose aloud to a Year Eight class which had the words 'Jesus Christ' in it, half of them clapped their hands over their ears as if he'd blasphemed.

'You know, the Prophet accepted Jesus as a wise man,' he told them.

'Our imam says we should not listen to those words,' Falik said, to a general murmur of agreement.

'Is your faith really so weak that you can't even hear them?' Ian answered. He knew that even asking this could get him into trouble, and sure enough, a parent had complained – using his child as interpreter.

187

I could go back, he thinks; I don't have to battle on in this country, where white people never seem to have black friends and yet talk of multiculturalism, and where black people just don't seem to try. All his friends have got married and settled down. South Africa isn't doing so badly, whatever exiles say, and a lot of expats are coming back. What can he hope for here? Quentin hasn't even bothered to ring him, though his American secretary had got in touch. That, really, is the worst thing. Listening to the winter wind whining and rain rattling against the big dingy hospital windows makes a return to South Africa unbearably tempting. In Jo'burg he has a nice little house, with a gardener and a maid and a car in his garage all waiting for him. Somebody else is renting it in his absence, but he could return to the sun, and the good life, where even if people attack you and rob you they aren't in your classroom.

Outside, Ian can see the crest of Highgate Hill, where Dick Whittington heard the bells of London ringing. *Turn again, turn again Dick Whittington; turn again, thrice Lord Mayor of London.* The real-life Dick had been the son of a nobleman, and had suffered no exceptional poverty, but nevertheless the story had grown up, with its cat and its exotic voyage that, thanks to the cat's skill as a mouser, became the foundation of a great merchant fortune. Turn again . . . But where should he turn?

Nowhere in Ian's body is comfortable. The drip in his hand throbs. The sweat-soaked sheet on the plastic-coated bed beneath him is rumpled, and his neck hurts. Stale air brings a wash of institutional food smells. He can hear trolleys being wheeled up and down, whining on the worn cream linoleum. 'Thanks,' he says to the nurses who (eventually) bring his food or who change his bandages and, as a result, his water jug gets filled more often, and they plump up his pillow. Damien, sullen and porky, never says 'thank you', although his sister and mother and girlfriend have all brought him shiny foil balloons with 'Get Well' written on them. He recognises the type. His pupils never say 'please' or 'thank you' either, although it would make their lives easier, as well as pleasanter, if they did. It isn't as if

188

they lack examples. Ian and all the staff praise pupils continually for doing the smallest thing right ('Thank you for walking across the room' was one of the more absurd examples) – but it never seems to strike teenagers that what goes around, comes around.

Another woman patient comes by, and stops, seeing his curtains open. She has one of those nice reddish faces and greying hair that seem so common here. She is attached to a drip on a stand.

'Hello,' she says. Desperation has made her break the British taboo about speaking to strangers, Ian sees.

'Hi.'

'You've just got here, haven't you? Car crash?'

'Fell off my bike.'

'I've been here for six weeks, and it's hell, utter hell. That old woman never stops talking, she shouldn't be in here but there's nowhere else. If you have any money, get a private room,' says the woman in a vehement rush of words. She looks almost mad – perhaps she is mad, he thinks. 'I haven't seen the floors cleaned more than once a week, no wonder there's MRSA – you know, flesh-eating super-bugs crawling all over us.' She makes a sudden convulsive movement, as if brushing something invisible off.

'I'll bear it in mind,' says Ian, warily.

He does have health insurance; every South African traveller does, but it hasn't occurred to him to use it. Would it get him a private room? He feels half-embarrassed, half-defiant about asking for it. But this ward is intolerable.

'How are you feeling?'

It's Katie, smiling. He ought to be grateful to her, but she depresses him with her plain, solemn looks and drab clothes. How could she possibly be working for his father? Ian thinks, meanly. Maybe she gets a kick out of hanging round invalids.

'I was wondering if it's worth having a private room.'

'I'll take a wild guess and say yes. You want me to ask at the desk?'

Within minutes of asking, Ian is being wheeled into a lift and taken up to another floor, and another world. Here the linoleum is new and clean, the walls freshly painted, and there are vases of flowers by the nurse's desks. His spirits improve immediately. Maybe Candice is right about the difference between state and private schools, too. Katie unpacks some fruit from Marks & Spencer and, blushing slightly, a bunch of yellow freesias. Their fresh, peppery scent makes him suddenly aware of how much he longs for the outdoors.

'Thanks. That's really – you're very kind to keep coming.'

'You're OK to have food? They're not going to operate on anything?'

'Not as far as I know,' he says. 'I can't understand how my accident happened.'

'Missing drain cover,' she says. 'Apparently all removable iron is getting stolen and sent off to China and Africa.'

'I shouldn't have been riding on the pavement, I guess.'

Katie says priggishly, 'No, you shouldn't. But the police were furious about the theft. The English seem polite, but they're seething with anger, like Jane Austen.'

This is someone from my country, he thinks, surprised. 'I'm interested to see what you brought me to read.'

Suddenly, his mobile rings so loudly they both jump. Ian swears, and Katie fishes it out of the plastic bag that still contains his clothes. It's Candice.

Guiltily, because he can see the signs telling patients not to use mobiles, Ian explains. While he is dealing with her horrified quacks, Katie goes off. What an odd girl, he thinks, but she has left him a note with her number, saying she'll come by again if he needs anything. No way, Ian thinks; although now he's talked more to her, he has to admit that she isn't quite as dreary as he first thought. There's a TV set bolted to his wall, but when he turns it on it's full of boring stuff – *Big Brother*, golf, quiz shows. He investigates the books Katie has brought. There's a biography of Keats, a novel called *Small Island*, and *The No. 1 Ladies' Detective Agency*, which he's always meant to read, and immediately loves because he recognises it all. How odd, that it's taken a white man to write about a black woman so convincingly . . . Once again, Ian's mind drifts back to his play about Dick Whittington.

He can imagine the boy, walking along the road to London, because he hears that the streets are paved with gold. All the people he passes – tinker, tailor, soldier, sailor, rich man, poor man, beggar man, thief – tell him otherwise but still Dick believes. Paved with gold . . .

There's a tap at the door.

'How are you doing, sweetie?'

Candice has brought white lilies. He hates their sickly smell, which makes him feel as if he's in a funeral parlour, but he pretends to be grateful. Katie's frail yellow freesias make his cubicle seem brighter, and smell sweeter. I was mean about her just now, he thinks, and an unaccustomed feeling of regret crosses his mind.

'Oh, but it's so nice having you just up the road, darling,' Candice says, after commiserating over his accident. 'I don't get to see enough of you. It really would be best if you stayed with me when they discharge you, you know.'

'Candy, I really appreciate all you do for me,' he says slowly. 'But—'

'I nearly forgot,' she interrupts, playfully. 'I brought you a present.'

He has forgotten her birthday, Ian remembers, too late. She won't mention it. She's funny about her age, and keeps going on about how she's becoming an old maid.

'I'm so sorry, I meant to get you something, Candy, only . . .'

'Hey, how could you?' To his horror she brings out a small box.

'You'll have to unwrap it for me,' Ian says, with a forced smile. 'My arm . . .'

'You see,' Candice says, her pink polished nails getting busy on the box's wrapping, 'you can't possibly go home to that dirty house. How will you feed or wash yourself, sweetie?'

Although Ian lives with a doctor and a nurse, he is uncomfortably aware that what she says makes sense. The house is a tip, and he is unlikely to get much rest with people coming and going and Mick's beloved rock music blasting out of the speakers. A week in Candy's flat doesn't mean they're living together . . . She makes it so easy, so pleasant . . .

Maybe it should happen, Ian tells himself, watching the layers of airy tissue paper crackle and hiss. Maybe the only way he'll become a man is by acting the part and growing into it. Although it's been lovely not to have responsibility, he's always known that sooner or later, real life reaches out and touches you, no matter how many layers of protection you put between yourself and the world. His mother and stepfather don't just lock up and live behind gates, they have iron bars that come clanging down inside the house, and a gated estate with Alsatian dogs in order to keep them from the kind of violent robbery that is commonplace in South Africa. They were liberal people, who had protested against apartheid, but this was the price they paid for staying on.

And now, just as he's got used to washing his own clothes and buying his own food, and not being afraid to walk around the city, here is Candice offering to featherbed him once again. He looks at her pretty face and healthy glow; she's so like Charlize Theron that her dad has even bought her a Mini, because of *The Italian Job*. What man in his senses wouldn't want to move in with her?

'That's great, Candy,' Ian says. 'I'd like that.'

A box stamped with the words TIFFANY & CO. comes into sight. Inside is a pair of heavy silver cuff links, shaped like truncheons, or possibly dildos.

'I won't be able to wear those to work,' he says, trying not to laugh.

Candice leans forward, her eyes wide. 'You're not thinking of going back to that awful school, with a broken arm?'

'I can always beat them down with my cast,' he says. 'The kids aren't so bad. Besides, I've got a week off for half-term. I'll be fine.'

Candice gives him one of her looks, and he knows she's going to trot out something from *Oprah* or one of her self-help books (the only ones she ever seems to read) about the difference between men and women.

'You know, you should see your father. I mean, it's important to

192

you, right? You have unresolved issues, sweetie, and that's what he is. And now you've made contact, I bet you'll get along just fine, though I still don't understand why you rang him, rather than me.'

'I didn't. He's my next of kin in this country, so my mom insisted that his number was on my mobile.'

But what I got instead, Ian thinks angrily, was his secretary.

24

A North London Dinner Party

Job, unusually, keeps both hands on the wheel. Frost is coming on the February winds, the council are gritting the roads, and every now and again he can feel the Ford start to slide slightly out of control.

'Would you mind driving a tiny bit more slowly?'

'Of course, madam.'

He will not stop calling her madam, not that she's asked him to. Maybe it would hurt his feelings if she asked him to stop . . . or maybe she secretly quite likes it, because it does annoy her terribly to find herself called not even 'love' these days, but 'mate'.

Polly rarely goes out in the evening when Bill isn't around; but this is probably her last chance to see Hemani before the baby arrives, and she has to seize it because she hardly ever sees her friends. The cleaner, Teresa, is booked to do babysitting for the first time, much to her children's disgust.

'She's got such awful skin, Mum,' Tania complains. 'Why doesn't she at least get her teeth fixed?'

'Because she's poor,' says Polly, patiently. 'Looking good takes money, darling.'

'So how come she got here?' asks Robbie.

'Because she's enterprising,' says Polly. 'Haven't you seen how she goes around listening to language tapes all the time when she does our cleaning? I think it's amazing.'

'She only works for us because she's not pretty enough to work in a café,' says Tania.

Polly resists the impulse to snap. She hates the merciless centrifuge of London life that whirls out all but the luckiest, cleverest, prettiest and richest. Of course, it's also what makes the city so dynamic – and so dangerous. She hopes she isn't going to spend the whole evening worrying about leaving her children.

As a divorcee, she has returned, in some ways, to a simulacrum of the kind of life she might have had as a single woman had she not got married straight out of university. Hemani, too, had married young and divorced the father of her first child; Polly had been instrumental in getting her fixed up with her second husband, Daniel. She hopes Hemani hasn't asked along a spare man for her, which would only be humiliating.

'Are you busy tonight, Job?'

He grins at her, his white teeth flashing in the orange gloom of the street lights. 'A little.'

'Would you be able to pick me up at eleven?'

'Of course.'

'I have a feeling I might drink a bit more than usual.'

'I do that myself, when I feel lonely.'

'Do you?'

'Only a beer, and not when I drive.'

'No, of course not. The minicab company wouldn't like it, would they?'

'Oh, one or two of the young ones drink alcohol. Their fathers aren't supposed to know.'

'My children aren't supposed to know, either.' Polly smiles, guiltily. 'They're so censorious. They think I'm an old woman. Robbie says things like, "Back in the olden days when you were young, Mum, did people have carriages?"'

Job laughs. Again, their gazes meet in the mirror. I shouldn't be sitting in the back seat, Polly thinks. Yet if she were to sit in front, she wouldn't feel at ease. She talks to Job more than she does to Bill, or to Theo: an odd thought.

A straggle of small shops along the Caledonian Road selling pet food, mirrors, ironware and food flash past. It's always a bit of a shock, leaving her own quiet street and seeing what lies just a block away; the poverty and squalor, the ugly council buildings and run-down commerce. Polly is just old enough to remember how English shops had once closed for half of Saturday and half of Wednesday as well as all day on Sunday. She can remember her mother coming back triumphant from the corner-shop saying, 'Open at eight p.m.! We've just become like New York!'

It is unthinkable now, to live as her parents had done, going to work only from nine till five and enjoying the benefits of newly formed education and health services. What paradise it had seemed! Now, in order to pay their exorbitant mortgages, and ever more exorbitant fuel prices, British adults have to work long hours – the longest, it's said, in Europe. Unless they are very rich, women are expected to work as well as have children; without the little cafés, the cleaners, the au pairs, the builders, and the late-night shops – all dependent on migrant labour – the professional classes could not manage. But we too are being squeezed, Polly thinks. Even to get into a good prep school, Robbie had had to compete against the sons of oligarchs and ambassadors, and every year her children have to sit gruelling internal exams in order not to be chucked out to make way for more.

'Job, how did you get to school?' she asks.

'I walked. Over hill, over dale, thorough bush, thorough briar.'

'Was it far?'

'Only five miles.'

'Wasn't it dangerous?'

'Sometimes there were snakes.'

'Oh.' Polly closes her eyes, imagining a small boy in the bush. 'How horrible.'

'There are many snakes in Africa,' says Job, laughing. 'They are less dangerous than men.'

'I suppose so. I'd still hate to live with them.'

'They like to crawl into car engines if you stop, because of the heat, and then when the engine goes wrong and you open the bonnet to check—'

'Don't,' says Polly, from the back seat. 'Would you go back, if you had a different leader?'

'Of course. I love my country, and my people. But until something changes, I have to stay here, praying the police never stop me.'

'If they do, Job, I'll try to help you. You do know that, don't you?'

'Thank you,' he says gravely. 'I hope I will not need it, madam.'

They arrive in Muswell Hill, where Hemani and Daniel now live. Despite being further away from the centre, it is more solidly middle-class than Camden Town and Islington, its large, ugly red-brick houses having been colonised for over a decade by aspiring professionals at the breeding stage. There is scaffolding outside, and inside is the smell of fresh paint and plaster, but the place has still been transformed into somewhere bright and colourful.

'I can't believe this is the same house!' Polly says, kissing them both. 'You're looking wonderful, Hem. How much longer before you're due?'

'About three weeks,' says Hemani. 'I'm looking forward to seeing if I get a girl.'

Ellen and Ivo are there already. Polly is delighted; alongside Daniel and Hemani they are her favourite couple, for Ivo is always entertaining and full of good gossip, as is Ellen.

'How's work?' Ellen asks, and Polly sighs.

'Grim. I used to be proud of living in a country which helps refugees,' she says. 'But now people think I'm doing something bad.'

'Does it ever occur to you, honey, that they might have a point?'

'Ellen, you have a foreign nanny, don't you?'

'Sure,' says Ellen, oblivious. 'You know, Tamara's first words were in Mandarin?'

She shows her a picture. Polly, like Hemani, is a godmother (though neither of them believes in God) and coos dutifully over Ellen and Ivo's daughter.

'Beautiful,' Polly says.

'Ah, but you know why that's so,' says Hemani. 'The more you mix up different gene pools, and different nationalities, the more you get children in whom faulty genes are suppressed.'

'So *that's* why we're drawn to beautiful people; it's really our individual quest for genetic health,' says Ivo, accepting another large glass of red wine.

'Ultimately, all Darwinian selection,' Hemani says primly.

'You know, I often feel the big mistake the Nazis made was to focus on the wrong end of the genetic stick.'

'Ivo, darling, there might just have been one or two other serious flaws in their philosophy,' says Ellen.

'That's our problem, Polly.' Ivo is on form, she sees. 'We're too English.'

'Ivo, don't be an idiot,' says his wife.

'Anyway, Ivo, I'm more Jewish than English,' Polly retorts.

'Nobody is English any more, have you noticed?' Ivo says. 'We're all British.'

'Excuse me,' says Daniel. 'Whenever there's a World Cup match you can't move without seeing St George crosses hung from cars and council flats. The problem is that the English have become the underclass, covered with colonial guilt.'

'What, we should be singing the national anthem in front of the Union Jack in schools?'

'At least reimpose proper border controls and ID cards.'

'How can you say that, Hemani?' Polly asks.

'Because, obviously, too many new immigrants makes it bad for those of us who got here first,' says Hemani. 'There's a limit to how much a culture can absorb, and we're long past it.'

'Oh, I *hate* all this us and them!' Polly exclaims passionately. 'When we invaded places like Africa and India, we broke down a door, and now we don't like it that they can come over here, just as we went there. Well, tough. It's not just a question of morality. There is no us and them. There's just *people*. We're all migrants from somewhere.'

'I agree,' says a young woman with an American accent, who has been listening.

'It's Katie, isn't it? We shared a taxi recently,' said Ivo, beaming at her.

'Very unwise to share taxis with Ivo,' Hemani remarks. 'There's something called the Sponge Lunge which—'

'Which belongs to my bachelor past,' says Ivo.

'We've also met before, haven't we?' says Polly, hesitantly. She couldn't think where.

'Yes,' says Katie. 'Briefly. I used to go out with Theo and Daniel's half-brother, Win.'

'Oh, yes, of course.'

Polly is deeply embarrassed. Katie is almost unrecognisable as the person who had been Winthrop's longest-lasting girlfriend. Polly hadn't liked her then; she had seemed so triumphantly, glossily attractive, just when she herself had been exhausted by two children and a transatlantic flight. But now, almost four years later, Katie looks haggard and dowdy. Poor child, Polly thinks. She had heard the split had been unpleasant, but had never expected Katie to wash up in London.

Hemani bustles around the newly built kitchen-conservatory. It has potted palms, and spotted orchids; the house is a stylish fusion of East and West.

'The construction was a nightmare,' Daniel says with melancholy pride.

'We're having our own builder hell,' Ivo remarks. 'Every morning, I trip over a dozen muscular Poles on my way to shave.'

'What are you having done?'

'Underfloor heating,' says Ivo. 'Like the Ancient Romans, you know.'

'Poles are *terrific*. So honest, so hard-working,' Daniel says.

'Yes, everyone says that, but what about the long-term effect?' Ivo is definitely getting drunk. 'Have you seen the street signs in Polish, and the notices in bank windows? We're sleepwalking into making the poor old British working class completely unemployable.'

'Oh, I don't feel remotely sorry for them. When I've had English workmen, they never work hard enough, they have their radios blasting out pop songs, and they leave the toilet seat up. The Poles are all, well, people like us.'

Ivo laughs. 'Hemani, my darling, they probably *are* people like us. We're just creaming off all the most talented young people in Europe, without even having to train them, simply because we're not an economic basket case any more.'

'Yes, and one day our children will be their au pairs and builders, if we aren't careful.'

'Delicious curry, Hem,' Polly says tactfully. She notices Katie push the food around; it's probably too spicy for her bland New England palate. 'Try the nan bread,' she murmurs. Katie smiles at her, and her face is suddenly transformed. Why, she's lovely, Polly thinks; just far too thin and sad. Compassion and curiosity stir her to conversation, and to finding out where she works and lives. Katie is gentle and modest; perhaps she always has been, Polly thinks, or perhaps like all of us she's improved by setback.

'The thing about the Romans was that they didn't have racism as we know it,' Ivo is saying. 'They were perfectly happy to make Spaniards or North Africans emperor, because they'd been brought up as Romans. The only country that has that kind of confidence now is America.'

'It's moving closer to America that's got us into diabolical trouble,' says Daniel indignantly. 'Most of the world hates us.'

'I don't know anyone who voted for that dreadful man,' says Ellen. 'Thank God he's nearly gone.'

'You can't say that any other country is doing a lot better. Look at France.'

'Oh, France is hilarious, isn't it? You know, the only reason why we were pleased to be hosting the Olympics was because we beat them.

They're family, really. You always have your worst quarrels with family, because you're intimately acquainted with their faults. Not that they aren't perfectly ghastly, really.'

'Personally, I loathe everyone in London who doesn't live within two miles of the Heath.'

'That's just middle age speaking, Ivo.'

Polly looks around the table. These are people she is deeply fond of; and yet their conversation fills her with unease. Everyone they know, everyone they see, is just like them, living in houses like these, reading the same papers, seeing the same films and TV programmes and plays, buying from the same shops and sending their children to the same schools; and they think it will go on for ever, with ever-mounting property prices cushioning them. But it can't. She looks out at the frosty darkness, and shivers. They're so exposed, somehow, in this glass room.

'And you're working at the *Rambler*?' Hemani asks Katie. 'Why there?'

'I guess I was hoping to meet Mr Darcy,' Katie says lightly. 'In a wet shirt.'

'Sadly, you're more likely to meet Mr Toad,' Ellen tells her.

'Can you make generalisations about national character?' asks Daniel. 'Surely – that's too reductive.'

'Really? Then why is it that when you define heaven as a place where the lovers are Italian, the cooks French, the police English and the mechanics German, and hell the police German, the cooks English and the lovers – well, everyone gets it,' says Ivo.

'Stereotypes appeal to the stupidest parts of us.'

'Not necessarily. I always judge by first impressions,' Ivo says. 'They're inevitably the most accurate.'

'Ivo, you hated me when we first met.'

'No, I didn't; I wanted to sleep with you.'

'Same difference, in an Englishman.'

It is a pleasant evening. Polly's burglary has become a story, to be commiserated over and filed away as an amusing anecdote, as is required by a North London dinner party. She doesn't tell them that she's still sick with fear in her own home, or that she twice leaves the table in order to telephone Teresa to check on the children. Katie earns her place with tales about the *Rambler*. She seems surprised they are so familiar with Quentin's career and private life.

'Oh, he adds to the gaiety of the nation,' Ivo says. 'Serial shaggers always do.'

'Seriously?'

'Well, obviously,' Ivo tells her. 'How dull if people are just good at what they do. So, Lottie actually knows about his mistresses? Well, she's been very discreet, I must say.'

Job drives Polly home, waiting patiently while she spends fifteen minutes saying goodbye to her friends. She offers Katie a lift.

'I didn't realise you were living over here, let alone so close,' she says.

'Oh, everyone seems to live in the same kinds of places in London, I've noticed,' Katie says. 'Or at least, the ones I meet do.'

Polly laughs. She is an eccentric, touching young thing, Polly thinks, ignoring Katie's fervent attempts to split the bill. How oddly punctilious Americans are about small sums of money! It must be their Puritan heritage.

'I hope we meet again,' she says, kindly, pressing her card into Katie's hand.

'I hope so too.'

Job drives off, bearing Katie to Agar Grove. Polly knows it well: it's an awful road, all humps and dilapidated houses on the very edge of King's Cross. She hopes Katie has a nice social life, and isn't still pining for Winthrop. She's probably well out of that relationship, she thinks. A voice behind her takes her totally by surprise.

'Mrs Noble?'

Polly turns, heart clenching. A man is waiting in the shadow by her front steps.

He is tall and thin; not the man who attacked her. She is still frightened.

'Who are you?'

'My name is Gheorghe. I am a friend of Iryna's. I—'

Polly says in her coldest voice, 'Perhaps you'd better tell me where she is, then.'

He spreads his hands. 'That's the problem, Mrs Noble. I have absolutely no idea.'

25

Lies Are What Everyone Survives On

For the first time since she arrived, Anna is out of the massage parlour. Three of the other girls, and two in Agar Grove, have gone
down with 'flu so badly that they can't work. No client will come
near their hacking coughs and streaming red noses.

'You must be bloody mental!' one of them shouted at Lena indignantly, seeing the row of sneezing, shivering girls sitting like sparrows
on a wire in the lobby. 'I wouldn't go near one of them if you was to
pay me.'

The result is that Anna is being transferred to the other brothel,
which is losing money. Lena is not happy about the split premises,
which had become available only because the landlord had found
himself with a flat nobody wanted.

'Dmitri, he thought he could have his own place and make more
money there from Eurostar,' she says. 'But is too old. I tell Sergei, we
need better place for Poshlust, but he wants to make big business.
And now the boss is fed up.'

Anna had had only minutes to gather her small bag of belongings
and, more importantly, her cache of rolled-up banknotes from their
hiding-place under the carpet. As she transfers this, she thinks what

each one has cost her. How light money is, and how heavy the price. It occurs to her, briefly, that her own mother, who had toiled uncomplainingly in order to keep her family fed and housed, might have thought this too; Anna had never thanked her, or admired her, thinking only that it was her fault for having children, and then for taking on those of her dead sister. How cruel she'd been, how quick to judge and condemn . . . She has heard nothing from Drita. Maybe she's out there, picking up men in cars, or maybe she's dead of an overdose. The seething steel cauldron of the city will give no answers.

Anna, bundled down the stairs in Dmitri's grip, memorises all she sees as the black Lexus slides through the streets, careful to keep the expression on her face vacant. Long hours of staring out at the same dull row of red-brick shops at the front of the massage parlour – a kebab joint, an optician, a shop selling offcuts of fitted carpet – have starved her eyes. On the corner is a white sign with a name: Kilburn High Street. It is a point of reference in the vast, anonymous city that seems so unending. There are signs everywhere, pictures and lights and advertisements and words; every shop window is piled high with a vision of plenty. The car stops by a shop selling saris, and just for a moment Anna breathes out in wonder, for the colours are richer and more lustrous than any she has ever seen, silk scattered with dots of gold and silver. If a rainbow had come down to earth, it could not be more beautiful, she thinks. There is colour in this city after all, even in the drizzling rain.

Dmitri laughs, abruptly. 'This place is shit. Wait until you see Kensington, Chelsea, Mayfair.'

Anna has no idea what he means. Yet the pills she has been collecting are a comforting lump in her pocket. Somehow, she must find a way to use them. If she doesn't use her head, she'll end up like Drita, or worse. Has the Albanian girl crawled into a hole like an animal to give birth in some hidden place? Has one of the brothers killed her for not having an abortion? Anna hopes not, but is more concerned that Drita should have posted her letter to her mother.

No matter that it was all lies: lies are what everyone survives on in this place.

Vera had grown up on lies. 'In the West, fairy tales begin, *Once upon a time*. Here, they begin, *It will be soon*.'

She had nothing but contempt for Communism. Vera had met Stalin once. She had done so well in her examinations that, as a great honour, she had been invited to the Kremlin. There, she had encountered a man who was small and with ugly, reddish hair who looked nothing like his posters. When she returned, everyone asked her, *What did Stalin look like?* And she answered, *Like a god*.

'Why didn't you tell them the truth?' Anna had asked.

'What do you think would have happened to me if I did? Who needs truth when they have *Pravda*?'

The tree-lined streets they are passing through now have houses for rich people. They gleam coldly, as if carved out of ice cream, and their windows are shining like jewels in the dull daylight. Many do not even bother to draw their curtains or shutters, but stand behind low walls or gardens, displaying the wealth within. Their fearlessness is a part of their luxury, Anna reflects, for in the Ukraine it would be locked away behind high walls and iron gates in case the people should want more than they have. She wonders whether there are even richer people than these, layer upon layer of them mounting up.

Her determination is revived by getting out. Even in the depths of winter people here are walking briskly, as if the acrid air has slapped their faces into a kind of alertness. Hurry, hurry, hurry, there is too much to do and so little time. Anna's own thoughts have sharpened, too. The dreamy, innocent girl she had been has become more calculating. Her mind spins like a rat on a wheel. The other brothel is mostly run by Dmitri, who is stupider than his brother and who likes to drink. There will be no Lena to guard them, and no video entryphone. There are bars on all the big windows, but if she can just get out of the flat, it will be easier to run away because it's on the ground floor. If, if . . . but for the first time in weeks, she feels a little quiver of hope.

'Never expect life to be easy,' she remembers her grandmother saying. 'Fate walks past everyone at some point in their lives, but he has only a single hair, and that you must catch. Everybody has to save their own life, little Anna. Nobody else will do it for you.'

Anna looks at the Russian in front of her, his thick hairy neck bulging over the collar of his jacket, and thinks with concentrated hatred that she will kill him if she can. He has her passport, and she has only the small bag she brought with her to Britain, and her wits. But she also has the pills.

The car draws up on the wide, shabby road that she remembers all too well. Anna is bundled out, up the steps and through the front door. It all looks pretty much as it did before, with dust and a pile of mail and a rusty old bicycle in the hall: even shabbier than the massage parlour – but then clients don't come here for the furnishings.

The two sagging double beds are still there, as is the black PVC couch, and the waiting room with its filmy grey net curtains and the traffic flicking past. Yawning and scratching herself, as well as coughing, Cristina slumps on the sofa, her roots showing like a dark road between the stiff blonde strands of her hair. She has dyed it since Anna first met her.

'Hey,' Cristina says, but Dmitri brushes her off.

'Is she still bad, downstairs?'

'You can hear her.'

'Shit. Every day, she loses me money. The boss is pissed off. I even get her antibiotics, but the stupid bitch coughs. Make her shut up – she'll put off even more guys.'

The sick girl is one that Anna hasn't met before. She ventures down the stairs to the basement. There are two more rooms down there, both smelling strongly of damp and drains, and in one is a girl, probably no more than sixteen and clearly feverish. Anna knows enough Russian to understand that she's begging for her sister.

'Shh,' Anna says helplessly. 'You must try to be quiet.'

She finds a cloth to wet and wring out, and bathes the girl's forehead, looking around. Damp speckles the walls and carpet, like the squashed bodies of small insects. The barred window is painted shut, like all of them, and the creeper obscuring much of the glass gives the light a dim greenish tinge, as if they were underwater.

'Are you thirsty?'

The coughing girl nods. There is not even a glass for her to drink from. In the corridor is a grubby, greasy kitchenette with a fridge, a microwave and a kettle. The only cutlery is plastic and snaps easily, but Anna finds a cracked red china mug, emblazoned with the words *Harry Potter*.

Anna makes the girl tea, black but with plenty of sugar. It seems to help. When she has finished it, Anna fills the mug with water and with her own comb brushes the girl's hair gently. It's lank, but thick and a natural blonde. She has small features and big, long-lashed eyes that make her pretty, even without make-up. Anna would have felt envious in another life, but now she just thinks impersonally how much more valuable it must have made her to the brothers.

The girl croaks, 'Who are you?'

'Anna. You?'

'Galina.'

So this was the girl the others envied, the one who had become the exclusive property of the oligarch. Either he'd got tired of her or he'd sent her back here because he didn't want to catch her illness. Or perhaps her coughing simply reminded him that she was human. Maybe if I could get sick, the men would leave me alone, Anna thinks. 'Where are you from?'

It is the question the girls all ask each other on meeting, as if the place which they have left still holds some essential part of themselves.

'Vilnius. Please, help me.'

Anna has not been thinking of helping anyone but herself. How can she? 'I try to make you –' she searches for the English word '– comfortable.'

She plumps up the meagre pillow – more dust than stuffing – and rinses the scrap of towelling with fresh cold water, then slips out.

'Is she ready to work?'

Anna replies, her eyes cast down. 'She has a bad fever.'

'Bitch!'

Dmitri is furious. He might hit Anna next. She momentarily hates Galina for arousing his anger, and herself for taking pity.

'I put her to work on the streets. Filthy, useless little *suka*.'

Anna, unable to bear the raw, repetitive sound of Galina's coughing, offers timidly, 'I make her soup.'

'No fucking point,' Dmitri mutters.

'It won't cost a lot. If I have onion and bone of chicken, I make.'

'What good will that do?'

'Is Ukrainian medicine. My granny make it for us when we sick.'

Dmitri grunts. 'Maybe.'

Soon Anna has other things to think about. Just as Lena told her, there are many more men who want a girl in the new brothel. How they find it is a mystery to her, but here she learns that Dmitri pays someone to go round pasting up postcards, and there is also a website. Anna sees the cards. They feature a Slavic-looking blonde with a voluptuous body who looks nothing like any of them.

'Who is she?'

Cristina says, 'Some model.'

'Who?'

'I don't know. Why ask me?'

Anna is silent. It's dangerous to talk to Cristina. She'll do anything for another fix. Anna looks for needle tracks on Galina's arms, but there are none. Maybe she, like herself, isn't an addict, but the brothers must have some hold over her, otherwise why return? If Anna ever got out, she'd keep on running, papers or no. Even if Sergei and Dmitri made good their threats to find her family and punish them it wouldn't stop her.

The main problem, really, is boredom, for between clients there's nothing to do but wait for the next meal or TV programme. Dmitri drinks whisky, talks into his mobile, demands sex, farts loudly and orders pizza. When the girls are alone, Anna drifts to the bathroom and opens its tiny window. The only one without bars, it gives onto a tangle of some kind of dead creeper, which has almost swamped the whole of the back garden. But the reason why it's unguarded is clear. It's too small to get more than her head through, though she tries, standing on the seat of the toilet.

Twisting and turning, trying to see if she can wriggle out, she looks up, towards the top floors of the building. She can see the blackened bricks and crumbling grey mortar stretching like a cliff-face, with occasional projections where window ledges are. It's all the same, but she remembers the woman who had smiled at her the day she first arrived. She had spoken about something to do with the house. Maybe she lives on another floor. Anna closes her eyes, and tries to remember the woman's face. So much has happened, and there is so much she doesn't want to remember. Yet that woman, who had smiled at her, she was almost certain, was from a different kind of world to the one that Anna is trapped by. Somehow it is important to keep this in her head.

Later, when the buzzer goes again and again, and the men come in, she thinks about the pills. There are one hundred and thirty of them, two for each day she has been imprisoned. When the last of the men has left, early in the morning, she tips them out.

The pills lie in her palm like little white moons. Some of them may be contraceptives, but if she takes them all at once some will undoubtedly send her into a deep sleep, for ever. She longs for this. It is the only power she has left, the power of refusal; but before she tries for the last exit, it occurs to her that she could try giving them to Dmitri instead.

26

Job Enters a British Home

Parked in Fitzjohn's Avenue, between several of London's most exclusive prep schools, Job has the leisure to observe a daily scene that he finds entertaining and mystifying.

It's like watching a kind of tribal dance, he thinks. From half past three onwards, cars arrive and women get out – manifesting anger, affectation, stress, patience and exasperation – to congregate beneath frowning red-brick buildings. The women themselves are largely of a type, being pale assisted blondes in jeans and jackets, clutching handbags so large that Job wonders whether they are displaced persons like himself. Then children appear, shepherded by a teacher. They wear uniforms in different combinations of navy, grey and maroon, and expressions of stunned exhaustion, blinking like prisoners just released from jail. Every garment they have on seems to be marked with the crest of their school, as if there were a danger that they might, for a single second, forget where they are. Some are greeted with hugs and smiles, but more with indifference. The show ends when the car doors open and close and the vehicles eventually move off to join a viscous flow of metal and glass.

The whole thing takes half an hour, and during that time Job witnesses more discourtesy than in the rest of his entire journey around central London.

'Who do you think you are, you stupid cow?'

'Move over, can't you?'

'It's my right of way!'

'Oh, get off your high horse for heaven's sake.'

How unhappy these white women look! Tired, tight-lipped and selfish, they vent their resentment from the elevated vantage points of enormous heavy cars like armoured tanks. Job is careful not to add to their anger. He is beneath their notice, he knows, for they have their own private feuds and rivalries which take no account of anyone else. The only young ones are the nannies and au pairs, who either drive small cars like Polly's or else use public transport.

Robbie slides into the car. 'Hello, Job,' he says in his high, clear voice. He grins at Job, and Job grins back.

'Hello, Mr Robbie.'

'You don't have to call me that, you know. Actually, I think Robbie is a bit babyish, don't you?'

'What do you prefer?'

'Rob. It's short for Robin, but I think that's a bit babyish too, don't you?'

'It is a name I like. You know, Robin Goodfellow? It is one of Mr Shakespeare's very best stories.'

'Does it have fighting?'

'Yes.'

'With swords?'

'It begins with a king conquering a queen, and taking her to his country,' says Job solemnly, and proceeds to tell Robbie a version of *A Midsummer Night's Dream* that has more duels in it than the original.

'I think I've heard that story before, somewhere, only there was more kissing and stuff,' says Robbie. He adds, 'You do know a lot, don't you? Why are you driving a minicab, if that isn't a rude question?'

'I'll tell you, if you tell me why you need a minicab to get home.'

Robbie looks surprised. 'Mum thinks the streets are dangerous. She's afraid of bad stuff like bombs and muggers happening to me. I don't mind because I don't like the Tube.'

'There is the bus, however. Have you travelled on the bus alone?'

Robbie sighs. 'Not yet. I'm still ten, and Mum thinks it's too young, specially in uniform. It is stupid, really, isn't it? I mean, we get up so early and travel for miles across London just to get to school, and I absolutely hate mine. Every day that's a school day is awful. Only Dad says that if I go to somewhere closer, I'll get beaten up and not learn anything. He and Mum are afraid that if we don't pass exams and go to the right universities we won't get jobs. So I'm sort of stuck, aren't I? I hope you don't mind.'

'No, I don't mind at all. Your mother pays me to do this, and I'm happy to help her.'

'I expect she's a bit of a helicopter, isn't she?' says Robbie.

'A helicopter?'

Job stops at the robot – or, as people say here, traffic light.

'You know, always hovering around me and Tania, whirring, because she's so anxious. Mum is the most anxious person in the world, don't you think?'

Job and his sister would play with Beth Wisden, running around in the big garden of the low colonial-style farmhouse, or in the bush, quite unafraid, and Mrs Wisden had laughed, believing it could only do them good. They would walk to the town emporium, with its sweet perfume of *kapenta*, or dried fish, to buy breakfast cereal: vanilla wheat flakes or chocolate maize. That emporium, where the women gossiped and the children hung around hoping for shortbread biscuits, had seemed to him to stock everything a person might desire – Tanganda tea, Marie biscuits, Tastic rice, Royco tomato soup, Mazoe orange concentrate. He remembers the wonder of the butcher's, with its pig carcasses hanging in the window and its slabs of biltong or coils of sausage, the bakery, the Indian tailors and bicycle shops. It had been worth a little fear to get to it. He remembers an old saying: the coward has no scars. But what parent would not want to protect their child from wounds? And in the end, no amount of common sense had helped them when the Zanu-PF supporters came.

'I don't know,' Job says, in his deep, quiet voice. 'All mothers are anxious. It is a part of their job. Maybe you should be glad to have such a mother, to care for you.'

'Oh, I am. She's a very nice mother, apart from working too hard. I love her very much, only don't tell her I said that.'

'Why not? She might like it.'

'She might think I was making a fuss. It's one of the rules, you know. Not showing whether you're sad, or you love someone.'

'Ah, yes,' Job says, sighing. 'But don't you ever tell people what you feel?'

'Do you, Job?'

'No,' he says. 'Perhaps I am more British than I knew.'

As a result of his small kindness to Amir and Chandra, Job has been invited to Tariq's home, and it is here that he goes at the end of his shift one evening. It is not far from where he lives, and is part of a row of new red-brick houses in a cul-de-sac. The houses are very ugly, with plastic window frames, but each has a tiny patch of garden in front and another out at the back past the kitchen, which Tariq and his wife cultivate.

'We are gardeners, we Bengalis,' says Tariq. 'We come from where the tea is grown, and many roses. You have heard, perhaps, of Darjeeling tea?'

Job pretends he has. At home, Tariq assumes a dignity that is different from his manner under the watchful, costive eye of Mo. His thin frame fills out as he sits cross-legged on a pale silk rug, relaxed and affable. When Job is formally introduced to Tariq's wife, he puts out his hand to shake hers, and is met with a graceful bow.

'We do not shake hands in our culture,' she says, smiling.

Job understands. 'In my country, some people embrace to show respect,' he says. 'But others do as you do, or bend their knees, to respect an elder or a host.'

214

'To touch can spread disease,' says Tariq. 'I believe this is what all people from hotter countries know, no matter what their religion.'

'You are right. However, I also think the custom of shaking hands comes from showing a friend that you carry no weapons,' says Job. 'I have heard that in some parts of Europe, there is no word for hello, only a phrase which means, "Don't kill me!"'

Tariq gives no reaction for a moment. Then, suddenly, his whole face changes. It folds, bulges, and for a dreadful moment, Job thinks he is angry. But he is not. Tariq slaps his knees with his hands and throws back his head, revealing long, stained teeth, and he laughs with a kind of delight that changes his appearance entirely. Job laughs with him. In that moment, Job thinks, they become not colleagues but friends.

Tariq's wife, who wears a scarf tied tightly over her head, serves them both amber glasses of tea, then retires to the kitchen from which spicy smells are coming. The house is spotless, if a little bleak. Job has followed his host in removing his shoes on entering, and is uncomfortably aware that both his socks have holes in them and that his feet smell. He asks if he can use the bathroom, and hurriedly washes and dries all the parts of himself that he is afraid are most in need of it. He thinks the Khans are aware of this when he returns, and that they approve, though it's hard to be sure. They drink their tea, and talk of small things. Job is intensely aware that this is probably the first time Tariq and his family have ever entertained a black man. For his part, it is the first time he has been inside a British home, and as he realises this he thinks of the ideas he had gleaned from the battered primers about Janet and John at the Wisdens'. That brightly coloured world, with its fathers in suits and its mothers in aprons, had been long lost even when Mrs Wisden had been a girl, and yet there is something pleasant about the Khans, who interest him. Tariq had greeted him with a blessing in the name of God, and thanks God before eating. Job prays with them. Although he is excluded from God's grace, he is impressed by the way Tariq says the word, 'Allah', as gently and caressingly as if he is addressing his wife. Perhaps I have

215

been addressing God in the wrong way, Job thinks; but in his heart he knows he is being punished for his crime.

Job, politely waiting, notices that Tariq eats and drinks with his right hand only, and copies him. The boys leave their game and sit quietly beside their father, doing the same.

He learns that Tariq had arrived as a small child from Pakistan.

'Do you go back?' Job asks.

'Yes, every other year,' says Tariq. 'I visit my family.'

Job sighs. 'Then I envy you. I cannot go back, and my family may all be dead.'

'Is there a war in your country?'

It is the most direct question that any of the drivers have ever asked him. He doesn't know how much they knew, whether they watched the news on TV – they watch the al-Jazeera channel, which they say is much better in Arabic. Amir is watching it now, frowning. The set shows an American tank, burning somewhere in Iraq, and it's clear from the newscaster's voice that this is not something to regret.

'No. We have a very bad man as our president, but there has been no revolution. People are starving in what used to be the best farmland in Africa.'

'My father was a farmer,' says Tariq.

'So was mine,' says Job. He looks into the clear yellow liquid in his glass, inhaling a fragrance of flowers. 'I am glad I did not follow him.'

'I am glad I did not follow mine,' says Tariq. 'This is my country now. My children are British, though they do not feel it.'

He glances at Chandra, who is playing on some kind of computer – shooting down soldiers and laughing.

'They are good sons, but the temptations of the city are many.'

'Yes,' says Job, and he flushes darkly as he remembers his attempt to buy a woman's body. I promised to go back to her, and I haven't, he thinks. In this calm, respectable house he acknowledges the real reason: he doesn't know whether he can trust himself. His desperation for sex is sometimes far worse than hunger. He clears his throat.

'But it seems to me, there is always a choice between a good action and a bad one.'

'That is what I tell my children,' Tariq agrees. He smiles at Job. 'Love your father and mother, study hard and follow Allah, and you will lead a good life, a life of peace and blessings.'

'You are wise to teach them this,' says Job politely.

Encouraged, Tariq confides, 'I am worried about my sons. They are good boys, but in a rough school – that is the problem. They keep their heads down, but I lost control of my eldest. I had to send him away to Pakistan to put him on a better path.'

He shows Job a photograph of Selim.

'He works for the company, doesn't he?' Job asked.

'Yes, sometimes. He passed his driver's licence, and he earns some money. But he no longer listens to our imam, and now he will not talk to me. He says we are corrupted by the West.'

Job looks at him with compassion. 'All is not lost, as long as your family is alive,' he says. 'Children do not always obey their fathers, but one day they become men, and return.'

'I hope so, *inshallah*.'

Slowly, carefully, they discuss what preoccupies Tariq most: his children's slowness at reading or writing in English.

'We take education very seriously in my old country,' says Tariq. 'You know, Pakistan has given the world many great thinkers and writers. You are a learned man, we all know this.' Tariq pauses. 'What would you do?'

'They are clever boys,' Job says politely. In the background, he can hear the sound of gunfire and explosions, and Amir laughing.

'Mathematics is no problem. It's the language, the books, the spelling. Their teacher tries to help but the class is too big.'

'How many children?'

'Thirty,' says Tariq.

Job almost laughs, for he himself had learnt in classes three times as large. But his real lessons, it is true, had come from Mrs Wisden. She was the one who had lent Miriam and himself books and encouraged them to read; he had grown up speaking more English than Shona.

'Perhaps they need extra lessons,' he suggests.

'I could pay,' Tariq says. 'You know, some of the other drivers have had tutors for their children.'

'Maybe you should ask their English teacher first,' Job suggests.

Tariq shakes his head. 'Their teacher keeps changing. Amir had quite a good new one, but he has been off sick after an accident. So many teachers at their school go sick.'

'They don't want to teach us,' says Chandra. 'They think we're all shit.'

'Mr Bredin doesn't,' says Amir. 'He's OK.'

Chandra says something in a mocking, unpleasant tone, which makes Tariq rap out a reprimand.

'You see? This is the problem.'

Job himself has other ideas about what might be causing the boys' reluctance to read. The screen that hums and responds to buttons being pressed is always going to be more attractive than a printed page.

'Do you read with them yourself?'

Tariq gives an embarrassed smile. 'I don't have the time.'

'Not even for half an hour before bed?'

Tariq's shift work, upon which the family is dependent for an income, makes this too hard, he claims.

The two men begin to haggle, pleasantly, about the possibility of Job coming once a week to do reading practice with the boys. It's a small thing, but it will cement their growing friendship and Job is happy to help.

Only when he leaves the house and hears the boys' high, clear voices shouting, 'Die, infidel, die!' does a tremor of unease go through him. Tariq and his wife are one matter, but the expression of concentrated hatred on the faces of their sons is another. Still, he thinks to himself: what can a child do?

27

They Know So Much About Us

'I know nothing about Iryna, except that she's vanished,' Polly says, almost gasping. She is afraid of this man, and of what he might be about to tell her. She wishes Job were still here – or Bill, or even Theo. Being alone is almost more than she can bear.

'Please, I must talk with you. Just a few moments, is all I'm asking.'

He puts a hand inside his coat and Polly tenses, expecting him to pull out a weapon. Instead he produces a passport, which he hands over to her. Reluctantly, Polly takes it, trying not to let her guard down. It is Romanian.

'I am Gheorghe. Iryna's fiancé. I am very sorry to call so late. It is my one time between my jobs when I can come,' he says, his voice low and anxious. 'I tried earlier, but the babysitter inside said you were out. So I waited.'

He is shivering. Polly makes up her mind. This is not the man who had tried to break into her house before, but she's still trembling with fear. What should she do? She doesn't want to let him into her home, where he might attack her. Talking to him out in the street, however, feels no safer than talking inside, where she has her panic button – and Teresa.

'You'd better come in.'

Teresa comes bustling up when she hears Polly's keys. Her broad pockmarked face is flushed with indignation.

'Mrs Polly, this man, he say he know you,' she says. 'Is OK? I go now?'

Polly hesitates. 'Would you mind waiting just twenty minutes more, Teresa? I'll pay you extra.'

'OK,' says Teresa. 'There is more ironing to do. You need any help, you call me.' She glares at Gheorghe. Teresa looks far more capable of knocking an intruder out with an iron pan than Polly. She had told her, in one of their stumbling conversations, that she has done capoeira, the Brazilian form of martial arts, and Polly takes comfort from this.

As Teresa goes down to the basement, Polly and Gheorghe go into the kitchen.

'You were going to get married?' she asks, prompting.

'If Iryna got Romanian citizenship, she would have the right to work in this country now we join the rest of Europe,' says Gheorghe. 'She would be legal. However, she has disappeared. I am very anxious for her.'

'Have you told the police?'

'Have you?'

Polly is surprised by his self-assurance, but answers, 'We had an attempted burglary recently, and the police want to interview her. Perhaps you should contact them.'

'The police will do nothing about an illegal,' says Gheorghe. 'You know this, Mrs Noble.'

'How do you know she hasn't been deported?'

'I thought at first that might be what had happened to her. But Iryna would have telephoned me. So this concerns you also.'

For a horrible moment, Polly thinks he is trying to blackmail her. Then he says earnestly, 'Mrs Noble, Iryna has not been to church or to any of her jobs for six weeks. Her family have heard nothing. Did she leave no word for you?'

Polly frowns. The Iryna she thought she knew – the pretty, competent girl who could use a sewing machine and coax tomatoes out of her small, sour back garden – rises in her memory. Yes, that Iryna, though she hardly knew her, was always responsible and responsive. She had never hesitated to call if she thought one of the children was ill. 'How long have you two been together?'

Gheorghe gives a tired smile. 'Two years. It took her a long time to trust me, Mrs Noble.'

'Why is that?'

'I work two jobs, she worked three.'

Polly stares at him, across the hall. 'How is that possible? Iryna was here every afternoon, and often babysat for me too.'

'That wasn't her only job,' says Gheorghe. 'She worked in the mornings, you know? And at weekends, and in the evenings. Every day, she worked fourteen, fifteen hours. So do I.'

No wonder he looks so exhausted, Polly thinks, and no wonder Iryna's cleaning was sometimes erratic. She remembers that during the afternoon, on the rare occasions when Polly was working from home, Iryna would make herself a strong pot of coffee. Polly had felt a bit annoyed about this – it was Fairtrade, and more expensive – but had said nothing, assuming that afternoon coffee-drinking was a Russian habit.

'What did she do?'

'In the evenings, office cleaning. I deliver food for a supermarket, and I do office cleaning, in the City and the West End. That is how we met. We both worked at night, after everybody has gone home. Without people like us, you would drown in dust. Do you think toilet paper is renewed by magic, and light bulbs never fail?'

'No,' says Polly, defensively. 'She had a comfortable home here.'

'Yes, I know. She was grateful for it, believe me. She respected you, and she loved your children.'

'Well, we all liked her very much too.' Polly is conscious that her voice sounds prim. 'That's why we've felt so jolly let down since she vanished. I'm surprised she needed the money.'

'Iryna's wages were sent home to keep six people in food and clothing.'

'*Six* people!' Polly exclaims. 'But I thought her parents both worked. I remember her telling me.'

'Yes. Her mother is a nursery teacher, and her father is a baker, and their parents are alive. Have you seen those books American tourists are so fond of, Mrs Noble? *Europe On $10 A Day?*' Gheorghe laughs, without humour. 'They should come to my country, or Iryna's, and live on ten dollars a week.'

'I do know about these things,' says Polly. 'I work with asylum seekers, you know. But these are vast problems, beyond any individual. I'm not responsible.'

Gheorghe's angular, mobile face looks apologetic. 'We had the misfortune to be born into Communist countries, that is all. Now we are free, but a hundred years too late. For an adult to live like a child is not an easy thing.'

'You visited her when she was babysitting, however,' says Polly, remembering her annoyance. 'My children met you.' She can smell the rank, damp smell of clothes that had been left too long in a washing machine coming off him, now that he is warmer.

'I came once or twice, yes. There was nothing bad, I promise. We are both so respectful of your family and home, Mrs Noble, we are Orthodox Christians, we—'

'I am not religious,' says Polly, annoyed.

'And also when you were away on holiday, I stayed here with her. She was afraid to live on her own.'

'I see. Yes, I suppose it might be a little frightening to be in a house alone,' says Polly, hoping they had not slept in her bed. The idea is deeply distasteful – though how would she have known? Iryna was the one who knew when she had slept with Bill, because she changed the sheets. They know so much about us, and we so little about them, she thinks. 'But – was she afraid of anything in particular?'

'I believe so,' he says, vaguely. 'Things from her past.'

'I know about the family she lived with before me, though I don't remember their name,' says Polly. 'She said they were unkind.'

Gheorghe looks surprised. 'Is that what she told you?'

'Yes – why?'

'There was somebody she was afraid of, a man. He was frightening her, but it's easy to disappear in a city like this. Change your mobile, change your address and . . . It would not be possible in Europe. No identity cards.'

'Not yet, at any rate,' says Polly.

'This is why I know something bad is happening to Iryna,' he says. 'She wanted so much to be legal. She had no reason to disappear.'

'When did you see her last?'

'Not since the first week of January.'

'That's when I last saw her. The week the children went back to school, she vanished.' Polly takes a deep breath. 'I must be frank with you. When she vanished, so did a diamond ring of mine. My engagement ring. It's very valuable – the only valuable bit of jewellery I have,' she adds. 'Its loss makes her disappearance very suspicious, in the circumstances—'

'Iryna is not a thief,' Gheorghe says quickly.

'We all think that, though, until someone has stolen something,' Polly retorts. The thought of her missing ring is making her angry again. 'What I know, and what the insurance company will find conclusive, is that both went missing on the same day. If she gets a criminal record, she will never be allowed to live here.'

This last isn't true: an astonishing number of immigrants with records for crimes as grave as murder, rape and paedophilia have been allowed to remain in Britain, even after conviction. It seems wholly random, who gets leave and who is refused.

Gheorghe puts his head in his hands, and sighs. 'Is anything more missing?'

'No.' Polly yawns, pointedly. 'I'm sorry, it's late, and I have to get to work tomorrow. I really can't help you. Her room was cleared out,

223

and I assumed that she must have decided to leave. I still think that's what she's done.'

'She was different over Christmas.'

'Was she?' Polly thinks back. She only saw her au pair for a few minutes every day, but Iryna had always been calm and cheerful. 'Maybe. I assumed she was homesick.'

'She was homesick, but she has not gone home. I talked to her mother.'

'How did you do that, if you're Romanian and she's Russian?' asks Polly, sharply.

'We all had to learn Russian at school.' Gheorghe's mouth twists, as if he tastes something bitter. 'English is the language of freedom. Iryna and I spoke English to each other.'

'You speak it well,' Polly says. She always says this to foreigners, to encourage them.

'I dream in English now, but it is like looking at a glass that was once a mirror,' he says. 'Iryna was my country. You understand this?'

'My own mother was born to refugees from Nazi Germany.'

'Perhaps that is why you don't seem, excuse me, totally English.'

'I don't know what being totally English is supposed to mean,' Polly says. 'People usually mean it to imply a kind of coldness, don't they, an unfriendliness? I am concerned for Iryna, and by what you say. But I simply don't know what to suggest. Who was this man she was afraid of?'

Gheorghe thinks for a moment. 'I didn't like to ask questions. So many of us have left behind lives that had bad things in them. But Iryna herself is a good person. Now I am afraid for her.'

'I think I am afraid for her, too,' says Polly, slowly. 'Gheorghe, I told you we were burgled. A man got into the house after midnight, only he didn't break in. He used keys. I never got Iryna's keys back, and unless there are copies floating around that I don't know about, it's probable that—'

'This man, did you see him?'

'Enough to know that he wasn't you.'

He looks pale, almost greenish-white with worry.

'I am legal. I have nothing to hide from the police.'

Teresa appears, silently asking if she can leave. For a moment Polly longs to say no. Being the only adult in the house has never seemed more lonely, or more frightening. Is this all the effect of the burglary? Should she ask her cleaner to move in? Teresa lives in a house somewhere in the outer suburbs of London, with other Brazilians who are horrible to her because she's poor and ugly and illegal. Even among themselves there is a pecking order of who is treated well and who isn't, and in the short time that her cleaner has worked for her Polly has learnt this. Surely Teresa would jump at the chance of moving into Iryna's old room? But Tania has her eye on it, and Polly has begun to feel that her family is moving forward into a new stage.

'Thanks, Teresa. I'll add it to your money on Friday,' she says. 'Would you like a minicab home? It's too late for the Tube.'

It's obvious that Teresa would like this very much, but would never have expected it. Her anxious humility touches Polly. Teresa has told her that her other two employers often 'forget' to pay her at the end of each week. She is utterly defenceless if they refuse; when they go away on holiday, they tell her at the last moment and do not pay her during their absence. What sort of reputation must we have abroad, Polly thinks, when we treat people so badly? What kind of trouble are we storing up for ourselves when the Poles and all the rest go home? But Teresa, who is sending half her wages back to Brazil in order to pay for her mother's diabetic treatment, is uncomplaining.

'Leave me your mobile number, Gheorghe. I'm glad you got in touch, and I'm going to think about what to do, but I must get to sleep.'

'I must get to my next job,' he says, writing down his number. 'Cleaning offices.'

'What did you do in your own country?' Polly asks politely, preparing to lock and bolt the door behind him. She looks out, seeing Job returning, giving a silent flash of his headlights to pick up her cleaner. Even after midnight there are still people walking down her street. She has a sudden crawling suspicion that she is being watched; that the silhouette of someone waiting inside a car opposite might not be her friendly neighbourhood drug dealer but a kind of spy. 'Did you train for something?'

'Yes,' Gheorghe says, with a faint smile. 'I was a lawyer, Mrs Noble. Just like you.'

28

Like a Ripe Fruit

Ian is now, at Candice's insistence, staying in her flat. He is not, he tells himself, living with her, but he can't deny that this is the most comfortable he has been as a Traveller. She has a very nice flat, with broadband and Sky, and he doesn't have to go to the launderette to get clean clothes. In one corner, a tall fig tree, pot-bound and over-watered, sheds its leaves and in the other Ian lies on the white sofa watching the Six Nations rugby on a giant flat-screen TV with a cold can of lager by his side, lapped in warmth and a cashmere blanket. It could not be more different from Finsbury Park, with its violently patterned carpet, battered sofa and tepid radiators.

'You lucky bastard,' Mick tells him when he visits. 'All this and her, too.'

Liza, wandering round the flat in bare feet, grins. She's a nice-looking young woman, or would be if she didn't have a scar running down her face.

'I bet he didn't ask for it, Mick.'

'That's probably why you've got the prettiest girl in London looking after you. Women! They're like bloody cats, all over you only when you don't want them.'

The Slug sounds despondent, and Liza gives him a friendly punch. They're visiting when Candice is at work, on the tacit understanding that she doesn't like any of Ian's friends.

'Well, I do want her, I suppose.'

'If you're not sure, let me know.'

Mick's crush on Candice is something else that makes Ian uncomfortable. The Slug has actually shaved and put on a clean T-shirt, but as Candice is out it's a wasted effort.

'Sorry you're crook, Ian. Was your nursing OK?'

'As far as I could tell.'

'What's this?' Mick says, picking up a tangle of wool on the white sofa. 'Don't tell me she's even knitting you a jumper!'

'Er—' says Ian.

Ian is like a ripe fruit invisibly invaded by a million floating spores, each of which is busily burrowing into his skin. Of course, he's very fond of Candice, but he isn't ready to settle down. He has to get qualified as a teacher, travel more and meet his father before anything can progress. His whole life is on hold, but she's so kind to him.

'I'm so glad you've seen reason about living here, sweetie, even if we can't have much fun yet,' Candice said tenderly, rushing back with bags full of nice things to eat from the local delicatessen. Sometimes, seeing her dazzling smile, he thinks he's a fool for not wanting to snap her up. But he can't imagine her ever enjoying sitting with him and his mates to watch the rugby.

When his friends leave and the match is over, Ian walks towards Hampstead Heath. Much as he dreads re-entering the run-down area where the Samuel Smiles is situated, there is something about Hampstead Village that makes his skin crawl.

'It isn't real, Candy. All this – all these stupid shops – it's froth.'

'But I like being able to buy croissants and a Starbucks,' she says. 'Don't you?'

Of course he does; prosperity is a good thing. Yet there is such a gulf between this world of Candice's and that of the part of London where he teaches that even the air smells different. Here it is scented with early spring flowers; over in Hackney it's hot chip oil. Why can't there be flowers where his pupils are? He looks at the pond by the parking lot, and remembers the anonymous body he'd seen being dragged out of the Ponds on the other side of the Heath. All around here it's a dream of loveliness, Georgian cottages set back behind wrought-iron gates and front gardens clipped and tended like something out of a picture book. How much would each one cost? Five million? Ten? How can anyone earn that kind of money?

His arm itching in its light cast, Ian turns back and wanders round Keats's House next door. Katie has recommended it, and he's ashamed never to have been.

'It's the kind of house great poets should have and never seem to,' Katie told him. As soon as he sees it, he knows what she means. It's a long, low, white-painted villa set back from the road in a garden; and it is perfection. Ian has never forgotten his own feelings on first reading 'Ode to a Nightingale', that passionate ecstasy. He loves Keats for his courage, his openness to feeling. He'd tried reading the poem to Candice; she'd yawned.

Perhaps I'm just a snob, Ian thinks, wandering round the rooms. He's older than Keats was when he died, and has achieved nothing. Nobody tells you that your twenties are as confusing and changeable as your teens, that you still go on groping your way forward. Was this the way Quentin had felt, leaving his wife and child? Perhaps, Ian thinks, I'll ask him.

He is meeting his father at last. Quentin had rung, and invited him to lunch at his club. Ian laughed, thinking it was a joke, before realising that it was for real. A club! He has seen them in movies, but he never thought he might set foot in one himself. Quentin is not from a posh family – his own father had been an army officer – but after Oxford he had risen rapidly in fashionable circles, especially after marrying into the aristocracy. The first marriage, to Ian's mother, had lasted less than a year and Ian has a strong suspicion that Nadine's family (at that time considerably wealthier than now) had paid him off.

All the way down into the thickening air and grinding gears of central London he wonders what his father will really be like. He has heard him on the radio – for Quentin is much in demand – though he has never yet caught him on TV. Katie has described him as good-looking.

'That doesn't help me,' Ian told her. 'You know, straight men can never tell if a guy is attractive. My housemate, Mick the Slug, is hideous, but girls are all over him.'

'Handsome and attractive are two different things,' said Katie's voice over the phone. She hasn't visited him since he left hospital, though he has called her to suggest meeting up for a drink or a meal. 'Quentin is something else.'

'I'll let you know how it goes.'

'Just don't let him charm you.'

'Charm is the English disease, isn't it?'

'But just think how awful they'd be without it,' she said, laughing.

He gets off the bus too soon, and walks down Regent Street. There is something ponderous about this part of London, though the stony exterior of Quentin's club is plain enough. Inside is another matter. The steps lead up to a palace of mahogany and marble where men talk to one another in quiet, cultivated voices. It is a vision of another century, filled with the confidence of Empire.

'May I help you?'

'I'm meeting Quentin Bredin,' says Ian to the porter, who stands, solemn as a priest in the confessional, to one side. Ian can feel him scrutinising his bruised face and his new suit.

'*Whom* shall I say is calling?'

'Ian Bredin.'

The porter admits that he is expected, then coughs and murmurs, 'Excuse me, sir, but guests cannot be admitted without a *tie*.'

Ian controls his features.

'Does it have to be an old school one?'

'No, sir. *Any* tie would do. We keep a selection here for those caught *short*.'

He chooses one at random, and puts it on, blushing. The porter considers him with a distant air of avuncular regret. It is, they both know, hideous.

'Upstairs, sir, first door on your left.'

It is all carved oak columns and deep red carpets. Overhead, a curved glass ceiling of diamond-shaped crystal allows daylight into a space the size of Ian's school's playground. A number of panelled doors lead off to other rooms – libraries, perhaps, or sitting rooms, or private dining rooms. His father is sitting in a leather armchair, reading a newspaper and wearing half-moon glasses. Their recognition is mutual, and instant.

'I was wondering whether you would look like me,' Quentin exclaims affably. 'Bad luck, your accident, hmm?'

He has dark, glossy hair and, just as Katie had told him, there is a surprising amount of it for a man in his fifties. It is disconcerting, like seeing an older version of himself. A tailored suit reveals a flash of blue silk lining, like the feathers in a jay's wing.

'Of course, I already know you don't *sound* the same. Good God, you're wearing one of the club's ties!'

'I was forced into it by Jeeves.'

'I haven't seen that thing since Bunty Evenlode turned up after a night in the clink.' Quentin embarks on a series of anecdotes about people Ian doesn't know and hasn't heard of. Ian smiles politely, feeling dull and provincial. Gradually, though, his father puts himself out to charm; he discovers Ian's passion for literature, and tells him a number of stories about famous people, all of whom come to the *Rambler* lunches. Despite himself, Ian is fascinated. To him, these men and women are heroes – even if none of them, in his opinion, can touch Mandela. A cheerful clink of cutlery on china, the Polish waiters, a pair of old buffers in bow ties discussing Afghanistan, all add to the amusement. Ian and Quentin's conversation picks up speed and enthusiasm; politically, they have opposing views, but it's enjoyable to cross swords. For the first time in months, Ian realises, he's actually using his brain again.

231

'So, last time I saw you, you were a baby. Fill me in on what I missed,' says Quentin.

Ian does so, briefly. He tells him about his schooling, trying to make it sound entertaining.

'Happiest days of my life were at prep school,' Quentin remarks. 'I was sodomised senseless, of course.'

Ian is unable to tell whether his father is joking or not.

'My school was private, but then everyone's is in South Africa. That's what attracts me about teaching here.'

'I went out to do a spot of teaching myself, when I came down, in the heyday of apartheid. A white man could walk around the streets thirty years ago and feel perfectly safe. Not that life has got any better for some, has it?'

'No,' Ian agrees dryly. 'Still, there is progress. When I was growing up we were advised to always carry a tampon in our pocket. It's the best way to plug a bullet hole.'

Quentin puts back his head and laughs. 'I like that. Women having a fanny shaped like a bullet hole,' he says. There is a gleam of slyness in his eyes, as if Ian has proved something. 'Best whores I had were in South Africa. Apart from the Russians, that is. They really enjoy their work.'

He sits back, with a complacent smile. Ian tries not to let his expression freeze. He can't believe what his father, whom he has just met, has told him. Is he being naive? It isn't just the knowledge that this man, with whom he had been getting on quite well, pays women for sex; it's the word 'whore'. Quentin, though, seems wholly unaware of his son's reaction.

'So, are you intending to stay in London?'

'I want to see the world—'

'You don't need to travel to see the world – in London the world comes to you.'

'How is Katie?' Ian asks, wanting to get away from this topic.

'Who?'

'Katie, your assistant. The American.'

232

'Oh, that Katie.'

'I thought she seemed nice.'

'*Nice*,' says Quentin, dismissively. 'Of course, niceness is all very well in its way, but nobody ever advances in life, or in London, by being *nice*. Niceness is for dullards, and the sartorially challenged, like my assistant. Now nastiness, that's what requires moral courage. Underneath, you see, everyone is nasty. That's what journalism's about.'

'If you never overestimate human nature, you'll never be disappointed,' Ian says, with irony.

'Yes, quite. I can see we have a lot in common.'

Quentin leans back. They have finished their second course, along with a bottle of excellent red Bordeaux. There is pudding, which is something called Spotted Dick. Ian hopes it's a joke. Perhaps this whole conversation is a joke, though he suspects not.

'Now, then,' says Quentin, looking hard at his son. 'What is it that you want? Money?'

'No,' says Ian, surprised.

'Well, that's just as well, because there isn't any. A job? You can't want to stay teaching at a state school.'

'I have to stay on for another term, or I don't get a qualification I need.'

'Is that your only ambition?'

'I'd like to write, one day,' Ian says. He has no idea why he suddenly blurts this out; the wine, he supposes. 'If I were good enough, that is.'

'Ah, now that I could help you with, perhaps.'

'Really?'

'You should come to a *Rambler* lunch. The good and great served on a plate, so to speak.'

'I haven't done any journalism since college.'

'Look, any fool can write, it's getting published that's the hard part. The *Rambler* is part of – well – all this.' Quentin waves a hand airily at their surroundings. 'Not that we can pay much, of course. But it's the place that launched the careers of countless chaps.'

'I'd appreciate that very much, er, Dad.'

'Oh, do call me Quentin. Why don't you write a piece from the coal face? What it's really like teaching in Bedlam?'

'It isn't always so bad,' Ian says defensively. A week of convalescence and a week of half-term have made him, once again, more optimistic.

'Well, just give us the worst bits. Our readers always love feeling that shelling out twenty k a year on little Tarquin's fees is worth it.'

'I'll see what I can do. It's very kind of you to ask me.'

Ian walks back to his bus stop, bewildered but not altogether disheartened. He has no desire to become a journalist, but his father has made it clear that he wants to see him again. Quentin is clearly a piece of work, but he's also a man of distinction, intriguing and at ease in this city in a way that Ian is sure he himself will never be. The hateful club tie returned, he is less self-conscious about his appearance. So what if he wears a suit from Boss, rather than Jermyn Street? He wishes his father hadn't said that about whores, but he is from a different generation. The wine at lunchtime is making him feel strange. He walks mazily through St James's, wondering whether there are really so many men who want pinstriped shirts, or Old Master oil paintings, and whether he will ever earn enough to be able to live like a grown-up. If he were to ask Candice to marry him, and if she agreed, then he would have money, instantly – he could join the club, after all.

The drizzle has made the pavements dark, the concrete slabs splashed with a treacherous slick of water and dirt. Ian can see the famous statue of Eros, balancing on one leg and pointing his bow with that effortful balletic stance which probably sums up the absurdity of love everywhere. Around its base, concentric circles of bedraggled tourists and teenagers have gathered, bewildered, like the survivors of a flood, while all around traffic wheels, and above on giant screens the promise of a world elsewhere shimmers and flicks. At the Underground, in a hot thick blast of stale air, a news vendor opens a mouth full of ruined teeth and bellows, as if in pain. Copies of the evening paper he has on display scream about yet another teenager dying from knife wounds, and flutter their pages like trapped birds.

Ian thinks again of the club he has just left; the way that, without a strip of cloth hanging from his neck, he had been made to feel somehow less of a man – and for a moment he understands why boys like the ones he teaches carry knives.

29

An Individual Lump Of Malignity

Up until now, Katie hasn't taken much notice of the other inhabitants of the house where she has her flat, but it's becoming harder to ignore the constant traffic in and out of the ground-floor maisonette. For one thing, her bell keeps getting rung at strange times of night and day; and for another, she meets such odd people in the lobby downstairs. There seems to be no rhyme or reason to them. Some are distinctly drunk, some are sober, some are dark, some white, some young and many more middle-aged. All, however, are men.

'Hello, lady,' some of them say, with a peculiar smile, when she passes. She ignores them, trying not to shrink into herself, but she has become increasingly antsy about the rings on her bell. Clearly, some kind of business is being conducted out of the ground-floor flat. There are odd sounds that float up from the back of the house – grunts and cries, and sometimes men shouting, and a regular thudding against the walls.

Slowly, a suspicion begins to form in Katie's mind. Surely this can't be possible, or legal? She knows about Soho being a den of vice, because people in her office have joked about it, but this is a respectable neighbourhood, isn't it? Yet now she looks at the skinny teenaged girls in short skirts whom she sees hanging around the bus stop late at night and never getting on the buses. Are they hookers? It's hard to tell for sure.

Katie hates confrontation; it makes her nauseous, and yet she is a born meddler – which may not, she gradually realises, have particularly endeared her to colleagues. They have not been impressed by her tackling the filing, just irritated. She longs for female friends, and thinks guiltily about those whom Winthrop had winnowed out of her life back home. She doesn't really have anyone in London to do stuff with. Justin is the one she is almost fond of, perhaps because, like her, he's into music and books and art, but he doesn't seem the type to hang out with anyone but gay men. Still, she tries. Her nebulous position as Assistant to the Editor has caused half the problem, she believes, because they feared that, as an outsider and a foreigner, she was being promoted over their heads. Now they have grasped that she's no threat to them, Jocasta, Cassandra, Minty and the rest are quite pleasant to her. They think she must be rich ('*All* Americans who live here are rich,' Jocasta has informed her, sharply) and only playing at poverty, just as they are only playing at having serious careers. They, too, consider themselves to be poor, though their salaries from the magazine are boosted by clothes allowances and free lodgings in what are referred to as 'the granny flat' in Pimlico, Notting Hill or a mysterious region of London known as 'the toast rack'. Katie's genuinely straitened circumstances are incomprehensible.

Lying on her landlord's thin mattress, every bulge of which is an individual lump of malignity, she listens to the noises of the house below her with half-closed eyes. She is used to the wail of sirens, racing up and down York Way, but often the night is pierced by the desolate, unearthly shrieks of foxes that make people start, and wonder whether they are hearing a murder. Another woman's body has been found in the canal just down the road, according to the free local newspaper which gets pushed through the front door. The new Eurostar terminal, for all its champagne bar and the sleek new blocks of flats being erected along the canal, is not enough to lift the neighbourhood.

Maybe it's this that makes Katie feel that the people who come and go all have the same furtive look. Could they be drug dealers? She thinks of the two men she had seen with the young girl on the day she got back from the States, and suddenly it becomes clear to her. Of course: they must be pimps, running a brothel from the downstairs flat.

Appalled, she jumps when her buzzer goes off. What has been just a persistent irritant suddenly seems threatening, invasive, frightening. No wonder she gets odd looks: the men must think she's a hooker too. Katie sits up, shivering. What if one of the johns assaults her?

Keep calm, she tells herself, breathing deeply. She opens her laptop, finds the local police station number, and after many pauses is put through to a bored male voice which takes down her details and promises to 'look into it'. She knows what this means. For a moment, loathing of her adopted country almost overwhelms her: this is a place where, when she goes into stores and asks for something out of reach, shopkeepers can't be bothered to get out a stepladder. Her landlord, whom she never meets, is even harder to track down, and her quest leads only to the answering service where she leaves a message. The money goes out of her account every month, into thin air.

'Who left that notice on the office board about my flat being to rent?' she asks Justin.

'What flat?'

'The one I now live in. Camden Town.'

'No idea. You don't think anyone else would want to live *there*, do you?'

When Katie explains, he shrugs. 'Oh, that kind of thing goes on all the time. Blink, and there's a knocking shop.'

On impulse, Katie rings Polly. She's a lawyer and a neighbour – she would surely know what to do.

'Listen, I've got a problem. I think the downstairs flat in my house is being used for prostitution.'

'How very unpleasant for you. Have you been solicited?'

'No,' Katie admits. She feels almost flattered that Polly thinks anyone would consider her. 'But – my doorbell keeps being rung, and I don't know what to do.'

'Would you like me to come round?'

'Oh, no!' Katie says at once. The idea of anybody coming to her flat horrifies her, though she is also obscurely touched by the offer. 'No, I just wanted advice, if you have any.'

'Well, apart from ringing the police and your landlord—'

'Which I've done, and neither of them showed any interest.'

'You could move.'

'Have you any idea how hard it is to find a reasonably central flat for a single person on the salary I get? Especially as my visa expires in June.'

'You can write to your MP, and your local newspaper. That may produce some results, eventually. Otherwise,' Polly says, dryly, 'get a large boyfriend.'

Katie manages a laugh. 'I'll let you know when I find one.'

In the skylight, streaks of turquoise, acid yellow, rose, apricot and indigo are punctuated by a single star. Staring up at it, Katie is able to acknowledge that she is lonely. Meeting Quentin's son had been weird – he was quite snotty to me, she thinks, and what kind of crazy person would cycle in a city this crowded? – but it had still reminded her that her social life is limited. There are only so many exhibitions, movies, recitals and cafés you can go to alone before solitude stops being a luxury. From her bedroom window, she can see the mad Victorian grandeur that is St Pancras station, recreated as the gateway to Europe. Thirty cranes pierce the skyline. The dust from countless building sites thickens the air, and coagulates on surfaces around her flat.

'I need to get out more,' Katie says, aloud. Hemani's dinner party

239

had showed her that she was still capable of making new acquaint-ances, although when she thinks of the Trollope-inspired fantasies that had propelled her move to England, she blushes with shame. Still, now she has met Ian she is curious. Quentin had asked her to keep an eye on him, so she had, while he was in hospital.

'Why are you in London?' he'd asked.

'I thought I'd try it out,' she'd said, ignoring the churlish tone. 'What about you?'

'I came over partly because it's a rite of passage and also to meet my father. So now I'm teaching in a crap school in the East End to kids who barely speak English.'

Katie had been unimpressed. Her own parents are teachers, and good ones because they always find something in their pupils to encourage.

'Do you think you'll stay, or go back?'

'I don't know. The weather doesn't help.'

'Yes, I know.'

There is nothing to do in February but endure. The soggy streets, the weeping skies, the skeletal trees are a daily dose of pathetic fal-lacy. Yet, even so, the days are lengthening. The sun is rising earlier and setting slightly later. There are sunbursts of yellow crocus along parts of the Outer Circle of Regent's Park. Birds are singing again; perhaps they always sang, only she was too unhappy and too busy to hear them.

Katie has lost all sight of the *Rambler* as something pleasurable to read, and only sees the anguish that goes into each issue: the piece which wasn't properly lawyered, the questionable grammar in another, the possible factual error, the misprints, the slip-ups and the dressing downs. However, she has enough self-confidence to tell Quentin to ring his son. He won't do it without nagging. After it's happened, she's pleased to hear that the lunch at his club ('I couldn't possibly invite him to my *home*!') has been a qualified success. 'He's really not too bad, for a colonial. At least he didn't want any money.'

'That's good.' Katie says, after a pause. 'He seemed like someone who might be worth trying as a contributor.'

Quentin gives her a penetrating look from behind his half-moon spectacles. 'Ha! I thought so too. A *Rambler* lunch, maybe. See he's invited on a duller fortnight.'

When Katie relays this, Ian is pleased but wary. He's got the habitual distance of young teachers, she thinks; or maybe he just doesn't like me.

'You think I should go?'

'He's your father. Yes, you should. I've never been to a lunch, but they're supposed to be fun.'

'You've never been? Why not?'

'I guess my face doesn't fit.'

She tries not to mind about this too much. Besides, food, so long a source of self-denial, has become a problem for her in a new way.

A short bus ride from her flat is a reconstituted-marble temple of the ethically sourced and soothingly presented. Waitrose is so unlike the bloated stores of her homeland that it's hard to remember it's a supermarket. She has found herself seduced into returning home with heavenly French bread, with a piece of Cornish cheese wrapped in nettle leaves, with a mango. These small indulgences, however, are nothing compared to the steak.

Meat is a part of everything she has given up; it makes her think too much of Winthrop, whose appetite for spearing moist tender cuts of meat over a barbecue in the Hamptons has become her enduring memory of their relationship. What did I ever see in him? she wonders for the thousandth time, but she knows the answer. Money is a kind of magic, as Wallace Stevens said, and she had been bewitched. Her lover's ease, the confidence, the charm had all been a corollary of wealth, impossible to disentangle from what he had, in himself, been. Hers had been the kind of story which she thinks Henry James would never have told, and she had punished herself for her error of judgement and feeling by denying her body more and more.

Only there, at the front of the chill cabinet, was a slab of pure

241

energy. No matter that it was a bloody chunk of dead flesh, hacked off an innocent cow, and something that should repel her as morally wrong. She yearned for it.

Katie forgot shame, forgot conscience, forgot misery and just pointed. When she got home, she went to the cooker in a trance and fried her steak with a dab of olive oil and salt. Then she began to eat. A purely physical happiness flooded through her, of a kind she hadn't had since her childhood. She felt an indescribable gratitude to the animal who had given her this gift. That night, for the first time, she had slept soundly; the next day she had even run down the street for the bus.

'Katie, you actually have some colour in your cheeks.'

'Do I?'

Patrick comes rudely close. 'Yes, you do. Are you having sex?'

'No – last time I checked I still preferred chocolate.'

He laughs. 'If you haven't, then you will.'

'Oh, go and take your hormones someplace else,' Katie snaps.

'Hmm,' says Quentin, scrutinising her over his half-moon glasses. 'You haven't been to a *Rambler* lunch, have you?'

'Well . . . no.'

'Time you came. You're organising the party, after all.' Quentin sighs. 'I've asked my, er, Ian, so you can keep him company. You do *eat*, don't you?'

'Yes.'

'Then I expect you to brush up a bit. You know – wash your hair, and so on.'

Even though she will miss the Emerson Quartet playing Schubert, Katie feels a little throb of excitement. 'OK, Quentin, I'll do my best.'

Ian is out of hospital, but she has his cellphone number and on impulse rings him to let him know.

He says, in his clipped South African way, 'I'm glad there'll be one face I know.'

'That's probably why Quentin asked me,' she answers humbly. It's probably true, too.

'No, I'm sure he's just accepted that you're worth it.'

'Oh, I don't know about that. I keep wondering, how did I exchange a power shower in Manhattan for somewhere with a toilet that only flushes if you pump the handle?'

'How did you?' Ian asks.

'I didn't want to appear to be one of those whiny Americans that everyone dislikes.'

'I expect you're the sort who makes things work properly, though.'

Katie is flattered. Maybe if she repaints her flat . . . In a burst of enthusiasm and energy, she goes to a Sunday-opening hardware store and buys white emulsion and a paint roller. My walls are the colour of English teeth, Katie thinks, opening the tin. Gingerly, she starts to paint. There seems to be such a lot of paint, and it's sticky. The smell is appalling, even with the windows open. Halfway across the next wall, she puts down her roller and opens the door to her flat.

This does the trick, although she's nervous about leaving her door unlocked. From downstairs she can hear shouting. Grimly, Katie wedges her front door with a clothes-peg, turns up Radio 3, and wields her roller in time with Mozart's *Requiem*.

'*Kyrie eleison . . . qui tollis peccata mundi!*'

It might be OK. She's actually singing when she gets a call from her mother, checking up on her.

'I'm fine,' Katie tells her. 'Really. Just very busy organising the annual party.'

'That sounds like a lot of fun, sweetheart,' her mother says brightly, and chatters on, anxious and affectionate and infinitely irritating.

'So, have you met anyone new yet?'

'What do you mean?' Katie knows what she means, and is instantly furious.

'You know, like, a guy?'

It's as if anger has driven Katie out of her body. The impression is

243

sufficiently strong for her to glimpse another face in the bathroom mirror. She grimaces at it. Her mother doesn't mean to be annoying, she just is.

'I have to go, Mom. Sorry.'

Katie puts her cellphone down. In the corner of her eye, she sees a movement that she knows she hasn't made. Her heart jumps into her mouth. She isn't imagining things. There, behind her, is somebody else.

30

Living on Trust

Polly is surprised at how punctilious the police are about informing her of the progress of the investigation into her break-in. The news is not good. Her intruder has left traces of DNA at other crime scenes (the investigating detective will not say where) but they have no name or known whereabouts for him. Tania pooh-poohs the whole incident, having slumbered through it all, but Robbie is so upset that he insists on sleeping in Polly's bed; she now keeps a poker next to it, feeling mildly ridiculous. Despite her rational, conscious mind telling her that lightning never strikes in the same place twice, every tiny creak has her waking in a hot, heart-thudding haze of fear. Increasingly, she is convinced that on the day she found Iryna gone she was woken by the same intruder as the one who had later broken into the house. She has never felt so vulnerable.

'I wish you were here,' she tells Bill. Privately, she is ashamed of sounding plaintive.

'I'll be over soon.'

'I know. I just wish it was now.'

A fortnight after the break-in, a DC Singh rings Polly at work to ask if she would be willing to identify a body.

'Yes, of course,' she says. Her voice remains steady, though her heart is not. 'Male or female?'

'Female.'

'Is this related to my break-in?'

'We're a different department.'

'Where did you find it?'

A cold bead of fear is travelling down her spine, like the mercury dropping in a thermometer.

'I can't tell you that, I'm afraid,' says the detective.

He gives her the address of the mortuary, and she drives there after the school run. When she arrives at the building, a bland suburban edifice, she is surprised it is so close, so normal. Singh, a slim, neat young man, comes out to thank her for her cooperation. They go downstairs together, Polly chatting nervously. He is as wary of her as she is of him, once he learns she is a lawyer.

'I'm afraid people like you aren't popular with my profession.'

'I don't do criminal law.'

'Then I apologise. But from our point of view, the cards are all stacked too much in your favour. Have you any idea how hard it's become to get a conviction?'

'No. But I do know how hard it is to keep the women and children I represent from being deported,' Polly retorts. 'They've done nothing criminal except to be born in the wrong country.'

Singh is silent, as she knew he would be. He's a pleasant young man – a chemistry graduate, she learns. She's never talked properly to a policeman before, and his fierce passion for justice takes her slightly by surprise.

'I see the results of crime, even petty crime,' he says. 'People who die a couple of days later from shock. So often, we know who's committed it but we just can't prove it.'

Bodies are always kept in basements. In the presence of one policeman after another, Polly signs forms, produces her driving licence as identification and, after passing through a glass door into a windowless neon-lit room, is brought face to face with death.

246

It is the first cadaver she has ever seen. The body has been kept in a kind of refrigerated cabinet, and for a moment Polly has a vision of her own filing system at work. Under its opaque plastic sheet, it forms a slight mound. She has imagined vividly what it must be like to be beaten so badly in prison that your internal organs rupture, or to hang yourself from sheer despair: yet she has never seen a real dead person. Death, for her generation, is still something far off that has barely begun to happen to their parents. The air-conditioning sighs invisibly, keeping the bleached room at a constant chilly temperature; but even in the cold, a faint sickly-sweet scent reaches her nostrils. She recognises the smell, and it horrifies her. It is the smell of slightly rotten meat.

'Do you need a moment before you see the face?' the policeman asks, motioning to the mortuary assistant.

'No. Thank you, I'll be fine.'

When Polly sees the body, not just limp and pale in the pretence of death like corpses in films but like an empty glove, so deflated, so absolutely lifeless, her first thought is to wonder whether there could be such a thing as a human spirit after all. She has heard stories from the people she tries to help, stories of suffering and cruelty and evil and sorrow that have made her wonder why they cling on to life. This is why.

'Take it easy, Mrs Noble, there's no rush.'

'No – no, I'm all right,' she says, staring.

At first she can't be sure. The features are not only bloodless, translucent as marble, but in some odd way collapsed so that she can see the skull beneath. The corpse could be that of almost any young woman. But then Polly catches sight of the mole on its jawbone. She had never even consciously realised it was there – a tiny round brown dot – but now she recognises it.

'Yes, that's her,' she says. 'That's Iryna, my au pair.'

The detective exhales softly. 'You're sure? I need a formal identification, Mrs Noble.'

'Yes. That's Iryna. I can't remember what her surname is, but I'll look it up.'

'Can you tell me how old she was?'

'Twenty-two.' The shame she had felt at not remembering Iryna's surname (something complicated and Russian) is lessened. At least she had always marked her birthdays. Polly adds, huskily, 'How did she die?' It's obvious she was murdered, but she wants to hear it.

'The coroner will tell you. She was found in early January.'

'Oh God. Oh God. And I thought she'd just dumped us. I should have known.' Polly feels the blood draining from her face, and suddenly she is sitting on a chair, while the detective gently presses her head down between her knees.

'I'm sorry, I'm so sorry,' she whispers, horrified by her own weakness, by guilt. 'I'd no idea.'

He crouches beside her. 'It's difficult even for us, and we don't know the victims. I'll bring you a cup of tea.'

The offer makes Polly smile, and yet when it comes she is grateful for the drink's heat, and the two plain sugared biscuits. DC Singh watches her anxiously.

'What can you tell me about Iryna?' he asks, taking out a notebook as another plain-clothes officer comes in.

Little fragments of memory come back to her as she sips: Iryna listening over and over to a CD of Arthur Rubinstein playing Chopin's *Nocturnes*; Iryna peeling potatoes with a knife, not a peeler, because she preferred it; the way she showed all her small, even teeth like a child when she smiled; her romantic love of deep red roses. Perhaps nobody else would remember these things now. Polly wants to say, 'She was fantastic with my kids. She made my house into a home. She organised us, sorted us, soothed us and kept me company during the worst three years of my life. She was – though I've only just realised it – a friend.' How to sum up these fragments of somebody's presence, their personality, into a whole? What are any of us, deprived of those who truly know and love us?

'She was an old-fashioned small-town girl,' Polly says at last. 'No pop music or short skirts, and church every Sunday.'

'Which one?'

248

'I think the Greek Orthodox one nearest to me. Or maybe it is Russian.'

'Did she work for anyone else besides you?'

'Yes. She went out in the evening, and sometimes in the mornings. I wrote her a reference, to say she was honest and hard-working. I – I don't know where she went – cleaning jobs. I found a box of matches in her room, from a pub, I think that was one place. I've been meaning to go there, too. You see, I thought she might have taken my engagement ring.'

'I see. Did you report this?'

'No. I didn't want to get her into trouble.'

Polly can see that DC Singh thinks she's a fool. To him, life is black and white, innocent or guilty. Trouble has come to Iryna, and maybe Polly's liberal uncertainties have been the cause.

'Any boyfriends?'

She tells the policemen about Gheorghe, and gives them his mobile number. 'I don't think he knows any more than I do, because he's been looking for her, too. He came to my house to ask if I'd seen her.'

She can see the detectives exchange glances.

'We'll need to take a DNA sample from him.'

'Why? Gheorghe wasn't my burglar, I assure you. I saw the man's face.'

'No. There are other reasons.'

The detectives say nothing, poker-faced, but she wonders whether Iryna had fought her killer, maybe got traces of his blood or skin under her nails. Iryna had been strong from all the housework; she smelt of sweat. She wasn't the kind of person who would have gone meekly; she was smart and determined, she had borrowed money to come to Britain, and had told Polly that she had paid it all off from her wages. Polly looks down at the corpse, wondering how she died. There is a degree of bruising to her face, still visible.

'Where did you find her body? I'll find out, you know.'

'On Hampstead Heath, in one of the Ponds.'

So Iryna was drowned, Polly thinks; or perhaps attacked near there.

'Oh, poor, silly cow, why didn't she tell me if she was in trouble? Did she think I'd turn her out into the street?' Polly pauses. Maybe that was exactly what Iryna had thought. 'Well, I don't believe Gheorghe killed her. They were engaged, according to him.'

'If he's innocent, he won't have anything to worry about,' one of the detectives says. 'Can you think of a reason why she might be on Hampstead Heath?'

'No.'

The implications of the questioning frighten Polly, and she wonders whether she should ring up her firm and ask for a lawyer to represent her. She hasn't been cautioned yet, but she knows how dangerous these informal interviews can be.

'Did you have any issues with her? Any arguments or difficulties?'

'No. I did ask her not to burn candles in her room on Sundays, in case she'd start a fire.'

'But you think she was stealing from you.'

'Not now!' Polly looks at DC Singh anxiously. 'We all liked her, I just couldn't believe she was a thief, that's the point. But she was amazed, I think, that we just had so much. That I could give her things like decent food, and her own TV. Her family had never had a private bathroom. Oh God, they don't know either, do they?'

'We would appreciate any contacts for her,' says DC Singh.

'I don't have their address, but I do have a couple of letters for her, if you can get them translated,' says Polly. 'She said she'd been with another family but they treated her badly, so I never asked for a reference. I just trusted her.'

Trust, she thinks bitterly. Maybe Iryna had trusted her killer, too. Every day, everyone in the world takes decisions to trust people they don't know: trusting those who prepare your food or deliver your mail, trusting those who drive their cars or aeroplanes, trusting the stranger at the door, the politician in the seat, the doctor in the surgery. Everyone lives on trust, but on what can that be based, now that the chances of knowing where someone has come from, or whether they share the same values, are so much less? Yet she had been right to trust Iryna. Her instinct hadn't been at fault, even if her ring is still missing. The sour taste that has tainted her life recently is replaced by guilt. She has still let danger into her family's life, somehow, and she has failed someone who, unnoticed and unthanked, had been essential – she has failed Iryna.

There are forms and more forms to sign, and it takes hours. Iryna's surname, mobile number, birthday, place of origin. Everything Polly can remember is written down, repeated, cross-checked, and she has to cancel two meetings. She wonders whether she will be reported to Immigration. The house will need more SOCOs all over it, and she and the children will have to make statements and give fingerprints and DNA samples.

'Do you think it's a coincidence?' she asks Bill, later that night. His image on the webcam looks uncomfortable. 'Her murder, and my burglary?'

'It wouldn't be, in a film script.'

He sounds distant. Polly looks anxiously at his face. It's late afternoon where he is, but she is ready for bed. Her big, chilly, lonely bed, she thinks. That's what she misses most in her life as a divorcee, just the kindly warmth of another body beside her.

'It's just that who on earth would want to kill a poor girl like Iryna?'

'You said she'd stolen your ring. Maybe she stole from someone else.'

'No, that doesn't make sense. There has to be a *reason*.'

'Polly, who knows where these people come from? You took this girl off the streets, and you're surprised when she turns out to be mixed up in something bad? You should get yourself a lawyer.'

'Bill, I *am* a lawyer.'

'You should know that you can't trust the law, then. It could turn nasty. Keep me posted.'

Polly stares at his face, and the vague, jerky image of the room behind him just before the webcam clicks off. Over his shoulder she can see an impossibly cerulean sky and, just for an instant, the outline of a woman's bare brown arm, before the screen goes blank. He was calling from his office, she thinks; it's his secretary. Yet deep inside her a worm of uncertainty starts coiling.

She has never understood what Bill sees in her. She isn't pretty or successful; she isn't even a partner at her firm. All along, she has been careful not to fall in love with him but it's hard not to. Bill makes her laugh; he has the kind of melancholy wit, as evanescent as it is apparently effortless, that makes small Jewish men irresistible to women. Their relationship has survived transatlantic crossings and recrossings; he had saved her from too much anguish after Theo left her for his new partner, and she in turn had rescued him from a mid-life crisis of his own. But Iryna's death and Polly's burglary has thrown up a void between them. She wants him here, now, and he can't or won't come.

The empty room overhead haunts Polly. She goes up to it that night. Its forlorn, tatty walls are a reproach. Perhaps it was never as nice as she thought, or perhaps it is the guilt about all that she has failed to do. Outside, rain falls in cold orange drops, out of darkness and into darkness, with a crackling, rending sound. Polly looks out at the streaming street, now a black river where cars are moored, at the council estate where Job lives, rising above the roof-line like an ocean liner ploughing its way through unknown seas, and thinks of all the desolate places of the city, of the comfortless strangers clinging to their existence. I can't help you, she thinks; I can barely help myself.

On the way out she sees Iryna's self-portrait on the door. Suddenly furious, she rips it down. It's only when her eyes clear that she sees something has been stuck underneath.

31

Job's Promise

There are a number of things on Job's conscience, but none weighs quite as heavily as his promise to Anna. He hasn't had enough money to go back, which is one excuse; but now he does because a week after going to the brothel he decided to stop sending the fifty pounds a month to Munisha that he had previously been doing.

There has been no word from his wife or sister for six months, and he is afraid they are either dead or in prison. Hundreds of thousands of people are now starving in his homeland, where shelves are bare and people walk around with bags of cash in the vain attempt to buy food. Even those who still have homes have to hunt for water in wells poisoned by arsenic, according to the BBC World Service (which he can hardly bear to listen to, it makes him so angry and sad). Four million have emigrated, and yet here they are refused asylum, even if they have, like Job, been tortured. And still the people do not rise up against their oppressor, and still Job himself does nothing. Each time he passes the Chinese Embassy, with its bowed figure of a silent protester drawing attention to the persecution of the Falun Gong sect, he feels ashamed.

Look at them, Job thinks. They have the courage that I lack. I am young and strong and I have not even joined the protesters outside the Zimbabwean Embassy on the Strand.

Fear has been hollowing Job out from inside ever since the events at the Wisdens' farm. He thinks how Nicholas Nickleby would have behaved, and in his nightmares Anna's extreme youth melts into that of Beth Wisden, staggering out of the barn, her legs as wobbly as a colt's on the day when the farmhouse boomed with flies, those huge black flies of Africa that cluster on the living as well as the dead, like evil spirits, when disaster strikes.

'What's your favourite line of Shakespeare?' Munisha asked Job once, when they lay in each other's arms.

'*She lov'd me for the dangers I had passed,/And I loved her that she did pity them,*' he said.

'Ah, *Othello*.'

'And yours?'

'The one about marriage. An *ever-fixèd-mark/That looks on tempests and is never shaken.*'

Job thinks of Munisha, and just for a moment he can see her, sharp as the acacia thorns rimmed with light at sunrise. She is wearing her nurse's uniform, and that gentle smiling expression of complete trust and love on her face. Then she's lost again.

In the back seat, Polly too is talking about constancy in love. Perhaps this is what draws them to each other as friends.

'It's an ideal, isn't it?' says Polly. 'We all know what love should be like, we can write the prescription but it never really comes true. Or it hasn't in my case.'

'Perhaps it's only by longing for the impossible that people get closer to it,' Job says.

'You mean, even if you fail you get further than you would if you hadn't had that ideal? Yes,' says Polly, sighing. 'I mean, I know that to other people, to my friends even, what I do is incomprehensible to the point of idiocy. What difference do I really make? Even when I win cases, it can sometimes seem just one tiny thing. But to that one person, or their family, it's enormous.'

'It is a good thing that you do, madam.'

'Oh, I hope so. I try. You know, that sounds awfully dull, doesn't it? Yet the older I get, the more I see how not only is goodness the hardest thing, it's the *only* thing.'

She sounds close to tears, and falls silent. The things which make people in this rich, fertile, lucky country feel miserable are paltry, although they complain about their Prime Minister, their taxes, their schools, their kids, their weather. At times, hearing them, Job wants to turn round and shout, 'Look, you have water! You have food! You have laws! You have those great expectations that were once only a dream in the head of Charles Dickens!'

But pain is pain. It can't be weighed and measured, exchanged or compared. The man sobbing in his back seat because his wife has left him, the couple returning childless from the fertility hospital, the boy who, like Robbie, is afraid of failing at school may not be starving and homeless but they are still tormented.

'It isn't so bad, you know, to fail an examination,' Job tells Robbie. 'There will be others.'

'Yes, but if I don't pass then I don't get into where they want me to go next,' Robbie sobs. 'It's so easy to fail, that's what Dad says, and then your life is horrible. I have to keep passing, or they'll think I'm stupid and useless.'

'A mother never thinks that of her children.' Job thinks of his own mother, and what he knows instinctively of Polly. 'She always hopes. She always believes. She always loves.'

'You're such a kind man,' Robbie says. 'I'm sure you'd never let anyone down.'

Job's soul, which has become as dried up as a nut without its shell, stirs within him.

Robbie's round, trusting eyes, their lashes spiked with tears, gaze up at him as he drives. 'You're worried about something, too, aren't you?'

255

'I am, yes. I have made a promise, which I haven't kept.'

'That is bad. Is it too late to keep it?'

'Maybe not. But if I keep it, it may be dangerous for me. I'm not sure that I can be brave enough.'

'I think you're brave,' Robbie says. 'I think you're like the Lion King.'

'Thank you,' Job says. He has no idea what Robbie is talking about, but remembers the old-fashioned traditional courtship phrase he had used when he first talked to Munisha: *If you love me, I will touch a lion.*

I can't touch a lion for her, he thinks, but I can help another woman.

The British police are different from the ones in Zimbabwe; they don't take bribes, or carry guns, but they will deport Job. He can't walk into a police station and tell them about the brothel because he can't risk drawing attention to himself. He does try the obvious, how-ever. When he calls from a public telephone (one of the few still working, though it stinks of urine and has had most of its glass smashed) and gets put through to the Kilburn police station, the bored voice on the other end asks if he visited Poshlust as a client.

'Yes – yes, I did. I wanted a massage,' Job says, blushing. 'But the girl I was given was almost a child, and she said she was a prisoner.'

'And did the young lady in question solicit you, sir?'

Job becomes so confused, angry and embarrassed that he rings off. He has given the police the name and address of the brothel, and maybe that will be enough. He knows, though, that the England that he had seen in books is long gone. There are no neat, smiling chil-dren like those in the Ladybird books; there are no Cheeryble Brothers or disguised dukes to save what is good and gentle and help-less. When he drives round the statue of St George and the dragon outside Lords in St John's Wood, he feels a kind of fury. *Cry God for Harry, England and St George!* Yesterday, on the way home, he passed a scene outside a supermarket in Camden Town where a gang of boys were beating each other up so badly that one was dragged under a bus. It is the kind of scene that had become all too familiar back home, but one he had never expected to see in England. Keep your head down, don't say anything, don't draw attention to yourself – the rules are not so different here from those in Zimbabwe.

Only, he won't.

'Have you had good news? You seem happier, Job,' Polly says, paying him for the week. She invites him into the kitchen now and gives him a mug of tea, as if they were equals.

'I have come to a decision about something that I must do.'

'Are you going to go back?'

'Back? No!' He's startled she should think this. 'If I had the money, I would go to South Africa, to Johannesburg. That is where my wife wanted to go, and where I pray she may have found her way. No, this is another problem.'

'Can I help?'

'No, madam. Thank you. It is a private matter.'

Job has lost some of the strength he had in his upper body, so each morning and evening he works himself into a dripping sweat by lifting his own weight again and again. The parallels between press-ups and sex strike him as grimly amusing, but he thinks too of the men at the minicab firm doing their prayers. Oh God, he says, if you have not forgotten me, if you have not become deaf as a punishment for my crime, help me.

There is no answer in his heart. Once he had prayed all the time, in the certainty of being heard and loved; he had felt that God was always there, in the immense skies, dispensing justice.

'Sokwanele,' he whispers to himself; 'sokwanele, Anna.'

Slowly, Job's will and body harden. He knows that Sergei is dangerous, with his temper and his knife and his cruelty. In a fight they would be evenly matched. Job hopes it won't come to that, hopes that he isn't being a fool by not arming himself with a knife of his own. Nevertheless, there are preparations he can make, and he makes them. From an old army-surplus store he buys a Kevlar jacket to wear under his shirt. Whenever he is near Kilburn, he cruises down its long, long high street and spies out the territory. Always crawling with traffic, it's patrolled by traffic wardens like every other street in the city. Job wants to laugh at the irony: the one crime for which all Londoners are sure to get caught and punished is that of illegal parking. All the drivers at Ace Minicabs have got tickets, and it makes Mo go absolutely ballistic even though there is often no choice. Leave your engine off for one minute, and some man or woman in a green jacket and peaked cap will descend.

'If there were as many policemen as there are traffic wardens, patrolling the streets and turning a blind eye to everything but a car overstaying its meter or occupying a residents' parking bay, then London would be the safest city in the world,' Job says in one of the many ongoing conversations at the car wash.

'True. They are the only Nigerians who never take a bribe,' Michael says.

It will be easier on a Sunday, Job decides, for that is the one day when you can park almost anywhere in the city with impunity. It is also the day he can be most certain of having free, because in addition to his other two jobs he has started to teach Tariq's two younger sons.

Job has never before realised how lucky he and his sister had been to have the little library that the Wisdens had let him look at, the battered copies of *Our Island Story*, *The Famous Five* and *Rupert the Bear*. Those stories, with their innocence and patriotic enthusiasm, had probably once belonged to Mrs Wisden, but they had been what got him reading in a country where a school library was often a single shelf in a place without walls. That love had been the great bond between himself and Beth, to her parents' growing unease. But Amir and Chandra live in a house devoid of books. There is the big new TV set, permanently tuned to al-Jazeera, and the DVDs and Playstation, but nothing printed – except a magazine called the *Rambler*.

'Who reads this?' he asks the boys. Chandra shrugs.

'It's Selim's. It's very boring. No pictures, just cartoons.'

'Would you like books with pictures?'

'Yes, as long as they're not baby ones.'

There is a public library not too far away, but Job can't get a library card of his own because he can't produce any proof of identity. The boys could get cards, but Tariq says he doesn't want his sons going out alone.

'There is too much traffic,' he tells Job. So Job has bought one or two books for them from a stall near Camden Lock, including one that Amir likes, about dinosaurs at a disco. It's for six-year-olds, probably, but not too insulting for someone of nearly thirteen.

'Selim liked books, but he got rid of them,' Amir says.

'Why did he do that?'

The boys shrug. 'Maybe he thought they were *haram*.'

Selim is someone Job has seen occasionally at the minicab firm, where Tariq's eldest son moonlights. He's a slim young man, clean-shaven and solemn, who doesn't speak to any of the other drivers. They are respectful towards him because he is said to be a scholar; something Job finds mildly puzzling because Tariq has mentioned that he had to leave school. Selim never visits when Tariq is there, but once or twice Job has been aware that the boy is present with Tariq's wife during his lessons. He suspects that Selim is anxious about Job's presence in the house, and wishes that he could reassure him. But, he thinks, how can I call myself an honourable man when I so nearly did a dishonourable thing? I will never be free of my sin until I have atoned for it.

Job circles a block, looking for a place to park on Kilburn High Street. There are shops selling Asian and African food, alongside expensive pizza places; there is a Primark, where women rootle for three-pound shirts brought to them from the sweatshops of Bangladesh and Manchester, and a handsome theatre opposite a boarded-up row of shops. He had noticed none of this the first time he'd visited the brothel, because he had been too excited. He remembers how rich even this street would have seemed to him when he'd first arrived two years ago, and how staggering the sheer quantity of food everywhere was after he'd spent weeks hunting for salt, sugar or cooking oil back in Zimbabwe. Job still can't believe that there are people who throw half-eaten burgers down on the pavement, or that supermarkets and restaurants even give away food at the end of the day. He hoards tins and packets in his tiny room because of the fear that food might disappear.

But this is about another hunger. Once again, he steps on the doormat to the massage parlour and hears a bell shrilling overhead.

Job takes a deep breath, and walks up the steps to the next obstacle, the glass door at the top. Behind it he can see the woman he had seen before, yawning under her blonde bob at the reception desk. She scrutinises his face, then buzzes him into the small lobby. All is as it was, with the same pornographic DVD playing out its grunts and gasps in the room beyond. Job averts his gaze, for what matters more is that there are no other men in the room. Sergei is missing. It is not yet midday, and the brothel has a somnolent air to it.

'I'm looking for a girl,' says Job, as he did before.

'Full-body massage, half an hour, fifty—'

'I know. I've been here. I want the same girl. She was very good.'

'All our girls are good,' says the woman automatically. Her skin is bright orange, and she has long bony nails like those of a witch, painted maroon.

'I want this girl,' Job insists.

'Do you know her name?'

'Anna.'

The blonde woman shrugs. 'Try a different girl.'

She presses a buzzer, and after a pause two other girls appear, snuffling miserably. Job barely glances at them. He can only save one.

'No. Nobody else.'

'Anna, she is busy.'

'Then I will wait. I have the money, but it is just for Anna.'

Job can tell this is not to the woman's liking. Perhaps Anna is with another client. The blonde flicks the pages of her magazine irritably, waiting for him to become impatient. Job sits stolidly on the leatherette seats. The luck of finding Sergei absent is giving him confidence. He keeps an eye on the video-entryphone screen, checking that nobody else comes.

'Anna is not here,' the woman says sulkily, at last. Job lets his eyes widen, a caricature of disappointment.

'She has left your business?'

'No. She is at the other place.'

'Then that is where I must go. What is the address?'

Job knows he is behaving oddly enough to make the woman suspicious, so he gives her a broad, innocent grin. A flicker of contempt crosses her bored face.

'She is at Agar Grove,' Lena says, giving him the house number. 'Flat C, in the basement.'

So close, Job thinks, as he drives through Camden Town. It is packed with the young of all countries, with wild, stiff dyed hair, multiple piercings, tattoos, studded boots and T-shirts, dressed up like children at a party. There is an air of frenzy, though the shoppers move lethargically. The smell of marijuana drifts through his window. The last time Job walked here, he was offered five different drugs in as many minutes. Why did they want to escape from their lives when they had so much?

But this is the world he must live in, however alien it is. He has to be patient. English people can't know or imagine what it's like to go to a market which consists of a few people putting out five tomatoes or a husk of corn on a cloth, where a butcher's is a corrugated metal roof on poles, with one carcass of a dairy cow turning green in the heat – any more than they can imagine what it is like to be Job, ringing on the door of the flat in Agar Grove and getting ready when it opens to fight for Anna's life, and his own.

32

The Taste of Freedom

The brothel is quiet on a Sunday morning. The constant buzz of the intercom that punctures Saturday nights has stopped, and there are only ordinary noises of traffic and water gurgling in the pipes from the flats overhead. Anna wakes from a brief, deep sleep. At this time of day she is able to have an hour of precious solitude, assuming Dmitri or Sergei have not decided to spend the night with her. They take it in turns at the flat, and the massage parlour, though what they do when they are away is a mystery. Lena has hinted that they do other work, for important people, involving favours and perhaps threats. Some of their time, obviously, is spent scoring drugs: cocaine for themselves, heroin and dope for the girls. Sometimes she smokes the dope. They have to think she's docile; and marijuana does help her stay detached from the thing she does, or has done to her.

The men, of course, don't notice the tracks up Cristina's arms or the glazed look in her eyes, any more than they stop to notice that Anna's figure is still that of a very young teenager. They think Anna is a lucky find, a piece of class.

'You could be a model' is something they tell her admiringly when she undresses. One of them has told her, as if justifying his actions,

'It's like going to Tesco's for me, luv. Seeing a working girl like you sets me up for the week. It means the wife doesn't get bothered, the family stays together, everybody's happy.'

Sometimes Sergei has taken her to private houses. Now that she has been working for him for a couple of months he thinks she can be useful for more expensive jobs – stag parties, or businessmen in hotels who know nothing of the squalor from which she comes. As long as she wears certain kinds of clothes, she looks as clean as a piece of fruit picked for a supermarket. Often, when Anna is driven to a job like this, passing English houses with their pristine plaster-work and fresh paint, she wonders whether she is in a separate world parallel to innocence and kindness or whether it's all sham. However they are dressed, there are still the drunks; the gross middle-aged men who grunt and sob and squirt uncontrollably into her mouth; the disabled ones, too misshapen or repulsive ever to find a normal woman; the bored husbands looking to spice up their marriage; the ones who just want to talk and cry. But for the past week in Agar Grove, there have also been four brown-skinned teenagers. They come in together, as a group, and night after night take turns with her and Cristina.

'Hey, Anna,' says Cristina. When the brothers are out and they are locked in the flat together, she is almost friendly. The weeks have improved Anna's English so that she is able to follow most of what is said on TV, and Cristina speaks good English, though her accent is thick, like soup made from potatoes. Galina still coughs dismally from the bed in the basement.

'Stupid bitch,' Cristina says. 'Maybe they get rid of her.'

'How?'

Cristina draws a finger across her throat.

'They kill us?'

'You want to find out?'

Anna shakes her head. She, too, is irritated by Galina, who begs for her sister in a tiresome way.

'Those Arabs, you think it was their first time?' Cristina asks.

'Were they Arabs?'

Anna is watching another food programme. Her stomach is knotted with hunger, and her teeth are feeling loose in their gums.

'I heard them say *Allah.*' Cristina snickers. 'Such thin, hairy legs!'

Anna tries not to notice, but she is a little curious too. The teenagers are nervous and exuberant, which makes a change. Maybe they have dared each other to do it together, she thinks. There is something odd about the way they look at her, something different from the usual glazed oxlike stare of other men. They all wear the same puffy jackets and round woollen hats, and they smell of oil and spices and alcohol, and are very clean. Two of them wait outside the bedroom, waiting for the first two to finish, and then they change over. They look disgusted, contemptuous and yet also ecstatic.

Every time, they bring a bottle of alcohol, which they pass around as if it were communion wine. Anna can taste the sour spirit on their tongues, and she doesn't think they are any more used to it than she is. It's visky, the stuff Sergei and Dmitri like.

'You like this?' she asks the one who wears glasses.

'Oh, yes!'

'You haven't been with a girl before?'

He giggles and squirms. 'Soon, I will be with seventy-two virgins.'

How many others are there like her in this city? How many more Annas, Cristinas, Galinas and Dritas? She thinks of those girls she travelled with in the lorry: all of them, she is now sure, enduring a fate similar to her own. She can well believe there are seventy-two virgins, stupidly trusting.

'You like visky?'

The boy makes a face. 'Not so much.'

'Will you leave some for me?'

The bottle is only a quarter full. He nods.

When he's gone, Anna thinks for a while. She can hardly believe that the plan forming in her head will work, but for a long time she has been thinking how to use the pills she has been collecting. Neither Sergei nor Dmitri ever drinks tea, or takes any food with the girls. This is a chance that will not come again. Quickly, before she can get too frightened, she takes the pills and pounds them up with the bottle. When she finishes, she opens the cloth to see a fine chalky powder, enough to fill a spoon. It's a surprisingly small amount.

What it will do to someone of Dmitri's size, she can't guess. Some of the pills may be contraceptives, but she knows that some are tranquillisers. Anna tips the powder into the visky.

The powder turns brown and forms a faint sludge on the bottom of the bottle. Anxiously, she shakes it up and down. The sludge swirls, its tiny specks reminding her of the shower of illuminated dust motes she had seen on her first day in England. Then it dissolves. Will the brothers taste anything different? Anna puts a drop on her finger and licks it, wrinkling her nose. It is as acrid as ever, but maybe there is something else beneath the burning amber that might be the taste of freedom. Her empty stomach churns.

How long will it take to work? She has no idea. All she can do is hope and pray, not to God but to the spirit of her granny: Help me succeed in this one thing. She has her bag, the one she brought all the way from Lutsk, but she might not be able to take that. What I need, Anna tells herself, are my shoes and my money. Her clothes are not respectable but she is less worried by that, having seen on TV the way British teenagers dress. All that matters is that she tries.

She goes into the reception room. Dmitri is sitting on a black sofa, watching a film. It's a romance, about two doomed lovers on a big ship, and very boring, although Cristina watches it open-mouthed. She must have been given some stuff, Anna realises. Dmitri is looking even more surly than usual. Maybe he's out of the white powder he calls *koks*.

Anna moves over to him very slowly. She has never been so conscious of this abominable place, with its grey filmy curtains and its pattern of spiders on the walls.

'You take too long,' Dmitri says. 'What are you doing to yourself?' He snickers.

265

'I needed to clean up.' Anna dumps the bottle down. 'He left this.'

Dmitri's small dark eyes rest on it broodingly. 'Those *chyornozhopa*, they drink like crazy men when nobody is looking. Fucking assholes, all of them.'

Anna shrugs. She doesn't want to look as if she cares one way or the other.

'Why are you wearing those things on your feet?' he demands, spotting her trainers. 'Wear shoes that make you look like real woman.'

'My feet are cold.'

'I can soon warm them up for you.'

Dmitri leers. Anna picks up the bottle, and waves it in front of his nose.

'Maybe I need some visky.'

'You think I'd waste any on you?'

'It's mine. He left it for me.'

She knows that this is what will make him want to take it away from her, and he does. His big, dark hand shoots out and wrenches it from her unresisting fingers. In a moment he has the top unscrewed and is swigging it from the bottle.

'Pah! Trust an Arab to buy fucking rats' piss!'

Downstairs, Galina coughs. Maybe she'll die in that barred room, Anna thinks; maybe we all will. The downstairs rooms always make her shiver. From the front she can see people in the street, just the portion between the top of the wall and the top of the window, as they walk past but they never look down any more than they look up. They are always in such a hurry.

Dmitri has drunk half the remaining whisky. He is about to take another swig when the buzzer goes.

'Shit.'

Dmitri goes over to the door and unlocks it but keeps it on the chain. He speaks a few words, as always, to the man outside, then slides the chain off and turns.

'Take your pick.'

266

The man enters, and Anna sees his face: Job.

He looks at her, and she struggles to keep her face immobile. Why has he come back? It's been weeks and weeks since she realised he had tricked her. She glowers at him.

'That one,' he says, and hands over the money. Dmitri counts it out with insolent slowness.

'Half an hour. Enjoy.'

Job staggers slightly and rights himself against Dmitri, who flicks him off. When Anna looks back, Dmitri is still swigging from the bottle. Job follows Anna down the corridor to the bedroom.

'You remember me?' he asks, when they are alone.

'Last time you weren't drunk.'

Anna is stripping off her top, contemptuously, but Job stops her.

'No, I don't want that, my sister. I swear by Jesus Christ, I've come to help you.'

At once she is frightened. What will his 'help' entail? Is he a lunatic? Cristina has told her that they get religious maniacs from time to time.

'How can you help me?'

'How many men are there in here?'

Anna looks at him mistrustfully, but makes up her mind.

'Just Dmitri, but his brother is close.'

'You still want to leave this place?'

Anna looks at Job for a long time. He is a fool, she sees: one of those men who think that women need rescuing. She nods.

'What do you need?'

'Money. I need money, and somewhere to go.'

'You'll go back to your country?'

'I don't know.'

Why does he want to know? She doesn't trust him – or any man.

'I have some money. Here.'

He gives her a hundred pounds. Anna counts the notes warily, then stuffs them down her bra.

'If I get out, where will I go?'

'With me. You can come with me,' Job says. 'My car is outside, unlocked. I'll distract him.'

'OK.'

Job's plan is very simple. He will stay inside the bedroom while Anna goes out and hides in the toilet along the corridor. Then, when he begins to thump on the bedroom door and make a noise to bring Dmitri, Anna can get out.

'He won't let me just leave the flat,' Anna says. If it were that easy, she would have done it weeks ago. Yet this flat, unlike the massage parlour, is on the ground floor and for its guard has just Dmitri, who may already be drugged. 'Besides, he locks the door.'

Job hands over a key. 'With this? I took it from him just now.'

She takes the key, amazed. 'What will you tell him?'

'That you tricked me. Do you have everything you need?'

She'd like her passport back, and she'd like more money, and she'd like to be the person she used to be. But none of these options are possible, so she slips out to the toilet. Behind her, Job wedges the bedroom door shut and begins hammering on it. Moments later, Dmitri has lumbered to his feet and come to see what the matter is. The two men begin an argument, shouting at each other through the jammed door.

Anna takes a deep breath. Job and Dmitri make such a noise that she is able to walk past Cristina to the main door of the flat, insert the key, turn it, run along the hall and open the front door. She has been out of the flat before, but never alone, never without one or other of the pimps keeping a tight grip on her. A blast of chill air swirls in. Anna looks out at the street, at Job's car waiting for her, at freedom. She has only seconds to make a run for it before Dmitri breaks down the bedroom door and comes after her.

She hesitates. Then, leaving the front door open, Anna turns and runs back, up the stairs.

33

Keeping On Keeping On

Ian can't cycle with his arm in a cast, which means that, instead of the joyous feeling of freedom while he cycles across Hampstead Heath, the beginning and end of his working day now consist of using the Underground. This is a very different matter.

The charred, cindery smell, the growing sensation of being buried alive as the lift sinks, the dim-lit platforms where people wait in silence for that blast of hot, foul air which sends mice on the tracks scurrying for safety is like a presentiment of disaster. Once on the train, it gets worse. No wonder people call it the Tube! It's like being reduced to toothpaste. Ian has always thought of himself as someone who likes other people or is prepared at least to give them the bene-fit of the doubt, but this city has changed that.

When he has looked down on London from Hampstead Heath, he has always seen it as veiled in translucent layers of history, mysterious and beautiful as a great queen. Now, close up, it has become a mon-strous body, violently active, with people swarming all over it like ants. Once on the Tube, people are locked in silent suffering, compressed into an essence of pure resistance and will. Perhaps what gives the city its energy is that its citizens are overcrowded to the point of madness.

During his sick leave, the Samuel Smiles seems to have deteriorated even further, and the talk of Special Measures has now shifted to the possibility that the school might even be closed down. The morale of both staff and pupils is terrible. Ian is always reading about the millions or billions being poured into education, but it seems to have made no difference to his own life. Just like the Royal Free Hospital, the place is run down. There are still hardly any books in the library, the meals are foul and the pupils are appallingly badly behaved. Sally is still being subjected to what Ian has learnt is called 'terroring'; in his absence, she is regularly pinned against the corridor wall by big Year 11s and assaulted. The Senior Management Team accused her of poor behaviour management when she complained. Ian's desk has been kicked in, and the small bribes he kept – like chocolate and gel pens – for the better behaved have been stolen. As ever, half the class arrives without a pen, which means he must keep a supply of pencils rather than pens (which will be taken to pieces and flicked at other pupils). These are always returned to him in a dreadful condition.

'Just sharpen them before you give them back,' he says. But they have no sharpeners, preferring to keep the blades as weapons.

There are one or two teachers trying to do more than stick it out until they collect a pension, but the majority can't even be bothered to fight for the photocopier. There is still no head teacher, because nobody wants to accept responsibility for the budget; half the teachers are on sick leave, even though Year 11 soon need to sit their GCSEs. The expectation is that few will even get passable grades in the core subjects of English, maths and science. Ian eyes the sixth form enviously; there are some boys who stay on, who make it through the system, but he never comes into contact with them as a teacher.

'It's unbelievable,' Sally says. 'Each time they get a good kid, their future gets screwed up. You know Amir, the boy in your year? He had an elder brother who was the smartest pupil they'd ever had in science. He had an offer from Imperial, and one from King's, and he never took up either.'

270

'Why not?'

'Because some of the other kids got to him, and he had to join some gang, which led to him getting into drugs. His parents took him out of the system and sent him back to Pakistan to get clean. The poor boy had some sort of breakdown, never took his A levels and now he's just a minicab driver like his father. And meanwhile the kids who bullied him stayed on because the school couldn't expel them, because they can't risk falling foul of the social exclusion business.'

Sally almost relishes these grim tales. She's probably venting her anger in a blog, Ian thinks. He wonders how long it'll be before she leaves.

Ian ponders again the fact that he doesn't need to be fully qualified to teach in a private school; as a graduate with an NQA he could switch, pretty much within a term, and go to one of those swanky-looking schools that he used to cycle past, schools where the budgets are devoted to building ever-better sports facilities or theatres or even to sponsoring scholarships; schools where at least some of the pupils may want to learn, and have parents who understand the importance of passing exams, and of manners.

Most of the ones he has now can't see the point in reading anything, even a newspaper. Why bother, when it's on TV? The liveliest are the Bangladeshi kids, who watch melodramatic Indian films, and sing the same songs. But the quiet ones, like Amir, are just as sad. He watches the boy, who is drawing more cartoons. His latest doodles are all of kneeling blindfolded men, some of them with gouts of blood exploding from their severed necks. He looks exhausted; maybe he's staying up late to watch horror movies.

'Look,' Ian tells them, and hands them a piece that Quentin has written. He is teaching a section on the media, something which has gone better than expected because he had photocopied pages of a book by Philip Pullman called *I Was A Rat*, satirising tabloid reporting. It's technically for six-to-eight-year-olds, but clever enough to amuse older readers, he hopes; at least his class aren't

271

openly rebellious. 'This is what my father edits.' They're more interested in his father being a journalist than they are in debating what Quentin has said about the dumbing-down of the nation. Ian plugs away. Keeping on keeping on is perhaps the single quality teachers most need, he thinks. Perhaps it's true for every profession: that virtue of doggedness which, long after the initial flash and dazzle of brilliance inspired you to turn up to do the job, means that you won't give up.

'Is he famous, then, your dad?' one of them asks.

'Not really. He just edits this magazine called the *Rambler*. Has anyone heard of it?'

To Ian's surprise, Amir puts his hand up.

'Really? That's great!'

Ian uses this as a way to tell his class a little about Dr Johnson and the early days of Fleet Street. He has prepared this lesson well, spicing it up with jokes and anecdotes, racking his brains for stories about journalism, before setting them their next piece of homework – bringing in different newspapers for the next lesson. For the first time he starts to enjoy himself, and gets the feeling that without him these kids might not be getting an education. His extra efforts and his increasing experience help him to make progress, even if it feels like pedalling up the steepest hill.

'I just want them to learn,' Ian says to Candice, at the weekend. They've gone for lunch at an Italian pizza chain in Highgate. Up on a hill east of Hampstead, it's perched between two or three of the kind of schools she wants him to apply to. The faces around them are all white, middle-class, contented, and remote from the desolate council estates with their wild, anarchic mixture of races, their lawlessness, their feral kids. Candice is right, he should be thinking of where to apply next, he thinks; and this has prompted him to buy the *Times Educational Supplement* for the first time in months and look at the advertisements for vacancies. 'You know, they love stories. If they had any encouragement they could do so much, but all they do outside school is steal.'

'It's the parents,' says Candice. 'If they took away their kids' mobile phones and TV sets they'd get rid of most of the bad behaviour. Sweetie, you can't solve the world's problems.'

He cuts into his pizza, a doubtful expression on his face. 'It's just that I've never experienced a world like this before. If I could make a difference to just one life . . . maybe I'm naive to even think it.'

'But you aren't even going to be *there* in six months' time! We're going to be travelling, remember?' Somehow, Candice has inserted herself into his vision of himself backpacking round Thailand and Cambodia. 'When we're watching the sun set on Phuket, this will all seem like another planet.'

Glancing round the restaurant, Ian notices that it's gone oddly quiet. Six big, tough-looking men, all black and wearing flak jackets, have come in and asked for the manager. Two are hanging around in the corridor, on the other side of the glass partition, blocking the exit, and three have sat down at a table with the manager, who is looking upset.

'Do you think we're in the middle of a hold-up?' Ian murmurs. He can see an array of weapons stuck into the men's belts, including what looks like a gun.

'No, not here, surely?'

'Maybe they're just off-duty security guards who want a pizza.'

They watch as papers are produced. Soon after, the men leave the restaurant.

'What was that about?' Ian asks their waiter.

'They were checking that everyone was legal. I tell them, this is an Italian restaurant, everyone is Italian, but they don't believe me.'

'Are they checking every restaurant?'

'I don't know. Maybe. The cook, he is very upset. He is English, and didn't have the papers to prove it. What is happening, when my customers can be upset for no reason?'

It's obvious: the transport, the schools, the streets, the public parks are crowded to bursting point. Ian's school never knows from one month to the next how many children will turn up speaking no English but demanding an education. Liza has told him about the GP surgery where she's a locum turning away hugely pregnant women because their lists are full. Yet there is no sign of decreasing affluence. On the contrary, people seem to be spending in a frenzy of consumerism. The high streets are packed with shoppers, buying bigger and bigger plasma TVs, smaller and slimmer laptops, skinnier lattes and bigger, more luxurious kitchens in which to eat their pre-prepared meals. A bank has crashed somewhere in the north, but it's far away, and nothing has changed.

Fifteen minutes have transported Ian, as if by magic, from a place where shops have metal grilles on their fronts to the plate-glass hub of wealth. Today, Friday, he has taken the afternoon off in order to go to the *Rambler* lunch and see his father again. He is curious, nervous and excited, less about seeing his father than about the magazine. The weight of history feels as if it's pressing down on his head; all those legendary distinguished men and occasionally women of letters who have written for it: Dickens, George Eliot, Mrs Gaskell, H. G. Wells, Graham Greene, E. M. Forster, Stella Gibbons, Penelope Fitzgerald, T. S. Eliot . . . the list goes on and on. Even if the *Rambler* in its latter days is not quite so august, it still impresses him.

A block away from Oxford Street, the Giant Bread & Cheese has vast Victorian windows etched with loops and swags. Inside, men huddle over their half-pints of warm beer; a fire glows in a grate. A framed series of *Rambler* covers by 'Felix' the cartoonist are the only signs of its literary connections. A grey-haired man polishing beer glasses grunts at him. 'Upstairs. Tell Quentin the Welsh rarebit is off.'

Ian promises to convey this cryptic message, mounts the stairs and enters a broad, bright room. Down the middle is a long table, and crowded around it is a group of people, talking and giggling over a photograph being passed from hand to hand. Nobody greets Ian, and he experiences a moment of sudden shyness as he stands unnoticed, wondering if he's got the right date.

'Hi there,' someone says quietly; and it is only because of her American accent that Ian recognises her.

'Oh, hi. Hi, Katie.' It occurs to him that it would be tactless to mention that he has noticed her improved looks. 'I'm very pleased to see you.'

'I'm as surprised to be invited as you may be to see me here.'

'No, I—' It occurs to him that it would be tactless to mention he had insisted on her being invited. 'I'm very pleased to see you.'

'You look different,' Katie says. 'Your face is healed up. I hadn't realised that—' She stops, and flushes. 'You do look like your father.'

'You look different too,' Ian says. Katie's hair is loose instead of being dragged back viciously into a ponytail. It has a pretty wave, he thinks. No: it's *she* who is pretty.

'Cleans up quite well, doesn't she?' says Quentin, in jocular tones. 'Amazing. Katie, I've put you next to Roger.'

'Oh, great,' Katie mutters.

'What's wrong with him?'

'He's the proprietor, and a bit of a creep.'

'Is that his car outside?'

Ian had noticed a large, shiny chauffeured car waiting, with its engine running, by the kerbside.

'I don't know. It could be Panga's. He's the man over there in the handcrafted suit.'

Panga's handsome head is sleek as a seal's; when he laughs, he displays dazzling white teeth.

'He does the Rich Pickings column.'

'The one that manages to be racist, sexist and reactionary while never offending his friends?'

'That's the one. But it keeps up our A-list readership, apparently.'

Ian does his best to circulate. Quentin, to his surprise, is introducing him to his staff. Cecilia goes into a flirtatious flutter, which he enjoys because she is so ravishing. When she hears he's merely a teacher, however, she turns her back on him abruptly.

'But I expect you write a bit, too, don't you?' says Jocasta, a handsome young woman who is wearing a bright pink jacket. 'Quentin said you're thinking of doing a piece for us.'

Ian smiles and nods politely. Somehow he gets cornered by the *Rambler*'s Political Editor. Crawley's face glows beneath his thinning lank hair like a beacon of anger. He spits his words out with such force that Ian can feel the spray on his own face, and half wonders whether it might contain venom.

'Rubbish!' he keeps saying; 'Dreadful man!' or occasionally, 'Dreadful woman!'

Yet Crawley also has the magnetism of the intensely ambitious. He knows whose nose must not be twisted out of joint, whose ego is in need of massage, whose memory is unforgiving. It's obvious that he hates Quentin, who seems coolly indifferent to him. Ian feels rather proud that his father is so aloof.

'How are you getting along?' Katie has drifted back, Crawley having decided that Ian is of no use to him. 'Everything OK?'

'I think I may have gone deaf in one ear.'

Trench taps his glass with a knife. 'Welcome. Just to remind everyone, we keep Chatham House rules. Nothing said here is to be repeated outside these four walls,' he says. His voice is treacly with self-satisfaction, Ian thinks, looking at the bouffant locks and the wide satiny tie.

'How did he make his pile?' he asks Katie softly.

'Commercial property, I think. He owns half the land around King's Cross – bought it years ago and made a fortune on top of his wife's money. She's some big French heiress.'

Everyone at this lunch strikes Ian as mildly peculiar. There is a tiny, wrinkled actress who is in a current production at the National Theatre; a peer whose claim to fame is that he collects Venetian palaces; a military historian who depicts the invasion of Iraq by means of everybody's bread rolls; an alcoholic who turns out to be an economic adviser to the Treasury; and an Indian novelist of immense distinction and even more immense ego. From time to time a Cabinet Minister answers a question put to him by Crawley, and everyone falls respectfully silent as if before an oracle, hoping for something other than the usual qualified non-committal response. It never comes. ('God what a bore!' Quentin says, as soon as the Minister leaves.)

The room is buzzing with conversations that aren't really conversation but a form of showing-off. Ian smiles until his jaws ache. Is this it, he thinks: the monotony of privation or the tedium of choice?

Katie has turned away to answer a question. Ian is conscious of being more aware of her than of anyone else in the room. He has thought about her surprisingly often recently. But there is something different about her that has nothing to do with her altered and improved appearance. She is actually laughing now, and suddenly, suddenly, Ian understands that she is real to him in a way that nobody else is, that everything that is his true self has become bound up with her. His mouth goes dry, his heart beats hotly – he is utterly confused and yet elated, as if he had been tethered all his life to the earth, and is now soaring vertiginously free.

34

Kept In The Dark

In the dim light of the stairwell, lit by an energy-saving bulb, the thing stuck to Iryna's door is revealed as a plastic and metal chip the size of a large postage stamp. Puzzled, Polly stares at it, Iryna's self-portrait crumpled in her hand. She knows what it is almost at once: a SIM card from a mobile phone, pressed deep into a blob of Blu-tack.

She hadn't asked the detective whether they had found Iryna's mobile, but she is pretty certain that she's looking at her SIM card now. Obviously this has been left deliberately, by Iryna herself. It's a childish hiding place, but also one that has proved surprisingly successful, given that the room has been searched by Polly herself, by the police and, as she now realises, by the unknown intruder on the morning of Iryna's disappearance. (Who else could have made it look as if she'd left?) Iryna would have known that if she did not come back Polly would take down her self-portrait, Polly thinks, and because it was outside her room it somehow didn't register . . . though the man who had attempted to break in clearly thought that Polly must have it. *Give it to me*, he had said. She had thought he meant the frying pan, but he must have been after this.

Whatever is on this chip must be important, therefore. It must hold information that made it worth breaking into her house twice. Polly knows that she ought to tell the police immediately, although they have her au pair's number and have probably traced her calls. There is nothing to stop anyone from buying another SIM card, however, she thinks. Perhaps Iryna had two mobiles, or switched cards around on just the one, or perhaps this chip hadn't belonged to her but to somebody else. So what exactly is on it? If she takes it off, very carefully, with a pair of tweezers to avoid leaving fingerprints, she can have a look, too; and by now Polly is too curious not to find out.

Nearby, the children sleep peacefully in their rooms. Polly hasn't told them yet about the murder. It would upset Robbie deeply, and probably Tania too, although it's so hard to tell what goes on in her daughter's head these days. Polly hopes that they'll go on believing that Iryna, like Mary Poppins, just went when the wind changed.

Guiltily, as if she were committing a crime (which she probably is), Polly goes downstairs. Iryna's card should work in her phone: they are the same make. She switches her mobile on, and the screen lights up with its logo of two grainy hands reaching out and clasping each other, accompanied by five tinny notes. So far, so good. But there is a problem, she sees at once. Iryna's account is protected by a passcode.

'Damn!' says Polly aloud.

'Mum?'

'Go back to bed, Tania.'

'I can't sleep.'

Without her make-up, Tania looks as young and innocent as Polly wishes she did all the time. Fourteen: such a difficult age.

'What are you doing?'

'Trying to get into Iryna's phone. I found her SIM card, and I want to see if it can help me find out where she might have gone. But it's got a passcode.'

'Oh. I know the number.'

'You do?'

'Yes,' Tania says importantly. 'It's 1812, like Tchaikovsky. We used to play games on it.'

Polly taps the silvery pads of her phone, and it works.

The menu board appears. As always, she is bewildered by choice. Does she want messages? That would be a good place to start. She scrolls down the Inbox. There are a number of short, affectionate texts from G, which she guesses are from Gheorghe, and some other messages in a language she guesses must be Russian. The last message, however, is different. It says, in maddening text-speak:

C U 2NITE

Polly checks the date. It was sent on the Saturday of the weekend when Iryna disappeared. She makes a note of the number, not wishing to use the ring-back facility. Now what?

'I wonder what was so important about this?' she says aloud. 'I mean, the police can probably trace who made this call, but there must be something else, some reason why she hid it.'

'Why do you want to know?'

'Iryna wanted me to find this. She hid it under her picture on her door.'

'Maybe it's a picture. Have you looked at her photographs?'

'No.'

Polly is ashamed to say that she isn't altogether sure how to use the mobile's camera. She fiddles with it, and Tania, impatient as ever, takes it out of her hands.

'Look, this is how you do it. Honestly, why are grown-ups so Neanderthal? This is so outdated, you know – you really ought to get a better one.'

A photograph blinks onto the screen. It shows a young girl's smiling face. She has dark hair, and the prim rosebud mouth of a *matryoshka* doll.

'Is that Iryna?' Polly peers over her daughter's shoulder.

'No, stupid, she's much younger. It's her sister.'

'I've seen her before, in a photo,' Polly says. She looks at the girl's pale face, shining up from the screen like a pearl. 'She looks the same age as you.'

'She's sixteen. Iryna missed her. She wanted her to come to London last year but she couldn't get a visa, so Iryna got really depressed about it. I'll just keep pressing this button. That's Gheorghe, that must be her mum, that's – ugh!'

'What?'

Tania silently hands the phone back to her mother. Polly looks at it and recoils, turning the phone over. It shows a naked young woman on her knees, in front of a man. His face is slightly turned away but remains visible, like his penis.

'It could just be a joke.'

'It's *gross*,' Tania says. 'Is it her? Iryna, I mean?'

'I don't know.'

'I think it's either her or her sister.'

They are both transfixed by the image, repelled and fascinated. Polly puts the mobile away.

'Listen, darling, don't tell anyone about this. I'm going to give it to the police.'

Tania looks at her mother.

'Mum, what's happened to Iryna?'

Polly is silent, preoccupied. It can't be a fake, she thinks; it has the queasy ugliness of reality. She wishes with all her heart that her child hadn't seen it; even if such images are far too easily available on the internet, she has tried to shield them from this kind of thing. It is a kind of pollution that has no place in her home and family.

'I'm afraid she's dead, darling. The police found her body, only they didn't know who she was.'

Tania nods, slowly. 'I thought something bad had happened. How did she die?'

'They don't know yet, but it looks like someone killed her.'

'Why?'

'I don't know. I had to identify her body, but I only saw her face. She looked quite peaceful.'

Tania doesn't cry. She has no concept of death, because she has never seen a dead person, any more than Polly had until recently.

'Are we in danger, then? Is that why someone broke in?'

'I don't think so, darling. Anyway, now we have our burglar alarm it's a lot harder for anyone to do that.'

'Don't tell Robbie.'

'Is that why you got the locks changed?'

Yes, Polly says, trying to reassure her, but she's not to tell her father. She's afraid that Theo will find out – he always thinks that everywhere outside America is unsafe, and keeps saying he's going to move back. She thinks again of Bill Shade's proposal. But it isn't a proposal; it's an invitation for her to come and live with him. If she were to ask the children about how they'd like to live in Pacific Palisades, Tania would probably be ecstatic; like all British teenagers, she aspires to going to a Californian high school. The fact that her mother's career would go down the tubes wouldn't count for an instant.

'You know,' Tania says, 'it might not have been Iryna who took that picture. It could have been sent to her by someone. She could have been, like, bullied. We're always being told about that in school.'

'The police will be able to find out. I'm giving this to them tomorrow.'

Carefully, she takes off the back of her handset, removes the SIM card and puts back her own.

'Poor Iryna,' Tania says. 'You know, she was always hiding things. Robbie used to say she'd got a pouch like a marsupial's and she'd stuff things like socks in it when we couldn't find them.'

The image of Iryna tidying away the clutter and detritus of domestic life suddenly rose vividly before Polly's eyes.

'She was a sweet girl. I wish I'd known her better. I used to think I was kind to her, and now I think I must have seemed like a self-obsessed cow.'

'You're not. Well, not completely. We do understand, Robbie and me, about your work being important.'

'Do you? Sometimes I wonder if it is, because the most important thing in my life is you – and I just don't spend enough time with you, do I?'

Tania looks at her gravely. 'Sometimes you don't. I just wish you didn't get so stressed. Iryna didn't.'

To herself, Polly thinks that maybe if Iryna had been a bit more anxious and watchful she might not have been murdered. 'She was such a crucial part of our lives for so many years, and I don't even have any photographs of her.'

Polly has sometimes wondered what her own children would remember about her. After all, it's always she who takes pictures of them, not the other way about; if she appears in photographs, it's as a shadow lying down at their feet before them.

'I do,' Tania says unexpectedly. 'Loads.'

'You do? Where?'

Her daughter sighs impatiently. 'On my laptop. You know you can download photographs onto your computer and send them to people?'

'Er, yes, I think so.'

'I'll find some and send them to you at work.'

'That's lovely, sweetheart,' Polly says, before packing her child off to bed with a brisk kiss. Despite her anxiety, she falls asleep almost at once.

In the morning, Polly telephones the number that DC Singh gave her and tells him about the card – though not that she has looked at it. He promises to come round for it personally, once he's got through some more paperwork. The police, like doctors, are drowning in bureaucracy. Hemani had told her that for every five minutes she spends with a patient she has to spend twenty more on putting useless information into her hospital computer.

'I just wish I knew why she kept that picture on her mobile,' Polly tells Hemani. Still marooned by pregnancy, her friend is grateful for any gossip. 'It's the most revolting photograph.'

'Was it porn? You know, boys send each other clips.'

'What woman would want to keep a photograph of someone doing something like that? No, you know what I think? I think she left the SIM card behind as evidence, as a kind of insurance. Perhaps she knew who the man was, or knew who had sent it. She was always asking me questions about the law. You know, about what a friend of hers could do to get a British passport, or the right to remain. Maybe she was blackmailing someone – possibly the man.'

Hemani says in her pellucid voice, 'That would be a motive for murder in itself, wouldn't it? Did she have email?'

'Not as far as I know. She had so little, really. I gave her an old TV and a nice room with its own bathroom, but it wasn't enough. Proper nannies are paid over twenty thousand pounds a year, for a quarter of the work.'

Hemani laughs sleepily. 'I should think most people would thank their lucky stars to find a home with you, Pol.'

'Oh, I do hope so. I feel so bad about all this. You know how it is, don't you?'

'Yes. I'd work even if we didn't need the money. Otherwise all my struggles to get a degree and my medical training would be pointless. But I can only be a surgeon because of having my mum living close by.'

'That's the rub, isn't it? We need a wife.'

Hemani laughs. Polly wishes she could see more of her; it's ridiculous, they live only a couple of miles apart but like most working mothers they hardly ever get to see each other.

'You know, the best thing about being divorced is that I get every other weekend free while Theo takes the kids. I can work my socks off, like a bloke.'

Polly doesn't really believe this; it's one of those things that divorced parents say to comfort themselves. In reality, she's distressed by the knowledge that Theo's decision to leave her has compromised her children's chances of future happiness and success; furthermore, she knows that, while her income has dwindled, his has probably barely been affected.

'I'm just thanking my stars that I got my consultancy before the present lot,' Hemani says. 'It's hard enough as it is to become a doctor in Britain, and now young medics have to compete with the rest of the world's doctors, too.'

'At least I don't have that problem,' Polly says.

Tania retrieves some photographs from her laptop, as promised, and sends them to her mother with the faintly patronising air that both children now display towards her. Polly has received photographs by email before – people with late babies are the most adept – but seeing her dead au pair's face smiling up at her from her screen at work makes her feel a kind of rage that is partly directed at herself. How could she not have noticed how young Iryna was – barely out of her teens? Her children, themselves younger (Robbie still with some of his baby teeth), smile up out of the past. There they are, sitting on a sofa that has travelled from the old house in Fulham to the new one in Barnsbury; a sofa which she and Theo had chosen over a decade ago from the Conran shop out of a particularly generous cheque for their wedding . . . Iryna looked more like their big sister than their carer, smiling with her arm round first Tania, then Robbie, helping Robbie build something out of Lego, smiling into the sun on a picnic on Hampstead Heath, and then making batter in the kitchen for a birthday cake which in another photograph is transformed into the cake itself, piled high with pink roses.

I never knew her because I never bothered to find out, Polly thinks. She has hunted for details of the girl's passport and home address but found none. She had expected a young woman to step into her shoes and keep everything running irrespective of that young woman's own personality or needs. Shame scalds her.

The lawyerly part of Polly's mind mounts a defence: surely she just hadn't had the time. Men don't suffer from this kind of guilt, so why should she? She knows what Theo would say: the people who cleaned her office, swept her streets, picked her fruit and served her coffee were only too glad to be able to earn a living, and wouldn't reproach her even if it meant they had to live in conditions that no Briton would endure. Yet this was different because of the ancient duty of care which a host owed a guest. Even if Polly had paid Iryna to be there, the girl had been living in her family like someone as anomalous yet necessary as a Victorian governess.

When the police detective turns up again to take possession of the SIM card, sealing it into a transparent plastic evidence bag, Polly shows him the door and the hiding place.

'Thank you, Mrs Noble. I'm quite annoyed that the SOCO officers missed it.'

'I'd be very interested in knowing anything you find out.'

'I have to follow procedure, Mrs Noble.'

Polly knows that this irritating mantra means she'll be kept in the dark, and feels no guilt about having looked at what was on the card. She thinks of the man in the picture. That thick, heavy torso, shaggy with greying hair, could be anyone's. Distorted with the effort or satisfaction of what he is doing, it's hard to identify. But the face is dimly familiar. She wishes she could remember where she has seen it before.

35

Katie Cuts Both Ways

The face Katie had seen in her mirror on Sunday was not, as she first thought, a delusion but that of a real girl. She looks terrified, far more so than Katie is herself, and it takes several moments to realise that she recognises her. It's the girl from the lobby: the prostitute.

Recovering from her shock, Katie exclaims in a loud, angry voice, 'What are you doing here?'

The girl cringes away. Katie marches over and blocks her exit in case she tries to bolt with whatever she's stolen. She is too outraged to be frightened. 'I'm calling the police.'

'No! Please, no.'

'You're a thief.'

'No. I hide. I hide for my life.'

Katie, about to ring 999 on her cellphone, stops. The girl's faltering English, her desperation, seem genuine. She is pale and bears traces of heavy make-up but seems far too young to be a prostitute. But then, Katie thinks, what do I know?

'What are you hiding from?'

The girl points her finger down and mutters, 'Dmitri.'

'Your boyfriend?'

The girl's face goes stiff with disgust. 'No! I am his prisoner.'

Now that she is confronted with the truth of her suspicions, Katie is both incredulous and curious. 'You're a hooker, right? A prostitute?'

The girl stares back at her mutely. Katie surveys her, in her thin, short zippered dress. This isn't the kind of thing that somebody from her world ever has to deal with. It is too ridiculous, too melodramatic, and she still thinks it is far more likely that she's interrupted a thief. However, even if the girl's tale is true, Katie doesn't want anyone invading her space. She herself is a damaged person: she is recovering from a breakdown and she needs her privacy.

'You have to leave,' she says. All the toughness and hardness she can muster is in her voice. 'You can't stay.'

'Please. Please, help me.'

Unexpectedly, the girl crouches down, and lets out a loud, wrenching sound. Katie, alarmed, wonders whether she is being sick. But then, with a lurch, she recognises it as exactly the same kind of vomit of hopelessness and grief that she herself had made, a while back, when she had arrived at her parents' house after leaving Winthrop. She looks at the girl's head, buried in her hands, and the big tears splashing onto her knees. She sighs. 'Would you like a cup of tea?'

The girl nods, though she doesn't stop crying. Katie goes to the kitchenette and puts the kettle on. At least I can find out more about the situation, she thinks. She brings the girl a roll of toilet paper. The girl mops her eyes, streaking them with black.

'What's your name?'

'Anna.'

'How old are you, Anna?'

'Fifteen.'

'Oh. My. God. You're a *child*.'

It should have been obvious. Anna's narrow hips and coltish legs, her high, tight breasts and the sprinkling of small spots around her hairline are all those of someone barely out of puberty. Katie has been talking to her as if she were a grown woman, but Anna looks at her with the sullen hopelessness of a teenager.

288

She says, in a much gentler tone, 'Where are you from, Anna?'

Anna says flatly, 'Ukraine. I have no passport. Sergei, he take. You understand?'

'Yes – yes,' says Katie distractedly. Anna is trembling, and she feels quite shaky herself. The man that this girl has escaped from is only thirty feet away, in the flat below. This could be a nasty situation, a part of Katie's mind warns her; back off. You are a single female lapsed vegetarian in a strange country: you do not need this. She ignores it.

'How did you get in?'

'The door is open.'

'I see.' Open because of the paint fumes, of course. 'How did you get out?'

Anna begins a confused explanation, something about pills and a fight, but her English breaks down.

'He is very bad man,' she says. 'With other bad mens. I see you, you not like them.'

To give herself time to think, Katie pours the tea.

The girl accepts it, gripping the mug with clawlike hands, but not drinking until Katie has several gulps from her own. Her wariness tells Katie more than words.

Katie's stomach rumbles, and so does Anna's. They exchange tiny, tentative smiles.

'Are you hungry?' Katie asks.

Slowly, Anna nods.

'OK. I'm not saying that I believe your story, but I was going to make something for myself. You can share it.'

Katie wonders what to cook. What *do* you cook in this sort of situation? It isn't the kind of thing you find in etiquette books, but her choice is limited anyway by ingredients and competence. She could fry a steak if she had one, or boil pasta, but that's about the limit of her abilities. She makes scrambled eggs, stirring briskly with a wooden spoon while Anna watches every move. When it's done, Anna bobs her head in thanks and eats with ravenous intensity.

'Toast?' Katie gestures at the loaf of stale bread. Anna nods again, and wolfs down two slices spread with honey.

What is she to do with this girl? Anna has arrived like a stray cat, but she is effectively a criminal. Assuming she isn't a thief, she has to be got into a place of greater safety. Katie, now her initial shock is over, finds herself thinking about the logistics. Organising people is one of her skills, although dealing with emotions is, she acknowledges, one of her failings. It's probably because of this – that she isn't so terrified of what the men downstairs might do – that she hasn't rung the police. Anna will need a lawyer, will need a doctor to check on her health, will need to be returned to her parents in the Ukraine . . . the thought of it all makes Katie quail. She might be prepared to put the girl up for a night, but what does she owe a total stranger? She would surely be putting herself in danger if she doesn't hand her over. Katie doesn't want to think about what having one or more violent pimps downstairs might mean for her, but nor does she feel that abandoning Anna to her fate is right.

Without being asked, Anna rises and washes the dishes. Katie, surprised, doesn't stop her. She has read endless self-help books at her parents' house, which encouraged women like herself to answer snippily 'That's your problem' when somebody tries to wriggle out of doing what she wants them to do, but she has never been offered help unasked.

Yet Anna, so terrified and so young, is indeed her problem. By offering her food, she has knowingly changed the relationship between them. Katie can just imagine Winthrop's voice saying, 'You shared your home with a teenaged Ukrainian *hooker*? Are you *nuts*?'

Yes, Katie acknowledges: she probably is. She hasn't been normal or entirely sane for a long time, but conscience cuts both ways. The same impulse that had made it impossible to turn a blind eye to her future husband's infidelity – something that, as he is six years older than her, she had thought likely to continue – now makes it impossible to turn Anna away.

The girl has finished the washing-up, and is looking at the floor, her head bowed. This is the point at which Katie could tell her, briskly, to leave. Instead, she asks, 'How long since you ate?'

Anna considers, then puts up two fingers.

'He didn't even *feed* you properly?'

There is a long pause.

'I think,' Katie says, 'that you should maybe have a bath. You can sleep on the couch.'

So, Anna has stayed. Not just for one night now, but for six. When Katie left to go to the office on Monday morning the girl was still deeply asleep, curled up under a spare duvet and looking no more than twelve. Katie had returned wondering whether her few items of any value would still be there. But they were, and so was Anna. What was missing was the dirt.

Every surface is now clean. Katie has never seen anything like it. Table, shelves, windows, floors: Anna must have been working all day. Something delicious is simmering on the stove. For the first time ever, her flat looks and smells like a real home.

'Well,' Katie says, aware that the girl is looking at her hopefully.

Anna has not stirred from the flat, but inside it she has been busy. Each day that Katie returns, something else is new. Her walls and ceilings are now a gleaming, lustrous white. Her curtains, which she had bought from John Lewis and never been able to hang properly, are now crisply ruffled instead of sagging from limp threads, and have instantly made the living room look cheerful and friendly. The shower hose, calcified into uselessness, now jets a radiant pincushion of hot water. Her books have been stacked neatly, in alphabetical order. A few framed prints, which had been propped up in a corner ever since arriving from New York, are hung up. All the dear, tatty things of her life before Winthrop, the things that when she moved in with him had been boxed away in storage as insufficiently smart or sophisticated, have magically reappeared, cherished and polished and reminding her once again of who she really is.

'Is better, no?'

'Yes, thank you, it is.'

Guilt and relief make Katie solicitous. Maybe this is how Anna deals with trauma, she thinks. Maybe she'll be able to leave now. She wants her to go simply because of the fear she now feels every time she goes past the door of the ground-floor flat.

'We need to find someone who can help you move on.'

Anna's expression, so eager to please, shuts off. In its place comes terror, and pleading.

'No, please.'

'You need a doctor. Anna, you might have an infection, or be pregnant.'

'I no pregnant.'

'How do you know that?'

Anna just looks at Katie, with that unfathomable remoteness.

She is so young, Katie thinks again, and yet she's been through things I can't imagine. How petty her own trauma now looks, and how remote!

'You help me.'

'No. I may be twice your age but I can't help you like a doctor can.'

'I help you.'

Their conversations have the surreal quality of an argument in a dream. Katie feels weird about returning to a flat that is no longer empty and bleak. She needs her privacy, and yet she also finds she needs company too.

Downstairs, she can hear a man's voice, shouting, and another voice shouting back. Both women freeze. I can't live like this, Katie thinks, listening. One voice belongs to the DJ who lives in the flat below, a thin man with dyed black hair and weird clothes – something called a Goth – who works all night and sleeps all day. The other sounds foreign. Katie looks fearfully at Anna.

'Dmitri?'

Anna nods, too frightened to speak. There is the sound of footsteps on her stair, and then a knock on the door. The women jump convulsively.

'Hello?'

There is another knock.

'Who is it?'

Anna is signalling to her frantically not to open the door but Katie, after a moment's hesitation, puts it on the chain and opens it a crack.

'Hello?'

In the gap between the door and its frame she sees a man looking at her, his eyes as hot and angry as a bull's. It's one of the brothers from downstairs. Katie puts on her blandest expression, the one she uses when she sees the poet skulking around the *Rambler*, though she can feel her heart throbbing with fear.

'May I help you?'

'I am looking for my girlfriend. She has little English, and she is sick – you know, in the head? You have seen her?'

'I'm sorry—' Katie begins, but then the man, Dmitri, puts his shoulder to the door and pushes. The chain pops off the thin frame, Katie staggers back, and he's in.

'Come out, Anna,' he says, and then shouts something in Russian. Katie stands there, trembling with rage and fright while he searches her flat. It's so small and sparsely furnished that it barely takes a minute.

'Get out,' she says. 'I'm calling the police, right now.'

Dmitri plucks her cellphone out of her trembling hands contemptuously, and throws it on the couch.

'You make trouble for me, I make trouble for you,' he says. His thick accent adds to the menace. She understands exactly why Anna is so petrified by him. Katie hasn't been this scared ever.

'There's nobody else here, as you can see,' she says. Dmitri grunts and goes out, slamming her frail door.

Katie sinks onto the couch, sick with terror. How has he missed Anna? Where can she possibly be hiding? She waits for what seems like a long time, then says hesitantly, 'Anna, it's OK. He believed me, and he's gone downstairs.'

Slowly, the back window creaks upwards. Katie hasn't even noticed it was fractionally open. Anna climbs in from the makeshift balcony, shivering and damp.

'I hide under the window.'

'That was real smart of you.'

Katie gets a blanket – thank heavens it had just looked like a throw – from the couch, and puts it round Anna's shoulders. Then she turns the TV on. At once a wilfully upbeat pulse of chat and music pours into the room, interspersed with the cackles and squeals of furry puppets. Under the cover of this cacophony, made by a black and purple striped cat, a mustard-yellow chicken and a magenta fox in a baseball cap, the two women talk.

'No police,' Anna whispers.

'Don't worry. I understand. We'll think of something.'

Katie does think; even at work, where the preparations for the party are now preoccupying her to the extent that the production of the magazine has become secondary. She has to organise the catering, wine and flowers, speak to the Special Branch policemen who are coming to check out the premises. Yet Anna's problems are more urgent.

'Do your family have a telephone? Would you like to ring them?'

Anna shakes her head.

'Would you like to write them a letter? They must be so worried about you.'

Anna is mute. Katie thinks she understands, because she has spent many of the past few years not talking about her own problems. Then Anna says, 'My mother, she has a letter.' She bows her head, and her hair falls over her face. 'I tell her lies.'

'You know what? We all tell our mothers lies,' Katie says. Unexpectedly, she feels more robust. 'They start off wanting to protect us, but then we have to protect them.'

All the same, she is appalled by how easily Dmitri might have found out her lie. Every time she goes past the flat on the ground floor now, she is sick with nerves. There has been no sign of life from inside, other than the sound of coughing from the basement, but the buzzer still goes as frequently at night. The vicious buzzing alarms them each time, and Katie has started picking up the intercom and shouting, 'Go away or I call the police!'

'How many other women are there?' Katie asks.

Two, Anna tells her. Five, in the other brothel.

Katie takes notes. Perhaps if she can write it all down and send it to the police then they will have to take it seriously. Maybe there are so many brothels operating out of private homes that they just can't cope. She's too frightened to report Dmitri's assault, but she buys bolts and a new chain.

'Are the other girls like you? Are they prisoners?'

'Cristina, she—' Anna mimes injecting. 'Galina, she sick. She had rich man, he liked her very much, but she too sick now to see him.'

One by one, she goes through the names.

'Are they all teenagers?'

'I think so.'

It's clear that she doesn't like talking about it. Anna's resilience amazed Katie in that first week. Her stubbornness and frailty, her solemnity and unexpected sense of humour are so much like what Katie remembers of her own teens that it's hard to remember what the girl must have been through. She seems normal. She likes clothes, and make-up, and when Katie told her about the lunch on Friday it was Anna who insisted on putting make-up on Katie's face.

'I try?'

'Don't put on too much.'

Anna's gentle, hesitant touch is impersonal and childlike. Katie can't help wondering whether she has touched men this way. How could a child be sexy? What had they done to her? There are many questions she wants to ask, but she feels it would be indelicate.

'Oh. That is better.' Katie stares at her reflection. 'You know, that's almost how I used—'

'Enjoy.'

A make-over by a hooker. How totally weird her life here is turning out to be. She thinks of the stories she had read as a child, in which children discovered other worlds at the touch of a ring or, just around the corner from her flat, E. Nesbit's Five Children, bored in the basement of Camden Terrace, had been instructed by a phoenix about the properties of their new nursery carpet.

'Why you no do every day?' Anna asks.

'I stopped living,' Katie says, and Anna looks at her and nods as if she understands.

36

Freedom Is Not An Absolute Condition

Job has become fond of Tariq's sons. He can't help liking children, although Amir and Chandra's behaviour each time he comes to give them a reading lesson is odd. The boxy little red-brick house looks the picture of calm, yet the wincing blue eye of their computer swarms with nightmares in which helmeted warriors battle invincibly against a host of foes. Job detests these games. How long, he thinks, before they see people as pixels? How can they understand that real blood isn't just a splash of red on a screen? Whenever Job arrives he finds them in front of the screen, their eyes glazed and their fingers twitching as if they're dreaming; every so often a tremor will go through them, and they'll press a button.

'Boom!' Chandra cries. '*Allah Akhbar!*'

'Die, *kuffars*!' says Amir.

Job tries not to show his loathing of the word. He remembers white people in Zimbabwe calling black people *kaffirs*, and he's pretty sure that the two words mean the same thing: alien, inferior, unbeliever. Yet the avatars that the boys kill on screen are white, not black. Does that make it any less offensive? The gaming is like a drug, he thinks, but when he says this to Tariq the older man shakes his head.

'I know what drugs can do. My eldest son, that was his problem. Now it is different.'

'What did you do?'

'I sent Selim home, to Pakistan. Here he had no discipline, he was running wild. He had lost respect for our faith and got in with a bad crowd. My two youngest are not like that. I prefer they stay at home, playing these games.'

Once Job arrives just as Selim is leaving.

'What are you doing here?' Selim demands aggressively.

'I am the boys' English teacher.'

Selim looks at him with narrowed, suspicious eyes. 'My father should not allow it.'

'With respect, your father invited me to teach your brothers.'

Job thinks of what he knows of the boy, who is probably only two or three years younger than himself. He can see that he is sensitive; his eyes make him think of a dik-dik, the little deer that runs so agilely through the bush, and which is every meat-eater's prey. When Amir lets him in, Job instinctively turns, checking Selim's retreating back. The grey bulk of his anorak has a reflective stripe on the shoulders which catches his eye; it looks like the stripe on a dik-dik's back, he thinks.

'Now, perhaps you boys are clever enough to remember where we got to in the story,' he says. It's always the hardest part of his time with them, getting them to turn their gaming off. But they are good boys, and polite, and as their confidence has grown Job has begun to read with them the second Harry Potter book. They like this because they've seen the film; discovering that the book has more details and scenes has intrigued them even if Amir insists that reading isn't cool. Their liveliness enables Job to forget about the disaster of Anna.

Job had never really thought about what he would do with the girl once he had rescued her. He had been so keyed up thinking about how he would save her that he hadn't given any thought to the next stage, and her total disappearance has come as both a shock and a relief. Anna has vanished; and Dmitri, to his amazement, had put up no fight because seconds after he had opened the door he had fallen over like a tree – drunk, perhaps, because he smelt strongly of whisky. Job had left, though not before relieving Dmitri of his – Job's – fifty pounds. He had even gone up to the other girl, who was sitting giggling in front of the TV, and tried to tell her that she was free to go; but she'd looked at him without comprehension, even when Job dropped her pimp's wallet in her lap. Since then he has cruised past the brothel in Agar Grove several times, looking to see if he can spot her. But the window is always bland behind its net curtain.

What could he have done if Anna had come back with him? His room in the council estate is so small that it might as well be a prison cell, and it is wholly unsuited to having two people in it. Yet as he himself knows, freedom is never an absolute condition. There are always degrees of freedom, in which you are at liberty but not actually free. This was what he had discovered in prison, in great pain and fear. The only true freedoms are those of the heart, and of the mind.

Tariq's sons feel just as frustrated about being at school.

'I hate it, I hate it so much,' says Amir, just like Robbie.

'What do you hate?'

'Everything. I can't explain. It's like prison. Half the boys is mental.'

'How are they mental?' Job asks, correctly guessing what this means.

'There's gangs, see. They hates you if you ain't in their gang, if you ain't from their country. Mostly, it's Somalis v Bangladeshis. They fight outside school, but inside too. We're picked on by both. Selim, he tried to side with the Bangladeshis, but it was no good. It's all gangs, and we ain't big enough. Every break, we gets hassled for our lunch money.'

'Do your teachers not do anything to stop this?'

'They ain't got no power, man. We knows they can't touch us, because of our human rights, anyone touches a pupil, we can have them in court for being paedos and perverts.' Amir looks miserable.

'My brother says it's all stupid, and a waste of time. He says Muslims can never get on with *kuffars*.'

'Why not?' Job enquires. Amir shakes his head.

'They are just too different. We go to a British school, because Dad thinks we're British kids, but then we go to *madrassah* school, and that has rules. *Kuffars* have no rules. They live without Allah.'

Job thinks of the schools that most children have in Zimbabwe, schools in the bush where teachers draw in the dust because they have no blackboards. They would love Amir's school, he thinks. Out there, a library is a plank on bricks under a tree, and even in Job's day books had cost a year's wages. Yet the desperation to read is such that people long to do it, even when they are starving. It is what the white man has given them, this great longing, this curiosity and thirst to learn more; but here, in the white man's own country, children have lost it.

Tariq and his wife are good people. Tariq has driven his sons round London in his minicab, pointing out places of interest: the house in Bromley-by-Bow where Gandhi lived when he trained to be a barrister, the Houses of Parliament, and Buckingham Palace. He told Job about this, without affectation or pride, because he wants to show that he is a good father. He seems to respect Job, now that he sees him as more than another driver and an African.

But if Job tries to tell Tariq that his beloved sons are full of hatred, he has no doubt that the other driver will turn against him. Job's conscience will not let him do it; Tariq is now the closest thing he has to a friend.

'Are you sure you want me to read with them?' he asks. 'It might be better for your sons to read with their father.'

'Yes, I am sure. You are a proper teacher; I understand that you have an education.'

Job sighs. These boys are eleven and thirteen, but he'd bet that Amir was probably having difficulty over books that Robbie had mastered at eight.

*

Yet Robbie too is convinced that he's failing. 'There are loads and loads of boys above me. I'm getting, like, mostly Bs, but they're all getting As.'

'Those sound like good marks,' Job says.

'No, they aren't! Not if you want to get into a good school,' says Robbie with deadly certainty. 'If you get into a good school, like I'm expected to, you have to get just, I don't know, As in everything and be really good at sport and stuff.'

'Most people aren't, I think,' Job says. 'Most people are happy to be good at just one thing, if they're lucky.'

'Yes, but we have to be good at everything to succeed, because we compete against the best, not the rest. That's what Dad says.'

Job is silent. Perhaps it's true; perhaps Robbie and the other children he sees pouring so docilely out of their schools are indeed the leaders of the future. However, he doubts it. Privilege may be passed down, like genes, but it can be just as suddenly snatched away from you, as he knows.

'What are you good at, Mr Robbie?'

'I don't know. Most of the time I'm so bored in school that I go into a daydream.'

'You sound like Winston Churchill. He was bad at school, and always in trouble there, but he became your greatest Prime Minister,' says Job.

'Did he?' says Robbie, interested. 'I've heard of him, I think.'

Job, sliding his car forward, instinctively probing for every opening in a line of traffic, executes a smart turn off Haverstock Hill. Robbie chats away to him, confidingly.

'My dad earns pots more than Mum. She's always working, working, working but I don't see the point. I wish he could live at home, but he won't.'

'But your mother is a very good woman,' said Job. 'She helps people, doesn't she?'

'I just wish she'd be more of a mum and less of a superhero.'

*

Job remembers the three men who burst into the Wisdens' farm, armed with just bricks and knives, demanding money, guns and the car keys. Nobody had been a hero then. Mr and Mrs Wisden had given them all they had, but still they demanded more. So they killed them, beating their faces to a mush. Then, forcing the girl's legs open and with a knife to her throat, they raped Beth, one after another. Job, terrified, had done nothing. He had hidden under the veranda, stuffing his fingers in his ears to block out the shrieks, while the men smashed their way through the lives of people he knew and loved, before loading up the truck with all the electric goods and pouring furniture oil over the bodies. After they left, Job had found Beth, and cut the electric cables binding her. They had walked five miles together, barefoot, bleeding and half-fainting, to the police station to ask for help.

Only later did Job discover that the person who had betrayed the Wisdens and let them in past the electric fence surrounding the farm had been his own mother.

She was dead herself now, worn down by trying to scratch a living out of the land given to her by the Zanu-PF men, which was as barren as if it had a curse on it. It was the same story all over Zimbabwe. Job's childhood paradise was gone, and the cattle and crops were dust. Beth had been taken away by relations – to England, Job always thought, though he never knew for certain because she had been too traumatised to speak to him again – and he had stayed in Harare, with his sister. Beth must be a young woman now, he knows; but he still thinks of her as fourteen.

There had been something so like her, around the mouth, in Anna. Job can't blame Anna for not wanting to get into his car. Maybe he should have tried to get the other girls out as well – he knew there must have been more, besides the girl sitting and giggling to herself in the front room – but it was Anna he had cared about.

Had Dmitri caught her? Job has no way of knowing. He has tried; God does not speak to his heart. Between the car wash, Ace

Minicabs, teaching Tariq's sons and private work for Polly he is kept pretty busy.

Tariq's life seems to Job to be an enviable one, but his sons don't see it that way.

'You know, Odion's mum is moving him back to her country to go to school,' Amir tells Job.

'Isn't it worse there?'

'His mum says not. She says they have more respect there, like in Pakistan.'

Their lessons go slowly, with many interruptions. Amir reads one paragraph, and Chandra reads the next, and Job, like Scheherazade, takes care to stop them just at the most tantalising moments.

'At our school, there aren't dragons,' says Chandra.

'No, but there's monstering,' says Amir.

'That's why we carry.'

'What do you carry?'

Amir feels in his school rucksack, and produces a knife. Its blade of stainless steel is stuck into a black plastic handle – a cooking knife, probably – and it makes Job shudder. Sixteen teenagers have been knifed to death in the streets of London so far this year, and there will be more. These beardless boys with their high voices and slim build are still children, without knowledge or experience.

'Why do you carry this bad thing?' Job asks.

'It gets you respec',' Chandra pipes.

Job closes his eyes, then says, 'May I borrow your knife?'

Reluctantly, Amir hands it over. He's afraid that Job will try to take the knife away. Job holds it, and then, very quickly, before he can change his mind, he slashes it across his forearm. The boys cry out in shock as a scarlet line across Job's dark skin flows from the wound.

'May I trouble you for a paper napkin?' Job asks, and Amir hands one to him silently.

'Are you mental? If our mum sees any blood on the carpet, we'll—'

303

'He wanted to show us,' says Amir.

'Yes,' Job says. 'Blood is blood. It is not like your games. If you do this to yourselves, the same thing will happen. You will feel it, just as I do, and if you cut another so will they. Words and pictures can be lies. What is true is the blood. If you cut in a different place – here, or here, or here – you will die.'

'There are people who deserve to die,' says Chandra fiercely.

Job says, 'Don't your prayers begin with praise for the compassion and mercy of God? Do you think knives are a part of that?'

'Compassion and mercy ent a help,' Amir says, as if Job were the child.

'How do you know?' Job asks. 'Have you tried them?'

37

Anna in the Light

Sometimes Anna thinks she can hear Galina coughing in the basement below. There's a faint, repetitive, rattling noise which might be
water in the pipes or might be air in somebody's lungs. Here she is, up
in the light and air like a flower and just down there in the dirt is
someone else who continues living as she had done. But what can
she do about it? She may have saved her own life but she can't save
anyone else. All the same, she finds her heart stumbling each time
that soft, persistent sound echoes up through the house.

She has not once been out, apart from her desperate scramble
onto the balcony to escape Dmitri. The stairs outside Katie's flat ter-
rify her, with their creaks and taps; sometimes she dreams that she is
out on the top tread and it tips into a long, curving slide that sends
her screaming and clawing all the way back to the ground floor. This
whole city is a place of pitfalls, traps and labyrinths from which there
is no exit; Anna has found a brief toehold, that's all.

If she is quiet, she can hear the soft sighing of passing cars that
sounds like the inhalation and exhalation of a great beast, punctured
by the wailing shriek of sirens. Every so often the buzzer sounds,
reminding her of an angry hornet about to sting, making her sick

with fright. Life always continues, and so does vice. Perhaps there is even a replacement for her downstairs. She herself must have come back as a replacement for another girl – Drita, perhaps, or another. There must have been so many girls like herself, tricked and sold, used and discarded. Anna doesn't cry, doesn't talk much, doesn't dream. The effort of remembering who she is, the effort of resisting taking the pills and above all the effort of doing what had been completely counter-intuitive and running up the stairs instead of out into the street has exhausted her.

For a long time, after Katie had left her to go to work, she had just looked up at the rectangle of sky in the pitched roof, thinking that it was the loveliest thing she had ever seen. It was as if she had never seen the sky before, or noticed its illimitable lustre. She could have watched it all day, its slow-drifting clouds building and subsiding like new continents in heaven, and the soft luminous blue crossed only by birds and the shining darts of aeroplanes. How could this be the same sky as the one she had seen in Kilburn? It is as if it has remade itself, for even when it rains she can see that the drops of water gleam and flash as they fall, like a blessing; and afterwards the air is fresh and clear.

Timidly, Anna has explored the two rooms, the living room with its dog-leg kitchenette and the bedroom with its equally minuscule bathroom. Despite its air of neglect and dirt, it seems more real to her than any of the places she has seen in the country so far. What reassures her most is the small portable TV set, which receives only terrestrial channels and no pornography. She had been terrified that not only would Katie send her back down to the brothel, but that Katie herself might be another prostitute – a strange one, because she makes no effort to wear make-up or show off her figure. Instead, she had been lent an old sweatshirt to sleep in. Katie has trusted her more than she could have dared to hope, although when she left on the first morning she locked Anna into her flat.

'You understand, Anna, this is only for a short time? This is my home, and I live alone.'

'Yes, I understand. I am respectful.'

Katie considered her with shrewd yet kindly eyes. 'OK. I must be crazy to be doing this. You don't smoke, I can tell, and I don't think you do drugs because I've seen your arms. I'll tell you what. My housekeeping sucks, and this place needs sorting out. You clean it for me, and we'll be quits.'

Anna understood only half of this, but nodded. Cleaning isn't going to do anything bad to her. There isn't a single part of her body that hasn't been bruised or scarred. Two of her teeth are loose from a time when Sergei had hit her across the face. One of her ears isn't working properly. The finger that Job had splinted still aches, as do two of her toes. Her pubic hair, which has been partially singed off, is still ragged. But the strangest thing of all is that when she looks at herself in the bedroom mirror, she still looks much as she did on leaving the Ukraine. Almost nothing of what she has suffered is visible.

'Is normal, is normal,' Dmitri had always assured her. Whatever the brothers and other men had done to her, however much she had whimpered with pain, they had wanted her to believe that it wasn't wrong or wicked or cruel. Did they do so because they knew that it was all a lie? Had the brothers ever been kind to anyone, even to their mother? Anna has given up trying to work out why men act as they do, but she thinks that if she ever forgets how contemptible they are she will have deserved her treatment. And yet, there had been Job . . . when Anna had tried to describe to Katie how she got out, she had omitted to mention his role, saying only that she had put pills in a bottle of whisky to drug Dmitri. She felt that if Katie believed her escape to be solely the result of her own efforts she might be more inclined to help her. Her surmise was correct. Katie, presented with such a tale, had been admiring.

'You know, if I'd gotten into such a situation, I hope I'd have been as smart as you,' she'd said.

It isn't so easy to escape from the memories, though. The first day alone, Anna had scrubbed herself with harsh, abrasive sponges meant for cleaning the bath. Even when she scraped off enough skin to make herself bleed it didn't satisfy her. She needs a new body; she would like to slough off her skin like a snake. But then, instead, it occurred to her to clean her surroundings, as Katie had requested.

The brothel had been dirty, too, but its dirt had been of a different kind. This is just dust, and neglect, and the lack (not the absence) of love. Anna doesn't dare vacuum because the flat is supposed to be empty, but there is a dustpan and brush, and some cloths. Slowly and silently, she moves through the flat, until everything is clean but the walls. These have the same spidery patterned paper as downstairs: a job lot, perhaps, from the last century. Seeing it, Anna shudders; it's another reminder that this sanctuary and the place of her torment are part of the same whole. One wall, in stark contrast to the others, is white and smooth, but it has not been finished. The roller has been left in the paint tray to stiffen and harden in lumpy clots. Carefully, Anna takes it to the kitchen sink and washes it; when it's dry, she finds it's made of some soft, fleecy stuff, like lamb's wool. She pours a little paint into the tray and dips the roller in. Pressed gently to the shabby surface it rolls smoothly forward, leaving a snowy wake. The ugly, dirty paper vanishes.

Anna looks at this miracle, and her thoughts stop whirling. She begins drawing the roller across in planes and arcs of purity. If she could bathe in whiteness, drink it, take it into herself then she would, but she knows it is only a thin skin. However, Anna has great respect for skin because she knows that it's all that lies between comfort and pain. If walls can be mended, then so can she.

All day, Anna paints, with the windows open and the cold spring air flooding in. Outside on the makeshift balcony, the plastic window boxes are full of hard green spikes, as some kind of plant pushes up into the world. The sun moves, and the walls are not just white but yellow, pink, blue – for the paint has a faint sheen to it which reflects light. Will Katie mind? Anna has to do something, not just sit and lick her wounds like a sick animal.

When it gets too dark for her to be sure she is doing it properly, she stops and thinks of food. Cooking, too, is something she knows how to do, though when Anna looks at the tins Katie has in her store cupboard she is appalled. No wonder she is so thin! The fridge – dirty, containing a jar of a kind of cream, a handful of stale bread, a single carrot, some potatoes, three eggs, milk and a couple of shrivelled onions – is equally dreadful. On a sheet of folded damp kitchen paper some beans are sprouting. Anna looks pensively at these ingredients. Unpromising though they are, she could make them into a meal, she thinks . . . there is a lump of cheese, hard as stone, which could be grated, and a bag of frozen peas in the freezer box.

'Delicious,' Katie says that evening.

'Is OK?'

'Yes. Sorry. I only realised when I'd left that there's practically no food in the flat. I'm not so good at shopping. Why don't you write me a list of ingredients? I'll go to the supermarket.'

Anna doesn't know what this odd word ingredients means. Together, they find a dictionary on the internet, and she translates what she needs. *Eggs, garlic, bacon, milk, lemon, flour, sugar, butter* . . . Can Katie afford it? Anna looks doubtfully at her. She can see that some of Katie's clothes, like her shoes and coat, are good quality, yet everything else about her benefactress is shabby. Is Katie rich or poor? Anna has no means of telling in this country.

'The flat looks amazing,' Katie says. 'You know, I meant to put it to rights when I moved in, but then . . . there just didn't seem much point.'

'I clean more tomorrow,' Anna says, seizing her chance.

'Are you sure you are well enough?'

'I am very strong. I am hotel chambermaid,' Anna says, remembering the phrase she had practised on the ferry over.

'Are you really?'

'No.' The two women look at each other, then smile. 'I practise English. But I know cleaning.'

'You need to see a doctor.'

'No doctor,' Anna says defiantly.

Katie sighs, but Anna knows she has won.

So they slip into a kind of routine together. Anna makes herself as unobtrusive as possible, aware that if she talks too much, or even breathes too loudly, Katie could change her mind. Yet she also realises that Katie has been lonely. She is no fool – she still locks Anna in every morning – but she is naturally, instinctively friendly. Anna's first impression of her had been right. She is an angel, but an angel who has somehow fallen to earth.

In the evening, after their meal, the two women watch the TV. The shows are always about how to change something in your life: your house, your garden, your appearance.

'Why is it always women must change, not men?' Anna asks.

'Not all men are bad, Anna. Everyone has good and bad in them.'

'You are good person, Katie.'

Katie laughs. 'I don't think I am. It's easy to be good when you have enough – when you're rich or happy. Much harder now. Tell me about yourself. Was your family happy?'

'My family, no.' Anna doesn't want to think about her own family, but she does want to practise her English. 'My family very, very poor. My father, he leaves, to work for Poland. My mother, she has five children – myself, my brother, and her sister children.'

'What happened to your aunt?'

'She dies. She has the cancer, from Chernobyl.' Anna touches her throat, trying to explain. 'My mother, she work all day, but there is not enough money.'

'Was that why she let you come here?'

'She not want me to, but my granny, she say any country better than Ukraine.'

Anna thinks of the girls who had come over with her on the boat, like sheep being lured into the slaughterhouse by the one that isn't killed, the Judas.

'You know, everyone in my country has come from someplace else.'

'You are not from here?'

'No. America.'

'I would like to go there one day. Why you leave?'

'Oh, a man.'

'You had a bad man?'

'Yes. Or maybe he was just bad for me.'

The two women smile at each other, cautiously.

'They're still downstairs, aren't they?' Katie asks. 'The other girls, I mean.'

Anna nods.

'Do you think that Dmitri will come up here again, looking for you?'

'I am quiet, like mouse.'

'OK.'

Katie frowns. Anna knows that she can't expect to stay much longer. She looks at her friend pleadingly.

'I tried complaining about it, you know. I called the police, but they did nothing, did they?' Katie says.

Anna shakes her head. Katie, with her large feet and her candid gaze, strikes her as naive, even though she's twice Anna's age. Yet that is what stands between her and the abyss beneath her feet. Katie's naivety, Katie's kindness, have given her a temporary refuge in which to find her strength, and Anna clings to it with all the selfish desperation of which she is capable.

Alone in the flat, Anna scrubs the wooden skirting board in preparation for painting the bedroom.

> 'Ti skazala shto v vivtorok
> Potseluyesh raziv sorok
> A ti meneh obmanula,
> Obmanula tai zabula.

311

You told me that on Tuesday
You would kiss me forty times,
But you tricked me
You tricked me and forgot me . . .'

She finds herself humming, then singing the song aloud as she works. It has a lilting tune which had been rediscovered by a pop group before she left the Ukraine, and although she remembers how she had sung it the last time in the shower just before her rape she pushes the thought away. She is safe here, surely? Anna pauses in her scrubbing, and listens.

Outside, there is a faint creaking sound, as if somebody is on the other side of the door. She holds the brush in mid-air, dripping foam, and then the hateful, familiar voice whispers, 'Are you there, little whore? Do you think you can keep hiding from me? Perhaps I'll tickle your friend with my knife. Or perhaps I'll use it on you.'

38

The Essential Injustice of Biology

However curious Polly is about the photograph on the SIM card, there is the relentless churn of work to be got through every day. It's like running in an eternal egg-and-spoon race, attempting to hurry while carrying something extraordinarily fragile. Yet even so, she is starting to feel that as her children have grown older the sense of extreme vulnerability (both her own and theirs) has become less acute. On the verge of middle age she has grown into herself and is no longer dependent on having a man in her life for her to feel like a person, for if she has lost the sense of boundless possibilities she had before children she has also lost the crippling self-consciousness that had once plagued her. When she stands up in court to defend her clients she is tapping into the tigerish protectiveness she feels for her children. Yet her children torment her with accusations of neglect and selfishness.

'Why did you bother having us if you hate us?' Tania has raged at her on occasions when she has been too busy to give her full attention to a question.

'I don't hate you; I love you. It's just that I don't have enough *time*.'

'Iryna had enough time,' Robbie said accusingly.

'Iryna was *paid* to have time,' Polly retorts; though it isn't really true.

Of course, she can never have a hangover because she has to keep work and family running with the same metronomic beat, week after week, even at weekends. She has become a machine, steadily devouring the days, months, years; or perhaps it is she who is being devoured, instead.

It isn't only Polly who feels this.

'You know, in Brazil, the time pass so slow,' says Teresa when Polly counts out the twenty-pound notes at the end of a week. Half her salary gone, in order for the children to have somebody there from three to seven p.m., do the laundry, cook them supper. 'You work hard, but you look at your watch and you say, is not even midday. In London, the days pass so quick.'

'Yes, I know,' says Polly, sadly.

Daily now, she wakes with the knowledge that she is probably halfway through her life; that at thirty-eight she might just be able to have one more baby but probably won't; that quite soon her children will be grown and gone. This knowledge, which only a couple of years ago felt like a bereavement, now seems like a promise. She might once again be *free*. She might be able to fly off to be with Bill Shade in the palmy luxuries of Pacific Palisades, might work hard enough to make Sam Stern take note of her, might even become a partner . . . But as long as she has dependants, none of this is possible.

Every half-term and holiday is an ordeal, because she has to pay somebody to be there while the children are at home. It's never Theo's problem, just hers. The children hate her for working so hard, and the partners hate her for not working hard enough. Polly hopes she isn't doing everything badly instead of doing just one thing well, but (even if she can pay Teresa to help, which is more than many women can afford) the essential injustice of biology precludes her from real choice. It will always be she who will cut into her working hours to attend a school concert, play or parents' evening, and always she who must deal with her children's homework, emotional problems and increasing bursts of teenage temper. It's only when she's on the juddering, creaking double-decker bus transporting her to and from work that she has time to think.

She still remembers Gheorghe's words: 'I was a lawyer, Mrs Noble. Just like you,' and feels ashamed of her self-pity. He has lost almost everything by emigrating in the hope of a better future. But Iryna has lost more.

Polly is haunted by the sense of a presence that is now an absence. She and the children still wear clothes that Iryna laundered and ironed for them; flowers that the girl planted are emerging in their garden, visible through windows that she cleaned. From time to time, Polly has wondered whether, if she herself were to disappear or die, she would have left any real mark on the world. Iryna had not been her right hand so much as her shadow.

How can Polly not try to solve the riddle of Iryna's murder? She thinks of the appalling photograph on the screen of the girl's mobile phone. Why had it been there? Did Iryna have a dark side? Could she have been a call-girl? All mothers told each other horror stories about nannies and au pairs, in which they were discovered to have stolen, worn your clothes, seduced your husband or had a parallel life as a prostitute; these were urban legends, fuelled by guilt and resentment. Yet nothing about Iryna's clothes or her behaviour in Polly's house had indicated that she was anything other than respectable. Gheorghe had told Polly that Iryna's other job was as a cleaner. What could have been more innocent?

Polly, accustomed to the conventions of detective novels, would enjoy puzzling out the card if she didn't feel quite so afraid. If only Iryna had left more of a clue! Was her burglar the man in the photo? Polly screws up her eyes. No: the burglar had been youngish, the man in the photo middle-aged. The police give her no information beyond the maddening line that they are 'pursuing investigations'. Well, so can she.

*

315

'I just wish I'd found out more about her,' Polly says to Hemani and Ellen when they meet. They are intrigued, excited and a little anxious for her.

'But how could you?' Hemani responds. 'Even if you'd got her through an agency, what do you suppose they'd have done that you couldn't? They can't check references, not unless they speak Russian or whatever, and even then how can they know they're speaking to someone genuine instead of an au pair's mum?'

'You know, I'd have kept her passport in my safe,' says Ellen. 'And I'd have asked her for her star sign. I always find I get on best with Librans.'

'I suppose that's as good a way as any of filtering out potential psychopaths, or their victims,' Hemani says gravely. (Ellen always talks in this nutty way, belying her shrewdness; it adds gaiety to their lives, Polly feels.)

What had Iryna done during all those mornings when she went out? Polly remembers the things she had collected from her room, and the books of matches bearing the name of the Giant Bread & Cheese. A misquotation from Thackeray, she recalls, about hunger acting as artistic inspiration. These people on the bus, pressing their cushiony and often malodorous flesh next to hers, whose ample buttocks, stomachs and thighs bulge with a superfluity of nourishment just as their iPods proclaim a superfluity of income are examples of economic success, an economic boom that seems unending. Surely that is a good thing? Everyone who has a house in central London has become a property millionaire, and the confidence this engenders has spilled out visibly, so that most pubs and cafés now have Continental-style pavement tables, and even crash barriers along the middle of the Holloway Road have flower-filled window boxes. Nobody, surely, goes hungry . . . An Asian barrister she likes working with had described how he and his mother were once so ravenous that they lived off frogs they caught. He had gone on to take one of the top degrees in law at Cambridge, after an epic struggle to get to

Britain. It's cases like his that make Polly proud to be working for her firm, and proud that the Law, despite its stuffy aspects, advances people of talent.

Iryna had worked the legal maximum for an au pair of twenty-five hours a week for her seventy pounds, which was barely half of the minimum wage (though she got five pounds an hour in the school holidays). Polly is guiltily aware that, even if she feels relatively poor, she can always lay her hands on a hundred pounds, and could cut her own grass and forget about paying for a laundry service to iron her sheets if she had to. Yet Iryna's earnings had supported the girl's family . . . so where *had* she worked? I must ring Gheorghe, Polly thinks.

Like Tania, she is convinced that the girl in the picture must be Iryna's sister. Therefore it must have been sent as a threat: look what your sister is being made to do. Polly sits up straighter as the bus rattles and thunders over a hump. Iryna had to have been blackmailed by someone who knew her well enough to have her number; or maybe she herself had taken it and was the blackmailer. But how would she know when and where to take the picture? The sister must have got the information to her. Maybe they both set up the man. Polly tries to think of the angles. The sister must be the key. How had Iryna herself got into Britain? Polly is sure that she'd at least checked that Iryna had a student visa when she'd offered her the job; she wasn't *that* foolish.

Of course, cleaners could discover a great deal if they chose. She had probably known every time Polly'd had a period; she had known when she'd been on a diet; she could have found out bank account numbers, computer passwords, and any number of mildly embarrassing secrets if she'd gone through private correspondence or even the rubbish. But then she would have left those as evidence, not the picture. Clearly, there was something else that Polly was supposed to work out . . . The man had to be someone she either knew or should recognise. Polly wishes she'd had the foresight to send the picture to her own mobile, rather than relying on memory. If only she had a name to go on! Google has made it easy to put a face to a name, but not the other way around. She thinks of Auden's words on private faces in public places – so much wiser and nicer than the opposite.

Polly looks down at the canal and at the thin fuzz of weeds or grasses covering the raw earth around the new Eurostar terminal. It has a dreary look despite the smooth, shiny new road that cars and buses swoop along into the centre of town. Ruined by the railways for a hundred years and redeemed by the Clean Air Act in the 1960s, what has been built here in the interim are council tenements, ugly, towering slabs of what is called social housing – meaning, of course, the opposite. Somewhere in here lives Job, as had her handyman Terry and perhaps a thousand other people all banged up together like battery chickens. Though Terry has, as he'd said he would, sold up and moved to Spain.

'When I need to earn, I just gets an easyJet flight back from Malaga and stay with my sons.'

'Are they handymen too?'

'Not interested. My kids, they've trained in computers. They've seen my life.'

'But what if you get sick?'

'The Spanish health service is better than ours.'

Terry and his wife will never be able to afford to move back. Polly's lover has a different version of the same problem.

'I can't get scripts bought in Britain,' Bill had said. 'It's impossible to get the finance together, whereas in Hollywood at least four or five studios can turn me down.'

He is depressed and frustrated. She has noticed that there has been a shift in the pattern of their calls. For the first two years, he had called her three times more often than she called him; then, for a year or so, they'd called each other up equally. Now, it's she who calls him most.

'It would be lovely if you could,' she said carefully. 'I miss adult conversation.'

'Any more news on your nanny?'

'Not really.' Polly didn't want to tell him about the photograph; it was too sordid. 'The police are trying to trace her family. I thought I'd drop in on a pub where she might have worked.'

'Leave that to the detectives. You don't know what you could be getting yourself into.'

'I won't be getting into anything,' said Polly, annoyed. Bill smiled, faintly. His face, framed by his neatly trimmed dark beard, always reminded her of the Chandos portrait of Shakespeare in the National Portrait Gallery, its shadowy sense of moral intelligence.

'How are you fixed in a fortnight?'

'Why?'

'I thought we might go away for a weekend, after the *Rambler* party.'

'Don't tell me you support that rag!' Polly exclaimed.

'It reminds me of all I'm not missing in Tinseltown,' Bill said. 'Actually, it's not so bad.'

'God, when I think that that crowd are probably going to be lording it over us at the next election . . . All right, I'll come to the party with you as long as we leave by nine p.m.'

'Sure. I'll stop off at my hotel when I get in, and swing by. It's sort of work for me.'

Remembering this, Polly sighs, looking down on a busy car-wash place. She loves London so much, and yet it is a city dedicated to work, not play. Even going to parties is work, for at the heart of power in this country everyone is a member of a very small club. A burst of tinny Mozart jingles from her handbag. 'Mrs Noble?'

It's Gheorghe, returning her call.

'You've heard about Iryna?' asks Polly.

'Yes. It's terrible news. I feared it because I knew she would not just disappear. Fortunately, I am not a suspect as I was able to prove where I was all weekend.'

'I'm sorry, Gheorghe. It was a shock for me, too. I had to identify her.' Polly pauses. 'Gheorghe, perhaps the police have asked you this, but I was wondering – where did she have her other jobs?'

His voice sounds vague and hopeless. 'One was in a big firm in the City – that was where we met. She stopped cleaning there soon after, however. The other was in an office north of Oxford Street. She went there in the evening.'

'Do you know the name?'

'No, I'm sorry. I know she wanted the job badly, because she told me she had paid the girl who did the work to move.'

'She did? How interesting . . .' More and more, Polly suspects that Iryna must have known where her sister was, and had targeted the man as a victim.

'Did she ever go to a pub called the Giant Bread & Cheese?'

'I don't know. Iryna did not drink alcohol, so it is unlikely.'

Polly can't go to check this out for a couple of days, but when she finds the place – a pleasant old gastropub of the kind that is popular – she shows Iryna's photograph to the barman.

'Nope. Definitely not one of our bar staff,' he says. 'You're not from Immigration, are you?'

'No. I'm just trying to find out about an au pair who disappeared and may be in trouble. I want to check she's all right,' Polly lies.

'OK. You can ask the kitchen staff.'

All the cooks are tall, thin black men, wrapped in white aprons. They are visibly tired, but smile, and look at her photograph, talking among themselves in some African language.

'Do any of you recognise her?'

Reluctantly, a couple of men nod.

'Did she work here?'

'No,' says one, economically. 'Nearby.'

'Do you know where?'

He grins. 'A newspaper. They have lunch here every week. Many famous people come.'

'What's it called?' Polly asks. But she already knows the answer.

320

39

Three Roads

Ian has never felt so much shame as he feels now. Though he has (he keeps telling himself) done nothing wrong, he feels as if he's inexorably going down a route that will take him further and further from what he knows is right. By moving in with Candice after his accident he has allowed her to think that their relationship has become more serious. It's no use telling himself that she made it too easy for him when he was concussed; like one of those nursery rhymes about how for want of a nail a battle gets lost, an instant's inattention has caused him to make a succession of choices. Candice is a very determined woman, and she has made it clear that she wants to get settled before she's, as she puts it, 'too old'.

'Too old for what?'

'Starting a family.'

'Candy, you can't be serious. Nobody here does that until well after thirty.'

'Yes, and I'm thirty-three.'

Ian shrugs, but Candice returns to the attack.

'When are you going to introduce me to your father?' she asks. 'I'd like to go to the annual *Rambler* party.'

'I'm not sure I want to go,' he says.

'Sweetie, why not? It'll be full of celebrities.'

'Exactly.'

If Ian falls in with her plans, his life will be transformed. Her parents will buy them a house. He could leave teaching, even; his tentative forays into writing could become a reality. He doesn't want to be supported by his wife, though, any more than he had wanted to be supported by his family. If he had been that kind of person, he'd have stayed in South Africa, and helped to run his stepfather's game reserve.

The alternative is that Candice will be very, very unpleasant, in a way that makes Ian shrink like a salted snail. He hates rows, and he knows, from the bitter way that she talks of previous men who let her down, that she never forgives or forgets.

So here he is, stumbling anxiously over the scatter of old shoes and coats in the hall in Finsbury Park, collecting his mail and feeling furtive. It feels like stepping back into a life he has outgrown. The shabbiness and mess, which once charmed him as an outward manifestation of irresponsibility, is odd after several weeks of pristine living in Hampstead, but these people are still his friends. Ian feels quite defiant about this. He doesn't have to watch himself with them as he does with Candy, any more than they will be uptight around him. There's Mick, unshaven and yawning over the wreckage of breakfast, and Liza brewing a pot of coffee, and the pianist next door practising yet another piece in a dazzling shower of notes.

'Hiya,' Liza says, smiling. 'Back from the living Barbie?'

'Mm,' says Ian. 'Long time no see.'

Mick grunts, and doesn't raise his head from the local newspaper and its blotch of dramas.

'Something wrong?'

'Oh, he's just hungover,' says Liza.

'No,' Mick says. 'My heart's bloody broken.'

'What by?'

'Isn't the usual question who?' Liza says, in her lightly acid tones.

'I'm off to South America,' Mick says. 'I've been in this city too long.'

'Candy and I are going to Thailand in the summer.'

'Yeah. Like I say, lucky bastard.'

Ian shrugs. Liza is smiling ironically. He looks at her square, pale face with affection 'What about you and Kim?' he asks her. 'When are you two travelling again?'

'Soon, I guess. We're both getting fed up with working in shitty UK hospitals. But it's also a pain, queuing with a load of blacks for a Schengen visa.'

Ian tries not to grimace.

'What? You think I shouldn't be offended that we're treated the same as them?'

'They're just people, Liza.'

'Oh, sure, like you or me are going to try and kill people we've never even met?'

'Why don't you think black people are frightened of that too?'

Liza laughs, shortly. 'Maybe because I grew up in Africa – the real Africa.'

Surprised, he asks, 'Which part?'

'West of Harare. I only became an Aussie later, as a teenager.'

Ian says nothing, but thinks he understands. There are white farmers in South Africa too who have that look; and over the past five years, his country has lost millions of young white people. No matter how fervently they want the Rainbow Nation envisaged by Mandela to work, they live in fear. Everyone knows someone who was murdered; everyone wonders whether they'll be next. This is why he wants to find out whether he could fit in here.

'Yeah, those queues are a pain,' he says, not wanting to quarrel. 'The best thing my father did for me was give me dual nationality.'

'Is he OK, then?'

'Pretty much,' says Ian.

His memories from the *Rambler* lunch are not making him eager to go to the magazine's annual party, but at the same time he's intrigued by Quentin. It's too late for them, and they are too different, but he has now caught him at last several times on TV where his father's telegenic looks and charm have beguiled him. Quentin is a rogue – but not, Ian thinks, vicious. Prejudiced against socialists, foreigners, women, the Welsh and the working classes, the magazine has an intellectual zest and sense of fun that he can't help enjoying. He has been writing his pseudonymous piece about his life at the Samuel Smiles, which has seemed almost impossible to render down into a thousand words but which has helped to crystallise his frustration.

'There's quite a bit of mail for you,' Liza says.

'Oh. Thanks.'

Ian opens the letters, and there, as he hoped, are three invitations to come for interviews. One is at a selective state school in a leafy suburb, an establishment which has excellent results. The other is at a mixed school in Camden, which is around the middle of the league tables. The third – which he is surprised to get – is an offer to stay on as a permanent member of staff at the Samuel Smiles.

The three roads, Ian thinks. Obviously, he won't stay on where he is. The bad smells, the fuggy staffroom, the deafening noise of corridors and lack of leadership have put a veil of anger between him and his vocation, making everything too difficult. He feels sorry for the kids. But he, unlike his pupils, can escape.

He has an uneasy suspicion that, if his father runs his piece, it will be less because he cares about poor children than because it's another stick to beat the government with for failing in its mantra about education. But Ian himself has no intention of ducking out. Here, in his hand, are three roads to choose from. He'll still have to finish this term and the next one before he qualifies to teach in the British state system, but just knowing that there might be light at the end of the academic tunnel is reinvigorating. If he gets fully qualified he can teach anywhere in the world. He can leave Britain, be free as air. It's a heady thought; and yet he finds himself increasingly attached to the place. Maybe I should just find a little flat of my own, he thinks; if Katie can rent somewhere, I could, too.

As Ian jogs through the woods of Hampstead Heath on Saturday morning, he notices that the trees now have a faint prickle of pale green, and all the daffodils nearer the lake are out. Dogs bark and frisk through the grass, and there are two exquisite white swans building a nest by one of the Ponds. This is the England of literature and fantasy: perhaps, like African wildlife, it can only survive in special fenced-off areas, but on days like today he can believe that the country he has read about isn't a dream. All through his run, he has delighted in seeing great old oaks and chestnuts, their boles rippling and twisting with age like heavy fabric round a dancer's body. On a sloping lawn overlooking the lake is the most beautiful tree he has ever seen, shapely as a Greek lyre and tipped with silver buds. People stop to admire it; it's like a tree in a tale, and must have been planted well over a hundred years ago. He goes past the tall arched windows of Kenwood House and down precipitous steps past a marble-lined bathhouse to its courtyard café.

Katie is reading at a small table. Ian is shocked by the rush of pleasure he feels at seeing her.

'How are you?'

'I'm good,' she says. 'How's your arm?'

'The cast is coming off next week.'

'Oh, great.'

They buy coffee, sitting outside in the weak spring sun to sip it, and then he gives her his piece – which was the reason why he rang up to invite her out. The sun makes Katie's hair glow as she reads, ignoring a number of dogs yipping for their owners. She reads with total concentration, and Ian watches her face surreptitiously.

'This is good. I'm sure we'll run it. Maybe cut that paragraph here, and go into more detail about what the boys are like.'

'I don't want them or the school to be identifiable. There's actually

325

one boy whose family gets the *Rambler*. The dad's a minicab driver, from Pakistan, so not your average reader.'

'Is there? I must tell Quentin. He'll be pleased.'

Katie looks tired again, Ian notices; there are faint violet shadows under her grey eyes.

'Is my father working you very hard?'

'Organising the annual party is quite a business, on top of the rest. Apparently, his assistants always leave shortly after it,' she says, with her New England lack of complaint.

'Oh. Maybe you should be applying for another job too, then.'

'I'd certainly like to be paid more! Not that I don't like my colleagues.'

'Really?'

'Yes. In the beginning, you know, they seemed a little strange. We have debutantes in the US too, you know, and I'd come across them because – well, my ex was from that kind of family, though I'm not. They were pretty snotty to me. But my colleagues are nice, once you get to know them. Everyone dreads the party because Quentin goes into meltdown, so that's made the rest get along better. Cassandra is in love with this actor, and they won't have a penny if they get married, and her family thinks she's nuts – and Minty's got this brother who's disabled, and she really loves him and takes him to Lourdes every year – and Justin, he's such a sweet guy – I suppose you just have to be better acquainted to get fond of some people.'

'Even Crawley?'

Katie makes a face. 'I guess he's more of an acquired taste than some.'

A robin, which has been busy pecking for crumbs, perches on the back of a chair beside her and suddenly bursts into a trill of song. They both laugh, and it flies off.

'Was he rich, your ex?' asks Ian.

Katie nods.

'He, you know, works on Wall Street, and his family all have trust funds and things. I met him when I came to New York, and I think

I was just . . . dazzled, though I was also in love. You know, people ask why rich people always want more money? It's because they can see what a vast difference being rich makes to their lives. Ordinary people can't begin to imagine it: what it's like to have a private plane, and all these houses and jewels. I thought it didn't matter to me, but even my work visa was easy to get because I was going to be Winthrop's wife.'

Ian is trying to think of a way to ask her what happened.

'But you didn't marry.'

'Oh, no.' Katie gives a sad, almost apologetic smile. 'I mean, I signed the pre-nup and everything, and then I called off the wedding. It was horrible and embarrassing because it was going to be this big event, but I figured less horrible than being with someone who would always cheat on me. In this case, with my best friend.'

Ian feels himself colour. 'I suppose people don't do these things to cause pain deliberately.'

Katie scrapes the froth off her empty cappuccino mug. 'It's very easy, not to think. I always wonder how many people go through life without confronting a single moral problem.'

All around them pleasant-faced people are gathering, with dogs and prams and children, as if coagulating out of the fine fuzzy spring air. Though some wear green wellington boots, and some wear trainers, and some have funny woollen hats and others well-groomed heads; though there is a seeming variety of faces and types, all of them inhabit a world which is essentially that into which Ian was born. It would be so easy to believe this was the only one, or the only one that matters, he thinks.

'Maybe you only get to recognise morality problems if you have an imagination,' Katie adds. 'That was really Win's problem. He's a smart guy, great at mastering facts, but unable to learn any rules.'

'All I'm doing is teaching my pupils how to extract the facts from fiction, not the feelings,' Ian says bitterly. 'I'm supposed to teach them everything in gobbets. It's pure Gradgrind. Whereas what I want, fundamentally, is to teach them to *think*. To understand why it's important to have a dream of your own, like the guys in *Of Mice and Men*. Maybe that's too patronising.'

'My parents are teachers. I think they'd agree with you.'

'I hope so,' he says, smiling. Katie flushes, and looks away. Perhaps she is regretting having told him about her past. 'Maybe I should lighten up. Candice tells me I think too much.'

'You *can't* think too much!' she says passionately. 'The problem isn't thinking. It's not acting on thoughts, when you know them to be the right ones.'

'I don't know . . .'

They watch the people at the café. A child is howling for an ice cream, and her anxious parents are in a frenzy trying to placate her.

Ian says, 'The kids I teach think that what they want can be got with a knife, or by selling drugs. If I tell them otherwise, I can see them looking at me and thinking *Loser*.'

Katie looks at him for a long time, then seems to make up her mind. 'There's someone I have staying with me who – who is an innocent person, a teenager, who has been through a very bad time. I think she needs help, but I don't know what to do. She won't trust anyone, not even a doctor.'

'Why not?'

'Well – for one thing she's an illegal immigrant. Actually, it's worse than that. You know I told you there's a brothel downstairs in my house? Well, she got out of it. She thought she was coming here to work as a waitress.'

'You're sure she's telling the truth?'

'How can anyone be sure? But yes, I think she is, unless she's an amazing actress. She's only fifteen, Ian, that's the worst part. I couldn't turn her out.'

'What does she do all day?'

Katie laughs. 'Well, she's completely cleaned my place up. Only she never goes out. She's terrified of meeting the guys downstairs. I'm not crazy about them myself.'

'You've tried the police, haven't you?'

'Yes. So far, nothing. I don't know if they don't care, or if they're too busy filling in forms, or what. I can't take her into the station, naturally. She's terrified of being sent back to the Ukraine. I think she's quite smart, because she told me that when she arrived three months ago she hardly spoke a word of English, and now she's picked up quite a lot from daytime TV. Or, maybe, from her clients.'

'Has she talked about them?'

'No. It's not, you know, a subject either of us wants to discuss. But I also feel – there must be somewhere she could go? I've tried looking on the internet, but so far what comes up is the most abominable pornography. Maybe I'm not typing in the right searches.'

Ian thinks. 'You know, I happen to live with a doctor and a nurse. Both women, and neither of them English. They might be able to help.'

Katie agrees to take Liza's number, and when they part Ian jogs off, preoccupied. Her news has surprised him. What a weird tale; maybe she's a bit unbalanced, he thinks. Or maybe she's that rare thing, someone with true courage. Ian has met people like that, in South Africa: people who had suffered in different ways in order to try to bring about justice. He has always wondered what he himself would do if the chance arose, and fears that he would fail at this, as at so much.

40

Social Safari

Katie doesn't need another complication, but she is enjoying living with Anna. Although lugging extra potatoes from the supermarket onto the bus and up the stairs is burdensome, like sharing her space, it is nice, in a simple, uncomplicated way, simply to share food, especially as Anna is an unexpectedly good cook. Katie has started to put on a little weight. Her colleagues on the magazine tell her she looks much healthier, and perhaps because of this she feels more confident around them. Having Quentin as a common source of complaint is, as she hinted to Ian, a bond.

'The thing about the *Rambler* is, it's really only a stepping stone to other things,' Cassandra explained. 'Of course, poor old Justin will never leave.'

'Why not?'

'Well, he's perfectly comfortable in his niche, and he's missed the boat. But the rest of us . . . I mean, Quentin has made a great go of it, but really, he ought to move on.'

The most common thing that Londoners say to each other, almost reflexively, is 'Come on!' Even those who seem comfortably settled are, she discovers, constantly in the process of trading up or sizing down. Katie is too poor to fall prey to such temptation: she literally has to calculate how many apples she can afford when shopping for food. Somehow she must find out how to help Anna move on, for both their sakes, but there never seems to be any time, and when she sees the thin young girls streetwalking below her flat she can't bear to turn her adrift. Work is frenetic, and as March progresses it seems as if the pulse of London has increased. Just as cicadas shrill more loudly on a hotter day, so the better weather makes people walk, talk and lose their tempers faster.

A thousand people have been invited to the *Rambler* party, and over five hundred are definitely coming. As these include the Prime Minister and several members of the Cabinet and Shadow Cabinet, the offices have had to be cleared by Special Branch. They arrive the evening before with equipment that looks just like metal detectors, and some keen, panting springer spaniels.

'Oh, the darlings!' cry the girls, and rush to pat them. Cecilia's pug dog Boswell is so jealous that he promptly pees all over the offices, bleaching the Turkish carpet in the editor's office in spots. Really, what the staff are more interested in are the Special Branch police-men, who are even better looking than Cassandra's boyfriend. Alas, the officers are stolidly professional.

'Excuse me, could this lift be blocked up?'

'It goes up to the proprietor's flat,' says Justin. 'He has a pied-à-terre on the top.'

'I see, sir. Are there any arrangements in case it fails?'

'No,' says Justin, looking like an ostrich longing to put its head in the sand. 'You always ask this, and there never are.'

'It's just that, in the event of the PM wishing to use the lift, we have to make quite sure it's safe, sir.'

'I doubt he'll want to. It's a private residence.'

The Special Branch officer murmurs into a device hooked into his ear. 'Health and Safety regulations require us to have an engineer standing in the shaft for the entire duration of the party.'

'Oh, Lord,' Justin mutters. 'Ridiculous!'

Katie and the rest of the staff agree. Special Branch must have a copy of the guest list too.

'In any case, it's a total waste of time,' says Cassandra. 'Half the guests are gatecrashers. You wait, there'll be twice as many people as guests, blagging their way in.'

'But none of them eligible,' Cecilia says, sighing.

Poor Cecilia is increasingly unhappy, and spends more and more time sobbing in the loos, repeatedly punching the hand dryer to drown out the sound when she's not talking on her cellphone in Italian, German, French and Spanish to her friends on several continents about Quentin's refusal to leave his wife. Her desk has been moved, so Katie is once again in the line of fire.

'Katie! This is a nothing list!'

'A nothing list, Quentin?'

'I want names, big names. I want celebrities! People who're in Debrett's don't matter any more, and neither do Justin's wretched little artistes. Get me that model from *Razzle*! You know, the one with the magnificent embonpoint – it'll put Trench in a good mood. Get rid of these idiotic *writers*, who on earth wants to meet *them*?'

Katie does her best. Perhaps it's that she can see Quentin's abundant dark locks are increasingly streaked with grey, or that he looks more strained when Mark Crawley, in his usual way, tries to bludgeon him about the political content of the magazine. Whenever Trench comes to the Friday lunch, Crawley attaches himself like a leech.

'You know, some people even think we're a publication for walkers?' he can be heard saying. 'Maybe we ought to change the title to the *New Rambler*.'

'You do realise what a nightmare it'll be if he gets to be the next editor?' Justin murmurs. 'I'd rather have Q shagging Cecilia on the sofa than that.'

'Surely Trench would never appoint him? He's so absolutely a face for radio.'

'I don't know. He has a lot of support in some quarters.'

Katie can't help thinking that if Crawley does take over she will get her own marching orders. He's typical of the journalists she has met so far. Few ever have a good word to say about each other in private; the women are always derided by the men as airheads, and the men are in turn castigated as bigots and dinosaurs. Even so, Crawley is peculiarly unpleasant. He pretends to be a shy man when he's occasionally made aware that his total absence of manners has grated on someone who might be useful, but is otherwise a bully.

'Maybe he'll go into politics himself,' says Minty. 'Any conversation with him is like swallowing the snake along with the snake oil.'

'He thinks politicians are coming to see *him*, because of his column,' Cassandra says.

Quentin frets over the invitation list. 'I'm not sure anyone is taking this seriously enough.'

'Is the annual party of *any* publication to be taken seriously?' Justin mutters.

Quentin fixes him with a withering stare. 'The media is a business, like any other,' he says. 'Simply because it's staffed by the few remaining eccentrics and misfits in Britain, as opposed to the little grey men everywhere else, means it matters more, not less.'

'Gore Tore?' suggests Minty.

'I've got him,' says Katie, checking her clipboard. 'Do rock stars really come?'

'Of course,' says Cassandra. 'The stupid ones want intellectual credibility, the intellectuals are all snobs and the snobs just want to have a good time with their friends.'

'It's the one thing that stops Trench from retrenching.'

'Which reminds me, Quentin, when are you going to put our wages up?' Minty says.

'Ha! Ask your father to increase your allowance, my dear girl.'

'You said that last year, too,' Minty mutters.

The day of the party arrives and the grimy ground-floor offices are transformed, with boxes and boxes of books dispatched to Oxfam in order to clear floor space. Computer terminals are taken upstairs, and a marquee is erected in the long thin garden at the back. The worn French windows are opened, patio heaters are lit and fairy lights switched on. Although Patrick, in charge of flowers, has annoyed everyone by ordering immense vases of green gladioli which impede sight lines, the effect is surprisingly stylish.

'What exactly happens at a *Rambler* party?' Katie asks.

'You work your way down to the end of the garden, and back again,' Justin tells her. 'It's the ultimate British queue.'

'How long does that take?'

'Oh, about twenty minutes, if you don't know anybody. You're on the hall.'

There are caterers who whisk white linen cloths over the desks, turning them into tables for trays of champagne and silver trays of canapés. In the basement, where damp-riddled copies dating back to 1750 are stacked in sheaves, more are busy opening bottles to take upstairs.

'God, it's exhausting just *watching* Poles work,' Patrick sighs.

Outside, by the front door, two Special Branch policemen check incomers with a minatory stare. An alternative party spills out into the street, in among the throbbing black cabs depositing ever more guests under the blossoming, sterile cherries. The sky has turned an exquisite shade of pale green, deepening into violet. Everyone has abandoned any pretence of work and is getting changed.

Katie feels a sudden deep shiver, of excitement or nerves. This is, after all, something she is glad to be seeing on her social safari. Within minutes of the starting time, guests are queuing to get in. There is a rattle and whine of flashbulbs popping off outside as paparazzi gather, searching for celebrities. Will they really appear at this odd, shabby little publication? Apparently so.

She stands in the narrow hall, ticking off names on a clipboard. All kinds of freelances who have just been voices on the phone appear. An Acropolis of columnists – the magazine's theatre, film, radio, art and TV critics; the agony aunt who gives such drolly misleading advice; a man in a pinstriped suit who turns out to be their Wine Correspondent, and a tramp who is their City Editor, plus numerous jolly, jowly journalists of both sexes baying like a pack of bloodhounds. There is an unending succession of former Tobys, instantly identifiable by their floppy hair and amiable expressions, and a handful of fragrant, elegant women who have made it to pinnacles of power and who wear stiletto heels to remind everyone of this fact. The waiting photographers go crazy over a young woman who reads the weather forecast on some TV channel, and another whose pride in her enormous breasts has been replaced by a burning desire for respectability as a children's author. Katie quickly learns how to spot the ones who should be shepherded through speedily: their teeth fluoresce in the poorly lit hall. The bearded figure of the persistent poet approaches.

'Hi,' Katie says, smiling at him. 'Invitation?'

'Er—'

'That's fine,' she says on an impulse of mischief. 'Go right in.'

Behind her, the roar of a good party thrums through the building as more and more people force their way through. Many are not on the list.

'But I'm a friend of Panga's!' a boisterous young man in a bow tie insists.

'Oh, let him in if he's shameless enough to have got this far,' says Patrick. He's there to check out the talent, he says, and also to inform his pet gossip columnist.

It becomes steamy and close, even with the door wedged open and the French windows into the garden allowing a flow of brisk spring air.

'Really, it's just an adult game of sardines,' Patrick says. 'Valeria! Darling!'

Katie wonders how many more people can possibly fit in. She looks up and sees Ian. 'Hi there. I didn't think you'd come.'

'I almost didn't, but I changed my mind.'

They look at each other. Ian has tied his long floppy hair back in a ponytail, which suits him, Katie thinks.

335

'Hello, Katie,' says Georgina Hunter. 'Could we just get past?'

'Of course,' she says apologetically. 'Go right ahead.'

At the entrance there is a kind of commotion. Ian turns, as do several others, and Katie cranes her neck to see what is causing it.

'Oh God!'

'No! No!'

'Stop him.'

'Get out, get out . . .'

Then, in the growing confusion, in a murmur that swells and swells like the sound in the trees before a storm, comes a gunshot, and screaming.

41

Tariq's Sons

His conversations with Tariq's sons disturb Job. They are just children, he thinks to himself; it's natural that they think of guns and
wars. He tries to remember whether his own dreams had included so
much bloodshed at their age; but whatever memories he may have
had are overlaid by ones of real violence, as a faint stain is overlaid
by a bigger, darker one. When Job dreams now, his dreams are of
sorrow and longing, fear and desire. He sees fragments: a child's eyes
crawling with flies, the wooden floor of the Wisdens' library, a
bloated poster of Mugabe, a man on fire, burning.

On either side of the thin, pockmarked partitions that divide
people on this insomniac estate he can hear the other lives, cease-
lessly churning. Forbidden to work, there is nothing for many to do,
and nowhere for them to go, only concrete and more concrete, brutal
boxes, and beyond it all the indiscriminate crawl of traffic. The baby
belonging to the Gambian family cries with a faint whispery sound,
like a dripping tap; its father is a student whom Job sometimes passes
on his way to work. Job envies him so much for having his family
there. Someone moans to themselves in another language. The two
Turkish girls have moved on, without warning, and have been

replaced by a young French Algerian, who has explained to Job that he has come to London because he can't get a job in France.

'*Le racisme*,' he says, as if complaining about the weather.

'What can you do here?'

'I can teach French.'

Everyone in the flats is restlessly searching like the scrawny pigeons that waddle and peck at invisible specks of food, roosting on such window ledges as do not bristle with wires to repel them. Below, in the muddy enclosure where a blistered red climbing frame is supposed to encourage young families to play between the looming blocks, a dog barks. It will be one of the many squat Staffordshire cross-breeds which shit on the grass, and are popular on the estate among the remaining white people despite their tendency to attack small children.

Job can understand the thirst for violence. His own childhood, blissful though it seemed, had been full of ambivalence, the consciousness that every gradation of skin colour brought with it different restrictions or possibilities. His mother had been one of eleven children, ranging from a brother so pale that he had married a German woman and could get into places for white people, to herself, so dark that a life as a farm labourer had seemed like the only one possible. Working as one of the Wisdens' maids had been more than she might have hoped for, but she knew that her employers could afford meat every day while her own family ate it once a week. Job and his sister were intelligent, but they were doomed to stop their schooling and work on the farm as labourers as soon as they were thirteen. Yet the Wisdens had paid for Miriam's training as a nurse in Harare. He looks at Tariq's sons. Blood, vengeance and punishment are words they use repeatedly. This, perhaps, is one reason why they don't want to read. They can't settle, in the way that all readers must. They have never been taught to keep still. How can they pray? Or maybe, when prayers are charged with anger they are something different.

'Who is telling you all these things?' he asks. 'The internet? The TV?'

'People. The Jews control everything, but the truth gets out.'

'Do you know any Jews?'

'How could I? They work, invisibly, to make our lives harder.'

'Why do they do that?'

'They are inferiors,' Amir says.

Job is surprised by this.

'Selim says so,' says Chandra.

'Does your priest?'

The boys exchange smiles and shrugs. 'He would like to, but he can't because the *kuffar* police bug the mosques. Everybody knows that!'

'But good Muslims make jihad, Mr Job, against the oppression of this country.'

'Where else in the world do you think Muslims are more free than in Britain?' Job asks in a tone of mild enquiry. They make no coherent answer. If Amir and Chandra were asked to find places like Saudi Arabia, Iraq, Iran and Israel on a map of the world, he doubts they would be able to do so. One of the first things he has done is buy them a jigsaw of the world from a charity shop, and each lesson, when they have done some reading, he reads to them while they fit the pieces together. It's a good map – although some pieces, inevitably, are missing – enlivened by ships, whales, wolves and even rockets as well as tiny figures of people. Over Zimbabwe there is only the figure of a rhinoceros. Britain has Big Ben.

They talk as much as they read. Job has the impression that although the boys are full of questions about justice, punishment, bullying and loyalty, neither Tariq nor their mother talks to them; all their information seems to come from their big brother.

'Selim says that's *haram*—' is how most of their sentences begin. So much is influenced by him. He gathers that Selim only visits when their father isn't there: that's why the boys' mother looks so sad. To Amir and Chandra, Selim is a hero.

'He's hard, Mr Job. Him and Dad, they don't get along. Dad thinks we're British Muslims, like, we read the Koran but we obey the *kuffar* law. Selim, he's different. He says Muslims are treated worse than lepers, that we have to show British people how we feel.'

'Why does he feel that?'

Chandra and Amir exchange glances. 'School.'

'Was that a bad experience?'

As they get excited, their words tumble out, slurring in a mixture of Cockney and Pakistani that Job finds hard to follow. He hears how nobody dares use the toilets because that's where you get beaten up, about the way during breaks the playground is criss-crossed with invisible territorial frontiers, about how Selim was bullied because his parents weren't from Bangladesh or Somalia.

'They's Muslim too, but they still hates us,' Amir says.

'Is your brother happier, now he isn't at school?'

'He is very religious,' Amir says. 'Going to Pakistan changed him.'

'Would you like to go there?'

The boys look identically doubtful.

'Selim says they're way harsh. They pray all the time. Do you pray, Mr Job?'

'I used to,' Job says.

'Why don't you any more?'

'I no longer believe that God hears me.'

Amir and Chandra look at him solemnly. 'If you pray, Allah always hears.'

Their conviction touches him. He relishes their enthusiasm, their dreaminess, their energy. Sometimes they break off reading because the boys want to hurl themselves over the back of the sofa like high jumpers, which makes him laugh.

'Do you do that at school?'

'No, but we want to.'

Job coaxes them through page after page, encouraging, correcting, praising. His old yearning to teach returns, and the boys are enjoying reading a story book.

'It's so different from school,' Amir says. 'At school we can never relax or be ourselves.'

'But the books are always the same,' Job says gently. 'They are always there, just as they were written, no matter how much time has passed. Every time you read a book your mind touches that of the person who wrote it – even if they died a long time ago.'

Chandra pipes up, 'What I'd like to do is make a big bomb, and blow up my school.'

Job laughs. 'Everyone feels like that, for a while. Are there no teachers you could respect?'

Amir says, 'Mr Bredin, he's OK. Lame, but not mean. He's stayed, not like the others.'

'What does he teach?'

'English, and sport. He's from Africa, like you, only he's white. Why is that?'

'There are many kinds of African,' says Job. He's supposed to be improving their reading, not their grasp of history.

Thanks perhaps to his friendship with Tariq, and to the regular custom he gets from Polly, Job is leasing a better car these days, a BMW saloon. It's second- or even third-hand, but he keeps it spotless, and now other drivers give way to him more often on the road. He has cut down on the car-wash job, going only on Saturdays when trade is busiest. Since Damien's absence, Michael has become their leader, and although the car wash looks no different it is better run, because tips are now shared out equally.

Everything is getting better. Job likes fetching Robbie from school, likes driving his new car, and likes chatting to Polly when she books him. She is dressed up today in a way he hasn't seen before, with perfume and diamond earrings and a soft red dress which makes her look prettier than usual. A bearded man is with her, and it's obvious to Job that this must be what Robbie calls 'Mum's boyfriend'. He nods and smiles when introduced, and speaks in an odd accent – half-American, half-English – about their destination.

'Do you know where the offices of the *Rambler* are? Left off Baker Street, past Manchester Square? I can direct you.'

'Yes, sir,' says Job. 'Perhaps if I could just have the postcode?'

341

He punches it into his new mobile phone, another improvement.

'Amazing what a difference technology makes,' says Shade. 'In the old days, becoming a black-cab driver took three years. Now anyone with a cellphone can find their way around, even if they can barely speak English.'

'Oh, Job's English is as good as yours or mine, Bill,' says Polly. She catches Job's eye in the driver's mirror and smiles apologetically.

It's clear that they are going to a party. Job is so used to seeing Londoners weaving in groups of three, bottle in hand, before throwing up or fighting, or walking in droves with that look of dour determination to work, that he's forgotten how they look when they're actually enjoying themselves.

'Look,' says Polly in a pleased voice. 'There's Justin! He hasn't changed since Oxford.'

'I can see Panga, too.'

'Where?'

'Over there, with a couple of pretty girls. Really, he's outrageous.'

'Well, he looks happy at least.'

'Look at all those politicians going in, snouts in trough,' Shade says.

Job is curious to see what a British politician looks like. Will they be surrounded by soldiers with guns? Will they have megaphones? He looks, and sees a group of men in suits, all white and middle-aged, talking. There is nothing to show who has power.

'They aren't *all* bad,' says Polly. 'I do believe some still work for the common good.'

'Sweet Pollyanna! Ever the optimist,' says Shade, and she laughs. Job wonders if she picks up the patronising note in his voice.

They aren't going to be long, Polly has said, and have booked him for the evening. Job cruises along the street, looking for a good place to park. Polly works hard, he knows, but she has no idea what it's like to be constantly behind the wheel, crossing and recrossing the city. To rest in his car and listen to the radio, knowing he will still be paid, is a holiday. He has packed a sandwich, tinned tuna and sweetcorn, and takes pleasure in eating it, slowly. Ah! Job thinks. For a moment, he is entirely happy because he can feel the good food descending to his stomach.

'Excuse me, sir, could I see your driver's licence?'

A policeman in a yellow flak jacket is bending down by his window. Job, sweating in an access of terror, fumbles for his fake licence. The man scrutinises it, and Job's photo, but it seems to pass muster because he hands it back.

'Thank you, sir. Why are you waiting here?'

'I am doing wait-and-return for two guests,' Job says.

'Names?'

'Mrs Polly Noble and Mr Bill—' He searches his memory for the surname. 'Mr Shade.'

Job is really nervous now, but the policeman speaks the names into his radio. Moments later, they check out.

'Thank you, sir. Have a good evening.'

It's clear that someone important is arriving because there is a flurry of movement and interest near the front door. A sleek black car, flanked by two others, draws up. Job barely glimpses him, guarded between two other men, but he recognises the stern craggy face of the Prime Minister, paler and more worn than he looks on TV. The waiting cameras rattle and whine, releasing another storm of brightness which reflects from Job's side-mirrors. He shuts his eyes, and when he opens them he can see somebody else walking along the street, reflected in his wing mirror. Idly, he watches the figure, and a piece of paper swirling around in an eddy of wind.

It is a young brown-skinned man, simply dressed in trousers and a jacket, and as he passes Job's car Job looks up and suddenly recognises Tariq's eldest son, Selim. Even though Job has only seen him a few times, he is completely certain. Selim is walking with a strange, fixed expression. How odd, Job thinks, and wonders whether he should get out of the car to greet him. The coincidence of seeing someone he knows, however slightly, in this street makes him feel childishly pleased. But the impulse passes. Londoners never behave in that way,

343

he tells himself; only Africans do. He watches Selim's figure retreat towards the crowd at the party door, the stripe on the back of his jacket like a crack in the darkening world.

Gird up your loins like a man.

The voice is so quiet, he can hardly hear it. What does it mean? The paper in the street twists in a miniature whirlwind.

Gird up your loins like a man; for I will demand of thee and answer thou me.

His fingers shaking, Job opens the car door and begins to run.

42

I Know This Man

Being part of a couple, Polly thinks, is like running in a three-legged race. When she lives independently of Bill Shade, she forgets how much time she has to spend pretending to be better or prettier or nicer than she really is. She had waxed her legs, shaved her armpits, tweezered her face, and is now so stiff with foundation, powder, blusher and lipstick that she feels that if she smiles too much half her face may fall off. Polly, whose normal appearance is that of a small woman who has had an unfortunate encounter with a tornado, has even had her hair done, and is also wearing the kind of reinforced underpants that women who have had babies tend to resort to on special occasions to flatten the stomach.

Such were the efforts she had once made as Theo's wife. She is a different person now: thinner, sharper, busier and perhaps more bitter. Polly can tell that Bill doesn't feel comfortable in Job's shabby old BMW; it doesn't go with his Hollywood teeth and manicured nails, but it goes with her. She feels quite defiant about it. This is who I am, she thinks silently. She doesn't want pity, or patronage, or even praise, but in order to come to this party she is having to pay Teresa, and will be working through the weekend to catch up on her briefs.

Polly looks at Bill sideways, at the red mouth and the weak chin in the nest of dark beard. She loves him because he's such fun in bed, and she never really enjoyed sex before; and also, if she's honest, she enjoys the sprinkling of stardust he brings from Hollywood. The cable TV show he's doing is good, and even if he's at the bottom of the food chain and feels he's a failure, he always has amazing gossip. Yet she knows that he isn't central to her life in the way that her children and her friends are. Would it be different if she were to uproot her family and move to LA? She's afraid that if she stays in London, the relationship will wither away; that she will wither too, and become one of those solemn, self-righteous divorcees, angry about everything and not even capable of choosing between different kinds of unhappiness.

'I suppose it's an institution, isn't it?' she says brightly to Bill as they walk up to the door of the *Rambler*. 'I'm just a little surprised you're willing to be a part of it.'

'Oh, I'm the opposite of Groucho Marx, happy to join any club that will have me,' he says. She hopes he's being ironic, but maybe it's true.

'It's always the way the English subsume other races, isn't it – by seeming to be exclusive, then quietly offering membership, provided you've learnt the rules.' Polly is speaking a little too loudly and self-consciously because she has just remembered how much she dislikes parties full of people she doesn't know.

'Just like Ancient Rome,' Bill replies. 'I never feel so much like the pork scratching at a bar mitzvah as when I come back to Britain.'

He's joking, she thinks. Bill always makes such a fuss about being Jewish and different, but the truth is that he slots right into a certain kind of glitzy media life; it's Polly, who looks so English but who feels so alien, who is the awkward one. Or perhaps everyone in the world feels that parties are something that other people enjoy, and which they endure because otherwise the alternative is another evening alone.

They hang back a little, because the entrance is crowded. Bill spots someone he knows, and they begin talking enthusiastically, with no more than a perfunctory introduction to Polly. He is at ease in the company of other men, she realises. Suppressed violence, the competitiveness that is barely concealed by smart clothes and affable manners, is his default setting. Underneath, all men are like something from an earlier stage of evolution, more brutal and more practical because, unlike women, they are allowed to be animals. Polly has always thought of Bill as a woman's man, because he can talk about feelings, but here she can see that he fits right in. It reminds her of her earliest days in the City, all these roaring men, their skins gleaming with alcohol and affluence, showing off to each other. They didn't need women, not really, not as women needed men. She wonders whether her son will become like this, when now he is so sweet, vulnerable and loving; Tania is always sneering at her for being soft on him, as if hardness were more desirable.

The party has been going for over an hour, and is clearly at its peak. Be calm, keep smiling, Polly tells herself. Her boss Sam Stern will be here; it's good for her to remind him of her existence – unless, of course, he looks at her with total blankness. The women here are at least fifteen years younger and two stone lighter than herself, and far more professionally distinguished. They wear tiny dresses, and are almost as slim as Katie – whom she can just glimpse inside. Oh, to be thirty again, she thinks, knowing that even that would seem old to them. She spots Ivo Sponge with relief.

'Polly my darling! I didn't know the *Rambler* was your sort of scene. Look, there's Dame Jane. Have you seen her at the National?'

'No – should I?'

'Well, yes. Completely mesmerising, even if she does look a little too much like an escapee from a Greek vase.'

Ivo is always good value, a fount of gossip and a sewer of information, especially when Ellen isn't around. He rattles off a story about a famously reclusive designer, explaining that it was due to his having had so many facelifts that, when he went bald, the scars meant he couldn't appear in public. Polly laughs, grateful not to seem too dependent on Bill.

347

'Really, Ivo, I do wish you'd come back to England to work.'

'I have been approached, my darling, but they couldn't afford me. No, it's permanent jet lag for a while yet. But apropos the dear old *Rambler*, watch this space. Moves are afoot, my spies tell me.'

'Really?'

She sees a young man, almost a boy, approaching them. He's wearing a padded jacket and looks odd. Then Polly wonders whether he's on drugs because he's saying something over and over again, something which she can't quite catch. Perhaps he's lost, she thinks, and she smiles at him enquiringly. She's used to being stopped by tourists and asked for directions; she must just have that sort of face, maternal and kind and – she fears – dull. The boy brushes past, ignoring her, and then, suddenly, she feels a violent blow.

Polly falls onto the pavement, banging her knee and the palms of her hands. The pain is so shocking that she feels like bursting into tears of anguished surprise. Someone is shouting.

'Stop! Stop!'

Polly lifts her head, and there, right in front of her, are two men on top of each other, struggling. Both are dark, and one, to her astonishment, is Job; the other is the boy who just passed her. Some people are tittering with embarrassment, and some are watching with imperturbable disdain.

'Break it up, and get away from the door, gentlemen. Move along, please, you're causing a public disturbance.'

Job is grappling with the boy's hands and arms, hugging him tight, and the boy beneath him is shouting something in a muffled voice, and Job says, 'No, Selim!'

'Put your hands above your heads,' says the policeman. To Polly's horror, he and his colleague have drawn guns and are pointing them at the two men. The crowd of party-goers is disturbed. Expressions of mild alarm cross faces, and more and more people are turning to watch or pressing against the windows of the office. A frantic one-way radio conversation is going on, conducted by a young man who must be a plain-clothes policeman because he's wearing an almost invisible wire in his ear. The Prime Minister's inside, Polly thinks; there are artists, directors and writers; controversial figures, and columnists who have called for animal experimentation, a secular education system and the abortion of foetuses. But the party is still roaring, as if none of this were going on.

The two men wrestle, illuminated by the street lights and the light over the door. Job is bigger than the boy, and heavier, and he is trying to hold on to his arms but somehow the boy rolls over. His look of calm is unfaltering, but he's also gritting his teeth and making a huge effort to get free. There is a belt around his waist, and something odd about this. Polly doesn't quite understand what she's seeing, but then a policeman shouts in a hard, panicky voice, 'Down, get down, everyone! Clear the area!'

There is a metallic clicking noise all around. It's as if the photographers are working again – and perhaps they are, because Polly can hear the whirr and click of cameras. But this sound is heavier.

They're going to shoot them both, she thinks.

'Put your hands above your heads, above your heads! This is your final warning!'

Words struggle into Polly's throat.

'Don't – stop – I know this man—'

There is a sharp cracking sound, then another and another. The air is filled with a smell of acrid smoke.

Then it stops. There is almost total silence. Even the photographers have stopped filming.

'Job!' Polly cries out, seeing how still he lies, and the blood spreading around him.

'Stand aside, madam. We're evacuating the area.'

'But I *know* this man, he's my driver,' Polly says. In the distance she can hear the pulse of sirens, and it becomes the throb of nausea in her throat. A policeman is bending down over the bodies, holding his hand down to feel for a pulse.

'We need an ambulance, an ambulance, over,' he says into his radio. 'Two men down.'

349

The building is being evacuated. The crowd around the entrance is streaming away in a patter of hurrying feet, with high-heeled shoes kicked off and abandoned. Two bodyguards whisk the Prime Minister into a black car, which streaks away. More and more police cars arrive. A helicopter is circling overhead, focusing a fierce bright beam of light which makes the crowd blink as if awakening from a dream. It has taken perhaps four minutes since the sounds of the shots, and Polly imagines the confusion that must be rippling out over the city as the news spreads.

'Job isn't a terrorist,' she says. 'He's just my driver. There's been a mistake.'

Nobody listens. People are calm, orderly, polite, but terrified. There is no pushing or shoving, but in every face there is now the knowledge that, just seconds before, they might have been killed. A couple of doctors have stepped forward to offer help, now that the other man has been dragged off Job. Polly feels tears rise to her eyes, because he's so still.

'The bomb-disposal team are almost here,' she can hear an officer saying. There is relief in his voice. *Is* it a bomb round the other man's waist? It's hard to tell.

She can see Ivo, and Katie, and then one face in the crowd swims up into the bright light as if out of deep water. He's a middle-aged man in a suit, standing behind a young woman whose mouth is open in an expression of panic, and perhaps it's that which makes her recognise him. Their gazes meet, and in that split second Polly knows who he is, because they've met, and she also knows where she's seen him since. It's the man from Iryna's mobile, the man whose identity was so important that she left it behind for Polly to find: Roger Trench.

'Can you identify this man, madam?' the policeman is asking. 'You said you know him.'

'He's a minicab driver,' Polly says, jerking her thoughts back. 'He drove me here – I use him often. His name is Job. I don't know his surname, but he's not an Islamist, he's from Zimbabwe. He was trying to stop the other one, don't you see?'

'We'll be taking statements from witnesses,' the policeman says. He's in shock too, the skin tight over his eye sockets. Job, Polly thinks, amazed. That cheerful, naive, round young face. She wants to run to him and tend to him like his mother. Beyond, where the road has been taped across and people are being checked by more police, camera crews gather like crows.

Polly looks around, wondering where Bill is, but then two ambulances arrive. How many times has she heard this banshee sound in the past few years, and felt unequivocal dread at the random misfortune or deliberate malice that they advertise? The two men are lifted onto stretchers – she's glad to see that the bomb-disposal men have taken the belt off and removed it to another vehicle.

'Where will they take him? Job, I mean?'

'I couldn't say, madam.'

'I need to get home. I need to let my children know I'm safe.' Polly is exhausted, and dreads another long interrogation and session of form-filling like the one she had after identifying Iryna. She thinks again of the face she saw, emerging from the party. How can she be sure? Maybe if I ask Katie who he is, describe him, maybe she'll know. Or she can simply type his name into Google. Easy to fit a face to a name, but not the other way around.

'Write down your name and details, please, and then you can go.'

Little tremors shake Polly's hand. She walks to the barrier, to the great crush of cars and cameras and questioners with microphones.

'Did you see him?'

'Is it true he was a terrorist?'

'Did he say anything?'

Polly desperately wants to go home, but she knows what she must do to help Job.

'Yes,' she says, loudly and clearly. The cameras and hand-held recorders swivel in her direction. 'I was standing right where the shooting happened, or rather I was until the man who saved us all pushed me to the ground, and I know him.'

She takes a deep breath. 'His name is Job, and he's an illegal

351

immigrant from Zimbabwe. He's a minicab driver, not a terrorist. I don't know how he guessed what the other man was intending to do – but what I do know is that if there had been a bomb, several hundred people at the party, including myself, would have been killed or wounded if it hadn't been for Job's actions. The police shot an unarmed man, and a hero.'

Ignoring the babble of fresh questions, she pushes forward, after giving her name and profession to the BBC crew. She's got her story in first; she will offer to represent Job in court if he gets prosecuted. Anger and sadness make her walk faster and faster.

'Polly, wait!'

It's Bill.

'Hey, are you OK?'

'Yes, fine. I'm getting a taxi home.'

'I couldn't figure out what was happening, and I couldn't see you anywhere.'

His eyes are shining with earnestness. It's as if something in Polly's brain has blown a circuit, because she just doesn't care any more. He looks like a gerbil that Tania once had, she thinks – a little, furry, big-eyed gerbil who spins all day on a wheel, in a cage.

'You left me.'

'I had to, the police moved everyone on.'

'Not us, you. *You* could have stayed. If you cared for me, you would have stayed. That's what this is really all about, isn't it? You didn't fundamentally care enough to check whether I was alive or dead.'

'I should have stayed, Polly, please, believe me, I do know that. I just freaked out, with the guns. Polly, don't get mad at me, don't—'

Polly says, with an anger made worse by humiliation, 'All my life, I've been taken in by men. If it had been me – if it had been you, lying there, and me on the sidelines, I would have stayed, you know. But you didn't. Now excuse me, because there's something else I have to let the police know.'

43

The Green Flame of New Leaves

Ian has his arm around Katie, and she has her face pressed against his body. The frightened crowd, pushing forward along the entrance in the rush to escape to the open air, is sufficient excuse. They are trembling as if their skins can no longer contain them. If I die this moment, Ian thinks, I want it to be in her arms. The thought has hit him like – the metaphor suggests itself with irony – a bombshell.

Once everyone is out of the corridor a genteel stampede erupts, past the two bodies and the knot of police and out into the chill evening. Arriving at the end of the street, they get stopped. There are police cars and lines of tape blocking their exit. Bureaucracy has taken charge, and the slow process through official questioning is like passing through the digestive tract of a boa constrictor. Beyond this there are lights and questions and camera lenses but luckily there are far more famous faces to give their accounts of the attempted bombing. Many have even seen it as a professional opportunity, and are preening and posing for the public. Ian is disgusted. He has glimpsed the two bodies, and the intense, grim expressions of the policemen guarding them while a bomb-disposal expert gets to work. This, then, is England now.

He had grown up with the anticipation of violence hanging heavy on him. The houses guarded by electronic gates and armed-response units, the necessity to lock your car from the inside when driving and never stop to help another person, the estates protected by high walls and wire and dogs – all this had been part of his upbringing. Ian had not realised how oppressive it was until he'd left home. He had seen the horror of the Twin Towers in New York, and the iconic image of a red double-decker bus with its roof blown off from 7/7, but it had all been melodramatic and remote, not something that could possibly affect him. Yet in the space of three months he has seen the corpse of a murdered woman, has had his arm broken in an accident and now has just survived an assassination attempt.

Ian wonders, fleetingly, whether his father has got out. He hadn't even got in to say hello to Quentin. Perhaps he should take comfort from the fact that nobody apart from the two terrorists appears to have been hurt – though some are saying that one of them wasn't a terrorist at all but a member of the public who tried to stop the other.

'Move along as quickly as you can, out of the cordoned area,' a loudspeaker keeps saying over the thudding whirr of helicopter rotor blades. Somehow it is more frightening out here than it was indoors. The noises are magnified by the buildings all around.

'Are you OK?' he asks Katie. She nods, and smiles, and they run, holding hands.

At last the sirens fade in their ears and they slow down. It's like walking in a dream. A block or so away is Oxford Street, but this is Fitzrovia, with small shops, cafés, a row of restaurants. Ian is acutely aware of the green flame of new leaves running along the trees. A kind of fever has seized him, in which he feels both intensely alive and alert, and also detached. At Manchester Square they stop and turn to each other. Ian thinks of all the other times he has kissed a new girl, the moment when indecision becomes decision, and knows that the moment has come.

Ian kisses Katie, and although the kiss has the same component parts – lips, teeth, tongues, hands, hair and flesh – as a hundred thousand others he has had between the age of thirteen and twenty-eight, it's also different. He is falling, or flying, he is falling into sleep or waking up for the first time. Yet there is also the growing awareness that it's going wrong, because she is pushing him away.

'I'm sorry. No.'

'No?'

'No.'

He refuses to believe her and kisses her again, a different kiss this time because he's trying to make her change her mind. The kiss is a kind of battle, advancing and repelling, and they both make stifled noises of frustration, greed, anguish and determination. Katie judders as if electrocuted, then breaks away.

'You have to stop. I don't want this, I don't need this. I thought we were *friends*.'

'We were – we are. It's just that it's more than that.'

Ian is conscious of sounding petulant, angry, despairing. No girl has ever denied him, and he has taken that for granted. Rejection is more mortifying than he could have imagined: for the first time he understands why some men force women; yet he can't. All the blood in his body has rushed from his head to his groin, and it hurts. He wants her, she doesn't want him. It's like being trapped between an immovable object and an irresistible force.

Katie is shivering. 'You're in a relationship already, anyway.'

'It's never been serious, if that's the problem. I've been trying to end it.'

Candice will be absolutely furious, and she has every right to be. But that's her problem, Ian thinks defiantly.

'I'm sure she doesn't know that, does she?'

'I'll end it.'

'Why do you think that would make you any less like your father?'

Her contempt stings him, and he steps back.

'OK, OK. I'm in the wrong, *ja*? Only – you feel it too, don't you?'

'No. I'm going to catch the bus.'

Katie breaks away and sprints down the street. Her long legs flash against her black dress like clappers in a bell. He's frightened her, misjudged her, he's a fool.

'Wait! We can catch the same one!' he calls, despairingly.

Could this surge of passion be the effect of shock? He has to consider it as a rational possibility. After all, people who survive danger together often find themselves attracted – he's sure he's read that somewhere. He thinks of how they had first met, and how plain and odd she'd seemed, the complete opposite to anyone he'd ever dated. Only now, everything that had annoyed him makes her desirable and intriguing. I'm in love with her, he thinks, astonished; this thing that I never thought would happen, has.

It isn't your fault, Ian thinks, trying to rehearse what to say to Candice. It really isn't, either. They've had a good time, as if they'd gone away on a beach holiday together, only she isn't what he wants. He is in love with Katie. He is in love. The top of the double-decker bus taking him back has plastic windows smeared with scratches which spin the passing street lights into perfect circles of orange luminescence. Only she has rejected him, just like that. He thinks of the rustle of her silk dress as they ran, and wants to weep.

'Oh, my God, Ian?'

It's Liza at the door, pale and stressed. He's touched by her concern. The bomb attempt must have been on the news, and he'd already forgotten it.

'It's OK, really. The police got him, I'm safe, everybody's OK—'

'I don't know what you're talking about – haven't you listened to my messages?'

'No. I haven't been checking my mobile. What's wrong?'

'It's Mick. He got knifed by some kid, and it's bad.'

'Oh, shit.'

'I've let his parents know – they're flying in from Sydney. Kim is with him, I've been on call. Not that there's anything she can really do.'

'Jesus. Where is he?'

'The Royal Free. He's in intensive care – I'm going there tomorrow arvo soon as I'm off shift. The stupid Alf. He wouldn't give this gang some money, so he got stabbed.'

'He wanted to travel,' says Ian; and now it seems to him that everything that has gone wrong is to do with money. He has got himself into this situation with Candice not because he loved her but because, deep down, he'd wanted the life that a rich wife could offer him. He's horrified by this realisation. All money is, is a substitute for something else, he thinks. It's what you settle for instead of something worth having – like love, like life.

What can he do? He's still reeling from the bomb, from Katie, and he has to teach tomorrow, and go for an interview at one of the schools that replied to his application. Everything is a mess, and yet his only real friend in the city is mortally sick. He hasn't realised just how fond he is of Mick until now. The whole house is in shock, and mates keep ringing when they hear the news. Mick has loads of friends, guys and girls – far more than Ian himself. Perhaps it's because he's so kind, always willing to help someone move or have a good time. There are worse things than being a slob, Ian thinks, and I've been them.

His mobile goes off; it's his mother, ringing from Cape Town to check that he's alive.

'I'm fine, Mom. No, really. I should have called you at once, I was just a bit . . .'

The voice being bounced off a satellite comes to him full of love and relief. She sounds as if she's in the next room, not half a world away. I should have gone to see her, he thinks, guiltily. She loves him, and he takes it for granted. He leaves a message for Candice, who, oddly, doesn't call back, and another for Katie.

'We need to talk,' he says. 'Please, ring me.' There's nothing else to say, in the circumstances.

Maybe it was just post-traumatic shock, he thinks. Maybe she's frigid. She could be a nutcase. But each time Ian thinks this, the memory of Katie's face, of the expression on it, comes back to him, and he knows he's wrong. Maybe the only girls who'll ever fancy him are South African. A month ago, that wouldn't have disturbed him in the least, but now—

There's so much to do and think about that when Ian goes into work the next day he doesn't notice the crush on the Tube. He goes to his classroom in a dream, not noticing that the boys snicker when he takes the register and calls out a particular name.

'Amir Khan?' he says again.

'He's not here, sir.'

'Maybe he's blowing up the school toilets.'

'Don't be silly,' Ian says automatically.

'Di'nt you hear the news, sir? His big brother's a suicide bomber.'

'*What?*'

'Police and TV's all over their street,' says Liam. 'My mum says she always knew.'

'They ain't fuckin' like other Muslims, you fuckin' racist,' says one of the Somali boys.

Ian continues with his register, disturbed. Is it just one of those coincidences? he thinks. He remembers Amir saying that his brother read the *Rambler*, and how oddly that had struck him at the time. Why pick on that, though? Had his father run any pieces (or cartoons) that were particularly anti-Islamic? Or perhaps it was the knowledge that, once a year, an unusual number of the good and great of the country would be gathered together in a single location.

'God, have you heard?' Meager says to him when he goes into the staffroom. 'You never know where these bloody towelheads are going to pop up next.'

'He just looked like an ordinary teenager,' Ian says.

'Don't they all? The enemy within, eh? You know, the phone's been going all day to ask what the boy was like when he was a pupil here. Nobody knew anything, except that he was a bit of a loner.'

The TV set in the staffroom is blaring with speculation, and Ian keeps quiet about his presence at the party because they all condemn the magazine, especially after his own pseudonymous piece. The whole school is thrilled by the notoriety, and although some Muslim boys are shocked and ashamed it's clear from the comments he hears that others are admiring. He thinks of the drawing that Amir did, the blood and bits of limbs flying through the air. Had he known? Maybe that was how it always began, this kind of evil: children picking on other children because they were a little bit different. Or maybe Selim had met another kind of teacher, one who had found him easier to reach and corrupt. Meager is very full of the evils of mosque school, but what does he know about what is taught there, other than what he picks up from hysterical articles in the press?

Meanwhile, Ian has his own career to think about, and the first interview.

Ian catches the Tube to the girls' school in the suburbs. It's so different from the Samuel Smiles that he can't believe it's a state school: green playing fields, a wonderful library, experienced teachers. He looks longingly at the pupils, their keen, clean faces, their look of confidence and fun. There's a mixture of every race here, and a mixture of abilities, too; but most of all there is a sense of purpose.

'What do you think?' the Head asks him over an informal coffee. She is tough and shrewd, and he knows instinctively that she would have no difficulty quelling even the worst kids at his school because she possesses that precious thing, a natural authority.

'It looks like paradise.'

'Oh, we can pick and choose here. But I wonder whether we'd be good for you. You're doing your stint at a tough inner-city comp – one of the worst in the country, I know – and now you want to spread your wings. I can see you're good; your South African experience is impressive. You could end up a headmaster. But if you come here you'll be teaching the same years you've just taught. You might want to think about extending your range first.'

'I see,' says Ian. He suspects that she is telling him he wouldn't get the job.

He would so like to work in this place, to teach kids who really want to learn. Maybe he's had enough of teenaged boys, or maybe he is, once again, being seduced by what is attractive and easy. Perhaps he doesn't stand a chance in this system. All this year he's been looking down his nose at it, and at the Samuel Smiles, thinking how badly run it was and how irritating it is that he has to waste his time there of all places; but maybe *he*'s the useless one. Maybe he is hopeless because he doesn't speak Bengali. But he remembers what Meager had told him: teaching at the Samuel Smiles isn't teaching, it's crowd control.

'Get out while you still can,' he'd said. 'If you stay more than a couple of years, you'll be unemployable anywhere else because you'll never have taught a proper lesson.'

Dejected, Ian goes back to the inner city, and then to Hampstead to see Mick. The Royal Free Hospital has been weirdly transformed since Ian's own stay there. The dingy entrances have been repainted, new doors put in and the linoleum floors replaced with wood. For the first time it looks like a world-class hospital, Ian thinks. Seeing Mick lying there, with heart monitor terminals stuck to his chest and tubes from a drip running into his arms, reminds Ian of when he himself had been concussed. There is even Candice sitting beside the metal bed, with another huge bunch of lilies and a basket of grapes. She has been crying.

'Hey, Mick. How are you feeling?' Ian says softly.

'Like a fish on a frigging hook. I heard you'd been in a bit of a situation yourself.'

'Yeah. No worries, though.'

'Are we making too much noise?' Candice asks, seeing Mick close his eyes.

'My head hurts.'

'We should go,' Ian says, standing up. 'Are you going to be OK?'

'I don't know, do I? Jesus, I never thought I'd become another statistic.'

The stitched gash in his neck looks like something out of *Frankenstein*. A machine begins to beep, and a nurse comes in.

'Everybody out, please. I'm paging the consultant.'

'Will he be OK?' Ian asks Candice softly. Her eyes brim with tears.

'He's had one complete blood transfusion already. He nearly bled to death, but a Nigerian couple helped him. Nobody else stopped.'

'Poor sod,' Ian says feelingly. 'Why do kids do these things?'

'Don't you know that there's no point asking that question here these days? They all carry knives, so they're going to use them. I never thought I'd feel as unsafe here as in South Africa, but it's happening.'

Candice is more upset than he would have thought possible, considering how hostile she had always been to Mick. She sobs on Ian's shoulder.

'Oh, God! Do you think he's going to die?'

'You really like him, don't you?' Ian says softly. He isn't at all surprised when she gives him a small, embarrassed nod.

44

The Best Revenge

Anna knows that she can't stay at Katie's much longer. What she will do or where she will go is terrifying to contemplate, but if she doesn't move away then she knows that her period of respite is almost over. If Dmitri really knows she's hiding in the flat, neither she nor Katie will be safe until she moves. She hasn't told Katie about his coming up the stairs because she's too frightened that it will mean instant ejection.

There are people in this place who would expect her to collapse now that she is free. She has watched TV shows and seen people tell stories about their sorrows, and she imagines each time how her grandmother Vera would have laughed at them. Under Stalin, Vera had experienced things far worse than has Anna, and she had always said that the best revenge was to survive. When she feels like crying, Anna remembers that tough, toothless, wrinkled face, framed in a tight headscarf. She too has survived, and now she has to rediscover that sense of momentum that had carried her from the Ukraine in the first place.

Anna's body has healed, but Katie wants to be sure.

'I'm going to ask a doctor to come and look at you,' Katie says, in her soft sing-song voice. 'A woman doctor, Anna, who is the friend of someone I trust. You may need some medicine.'

'Medicine?'

'Antibiotics.'

'I have no money,' Anna lies, frightened. It's not true – but she has taken risks with her health in order to earn the small roll of cash that she has hidden, so she won't give that up.

'She will do it for nothing. It's important, Anna. Please.'

Anna is about to refuse when she sees the look on Katie's face. All the light has gone out of it. Strange, Anna thinks, because Katie had been so happy the day before.

'You are sad?'

'Oh, just disappointed, I guess.'

'Your boyfriend is bad man?'

'He isn't my boyfriend, just a guy I liked.'

'Is a problem?'

'Yes. No, well, it's complicated. Plus, he's my boss's son. If he still is my boss, that is.' Katie gives a high, faintly hysterical laugh. 'I may be out of a job by the end of the month. Maybe I should have gone to Paris. All good Americans go to Paris when they die, after all.'

'You are sick?'

'Only in my heart. You understand?'

Anna nods. 'Is better not to speak about these things, make heart like stone.'

'You think?'

'That is what my granny say.' Anna pauses, then says, 'I am look-ing for job on the internet.'

Katie has given her permission to use her laptop, a measure of trust that has touched Anna almost as deeply as being allowed to stay in the American girl's flat.

'You are? That's good, but I don't think you'll find one that way. Listen, Anna, I'll ask around. Maybe the pub near the magazine needs a waitress.'

The doorbell buzzes, and as always, both women jump. Knowing that it could be another client for the downstairs flat always brings hideous thoughts into each of their minds. But it is the doctor. Katie puts the chain on the door, just in case, before letting her in. When the woman enters, Anna stares warily at the first new face she's seen in weeks.

'Hi,' says the woman. 'My name is Liza, Liza Wisden. I'm Ian's friend.'

'Oh, sure,' Katie says. 'Thanks for coming. This is Anna.'

The doctor has an air of brisk professional competence which Anna immediately recognises, although she's never encountered it before.

'Anna, I'm a doctor. Do you understand English?'

'You speak funny,' Anna says suspiciously

Liza is Australian, she explains. Anna sometimes watches a programme called *Neighbours*, which is all about Australia; everyone friendly and kind in the sunshine.

(But then so had London been, in the only film she had seen about it.

'What was it called?' Katie asked during one of their conversations.

'*No Thing Hill*. Does it mean a place that is not true?'

Katie gave a short laugh. 'Well, in a way, yes.')

Liza says, 'Anything you tell me, I have to keep secret. I am not going to ask you for money. I will not do anything to you that makes you uncomfortable, but I want to check that you have no infections and no broken bones. I need to take a blood sample and feel places which hurt. But if you tell me to stop, I will stop.'

'OK.'

The doctor gives her a direct, calm look in which sympathy is mixed with scrutiny. It's almost as if she understands what happened, Anna thinks – but how could anyone?

'Now then, let's go into the bedroom and have a look-see.'

Anna finds it painful to take her clothes off in front of yet another stranger. Liza is kind but impersonal, explaining everything and waiting patiently for Anna to stop shivering. It helps that she pulls on rubber gloves, and it helps that she's a woman. The doctor presses the flesh over Anna's ribs carefully but strongly, muttering that she ought to be X-rayed.

Anna shakes her head. 'No hospital.'

'If I give you a referral, they won't ask for anything more.'

'No hospital.'

'No worries,' Liza says. 'I am going to strap bandages round your ribs, in case. Can I listen to your heart?'

Anna suspects that what the doctor really wants to do is to check her upper body, but she agrees. She will not take off her bra. Liza sees the bruises and cigarette burns, and asks in a quiet, casual way how she'd received them.

'Men,' Anna says, and for a moment she sees the professional calm of the doctor's face slip as she nods and makes notes.

'Boyfriends?'

'No!' Anna is outraged. 'Bad mens.'

'Yes,' the doctor says. 'I understand.'

Anna looks at her face and believes her. 'There is no words for badness.'

'Can you tell me?'

Anna doesn't want to remember, so she says quickly, 'They tell me I am – I was coming to this country to be waitress. That there are many, many jobs, even if I am illegal. But I am made prostitute, downstairs. Like the others.'

'And there are still girls down there?'

'Yes.'

'How old are they?'

'Like me. Teenager.'

Next is a blood test. As the butterfly needle pierces her vein, she thinks of Cristina injecting herself with heroin, and of the strange symmetry of their lives. The doctor removes the needle deftly, gives Anna a blob of cotton wool to press down on the small puncture, and seals it off with a round plaster with a smiley face.

'There. You deserve it more than most.' Then she says, 'Anna, you know there are people besides Katie who might help you? There are other girls like you – you understand? I would like to send you to them, for help.'

Anna listens, but in her heart she knows that she won't go near the place. If she does, she will become like one of the people she sees on TV, crying and complaining. 'I want to work,' she says.

Katie and the doctor discuss her in low voices next door.

'And you've actually reported this to the police, and they've done nothing? Jesus wept!'

'I guess you could try again.'

'You bet I will, but if I do they'll want to interview your . . . guest.'

'She won't agree.'

'All the bloody coppers'd have to do is watch the house.'

'Yes. But so far, they haven't.'

There is a pause, then Liza says, 'Ian sends his love, by the way.'

'Thanks.'

'I gather you two were caught up in the attempted bombing.'

'Yes. We were.'

Another pause. Anna is puzzled by what she can hear of this talk, but then Katie doesn't tell her much about her life outside the flat. Is this man the one she likes? Although she understands her enough in some ways, Katie is adult in her reticence.

'You know, our housemate Mick has been in hospital too, in intensive care, and we're all really cut up. It's been quite a week.'

Katie's voice says, 'I'm sorry to hear that. You've been really kind, coming here out of hours, and I appreciate that. Are you sure you can get the blood tested without getting into trouble?'

'Oh, I can lose it in the system, no worries. I've brought some antibiotics, which she should take anyway just in case of an STD. Let's hope her samples are clear. Three times a day, with food, and make sure she finishes the course. I'll ring you as soon as I have results. And meanwhile let's both keep calling the police. Bloody Poms, they're unbelievable.'

The doctor leaves, and Katie comes back in.

'Hey, Anna. Are you OK?'

'Yes. I am OK.'

'Would you like some tea?'

Anna jumps off the bed. 'I make.'

'No, no, it's fine, I'll do it. You don't have to act like you're my servant.'

How long do I have? Anna wonders, thinking. Katie is visibly tired and anxious and shocked since the bomb attempt. Anna is shocked too, because when the TV news comes on there is a picture of the dead terrorist – and she recognises him. It's one of the boys who had come to the brothel downstairs. She stares at the photograph.

'So young, isn't he?' Katie says sadly. 'Barely out of school. It's the same as it always is: he seemed normal but he wasn't.'

'He made a bomb?'

'So they say. They think he must have had help, but nobody is saying anything. You know, there's some shocking statistic about the number of terrorist attacks that have been foiled by the police since the Iraq War. Like, at least thirty? This isn't a safe country to live in. Maybe I should quit trying to make a life here and go home.'

'I cannot go home.'

'Are you sure?'

'Yes. I have to make a new life here. I want to go out.'

'Maybe that would be good for you,' Katie says.

However, as soon as Anna is on the landing all her memories and fears come back. She cowers in the door frame.

'I'm sorry.'

'Don't worry, Anna. It will take time. Tell me about this other girl, the sick one, in the basement.'

'Galina? She is from Russia.'

'Where in Russia?'

'I don't know. She cries for her sister. She says her sister, she lives here, in London.'

367

'She does?'

'Yes. Galina, she has a number for her, but Sergei he take her mobile.'

'Do you know her name? Maybe she can help if we trace her.'

Anna tries to remember. She has paid little attention to Galina's pathetic attempts to make friends with her, because she is even worse off than Anna had been and therefore useless. It was a common name, a Russian name but also a Ukrainian one.

'Iryna,' she says.

45

Job in Prison

Job's injuries turn out to be less severe than everyone had thought. Selim's body shielded him from the worst of the bullets and nothing vital was pierced. He came round in hospital, under armed guard, and within a day he had been patched up, handcuffed and interrogated. When he finally convinced his questioners that he had had contact with Selim's family only as a tutor, and had been sufficiently disturbed by what he had learnt of the boys' older brother to understand that Selim might have been about to become a suicide bomber, he was moved to Harmondsworth detention centre, near Heathrow, to await the decision concerning his future.

Harmondsworth is a name that strikes dread into the hearts of men such as Job. Effectively a prison for asylum seekers, surrounded by a double fence of razor wire, it is a place where people are processed in their thousands every month for ejection from Britain. Such is the political pressure to return these unwanted foreigners to their homeland that few of those arriving by day and night will be sharing a room the following week, although some whose cases are contested can stay for years. Nobody knows how long they will be kept in limbo; that is part of the torment. The bitterness of detention is like a stain on the soul that will never be washed out. The worst affected of all are the children, innocent and imprisoned, speaking in British accents and British in all but name. The locked doors, the lack of privacy, the regular roll counts, the lack of possessions remind some of them of school, only worse, they tell Job. Nobody knows what is happening to them, and for every detainee like Job himself who has a lawyer there are dozens more who do not.

Yet it is in this place that Job has begun to pray again. He has heard God speaking to him out of the whirlwind, and if his own sufferings brought him to England in order to perform a deed of atonement, then they have a purpose. *Be thou a man* . . . He knows Polly dreads coming to this evil place, which reeks of despair, and where bullying by the staff is notorious, but he will not let it define him. He has let it be known that he was a teacher, and manages to help one or two teenagers who were about to take their GCSEs. They are bright, hard-working children, determined to make a future for themselves, and now they are adrift, with so much pain and anger in their eyes.

There are people here who will try anything. Suicide is common, although detainees have no cords or blades; such is their ingenuity that every month they discover new ways of hanging or cutting themselves. The last time Polly was in here, she tells him, was to try to help a father and his son. The son had been born in Britain and had absolutely no hope of surviving in Angola, where he would be dumped; so the father, on learning that they were both about to be deported, had killed himself in order to keep his son, as an orphan, safe in the UK for another five years.

'Promise me that you won't do the same thing,' Polly says. 'Whatever you feel, don't give up.'

'No, madam, I won't.'

'Oh Job, do stop calling me madam. For one thing, I hope we're friends, and for another you saved my life. Besides, I've been meaning to tell you for ages that it makes me feel like I'm in my eighties.'

He grins at her, but can't quite bring himself to call her anything.

Seeing the professional side to her is interesting, he thinks. As a person she is warm, chaotic, hot-tempered and forgetful, but as a solicitor she's like a terrier dog. Having her on his side is the one thing that gives him hope. Polly tells him that the BBC and the *Rambler* itself have taken up his cause.

'All the government ever wants to do with people like you is push you out of sight, so the bigger the stink the harder it becomes for them to do that,' she tells him.

The Home Office sees its job as a filtration system, Polly believes. Most people never get their medical evidence looked at, and asylum seekers with poor English and no legal aid are regularly asked to sign blank sheets of paper on arrival, which are then taken as proof that they are returning willingly. Interpreters are scarce and resented as a waste of public money; everything possible is done to browbeat the interned into giving up in the face of adamantine unwelcome. Polly reads Job the letter that the Home Office has sent her regarding his case:

'The Secretary of State is of the opinion that your client should have sought redress from the Zimbabwean authorities before fleeing Zimbabwe and seeking international protection. Furthermore, the Secretary does not consider the various measures of discrimination that your client claims to have suffered could reasonably justify a well-founded fear of persecution. By his own admission, the only personal harassment that he has suffered was that he was blindfolded, beaten, hung upside-down, hit with the butt of a rifle and shot at, all of which were incidents of Zimbabwean officials abusing their official positions. The Secretary therefore concluded that your client has not demonstrated a well-founded fear of persecution, and has failed to provide any evidence that he is here for reasons other than economic self-advancement.'

'So, it's hopeless,' Job says. His spirits, which have been low before, sink even further. To not be believed, after all he has gone through, is almost worse than the torment itself. It's as if they are mocking him.

'Not at all. Firstly, the fact they've sent this ludicrous letter so quickly means they're scared you might have a case. It's a standard letter, actually; all they do is change the name of the country concerned and the specific injuries. Secondly, I have my best barrister willing to take you on and fight them. He's really good – and the son of Filipino immigrants himself, so he really wants to help. Don't give in, Job. That's what the bastards want. I wish you'd come to me before. I had no idea you'd been through so much.'

'There are far worse stories than mine,' he says blankly. 'In my room is a man from Somalia who had his daughter raped on his wife's body. He cannot sleep. The other is an Iranian bookseller. He sold an illegal book, *Brave New World*, to one of Ahmadinejad's police, and was electrocuted in prison, so he has epilepsy.'

Job can see that Polly has heard stories like this before, although she grimaces in sympathy.

'But they haven't done what you've done. Do you realise that you saved the lives of the Prime Minister and, oh, at least half the Cabinet?'

'Is that a good thing?'

'There's no way they're going to deport you. It's shameful that you should be here. We'll get you out on bail.'

Job doesn't understand what bail means, but when he does he is so touched that he turns his head away in order to hide his feelings. 'I can never repay you.'

'Well, I hope you will by not running away. Besides, they'll be doing the running by the time my barrister and I have finished with them.'

Polly looks at Job and says encouragingly, 'We'll be pressing the government for damages.'

'It's hopeless.'

'Not if I can help it. Look, Job, stick with it. You could get quite a lot if you win a compensation claim. They had absolutely no justi-fication for what they did.'

There have been searching questions asked in the press and the House of Commons about trigger-happy policing; once it was established that he was not a terrorist Job has become, temporarily, a national hero, although there are some who point out that the police had only been doing their job.

'It's not impossible, after what has happened, that you could be granted indefinite leave to remain,' Polly tells him.

'You know,' Job says, after a pause, 'I do not wish to stay in this country. Once, maybe, I thought the UK was a good place. But if I cannot be in my own country, with my own people, I would sooner live in South Africa, and look for my wife.'

'Would you really?'

'Yes. I do not believe my wife and sister are dead. I think I would know it, in my heart. They are trying to make the crossing, that is all. God will protect them, as He has protected me.'

Truly, Job thought, my mother named me for wretchedness and suffering, though as a child he had believed his name to mean something quite different; he had believed that it meant, simply, that he would have what everyone most wanted: employment.

Polly is saying something. 'Job, this may not be in your best interests as my client, but if I got you some compensation now, out of court, so that you could go to South Africa instead, would that be better for you? I mean, we can ask for more, and fight for you to get the right to remain here, but it might take months or even years. You'd be here a long, long time.'

Job sighs. 'Yes, I think it would be better.'

'I understand,' Polly says. 'I would do the same.'

They smile at each other, a little sadly.

'I will miss Mr Robbie,' Job says.

'Do you have children? Or brothers and sisters, back in Zimbabwe?'

'My wife and I had not been blessed. But my relatives are not the only ones.' Job draws a deep breath. 'Ten years ago, there was another family, a white family but one I thought of as my own. I failed to protect them when robbers broke in. I believe God has punished me for it ever since.'

Polly is silent. All around them, the life of the institution echoes with its clangorous doors and human or metal shrieks. Then she says, 'Job, if there is a God, I don't think He would be so cruel as to do that. How old are you now? Twenty-two? You were a child ten years ago. What you've done since – that's something to be proud of. Your courage saved many people's lives. I'm sure that, even if you feel you were cursed, you're now forgiven.'

'Do you think that is so?' Job asks.

'Yes. I'm certain of it.'

She takes his hand, dry and warm. Polly has sat in on interrogations in which Job has been asked again and again to admit to converting to Islam. The barely concealed aggression and disdain with which he was addressed made him clench his fists sometimes, but he always answered calmly, and with dignity.

'I am not a Muslim,' he said. 'I believe that my God and the Khans' are the same, but I follow the Bible, not the Koran. I believe in Christ's mercy, and in redemption. I believe Tariq to be a good man and a good father. He tried to help his son by sending him to Pakistan. His other sons told me that he quarrelled with Selim because of religion. There are as many different kinds of Muslim as there are Christians. I will not say what is not true.'

About Tariq's other sons, he stayed resolutely silent. He wondered whether they too would continue to hate unbelievers; whether without Selim to foster their feelings of anger and the desire for revenge they would become calmer.

'I taught his sons to read books, that is all. We read Harry Potter,' he said. 'They are just boys, they go to a bad school, they needed help with their English.'

Job's guilt over Selim's death is another reason why he wants to leave Britain. 'I can never go back to Ace Minicabs,' he says to Polly. 'They will hate me. I do not believe that any of them would have wished the bomb to go off, but they will always see me as a spy now.

Yet they were the only ones besides you, madam, who showed me Christian charity.'

'It isn't particularly Christian, you know. And I'm Jewish, really.' She has tears in her eyes.

'Please, give my best wishes to Mr Robbie. I am sorry I can no longer be of assistance.'

'I will, Job. He's sorry not to have you pick him up any more.'

Job nods briefly. He knows as well as Polly that there are hundreds, perhaps thousands of others in the city who would do just as well, that he is infinitely replaceable. Only my family sees me as special, he thinks; my family, and God.

She lov'd me for the dangers I had passed,/And I loved her that she did pity them, he thinks, remembering *Othello*. How much of love is pity, really? Pity, and admiration for what another human being has endured?

'Can I fetch you your things from the place you were staying?' Polly asks delicately. Job doesn't want her to see that mean room, with its bad smells and poverty, but there are small treasures he would like to save. She doesn't believe him when he says that once he had a house, that he had a respectable life, even in Harare. In the backs of their minds, he knows, all white people believe that people like him live in mud huts or tin shacks.

'There is something,' he says shyly. 'I can give you the key. There is a photograph of my wife which I would like to have; and my books.'

'I'll fetch them, I promise,' Polly says. 'That much at least I can do for you.'

375

46

In A Small Country, Anything Can Happen

Katie has often thought that her colleagues' productivity might be improved by having a bomb put under them, but the literal truth of this experience is that the *Rambler*'s circulation has gone up by a third. The prolonged and extensive coverage of an attempted assassination of the Prime Minister has reminded people who buy magazines to try it again; by a happy chance, Katie had already planned a special cut-price offer which undercut their two main rivals in the market. For the first time in a decade, the *Rambler* is required reading again.

'If I'd known that all we needed was a teeny-tiny terrorist, I'd have volunteered to blow us up months ago,' says Patrick.

'I had no idea you were so loyal,' says Cassandra.

'Oh, I'm not. But it's even worse not being fashionable.'

'I've just got our figures. We've overtaken the *Spectator*, the *New Statesman*, and *Private Eye*,' says Quentin. There is a round of clapping and cheering. 'Clearly, there's something to be said for going out with a bang not a whimper. Or do I mean the other way about? Anyway, as some of you may have guessed, I'm leaving.'

The horrified faces that greet this news gratify him and he

bestows one of his rare charming smiles, in the manner of one throwing small change to the masses. Only Mark Crawley looks alert and pleased. Not him, Katie thinks; oh, not him! She can see his cold dark eyes flickering as he calculates his chances of becoming editor now that Quentin will be out of the way, and his heavy face flushes red.

'It really wasn't your fault, Q,' says Minty, loyally. 'I mean, how could it possibly have been? The police should have closed off the whole street.'

'Oh, I'm not leaving because of that,' Quentin says. 'Perish the thought! No, I've had enough of being paid peanuts to work with – well, absolutely charming people.'

'Like Cecilia, you mean?' asks Justin, with a touch of malice. Cecilia has suddenly decamped after her affair with Quentin was leaked by 'friends', and the tabloids have had a fine time doorstepping her, largely because she looks so ravishing every time she goes out. Her sudden departure (ascribed to increased security risks) has been lamented by nobody, apart perhaps from Justin.

'One enjoyed seeing her in the room, like a bowl of fruit,' he says. A new girl, related to one of the Hapsburgs, is now doing the blog. She isn't nearly so pretty ('the chin, you know,' Patrick observes) but she is efficient.

'Quite, quite,' says Quentin. 'Anyway, I've accepted a job in America on the *New Democrat*. Trench and I have been considering my successor, which is why I've been being shadowed by young Sebastian here.'

Everyone looks puzzled.

'Sebastian?' Justin asks at last. Quentin points to the person who has occasionally sat, despised and unnoticed, in meetings since the start of the year. 'Sebastian Smythe.'

'You don't mean – the *Toby*?' Crawley expostulates. 'But he's only about twelve years old.'

'Actually, I'm twenty-nine,' says Sebastian, amicably. 'I don't quite get why everyone keeps calling me Toby.' Bland expressions meet his

377

gaze. 'We thought it sensible for me to shadow Quentin in the beginning, but I'm a little surprised that nobody realised who I am. I suppose nobody here reads *The Economist*? No, I thought not.'

Sebastian sits back, with the pleased look of a small boy who has just kicked over an anthill.

'It was felt that Sebastian had the right mix of editorial flair and business acumen,' Quentin says smoothly. The staff is visibly torn between frantically trying to calculate just how rude they had been individually to their new boss, and amusement at Crawley's disappointment.

'He looks like he's going to have conniptions, doesn't he?' Minty whispers in Katie's ear. 'Maybe he'll leave too.'

'No such chance. He'll hang on until the bitter end,' Justin says. 'Why?'

'Because everyone else hates him, and he's over the hill. He won't get another job.'

Sebastian, meanwhile, is swelling with authority, like one of those flannels that look as small as a postage stamp but which expand in water. Katie can see that he'll be good. Sebastian catches her eye, and smiles.

'Katie,' he says warmly, 'I very much hope you'll be staying on as a key member of staff. I'll be reviewing salaries as a matter of priority, I may add.'

She blushes. 'I would appreciate that, er, Sebastian.'

It's good to know that she has done well enough to satisfy somebody. Katie glances at Quentin, who has never once thanked her. He jerks his head to indicate that he wants to talk to her afterwards. It's odd: she isn't frightened of him or even annoyed by him any longer. She remembers, momentarily, Ian trying to kiss her. It had just been post-traumatic shock, she thinks, with a trace of regret. He hasn't called her again, presumably out of embarrassment.

'You know, Katie, if you're thinking of returning to the States I'll be looking out for an assistant,' Quentin murmurs at the end of conference.

378

'Really? You'd hire me?' Her amazement seems to surprise him. 'But I thought you hated me!'

'You're the only assistant I've ever had who hasn't spent every lunch break behaving like a quivering jelly,' he says, looking at her over his half-moon spectacles. (She's always suspected they were an affectation, the kind of thing he wore because it's what editors are supposed to wear, but now she sees that he is, in fact, fifty and feeling his age.) 'You just got on with the job, instead of acting the usual shrinking violet.'

Katie is filled with an unaccustomed sensation of relief so profound that it could be mistaken for joy. She says politely, 'Well – thanks, Quentin. I'll think it over.'

'It'll be an exciting time to be in your country,' he says, with a faraway look in his eyes. 'The most thrilling political battle of our lifetimes is about to be fought, and I want a ringside seat.'

'You may find it quite crowded,' Katie says dryly. But it's true. When she had left America almost a year ago, hope had seemed even more distant than spring. Everyone had hated her country, it felt like, whereas now . . . now, it may be rediscovering its revolutionary soul. It may all come to nothing, she thinks, but it would be fascinating. Yet, at the same time, she's just found her feet in London.

She has to think what to do with her life. In a couple of months, her visa must be renewed. Sebastian would write a letter claiming she was uniquely necessary, she was sure (she had never felt this about Quentin) but whether she wanted to stay at the magazine was another matter. She actually has the beginning of a social life. Minty has invited her to come round for supper, and she has been out to the pub with Patrick and Cassandra. Patrick, it turns out, has been cut off by his family after coming out to them – which Katie finds unbelievably cruel and stupid, and which partly explains his bitter wit. They all get along much better than she'd expected.

'You know,' Patrick says, 'we expected some sort of ghastly New York debutante but you're really not too bad.'

'I'm glad you think so. I expected you all to be ghastly *London* debutantes, but you're really not too bad either.'

Daniel and Hemani had been in touch when they heard the news, as had Polly and the Sponges.

They were all interviewed about the bomb attempt, and the thing that had been intended to blow them apart has, at least in Katie's own case, brought her into a circle of new friends. Ivo and his wife are particularly kind; he has taken her under his wing, and claims to be putting her name about as someone worth having on the staff of his old newspaper, though with Ivo you never know how much is truth and how much is bombast. Katie thinks that she recognises the face of the terrorist, Selim Khan; Ivo is convinced that he must have been driven by him when they learn that he worked part-time for Ace Minicabs.

'Maybe I said something about the *Rambler*,' he says excitedly. 'I mean, it's such an unlikely target otherwise, isn't it? Careless talk costs lives these days, doesn't it?'

'Ivo, it would be too much of a coincidence,' says Katie.

'The whole of life is about coincidence. If you live in a small country, anything can happen.'

'London isn't small. It feels like a whole world.'

'Aha – you've decided to stay here?'

'Yes, I think so. If they let me.'

The police have released a press statement about Selim Khan: he had been born in Britain and raised in the northern suburbs of the city, where he had seemed to be an ordinary teenager. Nothing else is known, other than there having been more bomb-making equipment found in a house in Finsbury Park. Three men are arrested.

'Why do they do it?' Sebastian asks. 'That's what we have to keep asking.'

'God knows.' Cassandra is sombre. 'Their parents come here to better their chances and the children end up hating us, even when they get good jobs. Sooner or later, another one is going to succeed. What are they teaching them?'

'A lot of multicultural claptrap,' Crawley says. 'If we just said here we are, we have Judaeo-Christian laws and you'd better keep to them or you'll get chucked out, there wouldn't be any problem. It's pretending we're all equal that weakens our culture and makes them cling to theirs.'

'What do you think, Katie?' Sebastian asks. He is chairing his first editorial conference.

'I don't know,' she says. 'I don't think it's a failure of multiculturalism, or of Islam. Those can both be good things. But there could be a failure to, well, connect. I think the problem is always when one person is seen as less than human by another.'

Everyone stares at her.

'But Katie, don't you see? The only way we can cope is by putting up barriers and divisions,' says Cassandra. 'You know – class, education, creed, county. We define ourselves by all that we're *not*. It's just that one of the things we're *not* is the kind of person who won't live and let live.'

'Maybe that's too close to indifference,' Katie says. 'Maybe that's why they feel so angry.'

'What right do people like Selim have to take it out on random strangers? We aren't put on this earth to be happy, after all. Only Americans believe that, according to your constitution.'

Katie shakes her head. 'We only believe in the right to pursue happiness; not that it's attainable.'

She thinks of this whenever she goes home on the bus. So many people crowd on, and so few seem to notice those who might need their seats – the old, the infirm, the pregnant, the very young – that at times she feels a fool for repeatedly offering hers. But maybe she wouldn't think of it if she herself hadn't suffered, just a little.

'Did *none* of them have pity on you?' Katie asks Anna.

'There was one. A black man. He try to help me.'

Katie leans her forehead against the cold glass pane of the living room, and sighs. One man, in over a hundred. It didn't suggest to her that she was ever going to find a better husband than Winthrop might have been.

'What are you going to do, Anna?'

'I get new job.'

Katie looks up, a little anxiously. 'What kind of job?'

'I am thinking, maybe in restaurant. I like to cook.' Anna returns her gaze steadily. She knows perfectly well that Katie had wondered whether she was going to return to prostitution, Katie sees.

'You're very good at it.'

The little top-floor flat is always steaming with good smells. Katie has even bought pots of herbs, and bunches of spring flowers. With its clean, painted walls and cheerful curtains, its bright lamps and throws, the flat now looks like a real home. She looks round at it. If I go back to the States, all this will be undone, she thinks.

The doorbell buzzes.

'Another creep,' Katie says, but when she says, 'Hello?' into the entryphone the voice that echoes into the receiver is Ian's.

'Hi,' she says. 'Yes, I'm good. Yes, that's fine. Just hold on two moments first, will you?'

Anna watches her, apprehension in her eyes.

'I'm really sorry,' Katie says. 'There's a friend coming – a man who – who I need to have a little time with alone. Not for very long, I promise.'

'What do you want me to do?'

'Do you think you could try and sit on the stair, a little way down? Nobody will see you if you stay on the next landing.'

Anna considers this, then nods. 'Is OK.'

Katie drags a brush through her hair, changes her blouse, feels a fool but she has her pride. Looking down, she sees Anna pass Ian in the stairwell. Anna shrinks away from him as she passes, but he doesn't even notice her. Once past, Anna perches on the window ledge of the landing below, and flicks nervously through a magazine. She'll be fine, Katie tells herself, looking down. Nobody can see her from below, and it's a significant step for her to take.

'Hi.'

'Come in.'

Seeing Ian, unshaven and carrying a bicycle helmet, makes him real again. Katie, overcome by a strange feeling, waves him in politely before stepping indoors herself.

'I'm sorry I couldn't come before,' he says. 'I was interviewed twice by the police, because I teach Selim Khan's brothers, and my friend Mick is—'.

'Yes, your doctor friend told me. Is he any better?'

'It's too early to say. He has been pretty badly cut up.'

'I'm sorry. That's awful.'

There's an awkward pause. Katie offers tea, and Ian accepts. Tea, she thinks: the other fail-safe of British social life apart from discussing the weather.

'I've been looking for a new job.'

'What a coincidence. I've just started doing the same.'

'Really?'

It's as if they are polite strangers. Ian suddenly looks just like his father, Katie thinks. She can imagine him losing his temper and being grumpy in twenty years' time.

'Yes. You know Quentin's moving to America?'

'He did tell me, yes. I met his family. Cute kids.'

They look at each other, uncertain what to say. Ian says, unexpectedly, 'What's happened to your – your friend? The girl you helped get away?'

'Anna. You passed her on the stairs.'

'Did I? Oh, yes.'

'I suppose I'm committing a crime by sheltering her, but what else was I to do? She wants to get a job, waitressing or something. She's remarkably resilient. I just wish I could find her somewhere else to live. She doesn't know a soul apart from me.'

'You know, if she had a job she could live in the house in Finsbury Park. There's a room coming free. I know Liza and Kim wouldn't mind.'

Katie understands that he's telling her that he's moving in with Candice. So much for their relationship being trivial, she thinks.

'That's very thoughtful of you. What's the rent?'

'Fifty pounds a week, pretty good even for a dump. It isn't a permanent solution. We're just there until the developer gets around to modernising it. He likes Aussies and South Africans because apparently we don't make too much mess. Your flat is a lot nicer than I was expecting, from what you said.'

Ian looks round, and Katie feels a kind of sad pride.

'That's thanks to Anna, mostly. She decided to take it, or me, in hand.'

'Amazing people, Eastern Europeans.' Ian puts down his mug suddenly. 'I'm explaining this very badly. Katie, the point is that I'm—'

Two things happen at that point. One is that he is interrupted by the sound of someone hammering frantically on the door of the flat. The other is that the evening, which has crept up on them imperceptibly, is suddenly filled with a strange flickering blue light.

'I'd better see what that is.'

Katie opens the door. On the landing, Anna almost falls into her arms. Downstairs, through the front door, she can see row after row of police cars outside.

47

Indecent Assault

Ian starts downstairs as if released from a spring. It's a relief to do something, because his meeting with Katie has gone even worse than he thought. She won't look him in the eye, and seems cold and distant. I should have called her after I kissed her, he thinks, I should have asked her out on a date, a proper date, and explained about Candice. Stupid, stupid, to have kept to his policy of drift!

Below, in the entrance hall, uniformed men are hammering on the door of the ground-floor flat, saying, 'Police! Open up!' Then, without waiting, they slam a portable battering ram hard against the door. Thuds shake the whole building, and there comes the sound of wood splintering.

Everything changes at that moment, as if not just a door but a lock to his own heart has been forced. In a part of himself, Ian has never been able to believe that Katie's teenaged prostitute really existed, but as the door smashes down it's like seeing into the essential flimsiness of reality. He thinks about how, all along the street, there must be flats like this one in which other girls have been raped and beaten, flats that are perhaps now occupied by happy couples or successful professionals or pensioners, all with the same sash windows and lumpy corniced ceilings; and yet this horror has happened here. A sensation of lives layered on top of each other, which he will never know about, overwhelms Ian momentarily. The women hang back.

'Be careful,' Katie says, behind him.

'Don't worry.'

Inside the flat there is obviously some kind of fight going on, and a lot of deep voices are shouting. Some officers drag out a couple of men, one a scrawny middle-aged white man and another who is younger and looks Asian.

'I was just having a back-rub, officer!' the first is protesting.

'How dare you,' the other says. 'I know my human rights.'

'You can give your statement down at the station, sir,' says an officer in the imperturbable British manner that Ian always admires. 'At present, I am arresting you both for indecent assault of under-age girls. You do not have to say anything, but I must caution you that—'

His words are drowned by cries from within, and suddenly a flailing knot of men falls through the doorway into the hall.

Two are policemen, but the one who stands up first is big, with bristling black hair. He is wearing a black leather jacket.

'Sergei,' Anna whispers behind Ian.

As if he's heard his name, the man looks up. Ian looks down at his face, heavy and brutal, and now nothing else matters. It's like moments he experiences playing rugby, when he knows that he is going to tackle someone. The other man knows it too, so that instead of running out the front door, which is blocked by police and the other two men, he charges up the stairs towards them. Whether he's also seen Anna, or whether he's trying to escape, or whether he is mad with rage doesn't matter. The air seems to have turned glutinous, so that there is a slow inevitability to everything.

Sergei has a knife in his hand, and the police at the bottom of the stairs don't even seem to realise what is going on. Ian can feel his heart thumping in big, loud beats, a deafening sound that fills him with heat. He looks into Sergei's eyes and sees a total absence of good. Everything in Ian that has been diffuse snaps into place, like

386

the metal filings around a magnet. He will not let him pass. This feeling is so instinctive and so powerful and so clear that he actually laughs aloud.

'Come on, arsehole,' he says.

'*Zhopa!*' says Sergei.

'Piss off.'

The two men begin an awkward, clumsy struggle on the stairs. Sergei is trying to force his way upwards, and at the same time as he's trying to punch him Ian is trying to grab his arms to block a slash from the knife. Both of them are drenched in sweat. Sergei is slippery as a snake, and Ian is boiling with fury. He loathes violence, and yet underneath his surface calm there has always been the anger that comes from growing up in a country where you might be killed for just a few coins. The knowledge that this man has terrorised women, that he might hurt Katie, merges into a roar of aggression. Being fitter and angrier and quicker, Ian lands a punch to Sergei's kidneys, and the knife falls. Better, Ian thinks, grinning. He has Sergei's arms by the wrists.

'Prefer fighting a girl?' he says.

'Fuck you.'

The banisters creak and crack as they crash into them, and the handrail is wobbling loose, meaning that the whole thing could snap away and send them plunging into the stairwell. Dimly, Ian can hear shrieking and the shouts of the police, but he goes on punching and being punched. All his life he's had nightmares about fighting an intruder, and now that it's happening he feels a kind of pleasure. He's as close to Sergei as if they were lovers – he can count the blackheads on his nose and the bristles on his cheeks – and the best thing he can think of is to nut him in the face. But Sergei lowers his own head so they bounce painfully off each other. Ian's eyes water with the pain.

'Shit!'

Ian staggers back, falling up the stairs. His face is suddenly sticky and he senses, rather than sees, the Russian looming over him to push past. He grabs at Sergei's legs, ineffectually.

There is a soft rattling sound. Ian can't think what it is, but in the corner of his vision hundreds of small pale objects come bouncing down the stairs. They look like tiny balls, and as Sergei puts his foot on them he slips. With a look of astonishment he flings up his arms, falling backwards, and then Sergei can't stop himself, he's hurtling down the steepest part of the staircase, arms flailing. When he lands heavily, there is the sound of bones snapping.

Ian looks at the round brown pellets, then up. Anna has emptied a jar of something on the stairs.

'Thanks, miss,' a policeman calls up. Two men handcuff Sergei, ignoring his moans. 'Come along, no more of that. You're in enough trouble already.'

'Pity he didn't break his neck,' Katie says quietly. 'Well done, Anna.'

Anna leans over the banister and spits. It's too far away to tell whether it actually lands on Sergei. 'Pig,' she says, with utter hatred.

Katie puts her hand lightly on Anna's arm. 'Don't,' she says. 'They aren't worth it. He isn't worth a row of beans.'

Ian looks at the pale hard pellets, and smiles. That's what they are: beans.

They watch as the two remaining women are led out of the flat. Anna bursts into muffled sobs.

'You see – you see, now?'

'Yes, I do. Come away, Anna. The police will want to take statements – you don't want to stick around.'

A dishevelled head pokes out of the first-floor flat, yawning. He's a thin man, with dyed black and pink hair in a sort of quiff. He's dressed in tartan trousers and extraordinary purple leather boots.

'Oh man,' he says, seeing the police; 'I didn't see anything.' He shuts the door again.

Katie looks at Ian. 'You're hurt. Come in – we need to get some ice on that.'

The warm, wet substance that Ian had thought was sweat turns out to be blood, and he can taste it now, running down the back of his throat. His many bruises begin to stiffen and ache. 'You know, almost every time I see you, there seems to be some kind of violence involved,' he says to Katie.

'I could say the same about you.'

'My father was a bolder man than I thought to invite you to London.'

'Or I was bolder than I thought to come here.'

Ian looks downstairs. The youngest prostitute is crying.

'Galina,' Anna says softly.

She withdraws into the flat. I ought to tell them that there's another girl, living upstairs, Ian thinks; but then he thinks, no. It isn't any of my business, and it might get Katie into trouble. If Anna got herself out of hell, I'm not going to put her back into it.

He hears the policeman murmuring into his radio.

'Operation Daffodil, over. Two females, three males, coming to the station.'

Ian raises an eyebrow. 'Operation *Daffodil*?'

'Maybe they wander lonely as a cloud,' Katie murmurs, and they both begin to giggle.

The remaining policemen are looking up at Ian now. 'Do you need medical attention, sir?'

'I'll be fine.'

He goes down, and gives his name and address as a witness, as does Katie. A paramedic dabs iodine on the cut to his brow, which makes Ian remember how unpleasant going to hospital had been. Katie is talking to another policeman, being charming and helpful and carefully not mentioning the presence of another witness upstairs.

'Thank you for your help.' The policeman grins at them. 'Though it's always inadvisable for members of the public to intervene.'

'I gather that this was a prostitution ring of some kind?'

'Can't say, sir. We've been pursuing a line of inquiry.'

Ian thinks about what this waiting must have involved for the girls. How many more men they must have had to endure before being rescued – if rescue it was. The girls looked hopeless. No, he certainly isn't going to tell the coppers about Anna, he decides.

'Sure you don't need an ambulance? That gentleman in the van's got a couple of broken bones, but we're taking him in for questioning.' The policeman gives a grim wink.

'I hope you'll run him through your system pretty thoroughly,' Ian says.

'Oh, we will. If this gentleman has been involved in any other crimes it'll pop up. Wonderful thing, DNA testing. All right, miss?'

'Yes, I'm good,' says Katie.

'I'll need your name for my report,' says the policeman. 'We'll be back for witness statements. You'll be contacted by Victim Support.'

'That's fine,' Katie says, with a trace of irony. 'I don't need counselling – at least, not as much as those poor girls do, I imagine. What'll happen to them?'

'Couldn't say, miss. If they turn out to be illegal immigrants they'll get deported, I expect.'

Ian and Katie exchange glances.

'Constant problem in this area. You close down one brothel, another pops up a few weeks later, alongside drugs and burglaries. You might want to think about joining Neighbourhood Watch. Here's the card.'

Alongside a number of inquisitive neighbours they watch the police cars and van move off.

'Typical,' one old man says. 'Bloody typical. We've been complaining about this for weeks. Nobody gives a damn any more.'

'What'll you do about Anna?' Ian asks, quietly.

Katie looks at him, and he sees the arch of her brows, the curve of her lashes, the clear line of her lips. Everything about her is fine, as if drawn with a diamond. 'She'll be fine, I think, now they've gone. I must go and see how she is, though.'

She's as protective as a sister, preoccupied.

'I see. Well – I must be getting back.'

'Yes,' Katie says. Ian is taken aback by the coolness of her tone. 'I hope your friend gets better.'

'Thanks. So do we all.'

Ian hesitates, but Katie gives nothing away. The person he so intensely desires has withdrawn completely, and he's angry with himself. *Never want what you can't have* has been a good philosophy until now, but it clearly isn't going to keep working. Maybe it should be *Only want what you can't have*. How else, after all, is he ever to become something more than what he is?

'I'll keep in touch.'

'Yes, do. And Ian – thanks.'

'For what?'

'For being on our side when we needed it.'

He looks at her very intently.

'You seemed to take care of matters pretty well by yourself, Katie.'

Ian bends down and unlocks his bike from a railing, pleased to find that his hands are steady. His mended arm aches a little, but more from bruising than from any new breaks to the bone – he hopes. Tomorrow he will have another job interview; it's for a mixed comprehensive not too far away in North London. Not ideal, turning up with a cut on his face, but he can tell some version of the truth if he's asked. He's looked up the school's reports, and its website on the internet. It isn't selective, like the girls' school out in the suburbs, but its pupils are streamed according to ability in some subjects; and it is a beacon school for arts and drama. Of all the jobs he's applied for so far it's the one he'd most like to get – at least, in theory.

'Tell Anna to think about the room. It's a good house really, and as long as she can pay the rent she's welcome. Liza and Kim are great housemates.'

'How long before you move out?' Katie asks. 'Or have you left already?'

'It's not *my* room,' Ian says, surprised. 'It's Mick's.'

'Is he not expected to get out of hospital?'

'Oh, he just won't be living with us any more,' Ian says, swinging his leg over his bicycle and pushing off. 'He'll move in with Candice.'

48

Under Her Skin

Bill Shade has sent round dozens of bouquets, and has left voicemails and emails pleading for forgiveness. But Polly has not replied. Her hurt and anger at his behaviour during the party are compounded by the apprehension that this stage in her life is over. She is used to being alone, and sometimes, when she considers how little time she now has between work and family commitments, she thinks she's better off that way. The question nobody seems to ask now is whether sex is worth it, when it's so seldom something to do with real love.

'I hate cowards, and I hate lies,' she says, when Bill finally tracks her down in her office.

'Polly, you are actually the most irritating person in the world, but strangely, I'd do anything for you.'

'No, you wouldn't,' she says with asperity. 'You made your feelings for me perfectly plain when you saved your own skin. I can't share my life, and my children's lives, with someone who is fundamentally uncommitted.'

Privately, Polly wonders whether she is actually speaking for herself. The spell she has been under since meeting Bill – a spell compounded by genuine admiration, and relief at having found a new partner so soon after Theo walked out – has evaporated.

'But I'm not uncommitted. Why else would I be moving heaven and earth to start up my business here? We're good together. Just see me, meet me.'

Polly wonders whether there is genuine emotion in Bill's voice; like most people involved in show business he finds it hard to tell the difference himself. It's perfectly possible that he has made some enquiries about setting up a subsidiary office here, but she knows as well as he does that he could not operate from Britain. 'The talent has to follow the money, and the money is in America,' he's told her often enough in the past. But she doesn't want to just cut him off. She believes in forms and customs, and trying to stay friends with your ex is always preferable in civilised people.

'I'll meet you at the pub just along from the *Rambler*,' she says, with a sigh. It's as good a place as any, and the location will stiffen her resolve to be rid of him. Teresa is booked to stay on and babysit. Even breaking up costs me money, Polly thinks crossly.

She gets there first, and has leisure this time to admire the pub's high embossed ceilings and large etched windows, on each of whose inside ledges is a large vase of exotic tropical flowers flown in from Africa. There is absolutely no sign that anything strange or dramatic has happened outside in the street – but then, London seems to absorb everything into itself. There are no cellophane-wrapped bunches of flowers to mark the spot where Selim's body lay after he had been gunned down, none of the usual tributes that usually greet the untimely death of a young person. Polly has spotted one single piece of the blue and white plastic police tape that had cordoned off the street still flapping on a railing, but otherwise the frenzied serenity of her city has closed over the incident, like water.

'What are you thinking?' Bill slides onto a chair opposite Polly with the practised ease of a man who has soothed many angry women in his time. He is, however, chastened to the extent of having bothered to wear a sweater she once gave him.

'I'm still trying to work out the connection between my au pair and the proprietor of the *Rambler*.'

'Why do you think there is one?'

'He's the man in the photograph on the SIM card that she meant me to find. I knew I'd met him before, and I recognised him at the party.'

'Iryna must have been blackmailing Trench, then,' said Bill. 'It's the only explanation.'

'How would she know who he was?'

'Maybe she was sleeping with him too. Or maybe she met him in one of her other jobs. Didn't you say she did cleaning?'

'Yes, near here, apparently. She isn't the girl in the picture, though. I think that's her sister.'

'There you are. She gets a picture of her kid sister and some rich old guy she recognises. Maybe she took the picture herself. I mean, why else would she get killed?'

It makes a kind of sense. And yet Polly can't imagine that the Iryna she knew would have calmly stood there, photographing the pair. 'But how would she have tracked them down?'

'All her sister would have had to do was steal a mobile from a john and make a call, if she knew Iryna's number. The problem for these girls is that they arrive in a country without knowing anyone who might help them.'

'I think she must have got her cleaning job in the *Rambler* building in order to find her,' Polly says thoughtfully. 'She was so frightened of the police, though. I expect she thought she could sort it out by herself.'

Bill likes puzzles like these; to him, they are the elements of a plot. Polly thinks of Iryna lying with her eyes shut, the pale, pretty face under the long dark hair, like that of the heroine of a fairy tale; only the image is illusory, because Iryna had been a real person and could not be summoned back by a kiss. She is gone for ever. The figure of Justice, that golden implacable female form, blindfolded and holding up a pair of scales in one hand and a sword in the other, rears up in her mind's eye. Polly has never liked the vengeful, adversarial side of her profession: for her its appeal has always been about the balancing of different claims and laws. But she would like Iryna's murder to be avenged.

'If she was brought in illegally, maybe it was the same for her sister. Maybe they were both trafficked, but Iryna got away. You said you practically took her in off the streets, without a reference,' Bill says, a little reproachfully.

'I know, I know, and I feel a fool now. But I still believe her story about an unpleasant family. If you'd interviewed as many au pairs as I have, you'd know how common it is.'

'Which isn't to say it's true.'

'We all take people on trust, Bill. Better to give them the benefit of the doubt than not.'

The young waitress hovering in front of them pauses. 'Enjoy,' she says.

Polly smiles pleasantly, because foreigners never understand how much British people hate being told what to feel, and because the girl is so young and pretty.

Bill resumes his attack. 'Polly, how about giving *me* the benefit of the doubt?'

'I have. But I can't risk my children. That's the difference.'

He gazes into her eyes. Gerbil, Polly thinks austerely. She doesn't want to be reminded of how tender he is as a lover, or how amusing his company. In another year or two, she thinks, I could wear pillar-box red and I'll be mown down by cars at a zebra crossing because no one will see me, but at least I can see *them*. All her life, her hormones have led her into one pitfall after another: marrying the wrong man, too young, trying to become something she wasn't and couldn't be, and now struggling to get her life back on track with the kind of juggling that was never going to be an Olympic sport. She looks at their waitress: her slender, supple elastic figure and unlined skin will bring her years of male attention and courtesy, and she probably thinks that it's natural, and eternal. But one day she too will be able to wear pillar-box red and still be mown down at a crossing; and if by then she hasn't made something else of her life, then woe betide her.

Bill says, 'Sweet Pollyanna. Don't end this.'

'Rather than waste money on flowers, why don't you do something that I'd take seriously?'

'What? Tell me.'

'Did I ever tell you how my father's family got into England in the 1930s? No? Well, they were shopkeepers in some little town, and the Nazis made it impossible for anyone to buy from Jews. They hung on and hung on, always getting poorer until, almost at the last moment, they escaped – because someone here stood surety for them in order for them to come to Britain. It wasn't anyone they knew, or were related to. So that's what I'm asking you to do. Stand surety for Job. I haven't got it. He needs someone to put up ten grand.'

Bill grins. 'Is that all? Hey, the guy saved my life.' Polly lets out the breath she hadn't been aware she was holding and gives him her first real smile. 'Maybe I should option his story, too. I'm thinking Emma Thompson as you, Dominic West as myself . . .' he goes on.

Unwillingly, she laughs. Bill's gift for self-deprecation always gets to her. 'Just make sure you do what you say.'

'Polly, I have total respect for you.'

'I'm sure you do,' Polly says. 'Only you think I'm a sanctimonious prig. Well, maybe I am, but I'm also *right*.'

'That's what sanctimonious prigs always believe,' Bill says.

This is the paradox about her life, and work: the two do not connect. Polly sometimes feels that her work is perceived as a kind of moral luxury, even by her closest friends.

But what she will not give up is the belief in what human beings owe to each other. She has done for Job what she could not for all too many of her other clients, but the principle is the same. They are individuals who have turned to Britain for help just as one person turns to another. Do you kick them in the face, or pick them up? The argument that they are living on an overcrowded island whose infrastructure is falling to bits doesn't really wash. Even on the *Titanic*, Polly thinks, there were people who remembered *who they were*.

Of all the things she has seen in her work, nothing has moved her so much as going into Job's room in the tower block nearby to collect his things. Polly is ashamed to remember just how scared she had been even to enter it: on the assumption that she was entering a place riddled with muggers and thieves, she had taken off all her jewellery and carried no handbag. Yet the people she had seen there had been no different from anyone else – except possibly even more nervous of her, assuming that she must be a social worker or policewoman perhaps. The keys that Job had handed her jangled as they unlocked iron grilles, similar to those in the detention centre. Inside was a warren of rooms, divided and subdivided, almost exploding from the sheer, silent pressure of the people living there. Job's room was the smallest of all. So bleak, so bare, with just one battered cloth suitcase under its single bed, a kettle, a microwave and a row of paperbacks on the window ledge: it had stabbed her heart with pity even before she knew it. What he most wanted was a photograph. She looked at the picture of a smiling young woman, knowing that the girl was Job's wife. He had told Polly about her: how she was a nurse and had met him in his country's capital. Polly can see that she is lovely, lovely in the way that Job is with that shining quality of goodness that people despise until they realise how rare it is.

Job is determined to go to South Africa if he gets out of detention. Even if he gets the right to remain in Britain, he is leaving.

'Nobody wishes to remain here,' he tells Polly on one of her visits to Harmondsworth. 'We only stay here because it is the way to keep alive. That's all I wanted from this country: to be safe.'

'I know, Job; but London has stopped feeling safe even to me.'

In a year, she tells herself, Robbie will be old enough to travel by himself on public transport – assuming she has the nerve to let him try. Some newspaper has unearthed a story about the suicide bomber, Selim, having been bullied at school. There is speculation that perhaps this is what embittered him against the whole of British society, although most think that his mosque school is to blame. Hemani rings to find out how the meeting with Bill has gone. The shock and fear of the bomb attempt, following so much else in the past three months, have made Polly edgy and angry, and it's a relief to talk to her oldest friend.

'Sometimes I think we're living in the equivalent to the last days of the Roman Empire. I'm not surprised it disgusts Muslims – the public drunkenness, the greed, the filth.'

'But people tend to want things no matter what their religion,' Hemani answers reasonably. 'Religion is just an excuse.'

Polly can tell that she is tired; in the background the baby she has not yet had time to see gives a fretful hiccup. She's a girl, to everyone's great joy.

'Are you getting much help, Hemani?'

'My mum, and Daniel, and my son, and my cleaner. It takes a village . . . Only, having a baby at thirty-eight is quite different from having Bron at twenty-four.'

'You know, Robbie told me something he learnt in school: that in Ancient Rome, the least wealthy Roman had a better standard of living than the richest person now. It doesn't sound very probable, does it?'

'Well, it does if you have slaves,' says Hemani. 'Imagine, not having to pay for cleaners or childcare!'

They both laugh, the soft, tired laughs of women on the verge of exhaustion.

'Bill thinks Iryna must have been blackmailing Trench.'

'What for? Money?'

'I don't know. She didn't strike me as particularly greedy, but then . . .' Polly's voice dies away as she thinks about her diamond ring.

'Maybe she thought Trench could help her become legal or something.'

'She was going to become legal anyway if she married her

Romanian. No, I keep thinking she had some hold over Trench. If I knew more about him . . .'

Hemani is quiet. Then she says, 'Why don't you ask Katie? You know she works on the *Rambler?*'

Polly has been intending to ask Katie round anyway, but this is a good excuse; the neighbourliness of London counters its vastness, and Katie can easily walk to her house.

One evening, when both women are free, the American girl does just that.

They chat over a glass of white wine about work and the party. Katie is thinking of leaving; Ivo has been helping her find a better job, and this leads on to the question that Polly wants to ask. She gets out her page of photographs of Iryna.

'Katie, I was wondering if you've met this woman.'

'Her?' Katie picks a photo up and says at once, 'Oh, yes. She used to clean our offices, and the flat above, but she disappeared a couple of months ago. Why?'

'Weirdly, she used to be my au pair and I'm trying to trace her movements. Whose flat is it?'

'Roger Trench, the proprietor.'

'Nice man?' Polly asks casually.

'Not especially, no. It's supposed to be a service flat, in every sense.'

The two women exchange a wry smile.

'Did you ever see Iryna with him?'

'You mean, as in having an affair?' Katie grins. 'Well, he definitely used to bring girls back there. He has a place somewhere like Hampshire, where his wife lives, but the flat is where he goes if he's, er, working late. But I never saw her with him, no.'

She's clearly about to say more when Polly's mobile rings. It's the detective, Singh.

'Sorry not to have been in touch before,' he says. 'We've just had a bit of luck.'

'Oh?'

'We're still working on it. Turns out your burglar's got form. We arrested him for something else, ran him through the system and bingo, his DNA came up for your case.'

'For Iryna?'

Singh laughs. 'No, another nasty business. At present he's pleading not guilty, but once he's definitely going down other victims may talk. Would you be willing to try and identify him?'

'Yes, of course.'

Polly wonders whether she will, in fact, be able to recognise the burglar. The memory of his attack has dimmed, and she is glad of it. But the police are so eager to get her identification that they send round a different officer in a car to drive her from work and back.

It's a bright spring day, and she wears a light coat that she hasn't put on since her holiday in California. The officer who drives her knows nothing about the case and isn't allowed to discuss it with her anyway for fear of witness contamination. She won't have to identify the burglar through a pane of one-way glass, to her relief: it'll just be a series of photographs on computer.

'These are the rules you lawyers make,' he says dryly. 'Everything is stacked against us.'

In the presence of her burglar's solicitor and another policeman, Polly is shown photos of ten men, all similar, on a laptop slide show. Five can be immediately discounted, and then a further three after more scrutiny. She only glimpsed him for a second . . . Polly hesitates over another similar face, before remembering that her burglar had a thicker nose.

'Can I see five and nine again, please?'

Then it's obvious. His face stares up at her from the screen: the cruel, lightless eyes. What else had he done?

'It's number nine,' she says.

'Are you sure? Would you like to look at the pictures again?'

'No.' Polly feels a twinge of dread, just in case she's got it wrong. 'That's him.'

The policeman and the solicitor both sigh. She goes out, signs more papers, and drinks a glass of water, sweating. The officer who drove her there is waiting.

'Did I get it right?'

'I can't say.'

There is, however, a palpable air of jubilation in the police station. It surprises Polly a little, because she has never really thought of policing as a vocation, like the law. She remembers what Singh had told her: *If it were up to me, I'd put criminals in a Coliseum with a couple of hungry lions.* Well, she understands the satisfaction. He will go down for robbery, at least.

Before she gets out, Polly asks Singh, 'Could you make a note to ask the defendant something? I believe he has a connection to Roger Trench, the businessman.'

'Why do you think that?'

'Because Trench is the man in the photograph on the SIM card. I looked at it before I handed it over, and I'm sure of it. Iryna left me that compromising picture for a reason. I think the girl with Trench is her sister. Iryna was expecting her to come to England, and she never arrived. I think she may have been trafficked, and Iryna was trying to get her out. I think Trench had Iryna murdered, or killed her himself.'

'We'll make a note of it,' Singh says, blandly.

Polly thrusts her hands into her jacket. In a pocket, in a seam, she feels something hard, circular and lumpy. Before she draws it out, she knows what she has found. There, in her hand, is her lost ring.

49

As If She Belongs Here

Anna can smell a change coming as the days lengthen and warm. From Katie's bedroom she can see trees in the back gardens flush pink at their tips as if blood, not sap, were returning. With light and warmth comes the return of energy and hope in the world outside. Birds call for hours each morning, trilling and whistling as if trying to coax Anna to come out. One especially sunny day she even brings a chair to stand on, and pokes her head through the skylight to see more.

Out on the grey slates of the roof it's like a different landscape. A pigeon struts on slim coral legs, making a soft crooning sound in its iridescent throat. It looks at her with bright, black eyes. She remembers how the birds she saw in Kilburn when she'd been in the brothel seemed to be rejoicing in their freedom, how they had been tossed about by the violent winds. Now Anna can see a nest constructed inside a chimney pot, and another pigeon sitting on it. Both pigeons watch her anxiously.

'Don't worry, I won't hurt you,' she says aloud. The male pigeon swells its pink throat, and continues with its repetitive soporific song. 'Forget, forget,' it says. Sometimes Anna actually manages to, just for a few seconds. But then, every now and again, something slips in her mind and she is back in the tiny cubicle, in the waking nightmare. She so wants to be well and whole again, not the shattered creature she has become. Yet when she looks at the bird on its nest it occurs to her, quite suddenly, that these creatures too were once part of an egg, and that the egg had had to break in order for them to be free, to sail and glide. Maybe it will be like that for her, one day.

To know that Sergei, Dmitri and Lena are in prison, refused bail, rather than waiting to pounce on her downstairs does make her less terrified. Little by little, Anna forces herself out of the flat's door. If running upstairs to safety and Katie had taken all her courage, it was worse going down. Each step is a step towards freedom, yet it makes her temperature rise and fall so that she sweats one moment and freezes the next. Still, it's the only way she is ever going to get her life back. This private battle is one that she makes herself do each day, with the door to the flat on the latch while Katie is at work. It's as if she's building up muscle. She has never told Katie that the first time she left the flat, as Ian came up the stairs, her knees gave way at every tread as if she were sinking into mud. How she had thought of pouring the dried beans onto the steps she would never know.

It's clear to Anna that Katie likes Ian more than she has admitted, although Ian disappeared after the fight with Sergei and hasn't been back. To see him fight like that to protect them – well, what woman wouldn't feel something?

'He was like lion,' Anna says, as they watch a nature programme about a wildlife reserve together.

'Er – I guess so.'

'You like him?'

'Yes, I do. He's a nice guy.'

'He has girlfriend?'

'She left him.'

'So—?'

Katie shakes her head. 'I'm not looking for another man. I need to think about my career, and what to do next.'

'Will you go back to America?'

'Not yet. Would you go back to the Ukraine?'

'One day. I miss my family, my little brother, ver' much.'

'*Very* much.' Katie corrects Anna's pronunciation. 'I miss my family too.'

They talk over their evening meal – a mixture of conversation lessons and genuine curiosity. Anna surreptitiously copies Katie's table manners.

'You have been back?'

'I've been back once, in a year. I was too upset to enjoy it much.'

'Upset? What do this mean?'

'Sad. Unhappy. Depressed.'

'I know those things,' Anna says. 'They are bad things, but they pass, like weather. That is what my granny always say. Says? Said.'

To be an adult is like listening to the radio music that Katie likes, which Anna dislikes because it almost always makes her feel sad and yet which she can dimly understand is somehow *more*. Anna thinks of how greedy she had been only a few months ago to grow up, how fiercely resentful of being in any way treated like a child. Now that her childhood has gone, she understands how brief a period it is in anyone's life, and how precious. Even if she has been granted a temporary refuge here, it's increasingly clear to Anna that she needs to find a new place to live.

'I want to get a job.'

'That would be a good idea. I don't think you'll have problems, working for cash.'

'Maybe if I sound English I will be OK. But I no look English.'

'I *don't* look English,' Katie corrects. She scrutinises her. 'You know, nobody exactly looks English, or British. It's mostly clothes. That's what you need, I think.'

'I have no money,' Anna lies. The roll of cash is for food, and real emergencies.

'No, but I have a little.'

'Already, you have done so much.'

'Look, Anna: if I'd paid you for cleaning and redecorating my flat, it would have come to at least enough for a new wardrobe. I think I can afford a little.'

Anna is still not confident enough to go out shopping, but they are the same size, so Katie goes in her stead. She comes back triumphant, with coloured paper bags, and they spend an evening trying on jeans, T-shirts, skirts and jumpers. The cheap cotton and wool mixes are sumptuous to Anna's eyes and fingers; there is embroidery, ruffles, ribbons, stitching – she has never seen colours like these, the jewel-like greens, blues and reds. An ecstasy of femininity seizes them both.

'This is so much fun!' Katie exclaims girlishly. 'I'd forgotten how fun it is.'

Anna looks at herself in the long, narrow mirror inside the bedroom cupboard. She looks like somebody different: not the rustic girl from the Ukraine, nor the teenaged prostitute from Poshlust, nor the waif whom Katie had rescued. She put on a short red coat over all.

'It's good,' she says, and they laugh because she has finally got the phrase right. Lastly, there is something that delights her heart: a pair of big silver hoop earrings, just like those she had envied on the ferry over. They are light as feathers.

'Not my kind of jewellery, Anna, but I figured they could be yours,' Katie says.

When she has put them on, Anna draws a deep breath. 'I am ready,' she says. 'But I do not know to how find work.'

She has looked on websites like Gumtree and Loot and has found advertisements for hotel chambermaids, even nerving herself to ring up some of the numbers on the new pay-as-you-go mobile phone that Katie has bought for her. When she does get through, it's clear that either her English isn't good enough or her lack of papers will stop her. She has to find another way.

'There is the cleaning agency I use for the magazine,' Katie says. 'I don't think they're too picky. I could give you a reference, I guess. But I've also been thinking. There's a pub near where I work, called the Giant Bread & Cheese. They might be looking for staff. Why don't you come in with me?'

So they go down together, and this time it isn't so hard. At last Anna will be out on the street, the sloping, lumpy, tree-lined hill that has played such an important part in her life. She has seen it from below and from above but she has never had the freedom simply to walk along it like any other citizen, in a bright red coat and shoes.

'OK?'

Anna is trembling slightly, but she nods. Together, they go out of the shabby black front door and get onto the little red bus that she has seen go rattling past. Katie shows her Oyster card, and pays for Anna.

'I'll get you one of these,' she murmurs as they find seats together. 'It makes bus travel much cheaper.'

It's difficult to be looked at by so many people, and Anna wonders whether any of them are former clients. But they are all wrapped up in their own lives, or looking out of the bus windows. She carries one of Katie's dried beans in her pocket, to roll between finger and thumb, and it seems to help when she feels the panic well up during her interview with the pub owner, a big, ruddy-faced, white-haired man called Steve. Not the kind of man to have any interest in Poshlust, she thinks, relieved. Those eyes have seen a good deal of life, of drunks and despair, but they are kind eyes all the same.

'Have you waitressed before?'

'A little,' Anna lies.

'She's an excellent worker,' Katie says. 'I wouldn't suggest her otherwise.'

Steve grins. 'Can you understand enough English to explain dishes if the punters ask?'

Anna almost panics at the word 'punters' but guesses what this means.

'I hope so. I like to cook.'

'You do, do you? Well, I'm short-staffed so I'll try you out. I pay ten quid a shift, and you keep your tips. All right?'

'All right. I work hard.'

'Good. It's a quiet time now, so I'll show you the ropes. You can start today.'

Anna beckons to Katie, and whispers anxiously, 'Katie, what are these ropes?'

'How to do things. Don't worry.'

Katie goes off to work, promising to come in later.

For the next three hours Anna concentrates ferociously. How to work a credit-card machine, how to display slices of bread for a serving, how to pull pints are all new skills, but they sharpen in her mind just as the menu chalked up on the blackboard becomes clearer as it dries. Everybody seems to speak with a different accent, and many orders are unintelligible; by a miracle the only mistake she makes – a wrong dish – is accepted by the customer. She's too busy to feel anxious, relaying orders to the kitchen and balancing dishes on her arms in the way that Paulina, the other waitress, shows her. Paulina is Polish – placid, blonde and sweet, though the small gold cross round her neck and a certain primness to her mouth make Anna wary of telling her personal information. Not that she is asked for any: here, in the heart of the city, everything is transient, and when she goes out later and sees Oxford Circus with traffic swirling around it she feels she might faint. How can there be so many people in the world, swarming in and out of holes in the ground? People step off the pavements just to get past each other.

The pub too is full, and at its busiest people are eating and drinking outside, shouting and smoking and gulping down life in great mouthfuls. The noise makes Anna wish she could put plugs in her ears, and her calf muscles ache from walking carefully in order to sidestep the unwary. But she doesn't drop any plates, keeps smiling and when her shift is over she wipes down the tables, collects empty glasses and sweeps the floors without being asked. By the end of her shift she has made twenty pounds in tips. The manager, Steve, nods.

'Fine. You're on,' he says. 'See you same time tomorrow. Can you do Saturdays?'

'Yes.'

Steve looks at her, his grey eyes shrewd. 'This is just part-time work, you understand? And you are from . . . Poland?'

'Lithuania,' Anna says firmly.

'Fine. As long as you're honest and hard-working, you could come from Timbuctoo as far as I'm concerned. Anyone from Immigration comes round, you disappear.'

'I disappear,' she promises. Getting caught seems like a remote possibility. Her head whirls with sums. She can make thirty pounds a day, every day, or maybe forty pounds, that is two hundred and forty a week. (Anna remembers that her price in the brothel must have earned it that much or more in a day.) But this money will be *hers*. If she works longer hours, maybe she can even send some money home. Maybe she can pick up some work as a cleaner, too. She will do anything – anything, as long as it's not what she did in the brothel.

Anna is so elated that she almost fails to recognise the man squatting on the pavement to lock his bicycle to the railings further down the street. The long back and clear-cut profile, the well-shaped hands with their strong fingers are familiar. It's Ian.

For a moment, she's going to walk right by him. Why remind him of her existence? Then she hesitates, and stops just as he looks up. He smiles vaguely, half-recognising her, but more because she's young and pretty and he is a man.

She says carefully, 'You are Katie's friend. The one who fought Sergei.'

Recognition comes into his eyes. He stands up and holds out his hand. 'Hi, Anna.'

She won't touch him: it will be years before she touches any man voluntarily. But he is the second kind person she has met that day – the third, if she counts the customer who accepted the dish she brought by mistake rather than make a fuss. Timidly she nods, and asks, 'You are here to see Katie?'

'I'm here to see my dad, in his office.'

Anna isn't sure what to do. There are things she wants to say, and not enough words in English to say them.

Ian says, 'You still live with Katie, right?'

She can see from his face how much he wants news of Katie; too obviously, he has come to try to see her, rather than his father, again. Anna doesn't really know, though; inexperience weighs on her tongue like the stone from a bitter fruit. She could tell him that if he waits, then Katie could trust him more, but what after all does she know about love? Besides, she is too happy for herself to be sad for him.

'I have job – a job – now. I am waitress.' A flash of memory comes back to her, of crossing the Channel and practising her English with the other girls. *I am very strong.* Well, she is.

'That's great!'

Ian smiles at her, a little patronisingly.

'Your friend, she is – was – kind. The doctor. I want to thank her before.'

'No worries – I'll mention it.' Ian pauses. 'Did Katie tell you, there's a room coming free in the house? Kim thought that you might be interested.'

'How much?'

'Fifty pounds a week, including bills. Normally, we'd have another Aussie, but – well, if you've got a job you might like to think about it.'

Has she understood him correctly? Is he offering her an alternative to living with Katie? Of course she will take it. She will learn to speak English perfectly; or perhaps she will learn to sound Australian. Anna's big hooped earrings tap gently on the side of her neck. She will learn to jump through holes smaller than these if it means she can survive. 'Is a good price. How many peoples?'

'Just the two girls, and me. Though I may be leaving since I'll be working in a different area.'

'Why?'

Ian shrugs. 'Time to move on. I've got a new job in a new school.

It's a good one, a big mixed state school. It'll be a challenge, an adventure, but I think it's a good chance.'

Maybe everybody who comes to London has this dream, Anna thinks, as Ian strides away to meet his father. The thin afternoon sunlight stabs down, bouncing off windows. Anna checks her reflection in one of them. Distorted and wavering slightly, it makes her look a little heavier than she is, perhaps the way that she will look ten or twenty years from now, but it is smiling back at her. All around, the tall pale buildings with their neat soldierly railings, identical as days in a calendar, march forwards into the future and back into the past, and the city sighs its unending exhalation of hope, or exhilaration, or change.

50

From One Winter to Another

For the second time in his life, Job is getting onto an aeroplane. The crowds around him in the queue shuffle forwards, pulling their coloured wheeled suitcases, hefting their backpacks. So many people, he thinks, as their numbers overwhelm him yet again.

London stretches even further than he could have guessed. Seeing it from the windows of his train, he realises that had he spent all his life minicabbing he might never have learnt the name of each street, as the drivers of black cabs are supposed to do. The city is bleeding out into another town which has swollen and burst into rows of identical brick houses; it is cramped and yet unconfined, like some fabulous monster that is replicating itself in all directions. Only in patches, around the railway embankment, can he see much wilderness left – the trees, silhouetted against the evening sky, the bright splashes of flowers and grasses bobbing in the wind of the train's passing. The train rattles and chunters to itself in an insistent rhythm punctuated by pings. It's like half-listening to a nursery rhyme, interrupted by bossy announcements through the speaker system reminding them that the train is No Smoking and that Mobile Phones Are Not to Be Used in the Quiet Carriage. The one thing

Job will not be sorry to leave behind is the morass of petty, punitive regulations which irritate the daily life of Britons.

It will be winter now in South Africa; as Job sees it, he is going from one winter into another. Not such a bad time to arrive, though it will be almost as chilly as England in Johannesburg, with a dry wind hissing between tower blocks and shanties. But there will be the sky under which he was born. To see the sky of Africa once more, with its spray of white stars and the Southern Cross, its great glowing sunsets instead of the watery colours of Britain: this is what Job wants, almost as much as he wants his wife. The city is petering out, with more parks and greens giving way to farmland, and then the airport arrives in the blink of an eye. Such a small island, he thinks; yet all the time he has been in London, it's as if it contained the world.

Nothing has turned out the way he had imagined it would, and yet he will miss this odd, cramped, cold country more than he thought possible. What he will miss are his friends: Michael from the car wash, Polly, and Tariq's family. Though Tariq is lost to him. Job had gone back to Ace Minicabs to try to tell him about Selim, and none of the other drivers had spoken to him, while Mo had silently put out his hand for the keys to the BMW.

'I think the police will have given the company a hard time,' Polly had said. 'You're lucky not to have been prosecuted for having a Zimbabwean driving licence, which isn't legal in this country.'

'But I am a good driver. I have never had an accident, or even a parking ticket,' Job had replied, his heart sore.

They have arrived at Terminal Five, the new departure point for long-haul British Airways flights. The terminal's opening had been so chaotic that Job and Polly had expected to find scenes of misery, but instead it's cool and calm and bright, an admirable place entirely suitable for twenty-first century air travel – not, of course, that this can continue for much longer, for what nobody is saying loudly enough is that there simply won't be the fuel left to fly aeroplanes in a decade's time. Everything is running out, and people have begun to talk about something called the credit crunch.

412

'Remember, Job, you can come back,' Polly says beside him. 'You do now have indefinite leave to remain.'

'Yes,' he says, though he knows quite well that he will probably never use it. 'I am very glad to have it. But my life will always be in God's hands, not those of this country.' He smiles down at her, and thinks of the ways in which their lives have touched for a short while. Small and doughty, Polly reminds him so strongly of Mrs Wisden. Job wishes he could have seen Beth Wisden one more time, at least to find out whether she has made a life for herself. People are always more connected to each other than not, he believes, whether by greed or shame or love or fear, but finding the point of connection, that is the miracle. When he had come to London he had been another person, numbed into dullness, and afraid; and somehow, through a chain of perfectly natural coincidences, he is returning not only a free man but a rich one.

Not that Job's good fortune had been immediately evident. When he got out of Harmondsworth, on the surety paid by Polly's friend Bill, he had lost the room in the council flat. The rent he owed to the middleman who let it had, of course, not been paid, and there was somebody else in the room. To his great surprise, Polly then offered him the use of her basement.

'It isn't being used as a playroom right now,' she said. 'It seems only sensible, as long as you're quiet, for you to move in until everything is sorted out.'

'I promise you, I am very quiet. I play the bongo after midnight, but that is all.'

Polly smiled; she always understood his jokes. 'Actually, I'd quite like to have another adult in the house right now.'

Job couldn't help wondering if she was offering him something more; but she added, 'It's just a temporary solution, Job.'

'Madam—'

'No! No – you must stop calling me that,' she said. 'We're friends, aren't we? And friends should help each other, without obligation.'

413

He had looked at her for a long, long time, then put out his hand. She put out hers, and they shook on it.

'Thank you, Polly. I would like that very much.'

She had done well out of taking his case, too, he learnt, and although she reaped very little in terms of money from defending him, she told him that the attention it gained meant that her firm was going to make her a partner. Job had been interviewed in the British press about his life, and had excited genuine compassion – although there were still some disgruntled columnists like a certain Mark Crawley who bemoaned the loss of an opportunity to get rid of the Prime Minister on that day; and others who suggested, in apparent seriousness, that MI5 should recruit suicide bombers to rid the world of unpopular dictators such as Robert Mugabe.

'How can they write such foolishness?' Job asked.

'Because they are free,' Polly said. 'That's part of living here. You may disagree with what somebody says, but you defend to the death their right to say it.'

That time in Polly's house had been the best Job ever had in England. To be part of a family, to be able to read, talk to the children, drink tea in the kitchen, to no longer be alone . . . Polly's cleaner Teresa of course believed he was sleeping with her. Robbie had even asked him, hesitantly, if this were so.

'No. We are friends, that's all.'

'Oh.'

'Why does this make you sad?'

'Because everyone we like goes away.'

'I must go away too, Robbie. I have a wife of my own, in Zimbabwe. I have to find her.'

The British were kind, in their way. Even Harmondsworth, with its airlessness, its bad smells and its despair, had not been steeped in the corruption and cruelty of officialdom as it would have been in his own country. Nobody was beaten, or tortured, or raped. He had been allowed to read books from the library, and kept in a room with two other men, not twenty, with a toilet instead of a hole in the floor. As the moment in which he will perhaps face these things again gets closer, Job swallows the fear rising in his gorge.

'Are you nervous?' Polly asks.

'A little. But I have flown before, you know.'

'Yes. But I meant about going back.'

'I survived; I will survive again.'

He has to believe this. He thinks of the voice he had heard, speaking to him out of the tiny whirlwind of dust. Polly does not believe in God; she would say, if he ever told her, that the voice was a dream, or a memory, or an impulse from his subconscious. She thinks that life is random, and it's only people's perception of it that makes it seem in any way orderly or ordained. Job, though, knows what he knows. He has read the story of his namesake in prison. Why had he been named after him, if not to prove that God watched over him, and all of mankind?

Outside, huge cumulus clouds billow against a sky flushed with pink, orange, red and blue. They are beautiful, and soon he will be up there, looking down at them as upon a continent, so pristine and solid-seeming that he remembers his wonder at not being able to live there, like the hero of a tale. But it is an illusion. The casual wealth of England, the abundance of water, the greenness even in high summer, have become normal to his eyes. People say that soon nations will fight each other because the world is heating up and drying out, but it's hard to believe that sort of pessimism in this gentle green and grey landscape. Elsewhere there are shortages of staple foods – wheat, corn, rice – and whatever is bad here, Job thinks, will be far, far worse where he is going. Even in England rain has caused bad harvests and the economy is in crisis; the Polish people who did so many jobs here are going back to their own country because of the sinking exchange rate, and now English people are complaining about how difficult it is to find builders, plumbers and the rest.

'Do you have travellers' cheques?' Polly asks.

'I have enough.'

She has already spotted a couple in a nearby queue – a white man and his girlfriend who recognise her, in turn.

Polly is laughing. 'Katie, you must meet Job,' she says. 'You know who he is?'

'Of course I do,' says the young woman. She has a lovely smile that crinkles the corners of her eyes, and very white, even teeth. The man is looking at her. 'Ian and I probably owe you our lives. We were at that party, and we'd never have escaped alive. You were so brave! I'm so pleased the government saw sense about your case.'

'I am lucky,' Job says, and remembers all the people he has left behind in Harmondsworth who were not so.

'This is my friend Ian. He's just got a new job, so he's going away before he starts, and I'm here to see him off.'

'Hi there, Job.'

They shake hands and Job knows immediately that this man is part of the new South Africa. He looks Job in the eye as an equal, in the way that no white Briton has ever quite managed to do, and Job smiles at him.

'What is your work?' Job enquires.

'Oh, I'm a teacher. In fact, I worked for a while in the same school that Selim Khan was at.'

'You *knew* the boy?'

'No. But I taught his younger brothers, Amir and Chandra. Poor boys, their lives have been made hell by what Selim did, or tried to do. The family is devastated. They're going to move to Bradford next month.'

Job does not say that he taught them too; that Amir had barely been able to read. Perhaps his teacher hadn't known, or perhaps he too had tried and failed. 'But you are moving to a different school?'

'Yes. I'm really pleased, because it's the one I really liked, and the only one which offered me a good job.'

'I'm moving on myself,' Katie says to Polly. 'My boss, Ian's dad, offered to take me with him to the States, but . . . well, I thought I'd try something different.'

'What, a newspaper?'

'Something a little more serious, anyway.'

They shift their suitcases forward, inching towards the check-point. Polly says to Ian, 'Are you going on holiday?'

'Oh, I'm going back to see my mother and stepfather, really. I couldn't persuade Katie to come too. She thinks it's all lions and snakes.'

Katie is blushing. Polly smiles at her.

'After the *Rambler*, I'd have thought a few snakes wouldn't matter. Isn't it in trouble?'

'We all think that Trench has got some problem he doesn't want people to know about, because the police keep interviewing him,' says Katie.

'Ah,' says Polly, and Job wonders why she looks so pleased. 'That's very interesting. You don't know what it's about?'

'No – though, as you can imagine, all sorts of rumours are flying around, including one about some girl he kept in his flat. They've had a forensic team go through it, and we all had a day off while they did, which caused total chaos. Anyway, the new editor has sacked almost everyone.'

'Including you?'

'Oh, not me. He seems to think I'm OK.'

'Of course you are,' says Ian. He smiles down at Katie, but she shrugs as if ridding herself of something that has been placed on her shoulders, unwanted. Job can see the pain in the man's face, and a kind of patient resignation.

Politely, he moves away so that they can continue their chat about families and friends. His own experience of South Africa will doubt-less be very different from that of Ian, and he will have no family waiting for him. He will be a stranger there, as he has been here; another displaced Zimbabwean, looking for lost relations and a job. Admittedly, he will be a stranger with a little more money than most because now he has that most precious of things, a British bank account upon which he can draw. Just as Polly had told him he would, he got quite a substantial out of court settlement for being shot by the police.

'If people in my country knew what a few British bullets were worth, we would all volunteer,' he'd said to her, when she'd told him the amount.

He could go back to Harare, because in Zimbabwe that money would make him a multimillionaire – but then, anyone who can buy a loaf of bread is a multimillionaire there. No: he has seen the news on TV, and the stream of people walking miles to wriggle under the razor-wire fences to get out. If he can find news of his wife, it will be on the other side of the border, in South Africa. It's what they always planned, if things became worse, and Munisha is a very determined woman. Job wonders how she will have managed; whether she will have prostituted herself for food. Sometimes he can barely remember her, and sometimes she is so close that it's as if she is standing just behind him, and if he were to turn round he would see her. Whatever she has done, whatever he has done will not matter as long as they are together again.

Job had even returned to the brothels, once he'd been released from Harmondsworth, just to check on whether he could find Anna one last time. The Agar Grove flat had not responded when he rang the bell, and neither had the one in Kilburn. They sounded empty, and there was no movement behind the thick grey net curtains. He hopes that it means they have been closed down; but, people being what they are, Job thinks, there will always be others. No life is free from evil. He would never know the whole story of Anna, just as nobody would ever know his own story.

'Are you really going to cross the border if you can't find her?' Polly asks, quietly.

'Yes. It may not be so dangerous now.'

Things in his country show faint signs of change. There has been an election, and Mugabe lost; only he won't leave. I have to hope,

Job thinks. Even if he struggles with dread from the moment he wakes, he has to believe that he can achieve grace.

It's time to go. He has dreamed of this moment so often, always with fear; yet here he is, about to leave England of his own free will. He can see the uniformed officers scrutinising passports as people file past. The multitudes of people, all about to become foreigners in another country, flow through the artificial barriers that demarcate an area that is Britain from an area that is No Man's Land, where alcohol and jewellery and clothing are untaxed. Soon he too will be sitting in one of those white winged vessels, fletched with energy, arrowing up into heaven.

'Goodbye, dear Job,' Polly says. She reaches up and hugs him, and he hugs her back.

'Goodbye. I cannot thank you enough for all you've done for me.'

'Actually,' Polly says, 'you did far more for all of us.'

She watches as he picks up his shabby suitcase. Then, very firmly and without a backward glance, he walks forward, to be lost in the steady stream of people leaving Britain, like water sinking out of sight.

London, 2002–2008

Acknowledgements

Writing acknowledgements always feels like showing the underside of a piece of weaving, where the threads hang out in knots and lumps. *Hearts and Minds* has more than most, because it was delivered four years late due to long illness and multiple surgery. So my first thanks are to the doctors who saved my life: Mr Sharma, Mr Magos and Dr Collis of the Royal Free Hospital, and Mr Lynn of the Charing Cross Hospital. I would also like to thank Richard Beswick, my editor at Little, Brown, and my agent Antony Harwood for waiting so patiently for delivery when many others would have given up. A number of people have been my readers of *Hearts and Minds* as a work in progress, and I would like to thank, among others, Rob Cohen, Kate Saunders, Jenni Russell, Lorna Owen, Leonora Craig Cohen and Francesca Simon for particularly helpful remarks and questions. Both Linda Watson and Veronique Minier helped to coax me back to health, at times when it seemed like a distant country I would never reach. Of the many books I read as background on a variety of subjects touched on in the novel, I would especially like to mention Craig McGill's *Human Traffic: Sex, Slaves and Immigration*, which remains as true today as when it was written.

Much of what I discovered about the hidden lives of immigrants could not be put into a work of fiction, and much that I guessed turned out to be true. Of the organisations which I can thank, I would especially like to mention the Medical Foundation for the Victims of Torture, the Poppy Trust, and the charity Women for Refugee Women. Euan Macmillan, an expert witness in immigration cases, and the solicitor for Bindmans, Liz Barrett, both gave me precious time to enable me to build Polly as a human-rights lawyer, as did Anna Hossein. I also thank Christoph Wilding for helping me with some details about what teaching can be like, and Francis Gilbert for his many excellent books on this subject, especially *I'm A Teacher – Get Me Out of Here*. American friends and fellow authors such as Tracy Chevalier, Meg Rosoff, Douglas Kennedy and Alison Lurie generously lent me some of their impressions of England for Katie. Marina Lewycka sent me the Ukrainian song that Anna sings, and Rachel Polonsky helped with the Russian. Readers who have enjoyed this book may like to know that several of the characters have already appeared in previous novels.

It is my deepest sorrow that my father Dennis Craig died suddenly a week before the novel was completed, and will therefore never get to read it. Both he and my mother were opponents of apartheid and had as their motto 'Nihil humanum a me alienum puto' or 'Nothing human is foreign to me.' This novel is dedicated to him, and to all readers who hold such generosity high in their hearts and minds.